The Treasures of a Carolina Summer

A Novel by W. Scott Jones

This is a work of fiction from the mind of the author. Through the years he has met his share of unique "characters". The characters of this novel are not real people; however, there are fictitious references in the novel associated with historical figures. The conversations and events associated with these historical figures are entirely fictitious. Some of the places associated with this novel are a combination of real places visited by the author along with his vivid imagination. The timeline of this novel is intended to be as accurate as possible to coincide with the significant historical setting associated with it. Some words used may be offensive in nature, but are only used in a historical context with no intention to harm or offend anyone.

Dedication

I dedicate this book to my son, William (Will) Scott Jones, Jr. who was killed in an automobile accident two days after his 25th birthday. I miss him every day and I know that he is smiling at his old man. Mom, your sisters, and I love you "Willie Bear".

I would also like to thank my editor, Mrs. Liz Simon, who not only corrects my many mistakes; she inspires and pushes me to places that I could have never imagined.

Contents

CHAPTER ONE

"The greatest treasures are those invisible to the eye but found in the heart."

Judy Garland

The sun began peeking through a dense Carolina fog near Hogtail Swamp when a worker from Peabody Construction Company dropped a large crowbar on the ground next to an old farmhouse that was under demolition. A split second after the crowbar hit the ground a rotten portion of the structure's mortise and tenon joint became exposed when a 2x10 hand cut pine board tumbled to the ground. The veteran construction foreman looked at his young partner and said, "Well, I'll be... Look at those wooden pegs."

After carefully inspecting the exposed area of the structure, he then yelled at his boss to come over and take a look for himself. After only a quick peek, Ron Peabody made the decision to immediately stop all demolition.

It was only fifteen minutes later on that muggy Wednesday morning on May 30, 1979 when Mark James received a phone call at work. He immediately recognized the deep worn out voice of Ron Peabody. He listened for a few minutes and then replied, "I see. What do you think we should do?"

Mark could almost smell the cigarette scarred voice of Ron Peabody as he screamed over the phone saying, "I hate to say this, Mark, but what you have here is a well-kept treasure. It's a log cabin for Pete's sake. This may be the oldest standin' wooden structure in this county and maybe the entire state of South Carolina."

"What do you suggest we do?"

"I think we need to call Chad Emory from the Oak Bay Historical Society. He will know what to do. I know you said that you thought this house was built around 1865, but I am here to tell you that it is much older. This type of construction is from the pre-Civil War era. I even have a hunch that it may be as old as the Colonial era."

"Thanks, Ron. Let me know what Mr. Emory finds out."

By the time Mark's only son Roger, and his best friend Stewart (Stew) Turbeville, arrived from their last day of school at Oak Bay High School, Chad Emory and seven other people were inspecting the great find. News had traveled fast. Anyone in or around the small town of Oak Bay, who relished history, wanted to know what was under all those thick pine boards which had been hiding a log cabin from plain sight for many years. Once Mark saw Roger and Stew he immediately walked over to them as Roger asked, "What is goin' on here, Dad?"

"I'm not quite sure but while you were at school today, they found somethin' pretty incredible."

Roger asked, "What have they found?"

"They think that the main portion of Big Me-maw's house is a log cabin."

Stew looked at his best friend and said, "How cool is this?"

Roger was ecstatic about the news, but he was also still aggravated that his parents had decided to tear down the house that he dearly loved. His grandmother had only been dead for about two weeks last year when his parents informed him that they were going to tear down the old house and build a new modern brick style two story house. Roger begged them to renovate the old house which was built in three sections. His Grandmother Gwen, had told the family that the front section had been added to the original house in 1920 to accommodate two elderly aunts who had come to live with the James family. She also told the family that the middle and back sections of the home, which were adjoined by large glassed in breezeways, had been built around 1865. She said that Marks's father, Matthew James III, had been told by his father that Union troops had spared the newly built house in 1865 while they were burning down many structures during the last days of the Civil War. After the family placed a Masonic Symbol in the window of the home, Union troops who sympathized with their Masonic brothers decided to leave the structure standing after they took all of the valuables and destroyed the crops.

Roger loved the history surrounding his grandmother's house which had been home to at least three generations of dairy farmers. His father Mark was not one of them. Mark, who became a legendary high school football player at Oak Bay High School, wanted nothing to do with dairy farming the day he went to college at Appalachian

State in 1961 on a football scholarship. Two years later, a career ending chop block from a short, stumpy looking offensive lineman from Western Carolina College shattered his right knee. During the school's winter break that year he found himself back on the farm hobbled with a full-length cast and a pair of crutches. Recuperating with every intention of returning to Appalachian State, his father decided to take a nap one Sunday afternoon and never woke up. Suffering from a massive heart attack, Mark's father left a thriving dairy operation a lot better off than when he inherited it.

Less than a year later, the only child of the family supposedly persuaded his mother to sell the dairy portion of the farm and give up the family business altogether. He was still hobbled and heartbroken when he took over the milk business; a business which required ridiculous hours and a love for bovines which only a handful of special people ever possess. Mark was not one of them.

Once Roger was old enough to understand that his grandmother sold the dairy operation for a lot less than it was worth, he resented the fact that he never had the opportunity to decide if he wanted to become involved in the now defunct family business. Roger had been told two very conflicting stories surrounding that fateful decision to end dairy farming. His grandmother once told him that she sold off the operation because Mark didn't want to work on the farm. Roger's father, Mark told him that Gwen James decided to sell because she had no inclination to manage something that she had grown to hate. Knowing his grandmother, he believed his father.

None of the family history erased the fact that Roger wanted to keep the old house for more than sentimental reasons. He appreciated old things and loved history. He thought it would be cool to live in a house that was over a hundred years old. He wanted to live in the house where several of his ancestors were born and where most of them died.

Roger's mother, however, was totally opposed to living in a house which she believed was as haunted as a graveyard. Roger was convinced that his father really did not want to tear down the old house. He knew for a fact his mother would have burned down the place if it was up to her. She could care less about the ancient rows of hydrangea bushes and neatly laid out rows of monkey grass near the front porch which some said were planted before the Great Depression. She hated the Spanish moss which swirled in the large oak tree which sat dead-center in front of the house. Bearing the remnants of several rusted horseshoes and a large railroad spike embedded into its bark, the old oak was the oldest living thing on the farm.

To appease Roger somewhat, Mark agreed to use some of the boards of the old house in the new house they were planning to build. He also directed the construction crew to save some of the bricks from the original fireplace for the new home.

Living in a mobile home next to his grandmother's house his entire life, Roger longed for the day that his family could move into a real house. His mother had the same dream but she wanted a brand new modern home without any antiques or any of the old furniture her mother-in law left in the house. Mark had promised his bride a new home for many years, but he did not have enough cash to make it happen. He never once thought about asking his mother for a loan. Everyone in Oak Bay knew that Gwen James would have given Mark anything he asked for if he only asked. His pride would not allow it.

Driving a local architect almost insane, Juanita James was allowed to design the new home once Gwen passed away. Inheriting two timber lease agreements and a few shares of Wachovia Bank stock,

Mark's inheritance was significantly less than what he expected. He was mentally devastated when he found out that his mother secretly cashed in several life insurance policies he thought were still in full force. She had also secretly sold off a few parcels of land adjacent to the property which he was counting on for extra rental income. When Gwen's attorney told Mark that his mother's savings accounts were nearly dry, he could not believe it. Gwen had left him enough money to build a new home, but not nearly enough money for him to live comfortably. He soon realized that the property taxes were going to eat him alive.

Mark James was visibly worn down from a marriage to a woman who had pushed the envelope with an assortment of psychiatric diagnoses. He tried hard through the years to find his wife professional help because of her irrational behavior which started when Roger was a baby. Her diagnosed postpartum depression lasted for more than fifteen years according to one doctor while another said she had a personality disorder which was so severe he did not have enough training to provide her adequate care.

Having a religious awakening five years into the marriage, Juanita was now consumed with reading the Bible and participating with various prayer groups. Prayers and numerous hours of Bible reading did not offer relief from her disorders, but it did seem to calm her down at times. Her own pastor was forced to spend countless hours trying to resolve her tangled tongue which at times brought confusion among his flock. Simply stated it was not uncommon for her to tell a church member to go straight to hell during a church service. When Roger was only seven years old, his mother testified publically to the congregation of her church after the Children's Choir completed a Christmas play. Before Mark James could usher her away from the podium, she told the congregation that she too had been blessed to be a Virgin when she "miraculously" gave birth to her son.

Mark worked as the manager of the Oak Bay Hardware Store during the day and drank just enough at night to squelch the sting of a woman he knew was as crazy as a cheetah monkey. On top of having to deal with his psychotic wife, Mark had to deal with his mother who drove his own father to an early grave with her petulant demands and constant nagging. The friction between Juanita and Gwen at times was chaotic and extremely toxic. Even Mark knew that there was nothing that Juanita could do to live up to his mother's unrealistic expectations. Mark was constantly torn as he tried in vain to please two stubborn women who were as different as their homes. Gwen's overbearing meddling in the marriage caused Juanita to pack her bags on more than one occasion. Once Gwen found out that Juanita had psychiatric issues, she dubbed her the "deranged" daughter-in-law to all of her friends. On two different occasions the two women came to blows where Mark was forced to separate them.

Mark's uncanny ability to talk his wife into returning to their country home was as impressive as his ability to talk his mother into apologizing to his bride. Juanita's deep resentment of living under her mother-in-law's shadow had a powerful impact on the dynamics of the family.

In 1976, when Gwen fell in the old house and broke her hip, it was Juanita who was saddled with her care because Mark could not bring himself to put his mother in a nursing home. The prideful and elitist woman hated her predicament more than her daughter-in-law hated tending to her. Every time Juanita would try to wait on her, it was never good enough. Every time Gwen pitched a fit about her perceived lack of care, Juanita would sternly scold her like a child. Whenever people would visit, Gwen would tell them that Juanita was trying to kill her. Although no one ever paid attention to the old lady, Juanita utterly loathed her ungrateful comments and attitude.

Only a month after the big fall, Gwen suffered a massive stroke. She went downhill from there and lingered for months. The day before she died, Gwen James mumbled the words, "Go to hell" to her daughter-in-law.

Juanita whispered back, "I'm never going to visit the place where you are headed."

Chapter Two

A few minutes after Roger and Stew were able to get a look at the exposed section of the home which revealed two logs of the cabin, Chad Emory yelled at Mark James and said, "You need to come in the house and see what we have found."

Roger and Stew followed Mark into the main section of the barren house. Having removed the old wood paneling that had been on the walls since the turn of the century, they were all surprised to find the exposed wall in the living room covered with old newspapers. Mark asked the noted historian, "What is all this?"

"It is the old way of insulating a house. You would be surprised how effective it was, but then again you grew up in this house. These papers kept you warm in the winter and cool during the summer. Many times in these old homes, we find layers of newspapers that span many years."

Stew, who had begun closely inspecting the wall, said, "Y'all look here. I wonder who these ball players are in this drawing."

Chad Emory walked closer and upon clear examination said, "That is the front cover of *Harper's Weekly*, dated July 28, 1888."

Mark, who was only a few feet away from them said, "Here is the front page of the *State Newspaper* when the Spanish-American War started in 1898."

They all then began silently peering at the exposed wall, looking for even better finds. Chad Emory became a little giddy when he saw an 1859 editorial by the *Southern Watchman* opposing the election of Abraham Lincoln. To him this was the first proof that the home may have been built before 1865. When Roger found an article from an unknown newspaper about the death of famous composer Ludwig Beethoven, Chad Emory bent over and gasped before saying loudly, "He died in 1827. I will certainly be at the courthouse in the morning to research the title of this property. Who knows? We may find out this cabin goes back all the way into the 1700's."

Mark James asked, "What does all this mean?"

"It means that you own the oldest known standing home in Oak Bay County. I don't want to get into your business, but for the life of me, how is it that you didn't know this house was so old?"

Mark scratched his head and then replied, "I knew I had ancestors who lived on this property that pre-dated this house, but I just assumed that there had to be another home place on this property for the earlier ancestors that I knew about."

Chad Emory smiled and then replied, "That makes perfect sense. It appears that your family built right over the existing cabin. That was probably done in 1865. Pausing for a few seconds, he then asked, "Who do you think was the first person in your family who settled here?"

Mark replied, "From what other family members have told me, it was a man by the name of Matthew James. My father said that his father remembered seeing a painting of him when he was a child. He was later told the painting was stolen. My mother said that a lot of the old people in Oak Bay said there was a mystery surroundin' the first Matthew James. Nobody in the family has ever found out much about him or how he ended up here at Hogtail Swamp. My Great Aunt Clara did a lot of research on the family years ago. She hit a dead end when it came to the first Matthew James."

Chad Emory laughed and said, "Well, I'm not exactly sure right now when or if Matthew built this cabin, but I know one thing, he or somebody else was worried about some kind of attack. They were most likely concerned about local Indians."

"Why do you say that?"

"You see that hole in the corner of that wall?"

"Yes, sir."

"That is what we call a cabin musket hole. They were commonly used in log cabins of this same era for protection against possible invasion."

Roger spoke up and asked, "What happens next concerning this log cabin?"

Chad Emory paused and then replied, "Once we find out the age of this structure, your father will have to decide which direction he wants to go."

Mark asked, "What do you mean? We are supposed to start new construction in a few days."

Chad Emory with a puzzled look on his face quickly replied, "It's ultimately your decision, Mark, but if I were you, I would hold off for right now. You have a treasure that many people would love to see."

Roger looked at his father, but before he could say anything, Mark said, "It's your Mama I worry about. You know she could care less about any of this. For right now, I'm only going to tell her that construction has been delayed. Thank God she is at a prayer meetin' right now. She would not be happy."

"Good idea, Dad."

Roger then looked at Stew and asked, "You want to go up into the attic? We might find somethin' else of value."

Mark said, "We cleaned out everything. There is nothin' up there but old spider webs and a bunch of dust."

After getting a flashlight, Roger helped his best friend climb into the attic. Stew was not nearly as excited as Roger when he asked, "What are we lookin' for?"

"I don't know, but I have a feelin' that we may have missed somethin' when I helped my Dad remove all of the items that were up here. We were in such a hurry that we never looked for anything of real historical value."

A few minutes later Roger crouched down next to the exposed section of chimney and found a shoe box tucked away under a moth-eaten quilt. Searching frantically through the pile of papers in the box, he only found a few invoices from the farm which were dated in the 1940's. A few minutes later they unexpectedly hit pay dirt when Stew tried to stand up straight in the dark and musty room. Banging his head on the beam above him, Stew fell to the floor of the attic just as quickly as he had hit the beam above him. Grabbing the top of his head, he screamed, "Damit, Roger."

Mark James yelled from the main floor, "Are y'all ok up there? It sounds like y'all are about to come through the ceiling."

"We are ok, Dad. Stew hit his head but he is ok."

A few seconds later, something fell from the beam onto the attic floor, right next to Stew's head. Roger began to laugh and said, "You almost got the hell knocked out of you again."

Stew, holding one hand on the top of his head, rolled over and reached for the object next to him. Roger duck walked over to him and shined the flashlight on the object. It appeared to them both that it was a large book. Neither one of them had seen a book that large. Before looking at it, Roger slowly stood up next to the large beam above Stew. A few seconds later, with the help of the flashlight, he was able to see that Stew's hard head had cracked a shingle-looking box attached on top of the large beam. He then surmised that the large book had been ricocheted out of the box by the splintering of one section of rotten wood. Once Stew began opening the ancient looking text, Roger knelt closer to him. The beam of the flashlight immediately revealed a handwritten looking journal. Seventeen year-old Roger looked at his friend and said, "I have no idea what is in this book, but I am sure it has to be worth a few dollars to someone like Mr. Emory."

"You can say that again. Just look at the date on this first page. It says September 14, the year of our Lord 1786. This thing is about two hundred years old. I bet old man Davis at the Pawn Shop would give you a couple hundred dollars for this."

Roger looked at his friend and said, "You are probably right, but nobody is gettin' near this thing until I read every last page."

Taking a few minutes to read the first page with limited sight, they both were beyond excited when they struggled to read and decipher the following words: Thus I have recorded as testament thru my witness- Matthew James.

Long after his parents had gone to sleep that night, Roger quietly snuck out of the trailer and retrieved the large journal from the attic of the old house. The book was thick, and it was heavy. After almost dropping it on the front steps of the trailer, he was finally able to carry it into his bedroom where he began a historical journey which had him totally intrigued to the point where sleep became an afterthought. Reading from a book which was almost in pristine condition, Roger quickly began learning about his great, great, grandfather- Matthew James. Using a magnifying glass and a large standup lamp in the corner of his room, he began deciphering not only the small cursive handwriting but also the unique language of the time period. After about an hour of reading, Roger surmised that although Matthew James was indeed from the Virginia colony; the path he took to reach Hogtail Swamp in South Carolina was a mystery.

He quickly learned that Matthew was called to duty to help fight at the end of the French-Indian War when he was only nineteen years-old. In 1763, he and about thirty of his fellow Virginians were sent to Western Pennsylvania as reinforcements to help secure lands against Native American attacks.

Matthew wrote a detailed account of a small skirmish near Conewago Creek, Pennsylvania, where his small regiment was ambushed by a group of Indians on their way to Fort Pitt.

Roger was fascinated as he read about a battle which turned out to be utter chaos. It became each man for himself. Escaping with only a scratch from a grazing hatchet blow to the side of his face, Matthew found himself running through the woods alone, afraid, and completely lost. Describing that he walked and ran what seemed like "a day's journey", he hid near some large boulders which sat next to a smattering of wild bushes. He had no idea how far he was from civilization. His writing revealed the uncertainty and emotional anguish he was experiencing; knowing that many of his friends had been killed. He wept for his friends and relatives, including a "cuzin" named Eugene Barber. His written description of his cousin's death revealed the brutality of the battle. Matthew described in great detail the moment his cousin was almost completely severed in half while he groaned a loud plea for help during his last breaths. Matthew was heartbroken, confused, and all alone.

Not knowing what to do or where to go, Matthew waited for hours before he decided to move. Making his way down a small path to the edge of a creek before dusk, he was startled when he walked up on a somewhat camouflaged Lenape warrior who appeared to blend in with the local terrain. Squatting next to the creek and washing his face, the warrior did not hear Matthew's approach.

With the sound of Matthew cocking the hammer of his musket, the young warrior slowly turned around. Once he saw his face, Matthew realized that he and the warrior looked to be about the same age. Not knowing if he should shoot or allow the warrior to flee, Matthew stood motionless for a few seconds trying to think his way through the standoff. The young warrior then spoke up and said, "Dark comes. Shoot me or let me flee... Hungry."

Matthew could not believe that the warrior spoke English. After making the warrior put down his weapons, Matthew lowered his musket. The young native warrior then began telling Matthew that he had learned the "language of the British" from a Catholic missionary priest. He then spoke about his tribe and how his people were caught up in a war that would impact their tribe's survival. When Matthew asked him about the earlier ambush where he was almost scalped, the warrior explained that he had no knowledge concerning the matter. Matthew wasn't sure he believed him.

Matthew shared with him that he had journeyed a long way to help fight against people he did not know. On the edge of that creek the two teenagers found themselves sharing hopes and dreams that were not dissimilar. Matthew wrote the following which stood out to Roger: "Offer of a quaint sack of small berries, he smiled when I supped with him. I then knew God would offer protection."

The warrior named Nighthawk then extended his hand and told Matthew that he would be protected by his people if he wanted to follow him to his camp a few miles through the woods along the creek bed. Strangely, Matthew decided to follow knowing that he could be killed at any time. He had already witnessed the horrors of war. He now wanted to experience meeting a group of people who he had grown up believing were nothing more than savages.

Almost falling asleep after this last journal entry, Roger decided he better put the large book under his bed before he was caught. He did not want to turn it over to anyone until he had the chance to read further and find out more about Matthew James.

Chapter Three

The next morning when Mark James was driving to work, he thought about the log cabin which had been revealed from the demolition of his childhood home. He was reminiscing about some of his fond childhood memories playing under the old house when he suddenly had to apply his brakes to his beat up Chevrolet farm truck. In the nick of time, he was able to avoid running into the back of a brown station wagon which was the first of many cars that had come to a screeching halt about a quarter of a mile from the Billy "Cotton" Richardson Bridge on the outskirts of the Oak Bay city limits. Sitting in his truck for a few minutes, he began to wonder what was hindering the flow of traffic. He could not remember the last time he had seen traffic so backed up on the long bridge which spanned the Pee Dee River. A few minutes later as the traffic ahead of him began to move at a snail's pace, he was able to see his first glimpse of tragedy. The reflection of lights from the emergency vehicles at the bottom of the bridge along with the rising sun, danced off the deep dark waters of the river onto the old bridge pylons giving off a strobe light effect which momentarily hindered the sight of the drivers on the bridge. Once he came to the bridge itself, he could see a section of the bridge on the northbound lane where it appeared to him that a vehicle had crashed through the side railing. Creeping slowly up onto the bridge he was able to see a large county owned backhoe trying to pull something out of the river. Once traffic was stopped again by a young Deputy Sheriff, Mark was able to ask the deputy what happened.

The Deputy shouted out to him, "I'm not really sure. All I know is that somebody crashed into the river early this morning, and they have had a hell of time trying to get that car out of the river."

Over at the Oak Bay County RMC or Register of Mesne Conveyances, Sheila Biddle was busy placing a few document stamps on a newly filed Warranty deed of land title when she screamed at Chad Emory of the Historical Society, "Slow down, Chad, I have to get this deed stamped and recorded before I can help you."

Chad Emory patiently waited a few seconds and then replied, "I don't mean to be a pain in the rear this morning, but I need to find out about the James property at Hogtail Swamp."

Once she completed her task, she walked with him into the old deed book room which desperately needed better lighting. She asked in a librarian's whisper, "Are you talkin' about the property now owned by Mark James?"

"Yes."

Stopping next to a reading counter, she looked at him and replied, "We are in the wrong room. If you want to search deep into the line of title for that particular property, we need to go into the Wills and

Last Testaments Room next to the Probate Office. It will be easier to find the land title through testate distribution."

Digging through books which revealed the James family line of land distribution, Sheila finally looked at Chad Emory and said, "We are at a definite dead end."

"What do you mean?"

She sort of gave him a quick grin and then said, "We have the last will and testament of the first Matthew James. The Will describes land and title distribution to his offspring. We know he died in 1828, but as far as any record of how he obtained his land, we know nothing."

"How is that possible?"

"It's quite possible that Matthew James was an original settler of the property. That is highly unlikely but possible. Reading his will, there is no indication as to how he came to be the owner of his land. Unless you can find out something about his life, you will not find any records here about him obtaining his land. Based on the year of his death he could have settled on that property any time from 1728 forward to 1828. Of course, this would depend on how hostile the Indians were in the area. Surely, you people at the Historical Society, must have something in your records about this man."

"Not one thing. He is not mentioned as one of the founding fathers of Oak Bay. The oldest map of the area we have only goes back to 1840. For whatever reason he must have lived on the edge of the swamp without being too involved with other settlers in the area."

"Chad, your best bet would be to call someone at the South Carolina Archives and see if he is listed on any of the Census records. They have census records that go back to 1790."

While Chad Emory was still nowhere close to finding out the exact date of the James family cabin, Roger James was woken by his mother singing the tune to a gospel song loudly in the kitchen. Walking out of his bedroom into the small trailer's living room he yelled at his mother, "What are you doing, Mama? It's my first day of summer vacation, and the only day I can sleep in."

"The Lord doesn't like laziness. Besides, your father wants you to take the tractor down to the pond and bush hog around it before you head to Myrtle Beach this weekend. He also wanted me to tell you that you needed to change the oil in that old pile of junk."

"Stew is supposed to come over in a little while and we..."

Juanita interrupted her son and said, "He can come over, but the work has to be done. Speakin' of work, I wonder why the construction crew isn't workin' on the house today?"

"Daddy didn't tell ya?"

"Tell me what?"

"I don't know. I just thought he would know since he talks to the construction people every day."

"What aren't you tellin' me?"

"Talk to him. I have no idea about the construction."

Skipping breakfast, Roger hurried up and sprinted out of the trailer. He then made his way over to the old farm shed behind what remained of his grandmother's house. He slowly crawled up on the orange 1965 Massey Ferguson 135 tractor and cranked it up. The Carolina sun quickly began peeking its head from behind a few clouds, bearing down on the shirtless body of Roger James as he drove the tractor to the small pond.

While he began cutting around the pond, the starting pitcher for the Oak Bay American Legion baseball team began thinking about the upcoming season and how everyone in town had high hopes. The year before, they finished the season one game shy of making it to the state finals. Suffering from tendonitis, Roger felt he let his team down in the final game when he could only watch from the bench. It was one of the most disappointing moments he had experienced in his athletic career. Although he had helped his high school baseball team win two state championships, he personally wanted to win the American Legion state championship.

Roger or "Hot Rod Roger" was good, and he knew it. His father may have been a Oak Bay football legend, but Roger was quickly becoming a legend himself. Some people said he threw a baseball faster than anyone could remember. He could also throw a beautiful spiral as he also played quarterback for Oak Bay High. Although he knew that everyone in Oak Bay thought he was the man, he never let his sports' accomplishments go to his head. His father made sure that never happened.

Mark James loved being known by everybody, but he wanted more for his son than being remembered as a ball legend in the small South Carolina town. He wanted him to be prepared both athletically and academically. He pushed but never too far. His pride in his son and his accomplishments were tempered with genuine gratitude and enough self-reflection to make sure that fun never escaped the plan for success.

Roger loved the way his father had approached his God-given talents. He also appreciated that his father was not an overbearing jerk when it came to his development. He had witnessed some of his other friends' fathers who pushed their sons into hating the day they had ever picked up a ball when they were children. His father, however, would push him hard, but then would take him to eat ice cream or go fishing. Especially when he was still a small tot, he and his father always had a good time even through the bad games or heartbreaking defeats. At an early age, Mark taught his son that being humble was the most important trait he wanted his son to exhibit whenever he played ball. Once during a Little League baseball game, Roger laughed out loud when he accidently hit an opposing batter with a wild pitch. Sacrificing a big win over a rival team, Mark James immediately pulled his son from the game and told him he would rather him strike out every time at bat than to embarrass the family with such behavior. By the time he was twelve years old, Roger knew that bragging about his own accomplishments, publicly demeaning his opponent or exhibiting any action which would shine the spotlight on him would not be tolerated by his father. He also knew that no matter how bad he or his team performed, it was his father who was his biggest fan. Roger could always count on his father saying to him after a bad performance, “Hey, Big Guy, you just remember that the sun doesn’t always shine on the same dog’s ass. Tomorrow will be another day.”

Two hours later after making his last turn around the pond on the tractor, Roger suddenly thought about the treasure he had under his bed. He couldn’t wait to get back to the trailer and read some more out of his great-great grandfather’s journal. Making his way on the tractor to the old shed, he saw Stew pull up in his Plymouth Barracuda. Jumping off the tractor, Roger yelled at his friend, “Are you ready for the beach tomorrow?”

Stew yelled back, “David Jennings wants us to go out to a bar down there called the Bowery. He says everyone is fired up about a band called Alabama that is playing there.”

“I have never heard of them. You know that I’m not gonna drink while we are there so I don’t know about the bar scene. What is the name of the hotel where we are stayin’?

Stew smiled and then said, “We are goin’ to the Bowery. David says that all the girls from school will be there. You don’t have to drink a thing, but those girls will be hammered. Since you are officially a single man again, I think some new scenery will do you some good."

"Ok, but where are we stayin'?"

"The Sandy Shore Motel. It's only a few blocks away from the Pavilion."

"Hand me that socket wrench behind you. I have to change the oil in this old tractor."

Handing his best friend the socket wrench, Stew smiled and said, "Look, old buddy, this will be the last time all summer we'll be able to get away. With summer jobs and baseball starting next week, you need to let your hair down and have some fun this weekend. Don't be a party pooper."

"Ok, but I'm still not gonna drink. I don't care what y'all do, but I am committed to this year's Legion baseball season."

"That's fine. You don't have to drink. Did you have a chance to look at the book last night?"

"Did I? It's like a diary. My relative must have been one bored dude. He wrote about everything."

"Did you find out about when he built the cabin?"

"I haven't read that far yet."

"Are you kiddin' me? What did you find out?"

For the next hour Roger told his childhood friend what he had learned. Stew, who almost failed US History only a few days prior, was busy taking mental notes as Roger told the story while he drained the oil from the old tractor. Stew asked, "What happened when Matthew entered the Indian camp?"

"I have no idea. I stopped readin' at that point and fell asleep."

"Let's go find out now."

"No way. My Mama will never give us a moment's peace. You know she doesn't like it when I bring anyone to my room. I will have to read it later."

Later that afternoon, Chad Emory walked into the Oak Bay Hardware Store to talk with Mark James. Finding him sitting in his office, the town's most respected historian had Mark's full attention when he said, "We still don't know exactly how old the cabin is since the Census records for Oak Bay County before 1800 have disappeared from the state archives in Columbia. I am ashamed to admit that I forgot about those missing records. For whatever reasons the 1790 national census records for this area went missing in the 1950's. I totally forgot all about it. What we do know is that the last record of that cabin is a part of the record in the 1800 Census. I say that, but to tell you the truth, it just describes the family members living in a dwelling."

"What do we need to do now that you know this information?"

"How important is it for you that the new home is built on the same site as the cabin?"

"For my wife that is nonnegotiable. Don't think I didn't suggest that earlier. She thinks the new house would look out of place the way our property sits. She wants a new house and thinks buildin' one next to the old house would look stupid. We looked into renovation, but it was goin' to cost more to renovate than to build a brand new house."

"I see. Well, what if we could move the cabin to the back portion of your property?"

"How much money are we lookin' at?"

"I know we could get Mr. Peabody to give us a good deal. As a matter of fact he said he would do it for less than a thousand dollars.

It also happens that the Historical Society is willing to pay for that expense if you agree to one thing."

"What's that?"

"Allow people to come and visit the site."

"I don't know about all that."

"Look, Mark, this could be a money maker for both of us. We could set up a money box and ask for donations with a minimum two dollar donation. That way nobody has to man the place. You keep fifty percent of whatever is donated. I know it sounds cheesy, but we know that in similar setups, other people around the nation have made enough money to pay off their property taxes. With the right advertisement, you could be sitting on perpetual income long after we are gone. The historical society will promise to keep the cabin in good condition at no expense to you with the profits we acquire. It's a no brainer."

"That may be true, but I don't think my wife is goin' to like havin' strangers drivin' up to our place. She likes her privacy."

"I understand. You think about it for a few days. I will go ahead and draw up the contract in case you decide you would like to go through with it. I and many of the historical people of Oak Bay sure hope that you decide to keep the cabin because it is a...."

Mark interrupted him and said, "I know. You said last night it was a treasure, but right now it sure seems like a big headache."

Chapter Four

Roger ended up talking with his father most of the evening before his big trip to Myrtle Beach. Although the parents of the boys from Oak Bay had agreed to allow this adventure, every one of them only agreed after parental supervision became a reality. Mark was no different. If it wasn't for the parents of outfielder Josh Ackerman, Roger and his friends would not have been allowed to make the trip. Mark trusted his son to make good decisions while he was with his friends. Flashing back to his own adventures at South Carolina's busiest tourist spot, Mark wanted to make sure that his son didn't make some of the same mistakes he made when he was the same age.

Their conversation that night was awkward, but Roger understood why his father was so concerned. Although he wanted to shut himself in his bedroom and continue reading the journal, he knew it was more important to let his father get whatever was on his mind off of his chest. The last thing Roger wanted to do was to disappoint his father.

Juanita had already gone to bed when Mark looked at Roger before he changed the channel of the television for the Eleven o'clock News and said, "I'm countin' on you to be the leader down there. Don't let Stew and the rest of the boys talk you into somethin' you don't want to do. Remember, you have a lot more ridin' on this baseball season than some of those Bozo's. Don't let me get a call from the Myrtle Beach Jail because I will not come and get you. I love ya, but if you do somethin' crazy I will let you sit in that jail for a long time."

Roger laughed at his father then said, "Worry about somethin' else, Dad. I will be fine."

Mark looked at his son with a smile and responded, "I sure will miss you, and you know I love you."

Roger laughed before saying, "I love you Dad. You act like I'm shippin' off for the Marines. I'll be back Monday when Legion baseball practice starts."

Their conversation was then interrupted by a news reporter of the Eleven o'clock News from Charleston who was reporting from the bottom of the Billy "Cotton" Richardson Bridge. Mark yelled out to Roger, "That is the accident from this mornin'."

Roger said, "Hush up, Dad, so we can hear what he has to say."

The reporter then said, "Sad news to report tonight as authorities from Oak Bay County say they have recovered the body of State Senator Dennis Broadway from the Pee Dee River. The forty-two year old Senator from Moncks Corner drove off the Richardson Bridge sometime in the early morning hours, plunging to his death. At this time the Oak Bay Sheriff's Department in conjunction with the South Carolina Law Enforcement Division has not been able to determine the cause of the accident. The powerful Democratic Senator from the Lowcountry has served his constituents since being elected in 1966. He leaves behind a wife and three children. This is Mike Johnson of Channel Five News reporting in Oak Bay."

Mark looked at Roger and said, "That is a shame. I wonder why he was in Oak Bay so early in the mornin'."

Roger replied, "I don't know, but I bet he hates that he ever came to Oak Bay County. I love you, Dad. Have a good night."

The next morning, Roger found himself cramped in the passenger seat of Stew's Plymouth while third baseman Buddy Welsh's knees kept pushing him forward from the backseat. Stopping only a few miles from Oak Bay, at Tyler Crossroads, Roger yelled at Stew, "What are you doin'?

"Don't worry about it. I need to get somethin' out of the trunk."

Returning to the car with two six packs of beer and two bottles of wine, Roger said, "I told you that I was not drinkin'.

"I know. But me and Buddy are just a little thirsty."

Roger shot back, "You two are stupid. With all of the law enforcement people in and around this area because of that senator's accident y'all are not being very smart. You also know if y'all show up drunk, Mrs. Ackerman will send both of you home. If you are going to drink, let me drive."

"Come on, man. I will be fine."

"Ok but you two do not need to show up drunk. I don't want to be sent home."

Stew yelled out, "Hell, Roger, Josh's Mama drinks like a fish. I bet you five dolla's that she will already be passed out under an umbrella on the beach when we get there. That woman likes rum more than she likes her husband."

In a serious tone of voice Roger asked, “What about Mr. Ackerman? He is the one who told my Daddy that he would be callin’ parents if somebody got out of hand.”

Stew laughed before saying, “He’s a great guy, but the man is scared of his own shadow. That goofball will be so busy lookin’ at the young girls struttin’ on the beach; he will never pay us any attention.”

Buddy laughed and said, "He's right, Roger. Everyone in town knows Mr. Ackerman likes lookin’ at the eye candy.”

About an hour later after taking a curve way too fast on a secondary highway in a remote section of Marion County, Roger punched his best friend in the arm and said, “Find a place and pull this car over; let me drive!”

If it wasn’t for the fact that Roger’s two teammate’s bladders were about to explode, Stew would have never pulled off down a dirt road to let Roger drive his car. Secluded but in broad daylight, Roger’s friends began urinating next to the car right in the middle of the road while he threw out some of their empty beer cans. Right as they were finishing their last whizz of relief, Roger saw a car speeding down the dirt road. Before he could get his friends to climb back into Stew’s car, blue lights were flashing.

Deputy Barrett from the Marion County Sheriff's Department pulled up behind them and quickly got out of his patrol car. The overweight deputy with a big chaw of tobacco in his mouth yelled, “Don’t take another step.”

Stew, who was buzzing pretty good, smiled at the officer and asked, “What seems to be the problem, sir?”

“Where you boys from?”

Buddy replied, “We are from Oak Bay.”

“What brings you to Marion County?”

Roger spoke up and said, “We are on our way to Myrtle Beach.”

Before the deputy could reply, Roger took a couple steps toward him. Roger's movement spooked the deputy, who pulled his revolver out of his holster. "Don't you move another inch or I will shoot ya dead. Let me see your hands."

Roger put his hands over his head and said, "We're cool, sir. Nobody here wants any trouble."

"Is that right? Well, I hate to tell you clowns from Oak Bay, that here in Marion County, it's against the law to urinate in public."

All three of them replied in unison, "Yes, sir."

"Shut the hell up. My Mama lives on this road, and she would die if she knew that three clowns from Oak Bay were pissing on her road. Now why would you jackasses decide to pull down here and piss on my Mama's road on your way to the beach? Could it be because y'all have been doin' a little drinkin' cause I know beer when I smell it All of you hand me your driver's license or some official identification."

Stew then spoke up and said as he handed the deputy his driver's license, "Sir, we have only had a couple of beers. We are good."

Right after the words were spoken, vomit came flying out of Buddy's mouth as he began puking his guts out only a few feet away from the deputy. Deputy Barret shouted, "Oh, hell, no. It's one thing to piss on my Mama's road. It's another thing to puke on it. Y'all wait right here."

Roger began to think about what his father told him about calling him if he was put in jail while the lawman went back to his patrol car. Stew whispered to Buddy, "Damit, boy. What the hell? What is wrong with you?"

Buddy spit a couple of times and wiped off his face before saying, "I guess wine and beer don't like scrambled eggs and bacon."

Roger replied in a sarcastic tone of voice, "Not one bit. But don't worry, I am sure they will feed us real good in jail."

Stew looked at Roger and said, "He ain't gonna arrest us. He's bluffin'."

A few minutes later, Deputy Barrett made his way back over to them with three pieces of paper in his hand. He looked at the culprits and said, "Ok you clowns, y'all better be glad I don't have time to fool with y'all today. You can be on your way. Each of you can either pay this $75 fine for public nuisance and disorderly conduct or you can mail it in before you have to go to trial. Your choice."

Stew spoke up and said, "We ain't got that kind of money."

"You should have thought about that before you decided to piss all over my Mama's dirt road."

Buddy, who still felt a little sick asked, "Officer, does your Mama live at the end of this road? We will go up there and apologize to her right now, sir."

"Too late, vomit boy. The tickets have already been written."

Stew laughed and then said, "That's because his Mama don't live here. I bet there ain't a house within two miles of this soybean field. This is just a classic case of highway robbery." He then pulled out sixty dollars in cash from his pocket and said, "Look here, man, let's make a deal. Tear up those tickets, take this cash and you will never see us again."

Deputy Barrett didn't immediately respond as he gave Stew a long hard stare for a few seconds. Then suddenly he smiled and said, "I'll make this simple. Two hundred dolla's and y'all can be on your way."

Stew quickly responded, "Why don't we meet somewhere in the middle? How about one hundred?"

"No, sir, I have a better idea. It's gonna be one hundred fifty doll'as and the rest of that wine and beer you have in the backseat. If not, you beach boys can spend a night in our wonderful jailhouse while your car gets towed for another one hundred dolla's. This is the last offer you beach boys are gonna get today."

At first screaming at each other, Roger and his sobering friends quickly made a truce by the time they made it to the outskirts of Myrtle Beach. Buddy had just quit singing the newly released song, "The Devil Went Down To Georgia", by Charlie Daniels which was blaring on the car radio when Stew asked Roger, "I bet you thought we were goin' to jail. I know you don't believe me, but I knew all along he was bluffin'."

Roger kept his eyes on the road while only responding with a nod of his head. He was still mad about losing most of his money before making it to the beach. Buddy then laughed from the back seat and said, "I sure hope the first thing that deputy does is to chug that wine cause I would give the rest of my money to see his face when he does."

Roger looked in the rear view mirror and then asked, "Why is that?"

"Way before we stopped, I pissed in that empty bottle right here in the backseat. I almost filled that sucker up."

After all laughing, Roger asked Stew, "You know how to get to the motel?"

Stew ignored his question and said, "Pull up over there. I'm hungry as hell, and we are gonna get some hotdogs over there at Peaches Corner."

Roger looked at Stew and said, "Hot dogs? You are crazy as hell. I'm already broke."

Stew quickly shot back, "I ain't ever been to the beach without eatin' at this joint. Don't worry: I'll pay. It's the least I can do since I almost got y'all locked up for a night."

Sitting out on the deck which overlooked the crowded beach, they began eating their fill of the best chili dogs ever known to mankind. Stew then said, "My daddy says that he used to eat here when he was a kid."

Buddy pointed at a sign hanging on the wall behind their table which read: Peaches Corner- Established 1937. The place was so packed that neither of them noticed that there was a celebrity eating and drinking with some friends at a corner table only a few feet away. Buddy was the first one to notice the NWA United States Heavyweight wrestling champion, Nature Boy- Rick Flair. Stew idolized the man and may have been his biggest fan.

From where they were sitting, Stew could not clearly see his idol. However, from Roger's vantage point he immediately concluded that it had to be the Nature Boy because it wasn't every day you saw a man wearing a fur coat at Myrtle Beach in June. There was no mistaking who it was when the professional wrestler with his long flowing blonde hair shouted out his famous, "Wooooo" yell when one of the bikini clad girls in his entourage finished chugging a bottle of cold beer.

Stew whispered to Roger, "I'm gonna go over there and get his autograph."

Roger said, "Leave that man alone. He's on vacation. Only a jerk would go up to him and ask for an autograph. Besides, you don't have a pen or any paper."

About to make his way back into the main part of Peaches Corner to find a pen and some paper, Stew stood up and then quickly sat back down. With a very troubled look on his face, Stew muttered, "I can't believe it."

Buddy asked, "What's wrong, Stew?"

"Do y'all see who the Nature Boy is with?"

Roger replied, “Yeah some pretty hot chicks.”

“Not the girls… Look at the guy sittin’ across from him.”

Buddy looked hard before he asked, “Who is that?”

Roger asked the same thing before Stew loudly said, “Y’all may be the dumbest people on the planet. That is the Steamboat sittin’ at the same table with the Nature Boy.”

Buddy asked, “Who is the Steamboat?’

Stew looked at his friends and said, “Y’all must live under a rock. That is Ricky Steamboat.”

Roger threw up his hands and asked, “Ain't he a wrestler, too?””

Stew seemed aggravated when he replied, “You idiots don't get it. That is the Nature Boy’s mortal enemy. He hates Ricky Steamboat.”

Roger laughed and then asked his friend, “Stew, you do realize that professional wrasslin’ is all fake?”

Buddy looked at Roger with a puzzled look on his face and asked Stew, “Is it really fake?”

Stew quickly responded by saying, “Don’t listen to him, Buddy. It ain’t fake. There ain’t nothin’ fake about it.”

Roger pointed over to the Nature Boy’s table and said, “And that ain’t fake? I thought you said they were mortal enemies. Mortal enemies don't eat a couple of burgers together at Myrtle Beach.”

Stew looked at Buddy and said, “Roger is full of crap. You just wait; the Nature Boy is settin’ up old Ricky Steamboat. Believe me when I tell you, there is a method to his madness. Ricky Steamboat may think he is havin’ a good time today, but the Nature Boy will take him down when he least expects it.”

Roger laughed and said, “You two are a lot dumber than you look.”

Stew couldn't accept his best friend’s criticism about his belief in professional wrestling and the blasphemy he had thrown at the

Nature Boy. Without saying a word he stood up and walked over to the raucous table where his television idol was sitting. The junior from Oak Bay High, who was on track to graduate in the bottom third of his class, interrupted the private gathering by saying, "Hey, Nature Boy, I'm Stew Turbeville. I am, without a doubt, your biggest fan."

"That's great kid, but this is a private gathering."

In his nervous excitement, Stew stepped a little closer to the table and started to speak when he accidentally bumped Ricky Steamboat from behind. As Ricky Steamboat slowly rose up from his chair, it was obvious that beer had been spilt. Stew couldn't see Ricky Steamboat's face, but he could see the reaction of horror on the faces of everyone else at the table including his idol, the Nature Boy. As Stew stood frozen with fear and embarrassment, Roger jumped up and quickly made his way over toward the table of celebrities. Trying to shake some of the beer off of his Hawaiian looking beach shirt, the Steamboat turned toward Stew and said, "I ought to kick your…."

The Nature Boy interrupted him saying, "Calm down, Rick. This moron didn't mean to bump into you. It was an accident. Let him go."

Stew then tried to apologize to the mortal enemy of his idol before being interrupted by Ricky Steamboat when he said, "Piss off, moron."

Stew then looked at the Nature Boy who shook his head and pointed for him to leave. Roger then grabbed Stew by the arm and forcefully began leading his friend away from the table. Only a few steps away they could all plainly hear the Nature Boy when he said, "I love it down here at Myrtle Beach, but every now and then, I will run into a few morons who really believe that what we do is real."

They kept walking out of Peaches Corner without saying a word to each other. If Stew was emotionally crushed, he never said one thing about it. Instead, he continued to hold on as a true believer of the sanctity of professional wrestling when Buddy said to him in the car, "I guess we know the truth now. No more wrasslin for me."

Stew looked at Buddy and said, "You are the biggest moron ever. The Nature Boy just said that bunch of crap so nobody else in Peaches Corner would bother him while he butters up the Steamboat. You just wait, the Nature Boy, Rick Flair is gonna destroy Ricky Steamboat."

Roger did not say a word as they finally began making their way to the Sandy Shore Motel. He could not wait to get out of the car, unpack, and hit the beach.

Chapter Five

With Stew driving his own car, Roger was not paying attention when Stew took a turn down Ocean Boulevard. They had ridden several blocks when Buddy yelled from the backseat, “Aren’t we goin’ the wrong way?” Turning down a side street, Stew pulled into the parking lot of a convenience store.

“What now?” Roger asked.

“We can’t show up at the motel without some drinks and snacks. Y’all come on in.”

Ten minutes later Stew and Buddy were putting beer into a cooler in the back of Stew’s Barracuda while Roger stood in the parking lot sipping on a bottle of Dr. Pepper. Using a fake ID, Stew spent another good chunk of his remaining cash to buy a case of beer, a loaf of white bread, and a large jar of peanut butter. Roger laughed and said, “I see you fools are plannin’ on bein’ on a liquid diet this weekend. Can we now go to the motel? I am ready to get on the beach."

Two blocks later, still heading south, Roger knew that they were heading in the wrong direction. Right before he was about to let his friend have a piece of his mind, Stew took a quick turn next to an abandoned, rundown beach house that was for sale. Stew looked at Roger and yelled, "You want to go on the beach, well, good buddy, we are here."

Driving over a small dune, the nut job from Oak Bay drove his car right out onto the beach. Roger knew they were going to jail. Parking way short of the water, Stewart jumped out of the car yelling, "The water looks great. Come on you two, let's have some fun."

Chasing their friend out into the water, Roger caught up with Stew before Buddy. He almost tackled him as waves came crashing in around his ankles. He yelled at Stew, "We can't park on the beach. The cops will come here and lock us up. Look at all these folks lookin' at us like we have robbed a bank."

Stew laughed and then replied, "Hell, Roger, the only thing they will tell us is to move the car. Lighten up and have some fun, boy. This will be the last time all summer we will have a chance to get away. Startin' Monday it will be all work, baseball, and girls. This will be our last real fun together before school starts."

Roger gave in. He and Buddy took off their shirts and proceeded to follow the starting catcher of the Oak Bay American Legion baseball team into the waters of the Atlantic Ocean. Once they had enough swimming, they made their way back to the car. Pulling out some beach towels, they sat down under a blazing sun which was tempered by a stiff ocean breeze and some cold beer.

Roger watched his two friends guzzle beer as quickly as they had done earlier that morning. Several people walked up to them and told them they needed to move the car off the beach before the local police were called. With each warning, Roger tried desperately to talk some sense into his stubborn friend. It was no use. Stew was willing to gamble that the authorities would never notice since the car was almost hidden by a small sand dune on one side, a thick patch of sea oats on the other, and a series of large beach umbrellas perfectly placed in front of the car.

An hour later, Roger was convinced that Stew was right about the local authorities and finally began to relax. Leaving his friends to take a swim on his own, he noticed a single engine plane flying down the Grand Stand with a banner hanging from its tail. The banner read: America is Turning 7 Up. He laughed thinking to himself that the soft drink did not stand a chance against the big Two no matter how much they advertised.

After his long swim he made his way back to his friends noticing that many people were beginning to leave the beach. Leaning himself against Stew's car, he laughed when he noticed Buddy passed out and was roasting in the sun. Looking out at the ocean, Roger punched Stew on his arm and said, "We better move this car because it looks like high tide is about to roll in."

Stew laughed a drunken kind of laugh and then said, "That's what's wrong with you. You never know when to relax and have some fun."

With beer cans everywhere and Buddy passed out without a shirt on his farmer's tanned, white body, Roger kept his mouth shut as the waters from the ocean creeped closer and closer. Finally with the water only a few feet away and the sand becoming wet, Stew, like a general in the military, gave the order to retreat.

Hoisting Buddy up from his alcohol induced nap was a chore, but picking up all the beer cans was almost as tough. Once they were ready to roll with Roger appropriately behind the wheel, it was too late. The sand underneath the car was already wet even though the waters of the ocean were at least ten feet away. Roger mashed his foot on the accelerator while his two drunk friends tried to dig out the back tires of the car with their hands. Their efforts to extract the Plymouth Barracuda were all in vain.

Stew finally gave up and told Roger to quit trying as they helplessly watched small waves crash up against the front of the car. Sucked down like a plunger in a toilet, Stew's Barracuda was locked up in a sand dune that would not let go. Roger was more concerned about the consequences of the natural disaster because he began to wonder how he was going to make it back home to Oak Bay. Stew laughed and said, "Ah, the hell with it. I hope the ocean takes that car all the way to China."

Buddy yelled, "Wrong ocean, Stew. That would be a long trip from here."

Roger then yelled, "How are we gonna make it back home?"

Stew had a moment of sobering reality when he replied, "You make a good point. We better go find a tow truck to get this car out of the ocean."

Several people walking by them laughed and pointed in their direction. One man yelled, "Good luck. You may never get that sucker pulled out of here."

Walking back to the store where they had purchased the beer and snacks, Roger thumbed through the payphone's securely mounted phone book outside of the store to find a local towing service. Flipping through the Yellow Pages, he began calling several towing services. Using two dollars' worth of change making the calls, Roger finally looked at Stew and said, "Not one of them will go out on the beach to tow a vehicle."

Roger then went into the store and asked the old man behind the counter who they could call for help. After explaining the situation to him, the old man laughed and said, "You boys are out of luck. It's Friday afternoon. I don't know anybody in town who will come out here this late."

Standing in line to purchase a cold beverage and pack of crackers, a middle aged man spoke up and said in a loud confident voice, "I couldn't help but hear what you said. Let me pay for my items and I will help you boys out."

Roger turned, looked at him and immediately recognized the already legendary head football coach at Myrtle Beach High School, Doug Shaw.

"Aren't you Coach Shaw?"

"That's right, son. Do I know you?"

"Probably not. I'm Roger James from Oak Bay. I play quarterback and we scrimmaged against your team at football camp in Laurinburg this past year. I remember you yelling at one of your linebackers who missed a tackle when I gained a whoppin' three yards. I remember that guy because he wore duct tape around his arms and he kept yelling out that he was the Red-Eyed Devil. Coach, your defense is incredible."

"Thanks, son. I do remember you. I saw you pitch in an American Legion baseball game last year. It's none of my business, but it looks to me that baseball may be your meal ticket." The legend of Myrtle Beach shook his head and then asked, "How is that your car ended up on the beach in the first place?"

"It's a long story, but I am down here with some of my friends who like to drink a little. My best friend decided it would be a good idea if we parked his car on the beach."

"I see. Your friend doesn't sound like he is the school's Valedictorian."

"No, sir. He just loves to play ball and have fun."

"Nothing wrong with that, but I always say, be careful when you hang around stupid because stupid may decide to hang onto you. You seem to be a bright enough young man. Let me go outside and give a friend of mine a call. I think he can help you out, but it is gonna cost ya. I hope y'all have enough cash."

"How much are we lookin' at, Coach?"

"I can't say for sure but I'm guessin' that it will be about two hundred dolla's."

"Coach, just to be safe, let me ask my stupid friend if he has enough money before you make that call."

Walking outside of the store, Roger quickly introduced the famed coach to Buddy and Stew. Coach Shaw couldn't resist when he asked, "Which one of you geniuses decided it would be a good idea to park your car on the beach?"

Stew raised his hand like he was in school. Coach Shaw laughed and said, "I hope your wallet is bigger than your brain cause gettin' that car out of high tide is gonna cost you."

Stew shook his head up and down as Coach Shaw then walked over to the payphone and called a good friend. He then put his hand over the phone's receiver and yelled, "Do y'all have the cash before I send him out here?"

Stew yelled back, "Yes, sir."

In less than two minutes Coach Shaw hung up the phone and walked over to the boys in despair. He looked at Roger and said, "I was wrong. It will be two hundred and twenty-five dolla's. Do y'all have enough money?"

Stew spoke up and said, "I do, sir."

The veteran coach then smiled before he walked over to his car. He then turned around and motioned for Roger to come closer. Once Roger walked within a few feet from him, Coach Shaw said, "I can tell you are the smart one in this crowd. Don't listen to these fools the rest of your life because they will drag you down. Tell Coach Hutchinson hello when you see him. He is one of my favorite people. By the way, my friend Big Head Fred will be here in about an hour. If he is a little late, don't panic. Big Head Fred has never let me down."

"Thanks, Coach. I appreciate your help."

"No problem. Maybe one day when I am stranded in Oak Bay on my way to visit family in Winnsboro, you will help this old man out."

"You know it, Coach...Thanks again for your help.'"

It was almost eight o'clock when Big Head Fred arrived to pull out a car from the Atlantic Ocean. With lights flashing on his jacked up 1972 Kenworth C 500 semi wrecker, Buddy yelled at Roger, "That sucker looks like it could pull a battleship out of Hogtail Swamp."

Big Head Fred lived up to his name as the three hundred and twenty pound Black man jumped down from the wrecker. He was huge, but his head was a lot bigger than most humans. He was laughing from the time he jumped out of the wrecker until he walked closer to the friends from Oak Bay. He then yelled out, "I was told by Coach Shaw to come here and pull a car off the beach. He said, you boys, were from out of town, got drunk up, and got your car stuck on the beach. You better thank the Good Lord you know Coach Shaw cause I would be at the Western Sizzlin eatin' with my wife about right now. Y'all need to know this. The only people on this planet that would make me skip a date with my sweetheart are Coach Shaw and my own Mama." Knowing he had their full attention he then asked," So who is the fool that drove the car, and who is the man with the money who is gonna pay me?"

Stew spoke up and said, "That would be me, my fine man."

"Don't fine man me, son." Big Head Fred then got loud and began to preach. He said, "Y'all crazy white boys ought to be ashamed of yourself for gettin' drunk up and gettin' your car stuck on the beach. The Lord don't like ugly and drinkin' so much you forget to move your car before the high tide comes in is real ugly. Do your parents know y'all are drunk up and showin' out down here at the beach? I bet they would not be happy. Y'all need some Jesus in your lives." Big Head Fred then pulled his work pants up over his hanging belly and continued by saying, "Well, one of ya hop up in my baby and show me where this car is located."

Maneuvering his wrecker like it was attached to his body, Big Head Fred pulled up as close as possible to the sand dune before he looked at Stew and said, "We all make mistakes, but this one is gonna be expensive."

With the help of a winch the size of a small boat, Big Head Fred began pulling Stew's car out of the wet sand. Looking like the cable was about to pop, Buddy yelled out, "That cable will never hold."

Big Head Fred laughed hard and then yelled, "If I hooked a whale with that cable, I could drag it all the way down Ocean Boulevard with no problem."

Ten minutes later he proved what he said was right as the car was yanked out of the wet sand. Before he left them on the beach and collected his money, Big Head Fred said, "You might need to let it dry out a little before you try to crank it up. The salt and the sand is gonna be a problem. You might want to sell this car when you get back home before she rusts out. Don't forget, boys, y'all get some Jesus in your lives."

An hour later they were finally able to start the car. Riding down Ocean Boulevard, toward the Sandy Shore Motel, Roger told his friends, "Y'all know Big Head Fred was right about us gettin' some Jesus in our lives. We need to be thankful that we didn't end up in jail and that we have a car so we can get back home."

Stew laughed and said, "I have to give him credit. He knows how to use a wrecker and he should be a preacher, but we will all hear enough about Jesus when we get back home. The night is young, my friends. We are gonna make the most out every minute we have down here at Myrtle Beach or damn near die tryin'."

Chapter Six

Once they finally made it to the Sandy Shore Motel and checked in with the supervising adults, poor Buddy looked like a roasted lobster. An inebriated Mrs. Ackerman wrestled with a suitcase full of makeup and sundry items looking for some type of pharmaceutical relief for Buddy. Finding a half can of Solarcaine, she temporarily extinguished the fire on his body while Mr. Ackerman tried in vain to find out how to turn on their motel television. Buddy's sunburn was so bad on his face, stomach, and thighs it was apparent to everyone he wouldn't be able to go out with his friends. He had no choice but to spend the rest of the evening in the motel.

Stew didn't want to go to the Pavilion Arcade like Roger suggested. He wanted to head over to the Magic Attic and party with some of the other baseball players who were patiently waiting for them on the motel's second floor balcony. Before he walked out of their room, Roger asked Stew, "How much money did you bring here? "I'm already runnin' low, and you have been shelling out cash all day long."

Stew responded, "Just enough to have a good time."

While Buddy suffered, Roger went with some of his other friends to the Pavilion Arcade while Stew led a few others over to the Magic Attic. They parted ways on Ocean Boulevard when Stew yelled, "Y'all need to grow up and learn how to party."

Winning bonus points on the new video machine called "Space Invaders", Roger mentally blocked out the sights, sounds, and people around him once he began winning. When his friends decided to leave, he stayed. He was as laser- focused on that machine as he was when he was on the pitching mound receiving signs from Stew behind home plate in a baseball game. Every time he was declared a winner by the machine, he would slightly pump his fist in celebration similar to when he would strike out an opposing batter. He was so focused he was caught off guard when a girl from his high school punched him in his arm and said, "Ok, Hot Rod you can at least say hello."

Looking up from the machine he saw her and several other girls who had surrounded the machine to watch Oak Bay's most popular athlete in action. He spoke up and said, "Hey, Bridget. What are y'all doin' here?"

"We are down here with our youth group from the Second Methodist Church. I think you know everyone here."

Roger smiled and gave them a quick glance when Bridget continued by saying, "Do you know Crazy Daisy? This is her first time hanging with us."

"Crazy Daisy?"

Bridget Lee and the other girls laughed before she replied, "That is her CB handle. Her real name is Jeannie. Jeannie Branham."

Standing behind the other girls, Jeannie smiled and gave a quick wave to Roger. He at first didn't respond until he looked closer and saw the girl from Oak Bay who seldom spoke at school. Although never having talked much to her, Roger knew exactly who she was. Jeannie's family owned and operated a bar and pool joint on the outskirts of town called the One Spot. Most everyone in Oak Bay thought for sure that her mother was a prostitute. Some even speculated that Jeannie was also a prostitute. Roger's father had once told him that Jeannie's father was a twice a year practicing Mormon who liked to drink and fight more than he liked to gamble. Roger never paid much attention to all of the gossip surrounding Jeannie. He did however pay attention to her because she was the most gorgeous girl at Oak Bay High. Every boy at the school secretly wanted to know more about Jeannie Branham.

He had once tried to talk to her in his Biology class, but she was the only girl at Oak Bay High who intimidated him. He and the other boys at school seldom said a word to her because she was a full blooded, grown woman. Even some of the staff at school confused her for being a teacher. All of the boys talked about her and fantasized about her, but only a few ever had the courage to approach her without making a fool out of themselves. She looked and acted like she was untouchable. From what everyone knew about her, she was untouchable because she dated older boys who were out of school. Her quick wit and intelligent answers during classes along with more self-confidence than a corporate lawyer were as intimidating as her good looks. Roger thought Bridget and the other girls were good looking, but Jeannie was something special.

Before he could muster up enough courage to speak to Jeannie, Bridget said, "We just wanted to say hey. We are going back to the rest of our group now. Good luck with that game."

He looked up and replied, "Where are y'all stayin'"?"

"At the Sandy Shore Motel."

"So are we."

"We know. We ran into Stew and his crowd on their way to the Magic Attic before we came in here. They looked like they were already drunk."

Roger smiled and then waved goodbye to them, but he decided to follow them for a few steps before he mustered enough courage to talk to Jeannie. Although he was enamored by her good looks, he was also curious about her as a person. She was the mystery girl in his hometown.

Right as they made their way outside of the Arcade, Roger walked right up to Jeannie and asked, "Hey, Crazy Daisy, do you have a minute?"

The other girls stopped walking with their new friend and stared at Roger with looks of disdain because most of them could not believe he had made the decision to talk with her. He had dated a few of them in the past and had broken a few hearts along the way. Jeannie smiled and responded, "Are you talking to me?"

"Uh, Yeah."

"Well, before you start with your pile of crap you usually lay down on the other girls back home, let me just say that this girl is not interested in what you have to say."

"I didn't mean any disrespect.. I just wanted to get to know you. I know everyone else here except you."

She laughed for a second or two before she extended her hand and said, "I'm Jeannie Branham. Nice to finally meet you."

Before he could say a word or reach for her hand, she turned around and began walking away. Bridget and the rest of the girls began laughing as they looked at him like he was a complete idiot. He felt like an idiot.

Without a friend in sight and not enough money to continue playing games in the Arcade, he decided that it was getting late and he better call it a night. He waited for a few minutes before he walked back to the motel so he wouldn't walk up on the girls who made him feel so bad.

Walking down Ocean Boulevard, he could smell the scent of suntan lotions mixed in with the freshly made popcorn from the Pavilion; all brought to him courtesy of the Myrtle Beach sea breeze. Roger loved walking down Ocean Boulevard. However, on this night his mind kept drifting back to Jeannie. He wanted to know more about her.

The wind was blowing a little harder that evening when he walked through the parking lot of the Sandy Shore Motel. Way past midnight, his thoughts were quickly interrupted when Stew's car flew into the parking lot next to where he was walking. Power sliding into the very last open parking space, several boys from school piled out of the car along with Stew. It only took Roger a few seconds to realize that all of them had been in a serious fight. Shirts ripped along with bloody looking faces, Stew was the one who looked like he had received the worst of whoever they had been fighting. Roger ran toward them and asked, "What in the world is going on?"

Stew yelled at him, "Thanks to no help from you, we were ambushed by some boys from the base."

"What base?"

"The Citadel. You know- the military college in Charleston. Those boys dressed in blue, got mad and decided to open a can of whoop ass on us."

"I know where the Citadel is, but why did they attack you?"

"I don't know."

Roger smiled and then said, "Y'all must of have done somethin' stupid to get them all riled up."

Stew leaned up against the hood of his car and replied, "There I was standin' at the bar in the Spanish Galleon ready to order a cold beer and it hit me."

"I thought y'all were at the Magic Attic?"

"The place was packed so we headed over to the Spanish Galleon."

"You said something hit you. What hit you?"

"I had to pee like I have never had to pee before. I didn't want to lose my place in line to go and take a leak so once I made it to the bar tender; I ordered my beer and discreetly began to relieve myself while I leaned up against the bar's counter. I wasn't botherin' nobody while I waited for my beer. The next thing I know, some good lookin' gal standin' next to me begins screamin' her head off. Apparently, she felt a sprinkle on her feet and looked down and saw what I was doin'. I tried to apologize, but it was no use. A few minutes later, the boys from the base drug me out of the Spanish Galleon and decided to take turns whippin' up on me. These bozos here finally came to my aid to save my life. If it wasn't for hearing some sirens a few blocks away, I'm not sure those Citadel football players wouldn't have tried to kill all of us. Those dudes were not happy with me."

"You slung right there at the bar? Are you kiddin' me?" Roger then paused and continued by asking, "How do you know they were from the Citadel?"

"Every one of them was wearin' a Citadel Football t-shirt, and they sure as hell looked the part."

Roger shook his head and replied, "Boy, if you don't get right, you are gonna get killed doin' somethin stupid."

"Come on, Roger, it's not like it's the first time I've ever done that. I swear on my granddaddy's grave that I didn't know that I was splashin' on that nice lookin' girl. Hell, it's so dark in that place, nobody could see what I was doin'."

Roger shook his head again and then said, "Your desire to relieve yourself out in public has caused you a lot of trouble today."

Stew laughed and then said, "You mark my word, before we leave this beach, I'm gonna find that John F. Kennedy lookin' dude that suckered punched me and his bald headed friend who looks like General Eisenhower."

"Come on, man. You deserved to get your butt kicked. You better leave those college boys from Charleston alone before you get the crap kicked out of you again."

CHAPTER SEVEN

Roger and the boys slept in late on Saturday, eventually making their way toward the beach after a brunch which consisted of peanut butter sandwiches and some crackers. Walking through the lobby of the Sandy Shore Motel, Roger saw a copy of the Myrtle Beach News on top of an empty table. When he picked it up, the headline on the front page read: Foul Play Suspected in the Death of SC State Senator. Reading the article as he walked, Roger said to his friends, "They are not saying why they think the senator was killed. It is amazin' how the police can find out these kinds of things so quickly."

Stew laughed and said, "Yeah my old man told me one time that the FBI and the CIA are so powerful they could find out if you stole a piece of bubble gum from a Halloween bucket ten years ago in downtown New York. If you kill somebody, those cats will find out."

Buddy, who was still roasted, opted to park himself under an umbrella most of the day while Roger and Stew surrendered to the waters of the ocean mainly because Stew's body still felt like a used punching bag. The girls from the 2nd Methodist Church were laying out only a few yards away as Jeannie Branham had Roger's full attention most of the day in her white, one-piece swimsuit. He tried several times to talk to her with only minor success when she once asked him for a soda. He was enamored by her dark complexion and incredible body. She definitely snubbed him when he later tried to swim with her in the ocean. Her disdain for him was apparent and finally received by Roger with dejection and a hurt ego.

The afternoon seemed uneventful and quite peaceful until Stew talked Roger and Buddy into walking down the Grand Strand to scope out the bikini clad girls which seemed to be as numerous as the stars in heaven. They walked past the Myrtle Beach Pier when Stew suddenly stopped and told his buddies not to move. He cried out, "That's them over there playin' beach volleyball with those college girls."

Buddy, who was wrapped up like a sheik in the desert, yelled back, "Them who? What are you talkin' about, Stew?"

Stew grabbed Buddy's arm and said, "Those are the dudes who whipped up on me last night."

Roger said, "Now hold on, Stew. That gang of Citadel boys will tear us apart."

Stew began laughing and replied, "You don't think I know that? I don't know what I am going to do, but when the time is right, JFK is going down when I get him alone away from General Eisenhower and the rest of the troops."

Roger and Buddy both tried to talk some sense into their friend, but he had his mind made up and wasn't about to leave. Finally after standing in the same spot for about five minutes, Buddy looked at Roger and said, "This is stupid. I am going back to our place on the beach and sit under the umbrella and get me somethin' to drink."

Roger tried once more to make his friend leave with them; however, Stewart would not budge.

Two hours later as the Carolina sun began to ease its grip on the sunbathers on the beach, Roger and Buddy sat under an umbrella talking to a group of girls from Pennsylvania who had earlier decided to perch next to them. Buddy asked one of them, "Is this the first time y'all have ever been down South?"

A slightly overweight girl sitting next to them laughed and then replied, "My parents own a timeshare, and this is the second time we have come down here."

Buddy asked, "What is a timeshare?"

She replied with a question, "Do you people know how to read down here?"

Roger was about to be rude to her when Buddy spoke up and said, "We can read, but what in the heck is a timeshare?"

She laughed and then replied, "It's a new concept which allows people to buy into a property so they can vacation a few weeks out of the year at various locations instead of buying a condo or beach house. They have been around for a few years, but it is really catching on now."

Roger laughed and said, "It doesn't sound much different than rentin' a room at a motel."

Before she could respond, Stew startled them all when he ran up to the umbrella and dove on an open towel lying next to Buddy. Almost out of breath, he leaned toward his friends and gasped, "I..I.. I.. got 'em."

Roger, with a surprised look on his face, asked, "You mean to tell me you whipped that JFK looking dude?"

Stew shook his head back and forth and paused before catching his breath and then saying, "Better than that." He then smiled and opened up a beach towel he was carrying with him. Car keys and wallets came flying out onto the sand.

Buddy asked, "Did you steal his car?"

"No, you idiot." Stew then continued, "I stole all their keys and their drivers' licenses. I just wish I could have stayed to watch them look for their missin' keys and wallets."

Roger with a big frown on his face asked, "And you took all their cash?"

"No, sir, I took the cash out and left it there on their beach towels."

Roger frowned and replied, "Sure you did."

Buddy laughed and then asked, "How did you swipe them?"

"I was watching them play volleyball, plannin' on how I was going to get to JFK alone. After they quit playing, they all decided to take a swim. When they came over to their beach towels, a few of them pulled out their wallets and car keys from their swimsuits and put them under their beach towels. Once they hit the ocean, I took a quick stroll past their beach towels and did a clean sweep."

The big girl from Pennsylvania spoke up and said, "You stole from people on the beach? What a jerk!"

Stew looked at her and asked, "And who the hell are you?"

She stood up and began packing up her belongings before responding by saying, "I'm going to find a police officer. You are a common criminal."

Stew laughed and said, "Now hold on there, sweet thing. You have no idea what's goin' on."

Not responding to him, the rest of the girls from Pennsylvania began packing their beach belongings. Roger looked at Stew and then said, "You are stupid. When those boys from the Citadel find you, they will kill you."

Buddy laughed and said, "You are as good as dead."

Stew laughed back and said, "They will have to find me on foot."

Roger swiped up the keys and wallets and folded them in a beach towel. He then looked at Stew and said, "I am taking this back to them right now."

Stew screamed, "Have you lost yore mind? Don't you see that this is the ultimate revenge?"

Roger yelled back, "You need to get over it. We are not going to spend our last day at the beach wonderin' if the police or those college boys are about to catch up with you."

At that moment. Roger turned and saw Bridget and the rest of the church group girls from Oak Bay's Second Methodist Church standing behind him. Standing next to Bridget was Jeannie. She did not look happy. Roger was about to say something to Stew when Bridget suddenly pointed her finger at Stew and said, "Roger is right, you fool. I can't believe you. Y'all better take it all back before somebody gets in big trouble."

While Roger was looking at Jeannie, Stew jumped up, grabbed the beach towel full of keys and wallets and ran like a wild man toward the ocean. Bridget, Jeannie, and the rest of the girls followed Roger as they chased Stew to the edge of the water. Stew kept wading into the surf ending up with waves crashing around his waist. He then reared back and swung the beach towel like a helicopter blade. Roger screamed at him, "Don't do it, Stew."

Bridget screamed, "Don't be such an idiot."

Roger screamed once more saying, "Stew, if you throw those keys and wallets into the ocean then I am leavin' and going home tonight."

Stew stopped waving the towel for a few seconds, smiled big and replied, "Those boys have to pay whether you stay or go." As soon as the last word left his mouth, Stew swung the beach towel one more time and flung the wad of keys and wallets about fifteen yards into the deep water. Roger almost got sucked into an undertow trying desperately with Bridget and several other girls to find keys and wallets. With high tide rolling in and zero visibility in the water, they came up empty handed chasing after a few floating wallets which were carried in and out of the rough surf. Ten minutes later, Roger and the girls gave up the battle as their eyes stung from the salt of the ocean.

Walking back up to their spot on the beach, Buddy asked Roger, "Are you really leavin'?"

Roger, with a quirky look on his face, replied, "Beach time for me is now officially over."

Buddy laughed and then said, "That's a long walk home from here."

Bridget, who was now drying off next to them interrupted their conversation and said, "Roger, you are more than welcome to ride home with me and Jeannie . We have to leave this evening so that we can attend church services back home in the morning."

Stew did his best to persuade his best friend to stay in Myrtle Beach one more night. Roger, however, had no intention of hanging out with his crazy childhood friend. Having the chance to ride home with Jeannie Branham outweighed any of Stew's promises of another night of "fun". Never one to enjoy laying around on the beach for more than a day, for all practical purposes he was ready to make his way home to Oak Bay. Riding home with Jeannie sealed the deal.

Two hours later, after telling his inebriated chaperones that he was leaving, Roger stood outside Bridget's 1972 Volkswagen Beetle with his suitcase, waiting for the girls to come down to the car. Knowing that Bridget would be driving, he purposely decided to sit behind the driver's seat so that he could get a good look at Jeannie on the way home.

A few minutes later, Bridget stumbled from behind a low growing evergreen shrub on the side of the motel carrying a large suitcase and a canvas duffle bag. Roger walked over to her looking for Jeannie with every step he took. Once he made his way over to Bridget he offered to carry her suitcase. While Bridget opened the trunk of her Volkswagen, Roger kept peering around the corner of the building looking for Jeannie. After helping Bridget neatly place their luggage perfectly and slamming down the hood of the trunk, Roger said, "I will go ahead and crawl in the backseat unless you think Jeannie needs some help with her luggage."

Bridget smiled and said, "She has decided to stay with a few of the other girls. It's just me and you, Hot Rod."

With every fiber of his being, Roger wanted to tell Bridget that he had decided to stay, but he knew she would tell everyone that he was a nut job. He then reluctantly left Myrtle Beach that evening with Bridget.

Chapter Eight

It quickly became clear to Bridget that Roger's only interest that evening was to find out more information about Jeannie Branham. Bridget, who secretly liked Roger more than a friend, told him everything she knew about the mysterious girl who lived in a small house behind the One Spot Bar near the Pee Dee River. She said, "I guess for a Mormon she is pretty cool."

Roger laughed and then replied, "Her daddy might be a part-time Mormon, but from what I hear, she and her muth'a don't think the same way as the old man."

Bridget cracked her window before saying, "We have never talked much about it, but I guess you're right. She is hard to talk to at times. I was shocked when she decided to come with us to the beach. She never says much at school unless you ask her a question. All I know is that her Daddy and Mama have her workin' at the One Spot all the time. She told me that she was tired of workin' there. She said that a lot of those River Indians who live near the Pee Dee River love to hang out down at the One Spot. Some of the old guys like to hit on her while she serves drinks. She said her Daddy just laughs and her Mama just tells her to keep smilin' and shakin' her fanny for more tips."

"Does she have a boyfriend?"

"Not since she dated the Tucker boy last year. You remember Dale Tucker. He was twenty-one and worked for the Pee Dee Electric Company when he was run over by a pulpwood truck near River Road. Don't you remember?"

"Of course, I remember, but he was so much older than us. I really didn't know him. He lived on the Northside of the county. For the life of me, I forgot that Jeannie was goin' out with him."

"Oh, he was a really nice guy from what everybody says. Poor Jeannie had only been dating him for a couple of months when he walked out in front of that truck. He was chasin' one of his bird dogs across River Road. When the driver cleared Johnson's Curve, he said he never saw Dale standing in the road. The God awful thing about it is that Jeannie saw the whole thing while she sat in his pickup truck. It's been over a year now, but everyone says she has never been the same. My older cousin, Amy Lynne, who used to date Skeeter Jacobs told me that Jeannie and the Tucker boy were gonna get married once he saved up enough money to put up a down payment on a nice double-wide after she graduated from high school. According to Skeeter, Dale Tucker was doing his best to get Jeannie out of having to work at the One Spot and being controlled by her father."

"I never knew that."

"Well, that's just the gossip I hear. It may not be true at all. Skeeter Jacobs has been known to tell a few lies. He's servin' a year in prison for hangin' paper down in Charleston."

"Hangin' paper?"

"Writin' bad checks."

By the time Bridget pulled down the dirt road which led to Roger's trailer, Roger had said very little. Bridget had dominated most of the conversation. She talked about everyone at Oak Bay High and then gossiped more about the adults of the community. He liked her a lot, but at times he felt she talked a bit too much. Not only did she seem to know everybody in town, she knew who everybody was related to. He marveled at her ability to associate and connect a random person at school with their relatives or some juicy gossip about their family. Bridget, on the other hand, talked up a storm whenever she was nervous. He did not know it at the time, but she had been heartbroken in the eighth grade when he never again paid her much attention after their one and only date at the Oak Bay County Fair. Although they remained good friends in school, she secretly wanted nothing more than to be his girlfriend.

Ironically, during their ride home, Roger thought about the time when they went to the County Fair together; a date where his father dropped them off and picked them up. He remembered that on that one and only date, he felt intimidated by her outgoing personality. He was still embarrassed about how he had tried to kiss her on the Ferris wheel ride when she pushed him away, and told him he was moving a tad bit too fast for her liking. The memory of her rejection along with his eventual embarrassment still made him nervous whenever he was around her. Even being a local sports hero did not diminish his nervousness around her. In his mind, Bridget had long ago put him out of her mind when it came to romance.

Roger could tell his father had more than his usual share of Saturday night bourbons when he stumbled out on the porch of the trailer that evening. Glad to see his only son return home a day early, he gave Roger a big hug on the steps of the porch while Bridget waved goodbye and drove away. After telling his father that he was tired of the beach and ready to focus on his summer job at the Main Street Amoco as a gas attendant and the upcoming American Legion baseball season, Roger faked being tired when he told his father that all he wanted to do was to take a shower and flop into his bed. Mark then asked him, "Did you hear the news about Senator Broadway?"

"I briefly read in the paper that investigators think there may have been foul play associated with his death."

Mark replied, "They say around here that he was stabbed to death before his car crashed over the bridge."

Later that night when he finally heard his father stumble off to his bedroom, Roger reached under his bed and retrieved the old journal he had desperately wanted to read. Peering through a magnifying glass he quickly found the page he had last read. Deciphering the old written script he quickly picked up on the story of his great-great grandfather, Matthew James. Roger quickly became reacquainted with the story when he began re-reading that his relative made a fateful decision to follow a Lenape warrior named Nighthawk to his camp near Fort Pitt in the Pennsylvania wilderness in 1763. Reading a fantastic description of entering the camp, Roger learned that Matthew was not at first well received by the other Lenape people when Nighthawk interceded on his behalf. After much talking in a strange language, Nighthawk was approached by the Chief of the tribe named Turtleheart. The two of them spoke privately for a few minutes while Matthew awaited his fate among a group of people who seemed perplexed as to why Nighthawk had brought him to their camp. Thrusting a wooden club into the air, Turtleheart then spoke to Matthew through Nighthawk who served as an interpreter. Nighthawk then said, "Our Chief Turtleheart has spoken." Roger then deciphered that Turtleheart wanted to make peace with the soldiers at Fort Pitt. He wanted Matthew to help them convince the soldiers to honor a treaty which gave them control of all of the land west of the fort.

For the next few days, after Matthew agreed to help Chief Turtleheart, he lived in the camp with the Lenape people, learning their customs, their language, and eating their food. In his journal he wrote: Nitis'hëmëna yukwe which means, we are now friends.

Reading further, Roger learned that Matthew was prepared by Chief Turtleheart to be turned over to the British soldiers at Fort Pitt in a good will offering in hopes that the British commanders of the fort would look favorably on the Lenape people. Reading further he soon learned that the offering of Matthew to the soldiers did not produce the peace that Turtleheart expected. A few days after his ceremonial exchange for peace, Matthew learned that the British troops had concocted a plan that would eventually lead to disaster for the Lenape tribe. After having spent almost two weeks in the Lenape camp, Matthew was convinced that he would be able to persuade the British command that his new native friends did not really want war. Although the commanders listened to his story about living with the Lenape people with great interest, he later found out that the British commanders had no intention of making peace. Instead they devised a plan which would become history's first recorded account of biological warfare. Rubbing several blankets on infected colonial citizens and British soldiers who were infected with smallpox and housed in a temporary hospital for those infected, the commanders planned to give the blankets to the Lenape people as a gift, in hopes that the smallpox would spread rapidly among their tribe.

Matthew's objection to this plan was not only dismissed; it was considered by the British commanders as treason. They began to question his loyalty. A day before the planned visit from Turtleheart and other Native leaders to Fort Pitt, Matthew was locked up in the fort as a prisoner. When Turtleheart and Nighthawk asked to visit with their friend, the British commanders claimed that Matthew had returned home to Virginia.

Matthew later wrote that he was able to escape the fort on a rainy night about two weeks after his Lenape friends received the blankets with smallpox. Too late to warn them of the misdeed which had already taken place, Matthew set out on a journey across the Pennsylvania countryside in hopes of returning to his beloved Virginia. He wrote, “I am still haunted. I prayed many times that Nighthawk was spared.”

With only the clothes on his back and a large knife, Matthew survived in the backwoods eating wild berries, grubs, chickweed, and persimmons all while hiding from any people he encountered. Traveling on foot through mountainous terrain and streams for several days, he took a chance when he stopped a wagon full of German Baptists called Dunkards who were on their way to their settlement near Harrisburg. They took a chance on him and welcomed the sickly looking wanderer to join them on their journey to religious bliss. Taking advantage of their hospitality which included a bowl full of cabbage and potato stew along with a slice of wheat bread, Matthew could care less about their religious views as long as they were willing to feed him. Writing that he was wary of their peculiar religious practices which included celibacy and a diet which did not include the eating of meat, Matthew accepted their generosity and began traveling with the family of brothers and cousins who barely spoke any English. After two days of travel, Matthew wrote that he had never witnessed a group of people who seemed obsessed with praying and singing hymns more than making their way to their destination.

Not far from Harrisburg, while they stopped on the side of a creek to pray, a wagon driven by two young men stopped next to them. Resting their horses next to the creek, Matthew became acquainted with two struggling backwoods settler brothers of Scottish descent. They were making their way to Philadelphia to seek employment at the shipyard docks. With their parents killed in a morning fire at their remote farm cabin, the two teenage brothers barely made it out of the fire alive. Soured by the death of their parents and their isolative existence, they decided to move back to the big city instead of continuing to farm in one of the most remote places of Pennsylvania. After hearing their story and introducing himself, Matthew asked if he could join them on their journey instead of continuing to travel with the German speaking Dunkards. The two twin brothers, Jack and Glenn welcomed him to join them as they began a trek to Philadelphia.

Heading in the wrong direction from his parent's home in Virginia, Matthew described that he was hoping to find temporary work in Philadelphia before making his way home. He also wrote about how he and the twin brothers survived through the heat of late August and a series of drenching thunderstorms which halted their journey for two additional days. Sleeping under the wagon only about five miles away from Philadelphia, they were awakened when a Constable traveling with three other local watchmen, rode up to their makeshift camp. When the two brothers accidentally revealed the name of their new friend, the Constable informed them that they were traveling with a military deserter of the Virginia colonial army.

Before Matthew had time to make a move, the Constable arrested him and the two brothers. Matthew did his best to convince the

Constable that the twin brothers had no knowledge of his misdeeds before his pleas were quickly dismissed. Tied up in rope and made to finish their journey by walking to Philadelphia, the two brothers felt confident that their situation could be resolved once they were allowed to speak to a court official. Matthew, however, knew his walk into Philadelphia surely meant he would hang for treason.

As it turned out, they were both wrong. Later that evening, after having walked almost ten miles through the heat and dust of a hot day, the Constable released his prisoners over to a man named L. Weaver. Believing that they were being jailed to await a hearing or trial, Matthew and the brothers soon learned that the Constable had sold them as indentured servants to one of Philadelphia's most notorious criminal enterprises. Pleading for their freedom and the injustice that had been handed to them, the brothers were severely beaten and made to work on the docks handling lumber that was being shipped to England. As Matthew watched his new friends being taken away to another location, never to be seen again, he himself was taken to a cargo ship that soon began sailing for London.

Chapter Nine

The next morning, Roger yawned while he tried hard to listen to his pastor at the Oak Bay First Presbyterian Church. His pastor asked everyone in the congregation to pray for the family of state Senator Dennis Broadway. A few minutes later, when his mother shouted Amen very loudly in the middle of the sermon, Roger quickly woke up to the embarrassing looks he and his father received from some of the congregants. There was no doubt that Juanita James was turned onto religion more than the other members of the church. Most of the people in the congregation were sympathetic, knowing she had mental problems. They quietly forgave her sudden outbursts in their church; however, there were some of the very conservative congregation who secretly wished that Mark James would find another church for his wife so she could express herself somewhere else. Roger was always embarrassed when his mother would hold up her hands and swing them in a wild manner at various times during the sermon or when she would ask to pray out loud, something that nobody in the church ever thought of doing. Mark, on the other hand, accepted the fact that his wife had mental issues and dared anyone to say a word to her.

Later that afternoon, long after their Sunday lunch and a much needed nap, Roger James and his father walked down to the big pond behind his grandmother's old house hoping to catch a few bream off the old wooden dock. Roger couldn't help but think about his great, great, grandfather being shipped to London from Philadelphia. He couldn't wait to read more about his experience. Mark James, who knew nothing about his great grandfather, was only concerned about what to do about his mother's house. He looked at Roger before casting his Zebco rod and reel into the pond and said, "I haven't told your Mama about the house, yet."

Roger pulled away some fragments of a lily pad from his hook when he replied, "Dad, I sure hope you decide to keep the log cabin. It will kill me if you decide to tear it down."

Mark James then looked over at his son and said, "We can't afford to keep it up by ourselves. I'm afraid that if we allow strangers to ride up here and visit the cabin, your muth'a will go off the deep end."

"Dad, we have to try. Please promise me that you will give the Historical Society a chance before you decide to scrap it."

Mark James laughed and then said, "I promise."

Changing the subject Mark then asked his son, "So what time does Carl want you to show up to work at the station tomorrow?"

Roger shrugged his shoulders before saying, "The gas pumpin' begins at seven in the mornin'."

"Good, you can feed the hogs and chickens before you head out."

"I thought you were gonna handle that this summer, Dad."

"Like hell you did."

Later that evening when his parents finally went to bed, Roger dove right back into the journal of Matthew James. His writings revealed that he was surprised to find an entire crew of indentured servants working on the ship of his servitude. During the voyage he once thought about jumping off in the middle of the ocean to relieve himself of the pain he endured from the beatings he took from the cargo ship's overseers.

He wrote, "The noose around me neck for treason surely would be more solace than the hells I endured on thou ship of tortures."

Roger, then deciphered from the journal that Matthew became friends with an indentured servant of Turkish descent named Elijah. Only during times of rest and sleep, Elijah secretly informed him that their ship known as the Venus was part of an operation where lumber, barrels of sugar, and pork were exchanged for gold and silver so that the operators of the Venus could purchase African slaves. Elijah warned him that London was the first leg of the incredibly long journey which would take them to Africa. From Africa they would sail to the Caribbean to unload the African slaves in exchange for sugar and rum which they would then transport back to Philadelphia. He confided to Matthew that their job was to man the ship, load, and unload the cargo associated with it. Elijah knew this because he had already endured one such voyage.

Roger's excitement about these new revelations led him to continue reading the next few pages which revealed that Matthew and the crew of the Venus were attacked by a pirate ship near some islands halfway on the journey to London. Roger then peered hard to decipher Matthew's handwriting which stated, "Yis…The ship of Piracy fired one shot before the overseers surrendered without fight. Aye…The God of Mercy allowed me and the other indentures to be impressed into the confines of Captain Wingard, a man with nay apparent heritage. His vessel called the "Dynasty" pressed our service after killings of the overseers and the taking of bounties not to include the harvest of timbers."

Continuing to read, Roger learned that Matthew gained the trust of Captain Wingard when he confided to him his unfortunate ordeal at Fort Pitt. He did not know it at the time, but he later learned the pirate captain was married to a native girl from the Caribbean. His piracy came about after he witnessed first-hand, the mistreatment of her people by his own shipmates which were sailing for a Portuguese based trading company. Wingard, a man of a boisterous nature, led the mutiny of the Dynasty where he and his mutineers later transformed the ship into a battle worthy vessel of piracy.

Scuttling the seas for treasure provided them unlimited riches; however, Wingard and his crew were determined to disrupt the trade of slavery with planned high sea ambushes which ultimately led to the freedom of many souls never accounted for in any records of lost cargo. The mixed ethnic crew of the Dynasty and their captain were described by Matthew James as "the Robinhudes of the High Seas'.

The next day, Roger's radio alarm clock blared out the new hit song, "Rock n' Roll Fantasy" by Bad Company over AM radio station WOKB only a couple of hours after he quit reading the journal. He thought to himself that 5 o'clock in the morning came too early for anyone. As he showered that morning in his trailer's cramped bathroom, he did not look forward to making his way to the first day of his summer job at the Main Street Amoco in downtown Oak Bay. Although he dreaded his long hours which would culminate with him going to a two hour American Legion baseball practice, Roger was thankful for the opportunity to work at a place which paid him $2.50 an hour plus customer tips.

Already a veteran gas attendant of the station because of the weekend work his father secured for him during his sophomore year of high school, Roger knew that to be late on the first day of his summer employment would not make the owner of the station very happy. He also knew that if he did a poor job there would be an indictment on him and his father's character from the management, workers, and patrons of Oak Bay's oldest full-service gas station. Many of the men associated with the station were people he had known his entire life. The last thing he wanted to do was to impugn his family name by being considered unworthy at a job which at the time was coveted by many of his teenage friends.

That morning when he appeared in the station lounge, he was greeted by owner Carl Norman with less than enthusiasm. He looked up and said to Roger, "Glad you made it on time today. You always remember that a man who can't make it to work on time is a man who will eventually lose everything dear to him includin' his pride, dignity, and his woman."

For a seventeen-year-old boy, Carl's words of wisdom seemed at times to be directly associated with earth shattering events like winning the Cold War against the Soviet Union or the success of the American economy. Carl Norman was more than a tough minded boss; he was a stubborn old soul who believed that hard work at one's profession was as sacred as one's belief in the Almighty.

A few minutes after opening the station to customers, Carl took a big gulp of coffee out of a Styrofoam cup as he peered out through the station's double pane glass front window. Catching a brief glimpse of an unfamiliar customer who was driving a car with an out- of-state license plate, his train of thought was briefly disturbed by the sound of a dropped porcelain coffee cup hitting the floor of the station's lounge. One of the old-timers who had been a fixture at the Main Street Amoco Gas Station for several years was the culprit responsible for the accident. He and several other retirees spent most every morning at the place where local and national politics could be discussed, free cups of coffee would be consumed, tales of past achievements were welcome, and the juiciest gossip of the town was expected to be shared. Hanging over the door of the station's lounge was a handcrafted cedar wood sign which read: God Bless the O.T.C.C. (Old Timers Coffee Club).

The club was established so many years ago that none of the present members could even remember its inception nor could they believe that their lot in life had allowed them to join the club so quickly. With their lives once defined by their various professions, they now found themselves spending their days reminiscing about the past while trying to find hope in the days ahead. Each of them were fully aware of the hand carved notches on their club's cedar wood sign which were cut each time another member passed away. Those notches served as a clear reminder that their days were also numbered.

As the out-of-state customer came into the station to pay for his gas, Carl punched the keys of a slightly grease-covered, 1965 National model cash register. The old register teetered on the glass countertop of the station's customer lounge every time Carl hit a key. Before the cash register drawer popped open, the middle-aged, slightly overweight, balding owner couldn't help but notice the new, small, green and white, Mountain Dew advertising sign hanging on the wall next to the Oasis freestanding water fountain. With the sign slightly off center, he ordered Roger to adjust it back to perfection.

Already humid enough to make standing outside under the Carolina sun an undesirable task, the out-of-state customer wiped his forehead with a fancy looking yellow handkerchief. Carl then looked twice at the numbers on the cash register's pop-up, numerical monetary display before he said, "Good mornin', Partner, which will be seven dollars and ninety-five cents."

The more than middle aged, nicely dressed customer, slowly pulled out his wallet and said, "This gas is a little higher than when I filled up in Virginia last week."

Carl growled back at him, "Is that right?"

"Yes, sir. I paid only 74 cents a gallon right outside of Richmond."

"What ya gittin' at, Partner?"

"Oh, nothing. I'm just surprised your prices here in South Carolina are a little higher. Most of the time they are usually lower."

The station bell mounted above the entrance door of the lounge rang twice in rapid succession, signaling that another car had pulled into one of the two full-service aisles. Carl's response to the out-of-town customer was almost muted by the sound of the bell when he said, "It's sure hard to make y'all Yankees happy."

"Did you just call me a Yankee?"

Carl smiled while he reached for another gulp of his morning coffee. After taking a quick swig he replied, "I saw the license plate on your car when ya pulled up. Are you from Virginia or not?"

"Yes, I'm from the Chesapeake Bay area."

"Then you have to be a Yankee."

All of the members of the O.T.C.C. began laughing when the customer from Virginia replied, "A Yankee? I'll have you know that Virginia is as Southern as it gets."

With a haughty look on his face the customer then glared over at the old men in the station as he pulled his hands behind his back and puffed out his chest in a prideful gesture. Carl set down his coffee cup and spoke louder when he said, "Look here, Partner, I'm not gonna argue with ya. All I know is that if you are from anywhere above the great state of North Carolina then you are classified as a Yankee up in here. It's also a known fact that Yankees can never be satisfied. Might be all those cold winters... Hell, it might be the way y'all talk. I don't know, but don't get ugly with me up in here. We have Yankees come through here all the time."

Stumpy Sanders, retired former owner of the locally famous Big Pig Barbecue Hut, who was sitting in his special chair located next to the entrance of the station lounge, spoke up and said, "Don't pay Carl no attention. He's just tryin' to get a rise out of ya. He's a big ole shuga bear."

Hank Burrows, the town of Oak Bay's twice retired Chief of Police, added his two cents by saying, "His bark is a lot more dangerous than his bite. Old Carl woke up on the wrong side of the bed this mornin'; something he does quite frequently these days since his old Lady wants him to put in a swimmin' pool. He's tight as a tick. His idea of a pool is one of them Slip N' Slides and a garden hose."

Cane carrying, straw hat wearing, and half deaf, Gene Purdy, the eighty-nine year old retired owner of the Oak Bay Farmers Insurance Company, yelled out, "Wha'd ya say Hank?"

In unison everyone in the O.T.C.C. yelled, "Buy a new hearing aid, Gene!"

Harold Hutchinson, the retired legendary Head football coach, Head baseball coach, and Principal of Oak Bay High School, stood up and said, "Don't take offense, sir. I'm a Yankee from Upstate New York. I came down here to coach ball in 1948, and now I come here every morning just to be called 'The Big Yankee' by Carl. He thinks anyone who speaks like they are half-way educated is either a Yankee or a Communist."

The customer from Virginia forced out a nervous chuckle while Carl handed him his change along with a handful of Greenback stamps. He then looked over at Stumpy and asked, "Are those peanuts in that bag?"

"Yes, sir. They are bowl'd peanuts."

The customer asked, "Did you say a bowl of peanuts?"

Everyone in the station lounge began to snicker and hold back their laughter including Carl, who then jokingly said, "There ya go again. That proves it, Coach Hutch. If I were a bettin' man... "

Coach Hutchinson grinned and interrupted him saying, "Carl, you may be right."

The customer from Virginia asked, "Right about what?"

Carl yelled, "Bowl'd peanuts. Yankees don't know nothin' bout no bowl'd peanuts."

With a confused look on his face the customer from Virginia asked again, "Did you say a bowl of peanuts?"

Stumpy slowly rose from his chair and handed a bag of Pee Dee Farms boiled peanuts to the customer from Virginia and said to him in a mocking, nasally, Northern accent, "No...they are Boiled... You know, like a pot of boiled water." He then changed vocal gears and went back to using his slow Southern dialect by adding, "Try 'em. Yore life will never be the same."

"No, thank you. I've already eaten this morning."

Stumpy then pushed the bag of boiled peanuts a little closer to the customer and said with a grin on his face, "I insist. This ain't breakfast. It's just a snack. If you have never tasted a bowl'd peanut then you haven't lived."

The customer nervously proceeded to shell two peanuts and eat the treasures that had been revealed to him from the shelling. Chewing quickly then swallowing slowly he looked at Stumpy and said, "Gees, they aren't too bad. They are a little slimy, but they have a good salty taste."

Carl then walked from behind the counter over to the Coca Cola vending machine. The machine sat directly under a large metal shelf which prominently displayed several cans of Amoco 30 weight oil, an assortment of neatly stacked fan belts along with pictures of the 1974 and 1975 Main Street Amoco Little League baseball teams. Carl then popped a quarter into the machine which delivered a bottle of ice cold Coca Cola with a thunderous boom. He then retrieved the soda from the bottom of the machine and quickly turned to the customer from Virginia saying, "No man alive can eat those peanuts without a good soda to wash 'em all down. My treat, Partner... No hard feelings?"

The accused Yankee in question was momentarily hesitate to reply before he reached out and took the ice cold bottle from Carl. He then replied, "Thanks for the pop. No hard feelings."

Hank, who had already eaten more than his share of peanuts, sat down in his usual morning chair and then said, "If ya want to make it like a dessert, put those peanuts in your soda. Yes, sir... that might be better than sex."

Darryl Dukes, a retired postman and the only African American of the morning retiree crowd, sat in his chair reading the newest issue of the TV Guide. He briefly snickered at Hank then said, "Don't listen to him, sir. Boiled peanuts in a Coca Cola are revolting."

Carl then looked at the customer from Virginia and asked, "Where are you headed today, Partner?"

"I have business appointments in and around Charleston this week."

Stumpy sat back down and leaned forward in his chair before asking, "What kind of business?"

"I own a company called AAC or American Amusement Corporation. I'm meeting with several business owners from all over the Charleston area tomorrow."

Carl asked him, "You sellin' roller coasters, Ferris wheels or cotton candy machines?"

The customer from Virginia chuckled before he took another swig of his soda. He then replied, "No, sir. I am selling video poker machines."

Stumpy asked, "What in the hell is video poker?"

Roger, who had just walked into the station lounge, jumped into the conversation by saying, "I'm guessin' they are gamblin' machines with cash payouts."

The customer from Virginia nodded in agreement with Roger and said, "That's right. It won't be long until every convenience store and gas station from here to Mississippi will have at least one of my machines in their place of business."

Stumpy growled, "What the hell good are they?"

Roger then handed an Amoco credit card from another full-service customer to Carl. He then leaned up against the station lounge counter and replied, "Because those video game machines are so fun to play."

Carl asked Roger, "How do you know about these machines, Hot Rod?"

"I really don't, but I do know that those video game machines you play at the Pavilion Arcade in Myrtle Beach are a blast. I think I could play Space Invaders or Indy 500 all day long. If I had enough money, I would buy one of those arcade machines and put it in my house."

The customer from Virginia grinned and then said, "That's right, gentlemen. These types of arcade style machines are sweeping the nation. People can't get enough of them. As a matter of fact, I would say you have plenty of room right here in this station to have one or two installed."

Coach Hutchinson scratched the top of his head and asked, "How much money can you make off one of those machines?"

The customer smiled and then said, "Let's just say that with the right amount of foot traffic, two or three machines in this place could generate more income in three or four months than the sale of a year's worth of gasoline and oil. It's something to think about since it looks like we are about to have another gas shortage with what is happening in Iran. That revolution over there is about to put our economy in a tailspin."

Carl looked agitated when he handed back the credit card to Roger. He then spoke up saying, "Ok Mister… Uh whatever your name is…"

"My name is Paul Peters..."

"We're glad you came by Mr. Peter, and good luck with your bitness venture, but it's time for ya to head on down to Charleston now."

"Peters not Peter."

"Ok, Pete."

"But.."

"But I have heard enough. Enjoy your soda and nuts, Mr. Peterhead, before my hospitality wears thin."

Hank Burrows, self-appointed President of the O. T. C. C. hurried out of his chair and politely escorted the Virginia entrepreneur to his car. Once they were outside the station lounge, Hank said, "Forgive old Carl. His manners are sometimes lackin'. He's a Vietnam vet who is still tryin' to get his mind untangled from a place called Khe Sanh. He is a little gruff, but he has a good heart."

"I see. Well, I'd like to go back in there and tell him how much I appreciate his service to our nation. It's a shame how those boys were treated when they came back home."

"I know how ya feel, but I would highly advise ya to leave it be for right now. Now you have a good trip and stop by and visit with us anytime you are in the area. By the way, if you have a business card, I would much be obliged to ya."

While Hank was being cordial to Mr. Peters, Carl looked over at Stumpy and said, "Gamblin' machines…That will be day. No offense, Coach Hutch, but that Yankee is barkin' up the wrong tree with me. Nobody around here is ever gonna go for that bucket of hogwash he is sellin'."

After laughing at Carl, Coach Hutchinson began to softly clap his hands before saying, "Well, here he is... Let's ask Kirby what he thinks about Video Poker."

Unshaven with his pants and shirt riddled with holes, Oak Bay's most respected alcoholic vagrant walked into the station lounge with a broom in his hand and a smile on his face. A station regular, Kirby used the station's facilities to bathe at least once a week. He and Carl had a non-contractual agreement which for years had allowed Kirby to use the facilities only if he agreed to do some occasional janitorial work. On the coldest of nights, Carl gave him unlimited access to the heated mechanic's bay. The members of the O.T.C.C all pitched in as well, making sure he always had a pillow and plenty of blankets.

Bending over to pick up a piece of discarded paper towel off of the station lounge floor, Kirby looked up at Coach Hutchinson and said,

"I don't know anything about Video Poker, but if it makes you happy, then I say it might be a good thing."

Old man, Gene Purdy, laughed and said, "Well, there you have it. If it's good enough for Kirby, it's good enough for me."

Darryl stood up from his chair and pointed at Carl before saying, "Carl, you must not read the paper or listen to the news. The legislators here in South Carolina have already approved Video Poker to become legal. Gambling on those poker machines is going to happen with or without you."

Carl replied, "The only thing you find on the news right now is about the killin' of that senator from Moncks Corner."

Hank Burrows spoke up and said, "The boys at the Police Department say that he was stabbed nineteen times before he crashed that car."

Coach Hutchinson said, "At that time of the morning I wonder what he was doing up our way?"

Hank smiled and said, "Give those boys from SLED some time and they will have it all figured out. As a matter of fact, Chief Lollis told me that they were closing in on the trail. It won't be long until they make some arrests. He also told me that they were pretty sure that Senator Broadway had been dead long before that car crashed into the river."

While the discussion about Oak Bay's most publicized murder investigation continued with the members of the O.T.C.C, a dingy, orange colored, twenty-four foot U Haul truck rolled up next to the second full-service aisle, not far from the Main Street curb. Carl walked outside of the station lounge entrance, spit out a small wad of Beechnut chewing tobacco and yelled, "Hey Luther, you get the paperwork done on this one, and let Rainey fill her up and get her parked."

Chapter Ten

Luther Brown yelled into the Main Street Amoco station mechanic's bay number two for twenty year old Rainey Thomas. He yelled, "Hey, Colored boy, that brake job can wait for a few minutes. The boss man wants ya to fill up this truck and get it parked."

Rainey was only one brake shoe away from completing the work on an old Dodge truck. He muttered to himself, "Sh.. that old White man is one crazy clown."

Roger James overheard him as he walked into the mechanic's bay to get a can of power steering fluid. He laughed at Rainey and said, "Don't be upset with Mr. Luther. I heard Carl tell him to get you to service this U haul truck."

Rainey shot back, "Why does he always call me the Colored Boy? Doesn't he know that this is 1979?"

"I don't know. I guess he's just old and that is the way he was raised."

"I don't care how old he is. He keeps callin' me Colored Boy and I will..."

"Come on, Rainey, I'll help you get that U haul filled up and put away and I will talk to him later."

Standing in between the gas pumps on Full Service aisle number two, Luther Brown took out his black Bick pen from his blue station uniform shirt's front pocket and began filling out the paperwork associated with the return of the U haul truck. The sixty-five year old, retired factory worker had spent most of his adult life working at the Carolina Furniture Plant only about three miles from the Main Street Amoco.

The last three years of his life, the veteran of WWII came out of his brief retirement from the furniture plant, taking a part-time morning gig at the Main Street Amoco. Once a brief member of the O.T.C.C himself, Luther Brown became tired of drinking coffee, listening to the old- timers constantly complain about things that didn't amount to a hill of beans, and sitting around on his rear end. Working with his hands his entire life, Luther started pumping gas and taking customers cash one day when Carl was tied up on the phone. He offered to help out a couple days a week. Carl agreed. Part-time soon turned into full-time when Carl noticed that sales were on the rise and when Luther realized that the hell hacking he faced at home from his wife was a lot worse than pumping gas and washing windshields. He quickly became Carl's number one gas station attendant. The long-time American Legion Post member and former Worshipful Master of the Oak Bay Masonic Lodge knew almost everyone in town. Because of his affiliations, his personal relationships, and because he was a faithful member of the Oak Bay

Baptist Church, he was a valuable asset to Carl's business. Luther was the cordial front man whom customers trusted. His personification as everyone's grandfather served as a natural buffer to Carl's sometimes abrasive and ill- tempered behavior that he brought back with him after serving a tour of duty in Vietnam from 1966 to 1970. Carl's service to his country was the only mutually binding component of a business relationship where on some days; Luther wanted to tell Carl that he was the south end of a northbound jackass.

Rainey yelled out to Luther before he pulled the twenty-four foot truck behind the station, "Eleven dollars even for the fill up."

Completing all the paperwork associated with the U haul truck, Luther looked up at a newly married couple who were turning in the truck. They were waiting patiently for him to finish the business transaction as the morning humidity hung over them in a cloud of perpetual discomfort. He then slowly and deliberately folded the multi-colored contract pages and placed them in a U haul company brown envelope. Before handing the documents to them, he scratched his head and said, "I think this is gonna do it for y'all. I see on your paperwork that you two are comin' here from Columbia."

The long haired, unshaven man dressed in a pair of bright red gym shorts and a Mickey Mouse t-shirt smiled and put his arm around his very tanned, skinny, and curly haired wife. He replied, "That's right, I recently graduated from the University of South Carolina School of Law. I'm taking a job at the McCloud and Turner Law Firm. "

"That's outstandin'. I've known Kirk McCloud his entire life, and I have worked with Ben Turner in the Masonic Lodge for years."

"I've only met Mr. McCloud when I interviewed with him a few months ago. I did not have the opportunity to meet Mr. Turner. How is he?"

"All I can tell you is that ya better find a barber in town before you grace him with your presence."

"I've been so busy trying to pass the Bar exam. Now that you mention it I haven't even thought about getting a haircut. Please forgive my manners. My name is Shane Walker and this is my lovely bride, Dana."

"You don't say. Well, this ought to be an excellent opportunity for y'all. Oak Bay is a great place to live and raise a family."

Dana spoke up and said, "Thank you, sir. We are so excited to be moving here."

"No, mam, I thank y'all for your business. I'm Luther Brown by the way. If y'all need any service with your cars, y'all come on back and see us. We will take mighty good care of ya."

Walking fast with a slight limp he inherited from a fire fight in South Vietnam, Carl made his way over toward Luther and yelled out, "That's enough, Luther. We have customers who need attention."

The muscles in Luther's face tightened as he kept his composure and politely bid the newly married couple a good day. Once they made their way out of hearing distance, Luther walked over to Carl and asked, "Didn't you see I was tryin' to get those two to come back here for more business?"

"All I saw was you takin' your sweet time to talk those people to death. Now git a move on. We are gittin' backed up."

Over on the north side of full- service aisle number one, Roger frantically popped the hood of a Ford Galaxie as he yelled out to Luther, "If you can get the windshield on this one, I will start checkin' the air pressure in the tires of Mrs. Green's car."

Four cars and two trucks later both Luther and Roger were able to catch their breath and wipe the perspiration away from their foreheads with their red service station grease rags.

Roger leaned up against gas pump number two and said, "It is funny to me how one minute we are workin' like crazy men and then all of sudden it's like the world comes to a complete stop."

Luther smiled, nodded in agreement with Roger, and then put away his red grease rag. He then pulled out a smoking pipe from his blue, service station uniform pants along with an old worn out pocket knife. Scraping out the pipe with his knife, he looked at Roger and said quietly, "Carl don't have the first clue 'bout how to treat customers the right way."

Roger stepped a little closer to Luther in fear that Carl might hear their conversation. He replied in almost a whisper, "One thing is for sure. He don't take no crap off anybody in this town. He scares me at times."

In a more loud and defiant tone, Luther said, "He don't scare me. If he don't start treatin' people better 'round here he ain't gonna have no workers, and he ain't gonna have no customers."

After only nodding his head in agreement, Roger spoke up and said, "While we are on the subject..." He paused for a moment and continued by asking Luther, "Did ya know that you had pissed off Rainey somethin' fierce?"

"Bout what?"

"I'm sure ya don't even realize it, Mr. Luther, but you keep callin' him the 'Colored Boy'."

"Well, he is a colored boy ain't he? I've been callin' him that since the first day he arrived. Wonder why he is so put out now?"

Roger smiled at Luther and replied, "Come on, Mr. Luther, it's 1979, and nobody calls Black people Colored anymore."

"So he wants me to call him the Black Boy?"

"No, sir, he don't want ya to call him any kind of boy. He just wants to be called by his name."

"What name? Black Boy or Colored Boy?"

"No, Mr. Luther, just call him Rainey like you call me Roger. And you have to quit callin' him 'boy'. Rainey is twenty years old. He is a grown man."

"No, sir, he is a Colored boy whether he wants to be or doesn't want to be."

Roger interrupted him immediately and said, "Come on, Mr. Luther, I never hear ya call Mr. Darryl a Colored boy or Colored man. You always call him Darryl. Why is Rainey any different?"

"I don't know. Maybe it's because Darryl was my mailman for a long time. Anyway, he calls Rainey 'the Colored mechanic'."

"Not to his face."

"All right, all right.. I'm just jokin', Roger. If the Colored boy wants me to call him by his name, I will do it."

With a serious look on his face he then asked Roger, "I served in the Navy and worked the rest of my life in the furniture plant. When did it all of a sudden become a bad thing to call a youngster a colored boy or girl?"

Roger smiled and replied, "I'm not sure, but I'd say that all changed about ten years ago."

"Shut your mouth, boy...Why I'll be...I guess I am a little behind the times."

"Do ya promise to try not to call him the Colored boy anymore?

"As Carl always says- You got it, Partner."

Carl then stuck his head out of the station lounge and yelled at Roger saying, "Look here by God, I didn't hire ya to be no advertisin' billboard. Get the mop and bucket and give those restrooms some love when we don't have any customers."

Roger smiled and began walking toward the mechanic's bay when a very familiar car pulled up for service. He immediately looked at Luther and said, "I have this one."

Walking over to the driver side of a faded green, 1971 Ford Torino, Roger ran his fingers through his longer than usual sandy blonde hair. Dianna Branham, the driver of the car, rolled down her window. Full of personality and naturally good looks, the forty something long-legged lady smiled and winked at Roger before saying, "Why it's my favorite gas man, Hot Rod Roger. Please fill her up, and if you don't mind, could you pretty- please give my windshield some much needed love?"

"Yes, mam."

Roger then quickly ran over to pump number two to begin servicing the car of the friendliest customer in Oak Bay. For a moment Dianna waded through her large straw pocketbook like a mad woman. She sat straight up in her seat and peered into the rear mirror as she applied a healthy dose of lipstick to her parched lips. Roger then asked her, "So when is Jeannie coming back from the beach?"

"That is a good question. I think she is coming back today or tomorrow."

Dianna then opened her car door and began to make her way into the Amoco Station lounge. With every step she took, every man in the place couldn't help but notice all of the things about her that they shouldn't be noticing. Dressed in the tightest white shorts ever made, and an even tighter light blue Ralph Lauren Polo shirt, it was her bright red Stiletto high heel shoes that were barely noticed by the men as she entered the lounge. Tanned to perfection, Dianna walked into the lounge with a confident swagger. Carl quickly hung up the phone with an automotive parts company representative when she appeared in his view. Meeting her halfway around the lounge counter, he leaned over and gave her a hug while saying loudly, "Better hurry up with a quick hug before my wife comes up here and shoots me dead."

"Carl, you are one sly devil."

Stumpy sat straight up in his chair and said, "Don't forget about me, Dianna."

Carl laughed and then said, "Shut the hell up, Stumpy. Dianna wouldn't touch you with a ten-foot pole."

Turning toward Stumpy, Dianna noticed Rainey standing in the doorway of the mechanic's bay. She quickly winked at him and then walked over and gave Stumpy a big peck on his forehead. Rainey whispered to Hank Burrows who wanted a kiss of his own, "That is so disgusting. Kissing Mr. Stumpy is worse than kissing a muddy pig."

"I don't know…Yeah… What am I thinkin'? You're right, Rainey, that is disgustin'."

Luther then walked into the station lounge interrupting the love fest by saying, "Carl, there is a man out here who wants a price on a set of Firestone tires."

Carl put up his hand toward Luther and nodded in confirmation that his message was received while he kept his eyes on Dianna. She then walked over near the station lounge counter and gave Carl her Amoco credit card to pay for her gas. While he drug the handle of the credit card machine over the index card sized triplicate carbon copy purchase order, she smiled at him and said, "Well, Carl, I know you are an awfully busy man, but I have a little favor to ask."

"Anything for you, Dianna."

With a pitiful look on her face she continued by saying, "I hate to admit it, but business is not what it used to be these days."

"I'm not quite followin' you, Dianna. What do ya need? Do you need some new tires, a battery, or some transmission work?"

"No, Mr. Silly Pants, all we need is more business. Ever since that new Disco Bar opened up a few months ago, we have lost some of our regulars."

"I'm not quite sure I...

Dianna interrupted him and blurted out loudly, but in a dignified tone of voice, "Just keep reminding everyone that the One Spot is still the best place in this county to get a cold beer, shoot a little pool, and win some big poker jackpots. Don't forget that we have some of the prettiest girls in town working there as well."

Hank Burrows, Oak Bay's oldest living man of local law enforcement, cleared his throat and said, "You be sure to tell Sissy Roberts that I said hello. That girl can.... Uh, You know that she and I go way back."

"I know you do, Honey… I know you do. She is a lovely girl."

Carl briefly laughed and then said, "Speakin' of girls, how is your sweet little Jeannie doin'? I haven't seen her lately."

Before she could reply, Luther spoke up and said, "Well, looky here. I think all y'all have met Vince Smith. He is our new preach'a down at the Oak Bay Baptist Church."

Stumpy shrugged in his chair while a few of the men nodded and said hello. Others quickly pulled up a magazine or a section of the *Oak Bay Gazette* in front of their faces, hoping to avoid a conversation with a man of the cloth.

Dianna looked over at Carl, gave him a quick wink and then said, "Well, hello, Preacher Smith. It is so nice to finally put a face with a name. I've heard that you have been doing some remarkable things at your church." Dianna then began walking out of the station lounge before he could respond. She then stopped at the entrance door, turned completely around and said, "Remember to spread the good word." She then shook her head twice, whipping her long black hair into a rhythmic whooshing swoop before she made her way to her car.

With every eye of every man in the Main Street Amoco watching her every step, Stumpy whispered to Hank Burrows, "If I go blind right now, just go ahead and shoot me dead."

Once Dianna reached her car, Preacher Smith spoke up and asked, "Who is that woman?"

Luther quickly replied, "Her name is Dianna Branham. She and her drunken husband run a drinkin' and gamblin' joint down on the Pee Dee River called the One Spot. Some people say she is a prostitute."

Everyone in the station lounge began to cough loudly including Carl. Luther quickly caught on and yelled, "Well, it's the dang truth, and y'all all know it. The sinnin' in that place has been goin' on for as long as I can remember."

Carl then asked, "Luther, don't ya have a customer waitin' on a quote for some tires?"

"Nope. He left five minutes ago. I guess he got tired of waitin' on you."

The middle aged man of the cloth then looked at Luther saying, "Sounds like the Devil's work is alive and well here in Oak Bay." He then smiled and looked at Carl and continued his preaching by saying, "We all love the sinner, but us God fearin' people hate the sin." He then turned to the men sitting in the Main Street Amoco lounge and said as he grinned, "Maybe the Good Lord thinks it's time we dealt with this particular house of sin. I certainly will have my eyes on the One Spot."

After inviting everyone to church, Preacher Vince Smith walked out of the station lounge over to his shiny 1976 baby blue Lincoln Continental. He looked at Roger and said, "I appreciate you takin' care of my pride and joy."

Roger grinned before replying, "That is one smooth lookin' ride. I bet it cost ya a fortune."

Preacher Smith opened the driver's side door and began to sit down in the blue suede seat before he responded by saying, "When you are doin' God's work, young man, all of the gold in heaven is at your disposal. I hope you will join us this Sunday for some good old-fashioned revival style preachin' and teachin'."

"Thanks preach'a, but in my family we are of the Presbyterian persuasion. I don't want to hurt your feelin's, but my Daddy says that Baptist's are confused about the three D's- dunkin', dancin', and drinkin'. He says that all Baptists ever want to do is tell people that they are headed for a lake of fi'ya."

"No problem. You have a good day, and I will have you in my prayers." He then shut his door and pressed his fancy automatic window button. Once the window rolled down, he yelled at Roger, "I almost forgot to give you your tip, son." He then flipped Roger a shiny, 1976, United States, Bicentennial commemorative Quarter and drove away.

Back inside of the station lounge, two of Oak Bay's most respected living war heroes were arguing in front of the O.T.C.C. and a few customers who were waiting for Rainey to service their vehicles. Carl stood behind the station lounge counter as he yelled, "Damit, Luther, you have sunk to an all-time low today. I can't believe you brought your new preach'a up in here to cast judgment on Dianna."

"For Pete's sake, Carl, you are a married man. I see the way ya look at that woman, and it just ain't right."

"You can't fool me, Luther. I have seen you wipe your glasses many times so that you could get a better peek of her."

"Not true… Not true."

"You have the new Preach'a all riled up for no good reason. The One Spot has been a part of this community for a really long time."

"You're not gonna change my mind on this one, Carl. I've watched good men go down to the river over the years and end up broke as hell or losing their family."

"Now hold on just a minute, Luther. I'm pretty sure there is a scripture in the Good Book that says somethin' about castin' the first stone."

Hank Burrows could not hold his tongue when he butted in by saying, "Now, Luther, all those years I was the Chief of Police in this town, I want ya to know that our crime rate was very low because of the One Spot. The Branham family has always run a tight ship. I can tell you that over the past twenty years, I bet the police have not been called out there more than four or five times."

Stumpy jumped in and said, "Don't forget that they have been quite generous with their profits. Every year the One Spot gives money to the Recreation Department and the Oak Bay Hospital."

Definitely outnumbered, Luther stoically surrendered his fight by proclaiming that he was taking an early lunch break. He then walked out the door and over to the Main Street Diner, two blocks down the street.

Carl then looked at Stumpy and said, "Luther needs to get down off his high horse and remember that he is the one who once told us that half his deacons at his church drink like hell on Saturday nights.

Those do gooders sure like to look down on folks all the while they pretend they don't drink."

Stumpy laughed and replied, "Y'all know that is a big part of our Baptist heritage. We do our best to hide our sins. I've never met a Baptist who openly drank in public, and I have never met an alcoholic that wasn't a Baptist. The way we hide our drinkin' from others has become an art form."

Coach Hutchinson added, "This is the one thing I have never understood since the day I arrived here from New York. I am still baffled about all of the public opposition to alcohol in this town. When I was growing up, my own priest always warned us to never trust a man who wouldn't take a drink."

Darryl chimed in saying, "My grandmother always said there is no sin in a little gin."

After laughing, Hank said, "And my grandmother liked to say that licka was only good for sprucing up a dessert or to be used for medicinal purposes. Now that I think of it, she was either complaining about her arthritis or she was making a cake."

Chapter Eleven

Once Luther arrived back from the Main Street Diner with a pitiful look on his face, Hot Rod Roger and Rainey took their lunch breaks together in the back corner of mechanic's bay number two. Using a set of red, heavy, rolling tool drawers as their makeshift table, they both unfolded two gray metal folding chairs; creating a dining area for their bagged lunches.

Rainey took a bite of his sandwich and then said to Roger, "You do know that every one of those old men think you are the man. Every time you leave the station lounge, one of them talks about how hard you throw a baseball or how you single handedly won that playoff football game last fall against St. George High. They also talk about how they remember what a great ball player your father was when he played. They always call you the 'chip off the old block'."

Roger took a swig from a Nehi Grape soda and replied, "That's because Coach Hutchison used to be my American Legion baseball coach a few years ago. He also coached my Daddy. Because of that, our family has a strong connection to him."

"No, man, that's not all of it. You would have to hear a recording of the conversations I hear about you from those old dudes. It's as if they are living out their dreams through you. They worship the ground you walk on. To them, you are the Golden Boy."

"Stop it, man. Mr. Stumpy calls me the hippie boy and always asks me if he needs to take me to the barber shop. You evidently never hear the way Carl talks to me when you are not around. He has thrown more than one 'Damit, boy' at me just about every day."

"You do have a point. Carl has never cussed me; however, there have been a few times where I could feel the cursing without him saying a word. Remember last week when I forgot to put the oil cap back on that Chevy truck? I really thought he was going to kill me, but he never said a word. That look on his face was enough to send chills down my spine."

Roger laughed and then replied, "He was pretty pissed; especially when he had to give Mr. Johnson his money back."

Rainey took another bite of his sandwich before saying, "Carl is a rough dude at times, but he has never disrespected me like Luther."

"Now hold on, Rainey, I did have a chance to talk to Mr. Luther about calling you a Colored boy."

"What did that old fool say?"

"I got him straight. He promised me that he would change. I know this is hard for you to believe, but he has been usin' the term Colored for so long he really didn't know that you were offended."

"He better get straight because I have had it with the way he talks down to me like I am some kind of slave. I bet he doesn't know that I had to come home from college and take this job to help out my parents."

"I didn't know that. What college were you going to and how in the world do you know so much about workin' on cars?"

Rainey, in between chews of his bologna sandwich, smiled and replied, "I was majoring in pre-law at South Carolina State in Orangeburg. As far as my mechanical skills go, my father is a diesel mechanic down at Shorty's Truck Stop off I-95. He made sure that my brothers and I learned how to work on cars and trucks from an early age."

"It's none of my business, but why did you have to leave school?"

"It's ok. I don't like to talk about it to everyone, but my mother has cancer. The doctors say she has only a few months left. My poor father and my older sister are doing everything they can to take care of her. The least I can do is to lend a helping hand with the medical bills starting to pile up."

"That's a shame. I am so sorry."

Roger then tried to change the subject with Rainey who was three years older than him. He asked, "I hope you don't take this the wrong way, but I have never heard a black person talk like you. Why is that?"

Rainey laughed and then asked, "Are you trying to say that you think I talk like a white person?"

"Well, you sort of do, except you speak even better than most white people in this town. Are you from up North?"

"I'm an Air Force brat. We have lived on bases all over the country. When my Pops retired from the Air Force, he decided to come back here where he grew up. We moved here when I was in the 11th grade. Because I do try to speak clearly, I get teased all the time about the way I talk. My cousins here in Oak Bay call me 'Mr. Movin' on Up'. You know, like the theme song from the TV show, *The Jeffersons.* The reason I speak so clearly is because my mother used to be an English teacher. She was a stickler about clear diction and pronunciation with all of her children." Rainey then reached for a potato chip before asking, "I hope you don't take this the wrong way, but you don't sound as country as the rest of these Rednecks in this town. Why is that?"

Roger laughed and said, "I'm not sure, but it might have to do with Coach Hutchinson and his New York accent. He has been correcting my speech since middle school. I can still hear him yellin' at me about the proper pronunciation of this." Roger then reached into his pocket and pulled out a one dollar bill and said, "I used to always call this a doll'a. It drove him nuts."

Rainey laughed and said, "Don't get me wrong; you definitely still have a Southern accent, but it is not nearly as noticeable as most of these Rednecks."

Roger smiled and then asked, "Do you like workin' here?"

"You mean working instead of workin' don't you? Leaving off the g's in your pronunciation is what a dialectologist would describe as a regiolect or a dialect pertaining to a geographical area."

"I will take yore word for it."

Rainey smiled before saying, "What you actually meant to say is 'your' instead of 'yore' but to answer your original question, working here as a mechanic is a lot better than working at the furniture plant or in the tobacco warehouses. My Pops used to tell us when we were young that any kind of factory work not only wears out the body; it kills the brain."

"How did ya get this job?"

"I don't tell a lot of people, but my Pops and Carl served together in Vietnam for a couple of years, and they grew up here together. Pops heard that Carl needed a good mechanic and gave him a visit. The next thing I know, I am down here one Sunday evening while

Carl watches me service his 65 Chevy truck. He pulled up a lawn chair, drank a couple of beers and watched every turn of every wrench and screwdriver. He had me rotate his tires and change his air filter. I checked all the fluid levels, etc. When I was done, he pulled out a stopwatch and pressed the stop button. He looked at it and told me if I could promise to keep the same pace for every service job I was hired."

For the next twenty minutes the youngest employees of the Main Street Amoco shared dreams, talked about women, and began a conversation about race that was unplanned when Roger said, "I wish more Black and White people in our town would learn how to talk with each other like what we are doing right now. I'm pretty sure it would make a big difference in the way they would treat each other."

Rainey slid back in his metal folding chair and replied, "I know what you mean. It's almost 1980. You would think that the people in this town could move on."

Roger smiled and then said, "I still can't believe that at Oak Bay High we have a Black student body president and a White student body president. We all laugh when we have to vote for a Black homecoming queen and a White homecoming queen. I wonder when we will ever get to the point where we stop all this foolishness."

Rainey smiled and said, "The grown people in this town are the ones who can't seem to move on. I know this may sound racist, but it seems to me that the old white people around here can't quite put an end to the past."

"What do you mean by that?"

"I know that you have been to the Oak Bay Courthouse."

"I ride by it every day."

"Then you know that they have a statue of an unnamed, White colonial soldier which honors the Revolutionary War, a monument that lists the people who served in WWI, a statue of a White G.I. holding a gun to honor the vets from WWII, and of course, a statue of South Carolina Confederate General Micha Jenkins sitting on his horse. What a lot of people don't know is that General Jenkins wasn't even from Oak Bay. The biggest statue at our courthouse is one of a Confederate General who never lived a day of his life in this town and was accidentally shot and killed by his own troops. On the south side of the Oak Bay Courthouse we have a fifty-foot monument that was erected in 1910 by the Daughters of the Confederacy to honor the veterans of Oak Bay who fought in the Civil War. Along with those monuments, over in the Oak Bay Centennial park we have a statue of South Carolina native son, Preston Brooks who was a member of Congress in the 1850's. His great accomplishment was that he fought for slavery during his tenure in Congress. He became famous when he entered the chamber of the U.S. Senate where he took his walking cane and severely beat up an abolitionist Senator from Massachusetts named Charles Sumner. He may be a hero to white folks in this town, but he is no hero to me or my people."

Roger asked, "How in the world do you know all of this?"

"I know this state's history pretty well; not the white- washed version we were taught in school. You know that version of history which tries to make you think that slavery was good for Black folks because the slave owners were nice men who gave Black people food, clothes, and a place to live. I took it upon myself to do my own research a long time ago."

Roger replied to him, "To tell ya the truth, I have never paid much attention to those statues and monuments. They just seemed like they belonged. You know, like when you walk into a museum."

Rainey laughed for a moment and then leaned closer to Roger and said, "Out of all of those monuments and statues at the courthouse, the largest ones have to do with the one war that White folks in this town are still fighting."

"I don't know about all of that, Rainey. I do know that there are a lot of White people who are not racists who have respect for the Confederacy because they have relatives who fought in the war. I do know that a lot of people from this state were killed in the war."

"Well, all I know is that I still remember the separate drinking fountains and restrooms all throughout the South. I also remember seeing my Pops shed a few tears when he had to walk us into the back of a restaurant or find us another motel when he was told he and his family were not allowed. For a man who served this nation like he did, to only be told that he was not good enough to stay in a crappy motel was as low as you can imagine."

Roger quickly replied, "I'm sure that all that was awful for you and your family, but you would have to admit that this town has come a long way in the past few years."

Rainey leaned in closer to Roger before saying, "You are right. We have come a long way, but when I have to pass by that courthouse every day and look at those monuments it is not a good reminder of my heritage. Add to it, the Confederate flags flying on the back of White teenagers' pickup trucks, the tune to "Dixie" being played everywhere in this town, and this new crazy obsession with the *Dukes of Hazzard* doesn't make a Brother feel very welcomed. On top of that, I show up to work every day, and I am still called the "Colored Boy". From my perspective, we still have a long way to go."

"You make some good points, Rainey. I am hoping that we have taken care of the 'Colored Boy' situation with Mr. Luther. Roger paused momentarily and then continued by saying, "Now, removin' historical monuments at the Oak Bay Courthouse is another topic for another day."

Rainey bent over to tie one of his work boots before saying, "I agree. Don't get me wrong. I am all about history, but you have to admit that there is not one mention of the Africans that helped build this town or the Native Americans who were forced to abandon their homes. You do know that there were several tribes of native people who lived here hundreds of years before the first White settlers arrived? Don't misunderstand me. It wouldn't hurt my feelings in the least if one day those Confederate statues came down, but I am not advocating for that to happen. We can't erase history, but I think it would be good if our people were recognized for our contributions to society. Hopefully one day, the White people in this town will understand how we feel. No matter how you try to sugarcoat it, the South wanted slavery, and the North did not."

"I guess I see your point. Don't forget we could talk about the Romans, Greeks, Jews, Chinese and many other groups of people in history. Where do we draw the line?"

"I'm not sure, but it doesn't always have to be only the White people who are recognized for historical accomplishments. You have to agree that there have been some good non-White people from this nation who have contributed to society in a positive way."

"I can agree with that. The bottom line is that if we learn to sit down and talk, things would be better." Roger then extended his hand toward Rainey and said, "Thanks for talking to me today. I hope we are cool."

Rainey then shook his hand and said, "We're cool, Hot Rod... We are cool. I'm smart enough to know that not every White person is a racist or a member of the Klan."

Roger smiled and replied, "And I am smart enough to realize that we should judge people by their actions and not the color of their skin."

"Amen to that, Golden Boy."

Their lunch break talk abruptly ended when Luther walked into the mechanic's bay and yelled, "Hey, you two, we've got customers."

Rainey rolled his eyes as Roger replied, "Yes, sir."

Luther then yelled, "Roger, you take the Cadillac on aisle two, and I will get the Pontiac on aisle one. Rainey, Mrs. Dennis in the lounge needs an oil and lube job on her Chevy."

Rainey nodded his head, smiled at Roger and said, "Looks like we have made some progress, thanks to you. Now, once you are able to convince Carl to change the radio station from Country to Soul, then total progress will have been achieved."

Roger laughed and replied, "I took you for being a Heavy Metal guy."

Outside on the corner of the Main Street Amoco, Carl was having a serious chat with one of his old friends, Stan Hawkins. Known in the town of Oak Bay as one of the richest men of the county, he was the owner of the Hawkins Real Estate Company. The sometimes overly animated business man pulled out his lighter and lit up his second Winston cigarette a little too close to gas pump number two. Carl walked closer to the corner of the station and motioned for his chain smoking friend to follow. He waved his hand and cried out, "Step on over here while ya have that blow torch in your hand."

Carl's childhood friend laughed and then replied, "I guess that would be quite an explosion."

Carl, smelling the gas fumes coming off pump number two, moved a few more steps away and said, "Speakin' of explosion, what is the deal about the property across the street?"

Throwing down his cigarette and stomping it out on the concrete pavement, Mr. Hawkins then replied, "Nobody hates to tell ya this more than me."

"Don't tell me they are gonna build a funeral home over there?"

"Worse."

"How worse?"

Oak Bay's best known real estate tycoon replied, "It's a lot worse, my friend. An outfit out of Wilmington, North Carolina has already bought that property, and they are gonna put in a convenience store with self-service gas pumps. That outfit known as the Happy Mart is moving like wildfire. They are slingin' a ton of Slurpee's, hotdogs, and anything you can get from a grocery store along with self-service gas that is ten to fifteen cents cheaper than what you sell it for. They are building these stores and gas stations all around the Eastern half of North and South Carolina. They will have this one across the street built in just a few months."

Carl grinned and then said, "They may be some version of a grocery store, but they ain't no gas station."

"You are right, but Carl it looks like the days of full-service stations like this one are soon gonna be a thing of the past. With what has been happin' the past few years with gas prices, people have become obsessed with savin' a few pennies on the dollar when it comes to buyin' gas."

Carl laughed at his old friend and said, "Ok, Partner, I don't know what crystal ball you and your investment gurus are lookin' at, but as long as there are cars and trucks runnin' on gas and oil, then there will always be full-service gas stations."

"Carl, you know I usually agree with most everything you say, but this time you need to listen to me. In just a few years, these convenient stores are gonna run guys like you out of business."

Carl laughed again and replied, "No respectful woman in this town is ever gonna get out of her car and pump her own gas. Those heathen women in North Carolina might pump their own gas, but here in Oak Bay we have too many ladies who would never think of such a thing."

"Carl, I hope you are right, but as a friend I want you to think about sellin' this place before it is too late."

"Well, what in the hell do you suggest I do for a livin', Partner?"

"I don't know, Carl, but you are a good businessman. You might specialize in tires or open some type of mechanic shop. I saw a place in downtown Charlotte a few weeks ago that only does brakes and another one that only does oil and lube jobs."

"Hell's bells, Stan, we are a small town, By God. This is Oak Bay, South Carolina where real men still come to the service station to buy tires and batteries while ladies still come by so they don't have to get their nails and shoes stained from gasoline, grease, and oil."

"Alrighty then it looks like you have your mind made up. I sure do hope it works out for ya. You think about it because I know for a fact that this property will bring a pretty penny. You could sell, relocate near the Interstate and probably make a lot more money."

Carl then patted his old friend on the back, pulled down the brim of his sweat stained, service station cap and said, "You go and worry about somethin' else, Partner. This old station will be here goin' strong long after you and I have kicked the bucket."

While Hot Rod Roger was busy filling up a farm truck loaded with leaf tobacco on full-service aisle number two, Luther was making sure that local politician and attorney Ben Turner was getting his best service.

Luther politely said, "I met your new law partner and his wife this mornin'. They came by and turned in their U Haul truck."

One of Oak Bay's most successful attorney's replied, "That's great. He's not a partner yet, but from everything I've heard about him, he will do just fine. We are lucky to get him. He's top notch. He had some of the best grades we've seen in a long time."

Walking in a pair of thick, dirt covered overalls and wearing a long sleeve cotton button down shirt, Mr. Earl Grimes made his way from his farm truck and began talking to Ben Turner. He asked, "You got those papers filed down at Probate yet, Ben?"

"Not yet, Earl. How is your mama doing?"

"Whew boy, since Daddy passed we ain't been able to get her to eat very much."

"That's a cryin' shame. When folks are married for such a long time, it is a big shock to the system when one of them passes away."

"Yes, sir. Daddy was sittin' on the couch with Mama shellin' a pan of butter beans and the stroke done hit him like a bolt of lightnin'. One minute he was telllin' Mama how he wished she would make him a pound cake, and the next minute he was on his way to eat supper with Jesus."

"Well, don't worry, Earl. We will have those papers and the Will recorded with the Probate Judge first thing tomorrow. I can't talk ya into selling that good bird dog of yours can I?"

"Not a fat chance. Old Popeye has been with us too long. He's like family now."

Luther then stepped around the back bumper of the tobacco farm truck and said quietly to Hot Rod Roger, "This is what I love 'bout this place. We have all kinds of customers from many different backgrounds. I love listenin' to conversations like this one."

Roger laughed and said, "It is amazing, Mr. Luther. I thought I knew a lot of people in this town until I started workin' here."

Luther screwed on the gas cap to the tobacco truck and asked, "Is Rainey all right with me now?"

"Ya did good, Mr. Luther... Just keep callin' him by his name and everything will be good."

Luther smiled and asked, "When is your next American Legion baseball game?"

"We play Timmonsville Monday night here at home. Are you going to come out and watch me pitch?"

"Have I ever missed a Legion game?'

"I don't know. I never look in the stands."

"I know that is a bunch of bullcrap. I've seen ya look up when those ball park girls start chantin' your name."

"I hate to admit it, but they do get my attention every now and then."

"Speakin' of attention, I heard you talkin' to Rainey about that Jeannie Branham. You better watch your step with that girl."

"Why do you say that?"

"You do know that her family runs the One Spot on the river, don't ya?"

"Everybody knows about the One Spot, Mr. Luther."

"Have you been to that juke joint?"

"Heck no. My mama would kill me, and I'm not quite old enough."

"That's good, but be careful with that girl."

"She can't help where she comes from. All I know is that she seems like a good girl, and you have to admit that she is good looking. I just want to get to know her better."

"I don't know about her, but her family is as wild as a bunch of swamp hogs."

"Have you been to the One Spot before, Mr. Luther?"

"Boy, I ought to slap the tar out of ya. You know better."

Chapter Twelve

Later that evening at 9:30 pm, Roger and his parents had finished watching the television sitcom, *M*A*S*H** when Mark James decided it was the right time to have a family discussion about his mother's house. He leaned forward in his recliner and said, "Juanita, we need to talk."

Roger immediately knew where the conversation was headed once Mark said, "We have a little problem with the construction of the new house."

Roger was amazed at how his father explained to his mother that they were sitting on a historical treasure. Juanita at first seemed unimpressed when he initially explained that they could move the old house to the back of the property. Once he told her that the Oak Bay Historical Society would pay for the moving of the house she saw no problem with it.

He said, "That settles it. I will call Chad Emory tomorrow. The faster we get it moved, the faster our new house can be built."

As his father walked with his mother to their bedroom, Roger laughed, knowing that his father had cleverly avoided the most significant detail; allowing strangers to come and visit the log cabin.

Once he was certain that they were settled in their bedroom, Roger again began reading the journal of his ancestor, Matthew James. Finding the last page of his previous readings, he was shocked when he turned the next page and found two pages missing. He could see where the missing pages had been ripped out of the book, and he quickly concluded that the words written on the next page did not match the previous writings about Matthew's exploits on a pirate ship. The next page began with the following: "Thus my wife Sarah was taken to sickness with fevir on the coast of Carolina."

Disappointed that he could not read how Sarah came into the life of Matthew or how he ended up in Carolina, Roger almost fell off his bed when he read, "It was thou, my dear Sarah, who is the only one whom knows the change of me name. I, Lars Erickson of Sweden at birth had no choyce withstanding the rope of treason."

Those words were not only unexpected, they moved Roger emotionally in a way that he never expected. Roger felt betrayal, although he understood the element of survival associated with it. Reading those same words several times, he had to hold back tears. He immediately thought to himself that he and his family never knew they were descended from a man who changed his name so that he would not hang for treason. A lie concerning Scottish descent had now been revealed which Roger thought might kill his own father if he knew that their Scottish heritage was all a ruse.

Reading further, Roger learned that "Matthew James" was able to nurse Sarah back to health while they were living with a large family of tanners named Smith near Beaufort, South Carolina. Detailing a year which included a harsh winter and Matthew avoiding the movement of British troops throughout their region to avoid arrest, Roger learned that Matthew was desperately trying to find a way to move away from the South Carolina coast.

The rest of the week, Roger went through the same mundane routine. He would work at the service station in the morning, practice baseball in the evening, occasionally speak to Crazy Daisy on his CB radio on his way home, watch the news reports concerning the investigation of the death of Senator Broadway, and read the journal of Matthew James late at night. Nights of little sleep were beginning to take a toll on him. By Saturday of that week, he was exhausted. When he showed up to work ten minutes late, Carl lit into him like he had never done before. He screamed, “Hot Rod, don’t drag your rear end in here late. Do you hear me?”

Rainey noticed that Roger had his lip poked out after Carl’s rebuke. He smiled at Roger and said, “Carl doesn't play when it comes to being on time.”

Roger smirked and then replied, “I know it. These late nights are killing me.”

Rainey with a transmission seal in his hand, said, “Oh, the old love life must be in full swing.”

“Not exactly. I have been trying to get Crazy Daisy to go out with me all week. She finally invites me to church, and I know that my parents are not going to be too happy.”

“Why is that?”

“Let’s just say that my Mama does not think too highly of their faith.” He paused and continued by saying, “What I don’t understand is that Jeannie doesn’t even go to that church much. I have no idea why she wants this to be our first time together.”

Rainey laughed and said, "It really is funny when you think about it. From what I know about the Mormons they don't drink coffee much less beer and wine. I think it's hilarious that the owner of the One Spot is a Mormon. It just doesn't add up."

Roger laughed and said, "Yeah, I was thinking the same thing. Maybe he doesn't drink anymore."

Rainey shook his head and said, "Not from what I hear. They say that Teddy Branham can make Kirby look like a little leaguer when it comes to drinking."

Roger laughed and said, "Speaking of Kirby, do you see what he is wearing today?"

Rainey turned and Kirby walked into the mechanic's bay. Kirby looked at Roger and Rainey, smiled and then asked, "Do you have any trash that I need to take out?"

Roger replied, "No, sir." He then asked Kirby, "I don't mean to be mean to you, Mr. Kirby, but why in the world are you wearing a sweater when it's so hot today?"

"The skeeters have been bad the past two days. I can't stand getting bit by skeeters."

Rainey laughed and said, "Mr. Kirby, you are going to kill yourself in this heat."

Kirby smiled and replied, "I can take the heat, but I can't stand the skeeters. You boys be good. I will see you later."

Roger asked, "Where are you headed off today?"

"I've got some furry friends down at Oak Bay Park that need my attention."

Once Kirby walked out of the mechanics bay and hopped on his moped, Roger looked at Rainey and said, "He is a good old soul. You know that he goes down to the park and feeds the squirrels every day."

Rainey picked up a socket wrench and then replied, "For a drunk, the man really does have a good heart. About two days ago I saw him give a small kid in the station lounge fifty cents. I know fifty cents doesn't sound like much but for Kirby that was quite generous."

Carl then stuck his head into the mechanic's bay and yelled, "Hey, you two, we have a couple of cars which need a vehicle inspection. Don't forget that the new windshield stickers for the month of June are the yellow ones."

Roger looked at Rainey and asked, "I don't understand why the state makes everyone get a vehicle inspection."

"It's because the state makes $2.50 off every $3 inspection. The other reason is because stations like these make good money from the repairs that are needed once a vehicle doesn't pass inspection. I can't tell you how many times we have repaired a brake light or turn signal since I have been here. Sometimes I think that vehicle inspections keep us in business."

After completing the vehicle inspections, Roger walked outside to help Luther with a string of morning customers filling up for the weekend. Once he walked over to full-service aisle two, Luther was already filling up a bright yellow 1978 Datsun 280z sports car. Although the car itself caught Roger's attention, it was the Citadel Football bumper sticker along with the car's driver and passenger which caused Roger to want to assist his fellow worker.

With only one glance, Roger immediately recognized that they were the ones who had received the "ultimate revenge" from his childhood friend Stew Turbeville. To Roger, the JFK looking guy looked like he had just finished posing as a GQ Magazine model with his fancy haircut and expensive looking penny loafers. Roger also noticed that the "Eisenhower" looking dude was much bigger; wearing a pair of blue jeans and a Citadel Football t-shirt. Both now standing next to their hot looking ride, the JFK looking guy looked at Roger and asked him, "Is there a good place to eat in this town besides McDonalds or Hardees?"

"Sure. The Big Pig Barbeque Hut, a few blocks from here, serves the best barbeque on the planet. You can't miss it. They have a big Confederate Flag flying in front of the building, and the parking lot will be packed."

"Do they use Ketchup or Mustard based sauce?"

Roger smiled and replied, "Neither. They use an Eastern North Carolina vinegar style based sauce on their pulled pork."

"I have never had that before. Is it good?"

"Once you taste it, you will never want another kind of barbeque. We have people from all over who come here for the barbeque. By the way my name is Roger James."

"Did you say Roger James?"

"That's right."

"Do you play quarterback at your high school?"

"Yes."

"Look here, Mike, this is the quarterback that Coach Baker and the other coaches are always talking about." The JFK looking dude laughed then said, "My name is Tim. I actually play quarterback at the Citadel, and I am so glad to meet you. I have been hearing about you for over a year now. This is Mike; he plays Tight End."

"It's a small world. What brings you two to Oak Bay?"

"We are from Greenwood. We are on our way back home from Myrtle Beach for a few days before we report back to the Citadel."

"How was the beach?"

"We were having a good time until the crap hit the fan."

"What do you mean?"

Mike, the big tight end, then interrupted his friend and said, "Some dumb ass robbed us while we were on the beach."

Roger quickly walked to the back of the car and retrieved the gas pump nozzle as Mike continued by saying, "Some dude took all of our wallets and car keys. The crazy thing is that he left all of our cash."

"That is strange."

"You can say that again. It took us all week to get new keys and enough money to make it back home. Tim is driving without a license. We just hope he makes it home without being stopped by the law."

"Did you see the person who did this to y'all?"

"Hell, no. A couple of girls saw a short stumpy looking guy near our towels. I tell you one thing, if I ever find out who did it, that dude better watch out."

The quarterback named Tim began laughing and said, "It was an aggravation, but one good thing did come from all of it."

Roger asked, "What was that?"

Mike spoke up and said, "Romeo here may have fallen in love."

Tim smiled and said, "I wouldn't call it love, but I did meet the most beautiful girl I think I have ever seen."

"Is that right?"

Roger then dropped the windshield squeegee when the quarterback from the Citadel said, "Yeah, her name is Daisy Branham. She and some high school girl helped us out when we were trying to find a hardware store to buy a set of new car keys. She even gave us some money."

Roger regained his composure before asking, "Where is she from?"

"I'm not sure. She gave me her phone number, but I haven't been able to reach her. That is just my luck. I make out with the most beautiful girl for a few minutes at the beach, and I don't even know where she lives. She told me that she was in college at the University of South Carolina"

"That is a shame. What else did you find out about her?"

"Other than she is the best kisser I have ever met, not much at all. We were getting pretty heated up next to the Pavilion, and she left me high and dry. She gave me her number and bolted like she had seen a ghost."

Roger smiled and then saw disaster brewing in his peripheral vision. Pulling up to Full-service aisle number one was Stew Turbeville. Standing in between what could possibly become a big fight at the Main Street Amoco, Roger momentarily froze. He then quickly spoke up and said, "Y'all have a good trip. Good luck this year."

The quarterback from the Citadel said, "Not yet, Roger. I have to use the bathroom."

"Your best bet would be to use it at the Big Pig Barbeque Hut. Our bathrooms are out of order."

As the boys from the Citadel drove away, Roger noticed the quarterback from the Citadel looking over at Stew who was stepping out of his Plymouth Barracuda. He looked one more time before he drove away. When Roger finally made his way over to Stew, he cried out, "That was a close one. Did you see those guys in that 280z?"

"No, I did not. Who were they?"

"JFK and General Eisenhower."

"They better be glad I didn't see them. I would have…."

Roger interrupted his best friend and said, "No way in hell. Eisenhower who plays Tight End for the Citadel would have killed you. That guy looks like a beast."

Once Roger hurried up and filled up Stew's car, he looked up and saw his father pulling into the station. Climbing out of his blue 1967 beat up Chevrolet truck, Mark James headed straight for Roger. Not sure if he was in some kind of trouble, he walked toward his father, meeting him under the station's large awning.

"What brings you here so early, Dad?

With a big smile on his face, Mark James replied, "Mr. Peabody and his boys got it done this morning."

"Got what done?"

"They moved your grandma's house to the back of the property. It really does look pretty cool havin' a log cabin on the back of the property."

"That's great."

"I thought you would be a little more excited."

"I'm sorry, that is great news. It has been a busy day here."

"I didn't mean to keep you from work, but I had to tell you."

Roger smiled and replied, "It looks like you are pretty jacked about this."

"I am, son. I am. I think this is going to be a good thing for our family."

The rest of the afternoon, many of the customers at the Main Street Amoco were talking about the death of Senator Broadway. Roger and Luther noticed that several unmarked law enforcement cars passed by them on Main Street. When one of the cars stopped in for a fill up, Roger was lucky enough to be the one who serviced the car. The agent from the South Carolina Law Enforcement Division stretched his legs outside of his black Chrysler which sported a long antenna on the back. Roger asked the man with a stone face, "Are you a part of the Senator Broadway investigation?"

"Why? Do you know something about the case?"

"No, sir. I just..."

The investigator interrupted him and asked, "Then why did you mention it?"

"I was just wondering since you look like an investigator."

The uptight looking investigator then said, "Well, if you hear anything, you give us a call." He then pulled out a business card from his wallet and handed it to Roger before saying, "Put this in the station and tell everyone that this is the number to call if they hear anything."

Roger looked at the business card and replied, "Thanks, Investigator, Ivey. I will let everyone here know who to call if they hear something."

Luther, who heard the conversation, walked up to Roger once the investigator pulled away from the station and said, "Those SLED boys are a rare bunch. You better put that card on the station counter so we have it in case we do hear some good gossip."

Chapter Thirteen

Early the next morning, Hot Rod Roger was awaken from the sound of a woodpecker blasting his beak into a pecan tree outside of his bedroom window. The pecking sound, which seemed like machine gun fire, did not wake him as much as the aroma of bacon his mother was frying in the kitchen. Dressed only in a pair of Oak Bay High School gym shorts he had worn since he was a freshman, the tall, muscular athlete wandered half asleep into the kitchen. Eyes half closed, he immediately opened the refrigerator door.

"We don't have any more orange juice?"

Already dressed for church, his mother, Juanita, turned a fork full of bacon in an old black skillet that had been handed down a generation prior. She replied, "Ask your Daddy about the juice. He swears he never drinks it. It must be the orange juice fairy who comes into our house at night and drinks all of our juice. And then the vanilla wafers go missing and...."

Roger's father was slightly hungover when he was awakened by the same woodpecker. That smart bird had avoided two of his father's wayward shotgun blasts during the past two weeks. Stumbling into the kitchen, Mark James threw down a copy of the Sunday morning edition of the *Oak Bay Gazette* on the kitchen table, slightly raised his voice, and said, "Everything is good, Juanita. Now we don't need no hell raisin' today."

"I'll show you some hell raisin'. You both must think this is like the Burger King. Well, I've got news for both of you; you can't have it your way around this house. This is my house." She continued to ramble while the two males of the household rolled their eyes and pretended not to hear the verbal assault that was being unleashed upon them.

Mark then looked at Roger and asked, "What is this bill from Columbia House Records?"

Roger looked over at his father and replied, "I don't know, Dad?"

"It says that you owe them twenty-eight dollars and fifty cents. It has your name on the bill."

"I don't understand. They sent me eight album tapes and said it only cost a penny. I called them and ordered the eight tapes after I saw an ad in *Sports Illustrated.*"

"Did any more tapes come to this house after you got the first batch?"

"I think two or three, but I swear I did not order them."

"That is because that ad in *Sports Illustrated* is a scam. You better call them tomorrow and cancel. Whatever you do, don't accept any more tapes. Give them to me so I can send them back."

"I don't understand."

"The next time you decide to order somethin' over the phone, just remember that if it sounds too good to be true; it's not true. I've already heard some of the people at the hardware store complain about this mess."

Standing behind them, Juanita began pouring herself another cup of coffee. She said, "You both need to hurry up if we are goin' to make it to church."

Roger sheepishly spoke up and said, "Mom, about church today, I have been invited to go to another church."

Juanita looked at her son and quickly grinned before she asked, "Would that be at the Baptist or the Methodist church?"

Roger shrugged his shoulders and replied, "Not exactly."

"Don't tell me that you are going to the Catholic church."

"No, mam."

Mark James laughed and then said, "We are all ears? Which church is it?"

"Latter Day Saints."

Mark James almost spit out his coffee and said, "Are you talkin' about the Mormon Church off Highway Nine?"

Roger just shook his head up and down.

Juanita James shook her head as well and said, "No son of mine is going there."

Mark James then smiled and said, "Now hold on, Juanita. I'm curious as to how our son decided to attend the Mormon Church today." He then looked at Roger and asked, "Did two missionaries on bicycles have a talk with you at the service station?"

Roger smiled and said, "Not exactly. I think y'all have heard of Jeannie Branham. We started talkin' at the beach. She wants me to go to church with her today."

Juanita slammed her apron in the kitchen sink and cried out, "Oh no, this is not happening. No son of mine is gonna get involved with those people. For God's sake, do ya hear what he is sayin' to us, Mark?"

"Mom, you don't understand... She is a good girl."

"I don't care. Her family is..."

Mark interrupted his wife by saying, "Calm down, Juanita. They aren't goin' to get married. I don't think it would hurt for Roger to go with the girl to church."

"Have you lost your mind? I can't believe I am hearing this."

A few minutes later while his father continued to verbally wrestle with his mother, Roger quickly showered and headed out of the house with only one parent's approval. Jumping into his 1972, refurbished, Ford Mustang he could feel the morning heat coming off the steering wheel and the edge of his slightly cracked and worn driver's seat. Like he had done since the day he started driving, he came to a rolling stop at the end of the dirt road and squealed his tires as he put it into third gear and quickly let off the clutch. His father, who used to spend some of his time at the Oak Bay Dirt Track, taught him that trick when he was still a little boy. Stopping at the next stop sign he reached down near the center console and picked up the microphone to his CB radio, he yelled into the mic, "Breaker 1-9, Breaker 1-9, this is Hot Rod. I'm lookin' for a Crazy Daisy out there… Come in, Crazy Daisy."

"This is Crazy Daisy, Hot Rod...Go ahead."

"What is the name of the Road that I turn on off highway nine?"

"Lucky Road… It is your Lucky Day, Hot Rod."

"10-4 Crazy Daisy… I am on the way... I will catch you on the backside."

"10-4 Hot Rod... I will meet you in the church parking lot."

"10-4."

Nearing the Oak Bay city limits Roger took a right on Old Farm Road. He slowed down while he crossed the Pee Dee River over the old rust covered Billy "Cotton" Richardson Bridge. He knew absolutely nothing about the famous Senator who died in 1935. He thought how ironic it was that a recent state senator had lost his life on the same bridge. More swamp than river, this particular section of the long historical, black water, river always made him think about the first people of the area who must have had a difficult time trying to trudge their way through the swamp lands. Roger was also intrigued by the construction of the bridge with its reinforced concrete slabs and steel girders. He couldn't imagine any vehicle ever being able to smash its way through the steel guardrails.

Once over the bridge, he could see swamp and occasionally the river through the trees. On the left side of the highway he took notice of several large fields of healthy looking green tobacco, corn, and cotton plants. Some fields were riddled with an assortment of old pieces of agricultural machinery. Different types of discs along with a couple of tractors sat rusted and unused like they belonged in a museum or a junkyard.

As he approached the outskirts of the city limits, he noticed two old barns that were being dismantled. Behind the barns, construction crews had begun ripping away trees and clearing land. He slowed down to read the big sign at the construction site which simply read: Walmart Coming Soon. He had heard his father talking about the new Walmart and how it worried him that the Oak Bay Hardware Store might lose business. Seeing the Walmart billboard, and the first inklings of construction, Roger now realized that the new Walmart was about to be a reality.

Right before he entered the city limits, he glanced at the town's roadside historical marker. Roger had read the marker many times. He knew almost all of it by heart. It read as follows: In 1778 a group of settlers from Charleston began to settle this land; growing tobacco and cotton. In 1811 a town charter was created by the original settlers. They named the town Oak Bay because of its plentiful oak trees and because it sat on the edge of the Pee Dee River.

As he passed by the sign he thought about Rainey telling him that he didn't listen to the white-washed version of history that was taught in school. Roger then realized there was not one mention of the Native Americans and certainly no mention of African Americans on the historical marker. He kept driving.

Passing the large metal, green and white painted Welcome to Oak Bay Sign, Roger slowed down to take a look at the Oak Bay Auction Warehouses. They were a series of huge warehouses where generations of farmers gathered every July to sell their tobacco. When he was a small child, his Great Uncle on his father's side of the family took him several times to witness the parlaying of a unique style of language by the tobacco auctioneers. He could still remember being scared of the old men dressed in overalls who cried out a broken dialect of gibberish only to suddenly scream a selling price in the middle of a vibrant bidding war. He never could understand the rhythmic tune bellowed out by the auctioneers who sang out a series of numbers along with local slang which only keen ears could interpret. Designed over a hundred years earlier, the rhythmic chants were a way to ease the nerves of the buyers and sellers for a transaction which had serious financial implications. For many of the farmers the auction was their once a year chance to redeem the money produced with a crop which required intensive labor and complex agricultural skills. Sometimes lives depended on the sale at the auction.

After he passed the tobacco auction warehouse he knew he was coming up on what everyone referred to as the Bay. Several poverty stricken neighborhoods on the Southside of Oak Bay, used to be the section where the town's African American citizens lived. Still predominantly black, several poor white families now made the Bay their home as well. He couldn't help but notice several of the homes which needed extensive repair or needed to be demolished.

One block away he noticed the advertising war that was going on between the McDonalds and Hardee's Fast Food Chains which sat across the highway from each other. McDonalds had a big sign in its parking lot which was advertising their newly released Happy Meals. Hardee's had a larger sign that read: Steak Biscuits are Here.

Two blocks later, Roger noticed the sign on the Oak Bay Theater which read: The Muppets Movie, 5 pm and 8 pm. He had no intention of seeing this new movie as he kept driving. Turning onto Main Street he noticed the many cars and trucks parked at the Oak Bay Baptist Church; the largest church in the town. Driving slowly, he then reached down under his car seat and pulled out an eight track tape and quickly slid it into his car's eight track player. A moment later, the song, "Don't Look Back" by Boston was blaring from his newly installed Radio Shack speakers. He laughed when he rode by the Peach Basket Ice Cream Shop where several generations of Oak Bay residents had experienced an assortment of frozen dairy delights. It was also the place where he remembered seeing Bridget hanging out with some of her friends. On that particular afternoon, he found enough courage to ask her to go with him to the Oak Bay County Fair.

Only a city block away he thought of Rainey when he passed by the Oak Bay Courthouse. For the first time in his life, he gave a serious glance at the enormous statue of Confederate General, Micha Jenkins sitting upright on his horse. He began to wonder how out of all the great people from Oak Bay, this guy was awarded the best statue.

Braking at the stop light a block away from the Main Street Amoco he could see his place of summer employment. He took notice that morning of the large gable at the top of the station which had seen its better days. He had been told by Luther that the Main Street Amoco was originally named the Big Star Full Service Station. To Roger the place dripped with Oak Bay history as countless residents had at one time or another filled up their vehicles at the town's oldest service station. Pat King built and ran the place in 1937 until the day he died in 1970. That was also the same year Carl came home from Vietnam and decided to trade his gun chopper mechanical skills into running a gas station. Purchasing the station for a whole lot less than what it was worth at an estate sale, Carl revamped everything about the place except for the bulk of the exterior of the building. He painted over all of the old signage except for a faded blue star which had been the station's logo since before World War II. Luther told Roger that he still remembered that blue star when he left town on a Greyhound bus and headed for basic training before he was shipped to the Pacific to fight the Japanese. He also told him that Carl would not touch that blue star logo because he was superstitious. That blue star logo also reminded Carl of the boys and men he left behind in Vietnam. Roger then remembered being taken back the first day he began working at the station when he walked to the very back of the station. He noticed on that day that you could barely see the lettering through the white paint over padlocked doorways that read Colored and Indian Restrooms.

Stopping at the next street light, two blocks away, he laughed when he saw Stumpy's Big Pig Barbeque Hut restaurant where he and his family had eaten their fair share of ribs, pulled pork and hash. A few more blocks away he passed by his father's place of business which sat across from the Williams Furniture plant, Oak Bay's largest employer. Ten minutes later he found himself on Highway Nine. Only a few minutes away from the Northside Ward of the Church of Jesus Christ of Latter Day Saints, Roger became a nervous wreck. He not only wanted to impress Jeannie; he wanted to impress her family as well. Not more than five minutes away from the church he heard a call on his CB radio which said, "Breaker 19. How about it, Hot Rod."

Picking up his mic in his mustang, Roger replied, "I've got my ears on, Crazy Daisy."

"Sorry good buddy, but it's a no go today with the church business."

Roger, completely forgetting everything about CB radio etiquette, quickly responded by asking, "Is there anything wrong?"

"Breaker 1-9 that is a big Negatory. No deal, good buddy. Catch you on the flip side."

"Do you want me to come to your house?"

"That is a big Negatory, Hot Rod. Crazy Daisy going 10-7 over and out."

He tried in vain to contact her several more times before he gave up and headed toward home. On North Main Street he stopped at a payphone and tried to call her twice with no luck. With his feelings hurt he drove around the town and then in the rural areas of the county for about an hour before he finally drove home.

Later that afternoon after being absolutely bored out of his mind, Roger decided to take a chance by looking over the journal while his parents took a Sunday afternoon drive. Once he found the page where he left off, he turned on his bedside radio and began wrapping his mind around the written pages of his Swedish great-great grandfather. It did not take Roger very long to understand that his blood relative was in an emotional quandary as it pertained to him trying to reunite with his parents in Virginia while he was determined to find a safe place for he and his Sarah to live. Working with the family of tanners, he took a chance to relocate deeper in the backwoods of South Carolina in 1769 when the family of tanners suggested that he could make a good living by providing them much needed deerskins. For two more years, he lived off the land near the Pee Dee River in and around Hogtail Swamp. Leaving behind Sarah and their first son, with the Smith family, Matthew became quite successful in his rudimentary way of dealing skins and hides. Hiding his true identity for another year, he believed that the time was near for him to establish some type of homestead for his new family in one of the most secluded sections of South Carolina, next to Hogtail Swamp.

Unable to decipher some of the writings, Roger then learned that Matthew began building a "home of logs" using cypress and pines in June of 1772 on a small parcel of land next to Hogtail Swamp. Matthew was able to legally purchase a large parcel of land through a British land regulator named Simons. During this time Matthew not only increased his trapping business, he established a relationship with a scattering of Indians who lived in the swamp. According to the journal, Roger learned that those native peoples were called the River People; a group of Cheraw, Pee Dee, and Cherokees who braved the

harsh environment of the swamp in hopes of avoiding new White settlers as well as avoiding being forced to leave the area.

Chapter Fourteen

The next morning the phone at the Main Street Amoco rang several times before Stumpy answered it for Carl. He yelled over the phone, "Main Street Amoco. How can I help ya? No, sir. Carl is on a service call down near Cottonwood Road jumping off a dead battery. You did what? Uh huh… Well, that will be fine. I guess we can try. Just bring it on up here to the station."

Hank Burrows asked Stumpy, "What in the hell was all that about?"

"Another fish story. You all know Billy Bradford's boy Larry. Well, it seems that when Larry got married last week some of his friends decided it would be a good idea to put about ten Shellcrackers under the seats of his car. They also snuck a large Channel Catfish in the trunk of his new Camaro before he and the new Mrs. Bradford tied the knot. Y'all know this heat stewed them fish to a rancid smell by the time the weddin' reception was over. It was so bad they couldn't take the car with them on the honeymoon down to Hilton Head. Billy says that he tried all day to get the fish smell out of the car. He says it is God awful."

Hank replied, "Now those must be some really good friends. They are lucky Larry didn't whip somebody's ass before he left on the honeymoon."

Stumpy sat down in his chair and said, "If Carl and Rainey can't get the smell out of the car, nobody can. Remember last month when Mrs. Nugent had her cat die in the backseat of her Cadillac? Rainey and Carl got the dead cat smell out of that car's upholstery."

Coach Hutchinson, who was busy filling out the *Oak Bay Gazette's* Crossword Puzzle, piped up by saying, "Dead cat is a lot easier than dead fish."

Stumpy growled at him saying, "The hell you say. I bet you a doll'a that they have an easier time with the fish than they did with that cat."

Coach Hutchinson grinned and said, "I'll take that bet."

Hank Burrows poured himself his second cup of coffee as he said, "A dead rat smell ain't no joke."

Stumpy growled at him, "Cat or Fish are all we are concerned with Hank. So which one is it?"

Daryl spoke up and said, "Stumpy, there ain't no way you can judge a thing like that. That's no different than saying that you smell worse than old man Gene sitting over there."

Coach Hutchinson quickly replied, "That's a no brainer- Mr. Gene absolutely smells a lot better than Stumpy."

Luther walked into the station lounge from the mechanic's bay area and yelled, "I've got my money on Mr. Gene."

Stumpy yelled back, "Damit, Luther, we are only bettin' on the Fish and the Cat."

Luther laughed and asked, "Stumpy, are you the Cat or are you the Fish?"

Before Stumpy could answer, Hank yelled out, "Look who just drove up. Luther, it's your old buddy Crazy Bob Blankenship."

Luther snarled back, "I think I will let Roger handle him this morning'. Lord knows, I can't stand that fool. I have no idea why he decided to move back here from Charleston. Everybody in town says he is tryin' his best to speed up the death of his Great Aunt Essie who is worth a fortune. He moved in with her at the plantation mansion and is runnin' her round town like she is a marathon runner. I bet he is already runnin' through her fortune. "

Pulling up to Full service aisle number one, Bob Blankenship jumped out of his 1977 Oldsmobile Toronado and immediately began barking orders to Roger James. He said, "Fill her up with 3 dollars' worth of high test. When you are done, I need for you to check the oil, the transmission fluid, brake fluid, and the radiator. While you're at it, I need you to do one more thing."

"What is that, Sir?"

"She's just not running right today. I think it might have to do with stale air in the tires."

"Come again, Sir?"

"You heard me... I need for you to let out all the air in the tires and put in clean, fresh air."

"But..."

"I like to change the air in my tires at least once a month. It just makes the tires last longer."

Luther, who was listening from the open door of the station lounge, looked at Hank Burrows and said, "I can't stand it anymore. That fool will run Roger ragged and tip him a nickel if I don't go out there. He is pitching tonight and don't need all that on his plate this mornin'." Luther then yelled at Roger, "Hold on, Hot Rod. Put that stem cap back on that tire."

Mr. Blankenship walked from around the hood of the car and asked, "What seems to be the problem?"

"I'll tell you. We have had it with you coming up here buyin' a couple of dolla's worth of gas and wantin' us to service your car just short of waxin' and buffin' her out. No sir, today all this monkey business stops."

"Well, I...

"Well, I guess you better just take your business somewhere else."

"What is your name, sir?"

"Don't act like you don't know me, Blankenship, but just in case you forgot it is Luther Brown."

After paying for his gas and leaving Roger a nickel tip, Bob Blankenship pointed his finger at Luther and said, "You mark my word, you will hate the day that you ever messed with me."

Luther waved at him motioning for him to come closer saying, "Come on, big boy. Don't let your alligator mouth do all the talkin' for your mockingbird ass."

Carl, who had just come back from his morning service call, walked up from around the corner of the station and yelled, "Now hold on you two. What in the hell is goin' on out here?"

Luther, poking his chest out like a rooster, stood tall and then replied, "You know how this jackleg comes up here wantin' us to bend over backwards for him. Well, today takes the cake. He wants Roger to take out all of the air in his tires and replace it with fresh air."

Mr. Blankenship, who was a lot younger and seemingly more fit than Luther, took two steps toward Luther and yelled, "Who are you calling a jackleg?"

Carl, who thought the whole verbal exchange was quite comical, quickly placed himself in front of Mr. Blankenship, smiling as he interrupted him by saying, "Now hold on, Partner, I'm pretty sure you don't want to tangle with Luther over a simple misunderstandin'."

"There is no misunderstanding. Your employee refuses to offer me service and on top of that, he has called me a jackleg. So what are you going to do about it?"

Carl pulled out a worn bag of Beechnut chewing tobacco from his pants pocket and grabbed a small pinch before placing it in his mouth. He then calmly said, "I'll tell ya what I am gonna do… I'm gonna apologize for my employee's harsh tone with ya… Now it does seem like you do ask my employees to do a lot more than most folks when it comes to servicin' your vehicle. So from now on if you want special service there will be a minimum two dollar charge. Now don't that sound fair to everyone?"

Mr. Blankenship was not happy, but he held back due to Carl's calm demeanor. He then said in a calm and stern voice, "I will not pay an extra penny for service that should be rendered at a Full service station."

Carl sort of bowed up and interrupted him by saying, "Now, Partner, I have had enough of you today… The best thing you could do right now is to hop in your fancy car and take your business somewhere else."

"Alrighty, but everyone of y'all will hate the day that you messed with me. Just wait, one day…"

Carl interrupted him again by pointing to his car and saying, "Go on now before I lose my cool."

Roger, who was already pumping gas for another car on the other side of Full service aisle one, looked up and noticed that all the men from the O.T.C.C. and Rainey had made their way outside of the station lounge to watch the morning confrontation while Mr. Blankenship mumbled under his breath as he got into his Oldsmobile Toronado. Pulling out a windshield squeegee from the squeegee container attached to the station aisle metal support beam, Roger was only about three feet away from Mr. Blankenship when he opened his car door. Right before he closed his driver's side door he looked at Roger and said, "This is not over. You tell that bonehead boss of yours that Bob Blankenship will not be shamed."

Coach Hutchinson walked over toward Carl once Crazy Bob Blankenship drove away and said, "Carl, don't you think that was uncalled for?"

With a look of repentance, Carl replied, "I screwed the pooch on that one, Coach. I don't know why he got under my skin so badly."

Roger walked over to Luther and asked, "Are you all right, Mr. Luther?"

"Yeah, I'm good. Changin' the air in tires… Now that just beats all."

Carl then yelled at Roger, "Hey, Hot Rod, get the mop and bucket over to the men's room. I just saw Kirby make his mornin' visit to wash himself up. I'm sure that restroom smells to high heaven so help him out and give it a good mop down after he leaves."

On his way to get the mop and bucket, Rainey walked up to Roger from the mechanics bay and asked, "So how was the big date yesterday?"

"It never happened. She canceled on me."

"That is probably for the best."

"What do you mean?"

"You don't need to get involved with those people. There is something a little fishy about them. Speaking of fish… Oh my god… Do you smell that?"

Pulling up into mechanic bay number two of the Main Street Amoco was a dark blue Camero driven by Billy Bradford. Windows rolled all the way down; Mr. Bradford jumped out the car and yelled, "Rainey, I sure hope that you can do something with this smell."

Roger gagged a couple of times before Carl walked into the mechanics bay from the station lounge. Carl, held his hand over his nose and said, "Damit, Billy, this car may be a goner"

"You think y'all can get rid of this smell?"

"I don't know, but the first thing we have to do is to get it out of here before all of my customers get sick. Roger, you pull it around back. Rainey, you get the service truck and take Roger over to his Daddy's hardware store and get what you need to attack this thing. I looked on the shelf the other day, and I think Kirby helped himself to some of the Scope Mouthwash."

Just a few minutes away from the Main Street Amoco, Roger and Rainey walked into the Oak Bay Hardware Store. Once inside, they both heard Mark James yell from the back of the store, "Well, what a surprise. You two look like Mormon missionaries in your white collared uniform shirts and blue pants. What ya need, son?"

"You remember Rainey, don't you Dad?"

"Sure I do. How are ya doin', Rainey?"

"I am blessed, sir. It seems we have a small fish problem we need to take care of today."

"Is that right?"

Roger then explained their dilemma to his father who began laughing before saying, "I've heard some good fish stories in this store, but this is the best one I have heard in a long time."

Rainey laughed and then said, "One thing is for sure, if it can be done, Carl has an incredible recipe for this kind of trouble. He said to charge it on the station's account."

Chapter Fifteen

When Roger and Rainey drove up to the Main Street Amoco with the special ingredients for Carl's dead animal smell recipe, they were stunned to see a Oak Bay Fire Department truck, several city of Oak Bay police cars, and the car of the County Coroner parked at the station. A crowd had already begun to gather on the side of the building once they parked the service truck. Luther walked over to Roger and Rainey and said, "What a day."

Roger asked, "What the world, Mr. Luther?"

Wiping some tears away from his cheeks, the veteran of World War II replied, "It's one sad day. Our old friend Kirby was just found dead in the Men's Room."

Rainey asked, "What happened to him?"

"We are not quite sure, but it looks like he slipped and hit his head on the back of the commode. It's an awful sight with blood everywhere on the floor. God bless him, but it also looked like whatever he had eaten the past few days made its way down his pants legs. That restroom is one helluva mess. God rest his soul."

Rainey asked, "Who found him?"

"Carl had to pop the lock on the restroom door when he noticed that Kirby had not returned the Restroom Key. Y'all know he passes out sometimes from a big night of drinkin'. Carl just thought he was on another bender. Carl is over in the lounge pretty shook up. It's not every day you find a dead man in your restroom. Stumpy always worries that Carl might have one of his Vietnam flashbacks. He's watchin' him like a hawk to make sure he is all right. I know y'all have your hands full with the fish car, but it's gonna take all hands on deck to get that Restroom cleaned up after the Coroner finishes up his investigation."

Peeking into the station lounge, Roger and Rainey stood still when they noticed all the men of the O.T.C.C. standing in the middle of the lounge with their heads bowed. Coach Hutchinson was leading them in prayer. He said, "Lord, we want you to bless our old friend, Kirby. Yes, Lord, he was a good soul. He never bothered anyone. He tried to stay clean by washing in the restroom at least once or twice a week. We all know that when he drank he was a happy drunk. Thank you for allowing all of us to know this man who loved to drink a good bottle of Vicks Formula 44 or Scope mouthwash better than anyone we knew. May his kind spirit live on. Amen."

Stumpy tried to break the somber atmosphere by saying, "His spirit lives on by God... Just go in that restroom and you will know it."

Coach Hutchinson quickly interrupted by saying, "I never knew much about Kirby other than he always rode his Moped all over town and that he lived in a one-room camper next to Shiloh Creek. Does he have any family?"

Hank Burrows spoke up and said, "Kirby rolled into town about twelve years ago after hopping off a Seaboard Coastline freight train. I received a call one night that a vagrant was roamin' around Main Street. That was my first encounter with him. When I rode down Main Street, I saw him on his hands and knees on the street next to the Courthouse. When I approached him and asked what he was doin', he told me that he was lookin' for lost change that people may have dropped when they put money into the parking meters. I laughed at him until he showed me that he had already collected over two dollars' worth of coins. Through the years he has lived under bridges, in various abandoned houses and vehicles. That one-room camper he lived in came from the junkyard. He patched up that piece of junk and was able to have it hauled out to Shiloh Creek. The park ranger who oversaw the National Forest land next to Shiloh Creek has allowed him to live on that land for many years. Kirby never talked much, and I could never figure out where he came from. To this day I never knew his last name. A bad alcoholic, you would never find Kirby drinking wine, beer, or liquor. For whatever reason he had long ago acquired a taste for cough syrup and mouthwash. There isn't a drinkin' person in town who hasn't tried at one time or another to buy him a real drink. He never once succumbed to any of the offers. His drink of choice was Vicks 44 Cough Syrup. One day when I asked him about his family he simply replied to me that we were all a part of God's family."

Darryl said, "There is nobody in this town who could find loose change, collect soda bottles and aluminum cans better than Kirby. He could also whip through a trash can like a professional. He would eat a little for himself and then collect food for animals all over this town. He may have been a fool, but he was our fool. If anybody thinks they were better than him then they are dead wrong. I don't think there was a soul in this town who did not like Kirby."

Stumpy sat down in his chair and said, "When you think about it, we ain't no different than Old Kirby. We are all just one good crap away from eternity."

Hank Burrows cleared his throat and replied, "Stumpy, only you can turn a tragedy into a three ring circus."

"I didn't mean no disrespect, but you have to admit that in times like this we should all be reminded that all of us in the O.T.C.C. are on the clock. Time is ticking for all of us. It won't be long before we all have a new notch engraved for us on that wooden board."

Darryl shot back, "You got that right, Stumpy. Just look at old Gene sittin' there."

Gene Purdy held up his cane and said, "I heard that, Darryl. I'll bet you a hundred dollars I will outlive all of you sorry SOB's. Especially you, Darryl. You keep eatin' all those donuts and honey buns, and you will be drinkin' mouthwash and cough syrup with Kirby up yonder at the Pearly Gates quicker than you think."

Coach Hutchinson stood up and said, 'Gentlemen, Stumpy brings up a good point, but we can't sit here every day worrying about when our last day is coming. We have to live life the best way we know how and not worry about the last few hours of the eternal clock."

Carl wiped his forehead with his red service station grease rag and said, "Coach, I used to think about death every day in Nam, but when I got home it seldom crossed my mind. Today hurts."

Stumpy interrupted his friend by saying, "Y'all all shut the hell up. After hearin' all this talk I know more than ever that all you are bound to live for many more years. Who in their right mind would want to spend eternity with any of you, idiots? Satan or the Good

Lord himself would hate the day they came callin' for one of y'all. Eternity with any of you will not be any fun."

They all began to laugh when they noticed that the Coroner Calvin McDavid was standing in the doorway of the lounge from the mechanic's bay entrance. They all became quiet when he said, "I didn't mean to interrupt you, but I need a word with you in private."

Carl asked, " Me or Mr. Stumpy?"

"You, Carl. If you don't mind, we can talk out here away from everyone else."

While Carl and Coroner McDavid talked in private next to a parked U Haul truck on the side of the building, Roger and Rainey began the daunting task of cleaning up the Men's Restroom. Rainey pulled over the large red mechanic's bay water hose while Rainey pulled over the mop and janitorial sized bucket along with some Lysol and Comet cleaners. Before he entered the restroom, Roger looked at Rainey and said, "It just occurred to me that Carl wanted me to clean out the restroom before we got caught up with the fish car. It could have easily been me who found Kirby."

"Lucky for you that did not happen. I hate looking at dead people."

Back inside the lounge area of the station, all of the men of the O.T.C.C quietly speculated why the Coroner was talking privately with Carl. Coach Hutchinson wondered out loud by asking, "Do you think there could have been any foul play?"

Stumpy growled back at him, "Hell, no. Kirby slipped and fell. Case closed."

Hank Burrows walked over to the station's old television set and adjusted a homemade rigged up antenna made from several coat irons, a portion of a spoked Buick hubcap, two Budweiser beer cans, two big wads of aluminum foil, and copper wiring that ran through the top of the ceiling. Slowly and slightly turning the hubcap, Hank magically made the CBS soap opera, *The Guiding Light a*ppear clearly on the set's only viable channel. He then looked toward Stumpy and said, "There is no tellin' what he is sayin' to Carl, but the longer they are out there, the worse it will be."

Stumpy shot back, "With no Chief of Police here askin' a lot of questions- case closed. "

Gene Purdy, waking up from a quick cat nap, stood up and said, "Stumpy, I think Hank knows more about the law than you. So why don't you just zip it."

"Ain't it time for you to go home for your usual six hour nap? God knows you probably need to change your diaper."

Gene yelled back at him, "I ain't goin' anywhere till I find out what in the hell is goin' on around here."

Luther was trying his best to listen to what Carl and the Coroner were saying, but a steady stream of gas customers kept him hopping. He finally had to run into the lounge area of the station and ask Stumpy to go get Hot Rod or Rainey to come help him with the paying customers.

Hot Rod Roger quickly emerged on Full Service aisle number two to help Luther. He said, "We have the restroom cleaned. Rainey is now workin' on the fish car."

Luther nodded at him and then yelled, " I don't know why we have so much business right now. It feels like all hell is about to break loose around here."

As soon as the words left his mouth, an elderly lady waiting to pay for her fill up, spoke up and asked, "You haven't heard?"

"Heard what?"

The lady put her hands up in the air and cried out, "The news on the radio just said that we might be out of gas in the next few days. They are also saying that gas prices are about to go up much higher."

Another customer who overheard the conversation said, "This is incredible. Looks like 1973 all over again. We just need to go ahead and send our bombers to Iran and blow the hell out of those people and take all of their oil. The Ayatollah down the toilet bowl'a is what I say."

Luther then yelled over to Roger, "Go tell Rainey to put a hold on the fish recipe and get out here because we are about to get swamped."

For the next forty-five minutes the station's air bell in the lounge constantly rang as a steady wave of customers descended on the Main Street Amoco to get their last fill up of 79 cents per gallon of gasoline before the price changed and possibly spiraled out of control. Working like a pit crew from the Southern 500 at the Darlington Speedway, Luther, Roger, and Rainey pumped gas and washed windshields at warp speed. They sweated like pigs from the effects of the afternoon Carolina heat which bore down on the station's concrete driveways. The humidity mixed in with the fumes of the gasoline ignited tempers from several customers who waited anxiously to fill their vehicle tanks. One elderly lady yelled from her rolled down window to Roger, "President Carter needs to do something about this."

Luther was reluctantly forced to "deputize" all of the members of the O.T. C. C. to help with the cash register and to make sure the cigarette and Lance cracker vending machines were well stocked.

About five minutes later, Coroner McDavid left Carl, who walked up to Luther and whispered to him, "Go ahead and recalibrate the pumps to read 83 cents a gallon. Tell Hot Rod to put the price change on the main marquee with the magnetic numbers."

"Is everything all right with the Coroner?"

"I'll tell everybody about it when this crowd dies down."

Noticing the price change when he pulled up to the Full Service aisle number one, a deacon from the Oak Bay Baptist Church jumped out of his car and screamed at Luther, "Hey, man, what do ya think you are doin'?"

Luther smiled at his old friend and replied, "I hate it too, but I am just carryin' out orders from Headquarters."

Deacon Charlie Black was not amused. He slammed his driver side door and stood next to his car saying, "I don't know how y'all sleep at night. This is one ridiculous scam that is makin' y'all rich as hell."

Roger could tell Luther was about to lose his cool. He stepped closer to the esteemed deacon and said, "Mr. Charlie, nobody is gettin' rich here at the Main Street Amoco."

"Somebody's gettin' rich. Just a few months ago the price of gas was only 53 cents."

Rainey, wiping away the last squeegee streak on the deacon's passenger side windshield, laughed before saying, "Yeah, me and my boys are planning our next trip to Florida with all this profit we are making."

Deacon Charlie Black looked at Rainey and yelled, "You hush up, N... boy."

Before Rainey could make his way around the front of the deacon's car, Roger and Luther interceded by holding him back. Luther then let go of Rainey's left arm and turned toward Charlie Black and yelled, "You need to watch your filthy mouth. Nobody, and I mean nobody, talks like that to one of my partners. Charlie

Black, you either apologize to this young man or get your sorry ass on outta here and never come back."

As Deacon Charlie Black sped away from the Main Street Amoco without offering an apology, Rainey stood on the corner of the concrete pump aisle number one in awe of what Luther had done while Roger flipped the deacon the bird. Rainey then said, "Thank you, Mr. Luther."

Almost out of breath, Luther bent over and replied, "Don't think nothin' of it, Rainey. Charlie Black is one sorry SOB, and I am truly sorry that happened to you. Luther then paused and took a deep breath before saying, "Y'all mark my word, people who you would never expect are gonna act a fool over this gas. Yes sir, this could get real ugly."

CHAPTER SIXTEEN

At 5:30 that afternoon, Carl gathered everyone associated with the Main Street Amoco and told them to go ahead and close the station. While Luther turned the Open sign to Closed, Rainey and Roger pulled down the garage doors of the mechanic's bays. With one truck still on top of the rack on mechanic's bay number two waiting for a brake job, Carl hurried everyone into mechanic's bay number one. Cramped into the small area with some of them straddling that bay's lowered rack, Carl noticed that just about everyone except for Old man Gene Purdy was soaked in perspiration. He smiled and then said, "What a day. Thank y'all for the hard work."

Stumpy interrupted him and asked, "So what is the big news?"

"The big news is that we are gonna be hit with a bunch of customers tomorrow who are gonna want to fill up their vehicles."

Stumpy shot back quickly, "No, Carl. We want to know about Kirby."

Carl leaned up against the block cement wall of mechanic's bay number one and said, "They are gonna do an autopsy on Kirby. They have already sent his body to Charleston."

Hank Burrows asked, "Why do they need to do an autopsy?"

Carl smiled and replied, "They found some grease on the floor next to the sink. The Coroner says that from every indication it looks like he slipped on the grease before he fell on top of the sink. It appeared to him that when Kirby hit the sink, he bounced backwards causin' him to stumble. He then hit the back of his head on the commode where it split open like a ripe watermelon.``

Stumpy cried out, "Well, case closed as far as I am concerned. It was an accident."

Luther then spoke up and said, "Not so fast, Stumpy, all it will take is a good lawyer, and we could get sued."

Carl said, "He's right, Stumpy. They are gonna see how much alcohol was in his system when he died. If he wasn't drunk, then the station could be held liable for the accident."

Darryl cried out, "Hell, Kirby didn't have any kin. Who is going to sue?"

Carl smiled and replied, "The Coroner said the same thing but if they ever find any kin, this station could be sued if they ever found out the particulars."

Gene Purdy quickly said, "As long as we keep this a secret, nobody is gonna question anything. Carl, you need to worry about somethin' else."

Carl looked at all of them and said, "Tomorrow is gonna be hell. I just looked at the pump reservoirs, and we will run out of gas before the end of the day if we don't put a limit on how much folks can purchase. I will need everyone to be here bright and early. We will limit everyone to eight gallons per vehicle until we get another shipment in here."

Stumpy yelled, "It can't be any worse than today. At one point when I looked out there it looked like a barnyard full of chickens being chased by a pack of hungry wolves."

Luther winked at Roger and said, "Hey, Carl, we need to let Roger head on out of here. He is supposed to pitch tonight against Timmonsville."

Coach Hutchinson said, "I have to go too. I am helping them take up tickets at Legion Field."

Carl then motioned for them to leave before he said, "We all better have an attitude adjustment before we come back tomorrow. It is gonna be a long tough day."

Two of the old Legionnaires from Oak Bay American Legion Post 444 were still lining the batter's box with field chalk when Hot Rod Roger James entered the field that evening. Retired Coach Hutchinson had already informed his successor, Coach Randy Fugate that his star player would be running a little late. Oak Bay catcher, Stew Turbeville was busy putting on a pair of shin guards outside of the dugout when he looked at Roger and said, "I heard Coach Fugate tell some of the other players that you were gonna have to run a few foul poles after the game tonight for being late. He then turned and continued by saying, " Look over there at those boys from Timmonsville getting out of their bus. They all look like they are about thirty years old."

Roger picked up a game ball and began to rub it down with some sand clay as he replied, "Those boys must hit puberty when they are about six or seven years old. I bet half of them are already married and workin' full time jobs. I will give them credit. They just like to beat your ass, and they never ever say one word when they do it. Same thing in football. I can honestly say that I have never been hit harder by any other team. They will knock the crap out of ya, get up, smile, and then help you up."

Stew nodded his head and said, "The thing that always gets me is that almost everyone on their team uses the same bat. I bet if we got one of those Legion old-timers to swipe their bat they might not be able to play the game. The other thing that I have noticed is that those boys never spit when they chew their tobacco. They just swallow the juice. You have to be one tough sucker to do that."

Roger smiled and replied to his catcher, "Remember two years ago when their startin' pitcher pitched the entire game without wearin' a glove? The umpire first tried to say he had to wear one to play the game. Their coach pulled out a rule book and challenged the umpire to show him where in the rule book he could find such a rule. They argued for just a few minutes when Coach Hutchinson told the umpire that he did not object. I remember watchin' that dude every time the catcher threw him back the ball. I thought to myself that night those boys must be tough as hell or they may be a tad bit crazier than the rest of us."

Stew laughed and said, "Yeah, my daddy always says they are tough because their girls can and will whip most any man's ass."

While Roger and his catcher warmed up next to the fence on the leftfield side of Legion field, Roger couldn't help but notice that Jeannie and her mother were standing at the concession stand behind the home plate area. His pausing to stare over at them caused Stew to stop and look back as well. He then laughed before saying, "So it must be true. Everyone in town is sayin' that you like the Indian-Mormon girl."

Roger's smile disappeared from his face when he asked, "What did you say?"

"Now wait a minute, Hot Rod, you know I don't give a crap about any of that. Your old girlfriend seems to be the one stirrin' up this pot. You talkin' to Crazy Daisy for the world to hear on your CB radio doesn't help either. You know that people in this town love to talk; especially when it comes to their sports heroes."

"None of that bothers me, but I know it will bother my Mama if she ever hears that kind of talk." He went on to say, "I don't know much about her, but I sure would like to know more."

Stew smiled and said, "I really don't know her, but everyone in town thinks her mother is a prostitute."

"I have no idea, but I do know the old men at the service station sure do get worked up whenever she comes to get gas."

"Hurry up and get warmed up. Coach Fugate is lookin' over here, and he doesn't look too happy."

Timed to perfection, right after the playing of the national anthem, the most celebrated fan of Oak Bay American Legion Baseball could be heard entering the stadium. Like he had done for every home game since 1949, a Native American that everyone called Big Papa made his famous entrance into the stadium. He was a legend in the area. For many years he would stand on top of the Oak Bay dugout and allow teenagers not much younger than himself to unleash a retrieved foul ball right into the middle of his shirtless chest or stomach with all their might. He charged them a quarter to see who could finally knock the Indian off the top of the dugout. They would stand only a few feet away from him and let him have it. Grown men twice his age soon got involved in the throwing game which had many in town believing that Big Papa had to be liquored up to take such a beating. Nightly, he would take home at least eight to ten dollars' worth of quarters. Over the years, as his body began to wear, he became the unofficial mascot of all of the Oak Bay teams. Living near the river with his mother because he was born mentally challenged, he was most famous for his uncanny ability to imitate the sound of farm animals. He was blessed to be able to accurately cluck like a wild turkey or squeal like a fat pig. There wasn't an animal sound in God's kingdom that he couldn't imitate. Once he would enter the stadium, he would yell out,

"I'm a, I'm a, I'm a Big Papa."

The Oak Bay fans would then yell out in unison, "You are the Big Papa."

Sitting in a reserved seat right behind home plate, players from opposing teams hated Big Papa. For the entire game he would yell at the opposing pitcher as well as the opposing batters. He would say things like, "You ain't got no pitch, pitcher. You ain't nothin' but a duck." He would then begin quacking like a duck. His most famous line he said every game was, "Chicken feet-Chicken wings this is how the Rooster Sings." He would then cluck like a Rooster so loud it was almost unbearable if you were not used to it. Big Papa was one of the most loved people in Oak Bay. His popularity hit its peak in 1964 when it was said that Big Papa helped the Legion baseball team win the state title. That night he clucked like a rooster so loud it shook up the opposing pitcher who threw away the championship game on a wild pitch in Myrtle Beach.

Like he had seen many times before, Roger watched Big Papa as he entered the stadium that night making it sound like a circus was coming to town. Once he sat down in his seat he yelled out, "Ball Time.. Ball Time.. That means it's Big Papa Time."

Darkness was trying its best to push itself onto Legion Field when Roger James unleashed his first pitch against the American Legion team from Timmonsville. Stew Turbeville's catcher mitt sounded like a shotgun blast went off in it once Roger's fast ball hit it; estimated well over 90 miles per hour. The first batter from Timmonsville only heard the mitt. He never saw the ball. The old umpire behind the plate, a retired jailer from the Oak Bay City Jail, yelled out, "Stee-rike one."

Roger quickly wound up again and threw another fast ball that some in the stands said was the fastest pitch they had ever seen at Legion Field in all of their days of watching ball. The umpire hesitated to make the call as the crowd waited while Stew remained motionless with his mitt positioned right in the middle of the back of the plate. The umpire took off his protective mask and whispered to Stew, "I never saw the dang ball." After seeing that Stew's mitt hadn't moved an inch, he then yelled out, "Stee-rike Two."

The batter overheard him and without looking back at the umpire he said, "Me either. That dude is bringin' the heat."

As the home crowd began to clap before the next pitch, Roger James shook off the sign from his catcher. He then wound up and delivered a changeup which floated so long in the air, the batter would have had enough time to swing twice before the ball reached the catcher's mitt. Swinging way out in front of the ball which had perfect spin and rotation, the umpire became animated, throwing out his right arm like he was chopping down a tree when he then yelled out, "That's three- and that means you are done."

Big Papa yelled out, "Take yore seat- you piece of meat."

Exactly seven pitches later, Roger James retired the side with not one ball being touched by the bat of the next two Timmonsville batters. When he threw the final strike to end the first half of the inning, he could hear the crowd shouting, " Heat 'em up, Hot Rod… Heat 'em up."

As he walked off the mound and toward the dugout he glanced in the stands and saw his family and most of the people from the Main Street Amoco sitting behind the plate. He was very happy to see Rainey sitting next to his own father. Only one row away he then spotted Jeannie and her mother seated only a few rows behind his parents. He whispered to Stew in the dugout, "I hope my Mama doesn't act up here tonight."

Stew leaned over, taking off his chest protector and replied, "Don't even look in those stands. You are on tonight- just keep that flame thrower under control."

When Roger jogged onto the field at the top of the fourth, he reached down behind the mound and picked up a rosin bag. As he lightly dusted the top of his sweating wrists and forearms, he took a brief moment to look around Legion Field which had been in existence since 1938. The baseball/football complex was built as part of President Franklin Roosevelt's New Deal program called the WPA (Works Progress Administration) in an attempt to put unemployed people back to work. Roger loved the place his father once described as a cathedral built for legends. Forty years of kudzu and muscadine vines had long erased the visibility of the right and center field portion of the fence which left-handed hitters described simply as the "Vineyard". One of the football goal posts which sat only a few feet away from the right field foul line had for many years always been a part of the ground rule discussions before each home baseball game. Every player who grew up in Oak Bay knew from an early age that if a ball hit the top portion of the upright in the air it was considered a ground rule single which to this day has never been found in any rule book ever written. A ball hitting the lower portion of the goal post was considered a foul ball. Coach Hutchinson was the one who came up with the rule in the 1950's to protect players from diving after the ball when one of his star players broke a collarbone one afternoon running into the goal post at full speed. Roger thought to himself that he might be the only person who played on that field who had kicked extra points and field goals on that particular goal post as well as hit the upright for a ground rule single. He thought- what are the odds?

He then flashbacked to his early recollections of the place as a child where his parents would come to ball games leaving him to play with the other children from Oak Bay, next to the first base dugout fence. Pick-up games of football and baseball were played by elementary school aged children while the younger ones made mud pies in two huge piles of sand and red clay that were the secret to making Legion Field look so good. He remembered making mud pies as well as the first time he got punched in the face when he was six years old. Finding his father in the stands of a Friday night football game to cry on his shoulder, he was given the order by his mother to go back down to the "Pit" and knock the hell out of the kid who had busted his lower lip. He remembered her telling him, "Don't come back up here unless you knock his block off."

He did come back only a few minutes later to his dismayed looking parents who were ready to take him to the restroom and lay the belt to his backside. Right before his father grabbed his arm to take him out of the stands, he yelled, "I knocked his block off, Mama… I knocked him out."

A ten year old boy named Ralphie did get knocked out that night when six year old Roger James hit him in the head with a free standing iron water sprinkler which was leaning up against the stadium fence. Ralphie never knew what or who hit him until he came to at the end of the game. Poor Ralphie's father ended up whipping his tail a day later once he found out that Ralphie got knocked out by a six year old.

Cut deep into the side of a ravine on the third base side of the field, the blocked and cemented home bleachers of the stadium towered above the players on the field. Fans watching a game at the stadium had a great view as it appeared that the players were playing in a green and red valley. Looking back up at the fans, ball players couldn't help but feel as if they were playing in a professional sized stadium because the old ravine was so steep. One sportswriter for the Oak Bay Gazette in the 1950's once described the view from the top of the press box as the closest thing to heaven anyone in Oak Bay would ever experience before they met the Good Lord. Hot Rod Roger James, the son of a former Oak Bay All-Star linebacker and third baseman felt exactly the same.

Five innings later not one Timmonsville player had reached first base. Roger had already hit a single and a fourth inning triple which were all for naught as Oak Bay could not produce any runs. Before walking out to the mound at the top of the seventh inning, Roger said to Stew, "We can beat these guys tonight. We just need a run or two."

"Don't worry about that. Just keep hummin' that tater."

After taking his first warmup pitch, he noticed a commotion in the stands behind home plate. He couldn't hear what was going on, but he could see his father forcefully removing his mother out of the stadium. Roger stood motionless on the mound as the umpire then yelled for him to hurry up with his warm up pitches. He then intentionally threw a wild pitch way over the warm up catcher's head so he could buy a little more time to see what was going on. He then saw Jeannie and her mother leave the stadium.

The play-by- play radio announcer for WOKB later told his faithful listeners, “It was as if a demon jumped on the back of Roger James tonight as he fell apart in the seventh inning. A no hitter beginning in the seventh, he gave up three earned runs allowing the boys from Timmonsville to whip us with a final score of 4 to 1.”

The last concession workers at Legion Field were closing up shop when Roger finished running the last one of his ten foul poles for being late to the game. After each sprint from the left field foul line to the right field foul line, he would peek over at Coach Fugate who was watching to make sure the task was completed. Coach Hutchinson had tried earlier to intervene on his behalf, but Coach Randy Fugate was bitter after watching his team lose in the last two innings. It appeared he was taking his frustration out on his star player. Roger couldn’t believe that his coach made him pay the price for being late, but he didn’t say a word about it. Stepping into an empty dugout to get his glove and hat after he finished running his foul poles, Roger turned around and saw his friend, Stew standing on the top step, only a few feet away.

With a dejected look on his face, Roger said, “I thought you had scattered like everyone else.”

Stew replied, “I can’t leave my main man after such a rotten night.” He then paused for a few seconds before asking, “What happened to you tonight? I have never seen you lose it like that. You know I love ya, but I was relieved when Coach Fugate took the ball out of your hands at the beginnin’ of the eighth.”

Roger quickly replied, “If somebody I know could have hit the slowest curveball I have seen then maybe he wouldn’t have had to take me out.”

"Touché… I deserve that… You know me, I have never been able to hit a slow curve. I didn't mean to rag you, but I know somethin' happened out there tonight. You are better than that."

"I'm really not sure, but when I saw my parents along with Jeannie and her mother leave the stadium somethin' happened to me. My Mama was really upset, and I could tell my poor Daddy was havin' to make her leave the stadium."

"You know how your Mama gets. I bet it was all over nothin'."

"I'm afraid not. As they were walkin' away, I saw Patty only a few rows away from all of them."

"So what?"

"You know my old girlfriend always sits behind the dugout. She never sits behind home plate. I have a strange feelin' that she was involved."

About to make their way out of the dugout, Stew looked up and saw left fielder Jed Courson standing near the exit gate. Standing in his clay stained jersey, Jed had a wild look on his face when he stepped closer to Roger and Stew. He then threw up both of his hands and asked, "What the hell, Roger?"

Roger, who was in no mood for games, yelled, "What's your problem, Courson?"

Stew held on a little tighter to his catcher's mitt when he got closer to Jed Courson. He stared at him while he and Roger waited on a reply.

"If you wanted to get back with Patty, why didn't you just tell me?"

Roger looked at him like he had lost his mind. He laughed momentarily then said, "I have no idea what you are talking about. I haven't talked to her since we broke up."

Stew raised his voice when he asked, "What is all this about, Courson?"

Oak Bay's left fielder shouted back, "All I know is that after the game when I went up to talk to her, she told me that we were done. When I asked her why, she laughed and then told me that she was gettin' back with Roger."

Roger pointed at Jed and said, "That might be what she wants, but I swear that it is not what I want."

Chapter Seventeen

When he made it home, Roger James knew it was exactly 11:04 pm because right after the hit song, "Hot Stuff" by Donna Summer finished playing on his car radio, WOKB AM radio station's local Disc Jockey, Freaky Frank announced in a deep clear voice, "It's 11:04 right now in downtown Oak Bay with partly cloudy skies and a cool 84 degrees at South Carolina's Best Rock Station- WOKB."

Walking up the steps of the porch of his mobile home, Roger could see his father through the kitchen window. With his back to Roger, Mark James, poured himself a bourbon drink into a coffee cup. Pulling shut the door behind him with one hand while pulling off one of his tennis shoes with the other, Roger asked his father in a faint voice, "Is Mama asleep?"

"I think so. She got pretty wound up at the game. Speakin' of the game, what happened to y'all in the last two innings?"

"I blew it. All of a sudden I couldn't hit the backside of a barn. I was inside when I was aimin' outside. I was high when I was aimin' low. I even balked tonight, somethin' I haven't done since you coached me in Pony League." Roger then walked over to the kitchen table and sat down before he asked, "What was the deal with Mama tonight?``

"You don't want to know. It was a sad scene up in those stands. The saddest thing is that when the sun comes up tomorrow she may not remember one bit of it."

"One bit of what?"

"She was doin' so good, son. She seemed to be havin' a great time until your old girlfriend, Patty, walked up to where we were sittin' and stopped to talk to your Mama. I was busy watchin' the game and didn't pay much attention to what they were talkin' about. Between the blare of the speakers from the PA announcer and the crowd cheerin', I didn't hear what they were sayin'. All of a sudden your Mama punched the hell out of me. Before I could say a word she screamed, "Is our son really datin' that Mormon prostitute?" I was so embarrassed because I knew that Jeannie and her mother were sittin' only a few seats away from us. Dianna didn't hold back. She stood up and yelled at your Mama and said, "Hello… I said Hello, Crazy Lady. The Mormons are sittin' right up here behind you. We hear you loud and clear."

Roger asked his father, "Why did y'all leave?"

"Are you kiddin' me? I couldn't get your Mama to shut the hell up."

"What else did she say?"

"I don't know. She said somethin' about being Godless. No, as a matter of fact she called Dianna a 'Godless Whore'. To top it all off, she said that she would rather not have a son if he would stoop so low as to fall in love with a heathen prostitute. That's when the whole section of people in the stands jumped right into the screaming match. Dianna then yelled back that she would rather her daughter become a prostitute than for her to be involved with the family of a certifiable nut job. I finally had to haul your Mama out of there while she kept screamin' that Dianna was goin' straight to hell. I have wrestled with gators in the swamp more tame than your Mama when she gets riled up."

Roger wanted to cry, but instead he laughed for a moment and then said, "Oh, boy. I bet you were embarrassed." He continued by saying, "Maybe Jeannie will understand that Mama is just not right. I don't know how to even begin to talk to her."

Pouring himself one last drink for the night, Mark James looked at his disappointed son and asked, "Not to change the subject, but how about poor old Kirby?"

Roger looked up at this father and said, "I had to help clean up the blood in the Men's Room where he died. It was not a pleasant sight."

"You are a better man than me. I can't stand to look at blood."

"I really didn't have much time to think about it because we got backed up all day when folks started to figure out that gas prices were about to get higher."

Mark stirred his "coffee" with a spoon and said, "Yeah, I saw President Carter on TV when we got home, but I did not hear a word he said because I was tendin' to your Mama. I still find it hard to believe that a revolution in a country which sits in the middle of a desert could cause our gas prices to jump so high. I wouldn't be surprised if we find out that all of the big oil companies got together and made all of this up just to drive the prices higher. I remember the last time this happened we were told that we would be runnin' out of oil pretty soon. Back then the experts said we needed to get off the foreign oil in five years. We even changed the national speed limit from 70 to 55 miles per hour to save gas. Five years have passed by, and we are still guzzlin' foreign oil like no tomorrow. Now, here we are again bein' held hostage while the oil companies are smilin' like they just found a pot of gold at the end of a rainbow. We can't be that stupid. I am afraid that in the future, every time there is some international crisis, they will raise the price of oil just to make some quick profits. Prices will then go down for a while, and then they will come up with another excuse to raise the price again. Before ya know it, we will be payin' over a dollar a gallon for gasoline. People will get upset, and then the price will go back down a few cents. Good people will think that gas is cheap when it comes down to a dollar and fifty cents a gallon when it used to be two dollars a gallon. It will become an endless cycle where the oil companies will always be one step ahead."

Roger, who was looking through the fridge for something to eat, pulled out some leftover meatloaf and some really salty butter beans when he replied, "People today at the station were all bent out of shape about the price of gas."

Mark James then said, "Don't put that pot in the new microwave oven. You need to look in the cabinet over the sink and get one of those new microwavable containers."

Roger thanked him for the reminder and then said, "When I first started workin' at the station, I asked Mr. Carl one day how much money did he actually make off of the sale of the gas. I remember him laughin' at me. He told me that he only made a few cents off of each gallon of gas. I asked him how that could be, and he told me that his big profits came from the sale of oil changes, tune ups, battery, tire, and fan belt replacements. He said that if he only sold gas he would be livin' like Kirby."

Mark James took another sip out of his coffee cup and replied, "I don't know about all that. It is hard to believe that the people who sell the gas ain't makin' a killin' too."

Opening the door to the new microwave oven, Roger replied, "I have to be honest with you Dad, the price of gas is really the last thing on my mind right now."

Mark James knew his son was troubled, but he had to lay some of his own troubles on his only child when he said, "I know you have had a bad day, but I am sure that it doesn't quite rank up there with my bad news."

"What bad news?"

"Mr. Baldwin told me today that we were gonna have to start layin' off people at the Hardware Store. He said that the poor economy and the anticipated arrival of Walmart to our town gave him no other options. Right now my job is safe, but he wants me to be the one who gives three people the ax. Two of those folks are people I have known my entire life"

"That's a bummer."

"You don't know how bad I hate that I am the one who has to give them the bad news." Roger's father then leaned up in his kitchen table chair and whispered, "Come on outside on the porch. I need to tell ya somethin' that is very important."

Roger replied, "Really? I have to be at the station early in the mornin'. It has been a long day."

The look on his father's face gave Roger his answer without his father having to say a word.

Once they had quietly made their way out to the front steps of the porch, the two of them sat down like they had done many times before. It really wasn't a porch. It was more like a plywood deck wrapped with lattice and tiki torches.

Roger always loved it when he and his father had talks on the porch except for the times when his father was giving him unsolicited advice on girls or reprimanding him for something he had done wrong. He always knew that a talk on the porch was a signal that the conversation was considered important to his father. This night was no different as Mark James began to tell Roger something that had been a long-kept family secret. Roger could tell that his father was nervous because he kept pulling on the collar of his t-shirt; something Roger noticed about his father when he was a kid playing on his father's recreational ball teams. Mark James then cleared his throat before he told him, "This isn't gonna be easy for me to tell you this, but I think you better hear it from me before you find out about it from somebody else in this town." Before Roger could reply to his father, Mark James wasted no time in telling him, "When I was seventeen years old I rode into town with my grandfather to help him load some bags of fertilizer at the Dubose Seed and Feed Store down on Green Street. While we were loadin' the fertilizer onto the truck, I caught a glimpse of the most beautiful girl I had ever seen. She was so gorgeous that I almost fell off the truck when I spotted her. She was standing across the street by herself in front of Old man Thompson's Cotton Warehouse. Just when I was gettin' a good look at her, a Korean War veteran, named Dave Jennings, came out of the warehouse and grabbed this girl from behind. The girl began screamin' as he tried to pull her into his car. From out of nowhere, a grown woman came flyin' out of the warehouse and began kickin' and hittin' Dave. I jumped off the back of the truck and sprinted over toward them. The girl who was about my age was bein' strangled because Dave had one of his arms around her neck. I punched Dave in the face while the grown woman kept kickin' him. Crazy Dave would not let go of the girl. Suddenly, we all stopped and he let her go when a shotgun blast was fired up in the air. My grandfather had made his way across the street and fired a shell into the sky out of his double barrel shotgun that he kept in his truck. My grandfather lowered the gun and pointed it at Dave and told him to freeze before he blew him to Kingdom Come. Crazy Dave didn't move until an Oak Bay police officer showed up in his police car."

Roger looked at his father and asked, "Why are you tellin' me all of this?"

"Just wait and you will see." Mark James then stood up on the front step of the porch and leaned his hand on the step's railing. He then continued by saying, "After the police made the arrest, it took about thirty or forty minutes for them to sort out the whole ordeal. Crazy Dave, who had returned to Oak Bay from the war only a few years prior, believed that he had been hoodooed out of some money from gamblin' down at the One Spot. He wanted to recoup his losses so he had the bright idea of stalkin' and kidnappin' the teenage girl; holding her for ransom. I think you know the girl who I am talkin' about."

"I have no idea."

"Ok son, who owns the One Spot?"

"The Branhams'."

"That's right. The teenage girl was Dianna Skinner who is now Dianna Branham."

"So what does all of this have to do with you?'

"Well, let's just say that a week later, I found myself secretly meetin' up with Dianna down at Rust Bottom Creek. Having been a part of saving her life, she wanted to know more about me."

"You mean to tell me...."

"I hate it, but the truth is that we fell madly in love with each other that summer."

"You and Jeannie's mother?"

"That's right. We would meet up with each other at Rust Bottom Creek two or three nights a week in that big pasture that overlooks the creek. One of her older friends from the River would drop her off at my car. Once we spent the evening together, I would then drop her off at Haskins Country Store where she would have a friend pick her up and take her home." .

"What happened to you two?"

"It was awful. She was the first girl that I fell in love with, but we could not be seen together in public. You may not know this, but Dianna is part Cherokee. That is why she and Jeannie have such dark complexions. Times were different around this town. You know how it was back in those days. Blacks, Whites, and Indians were not supposed to mingle in that way. Dianna had to sneak around her mother who would have scalped me. On top of that, I have no doubt that my father or my grandfather would have shot me dead if they knew I was messin' round with an Indian girl. It was just not acceptable."

"How did it all end or has it ever ended?"

"Graduation came, and I went off to Appalachian State to play ball. Diana was a year younger, and she stayed here and finished her studies at the small River School for Indians. We met up one last time of my freshman year, during Easter Break. I hitchhiked all the way from Boone, North Carolina down to Monroe with only a few dollars in my pocket. When I made it to Monroe, I called her and waited about half a day for her to arrive. That evening we met up at a truck stop on the Charlotte side of town. We both had planned to spend the whole weekend together but in only a few hours all of that changed. I begged her with all of my heart to come to school at Appalachian the next year. That was when she told me that she had made up her mind to go out to Oklahoma to study about her Native heritage. We laughed, cried, made up and broke up all in a whirlwind of conversations which lasted for a couple of hours. Deep down we both knew it would be impossible to keep up such a long distance relationship. We also knew that our situation would be impossible in our home town. We mutually decided that the right thing to do was to end the relationship. Late that evenin' two of her friends came from Oak Bay, picked her up and drove her back home. I spent one of the loneliest and saddest nights of my life in the absolute worst motel room I have ever experienced. The next day I hitchhiked my way back to Boone. One year later I ended up back in Oak Bay after I busted up my knee on a muddy field where you know the story about my daddy passing away from a heart attack. That is when I cashed in all of my education chips and decided to stay home and help out Mama. Two months later I got introduced to your mother at Myrtle Beach, who at the time was a student at the College of Charleston. Of course you know she was from Goose Creek. Our worlds collided that day on the beach when I fell head over heels for your Mama. The next thing I know, your Mama is pregnant with you, and we are married. In front of Judge Clyburn and a handful of family members in a small room in the back of the Oak Bay Courthouse, your Mama shamefully tied the knot with a boy who got her knocked up one afternoon at the beach."

"I didn't know about you and Mama on the beach. Have you and Dianna ever...?"

"No, sir. When you were born those first few years with your Mama were some of the best years of my life. Now I'm not gonna lie to ya, when Dianna came back to Oak Bay from Oklahoma the thought did cross my mind. I saw her in town one day at the Piggly Wiggly Supermarket. At first sight, a lot of emotions overcame me.

I'm pretty sure that if she would have asked, I would have most likely done whatever she wanted me to do if you know what I mean. Then after we talked for a few minutes, I felt different. Her whole demeanor had changed. She was dressed in Native apparel and had the appearance of being a hippie long before anyone around here knew anything about a hippie. I also realized that she was devastated about the death of her mother. The reason she came home was because her mother was dying of cancer. What amazed me the most was that I could tell that she was sincerely happy for me and your mother. She never said it, but I knew by the way she looked at me that our times together in the past would always remain in the past.

I knew for certain that our worlds were too far apart. I didn't know it at the time, but she was already pregnant with Jeannie and only a few days away from marrying Teddy Branham. I couldn't believe it when I heard it, but it all worked out. Through the years we have always acknowledged each other, but we seldom go out of our way to speak to each other."

"Does Mama know all of this?"

"Yes but it is complicated."

"Why is it complicated?"

"When your Mama began to have her episodes when you were a little boy, I ended up spendin' a fortune on medical doctors, psychiatrists, prescriptions, and therapy sessions. I literally robbed Peter to pay Paul. Not many people know it, but I started bettin' on football and baseball games. Mr. Stumpy's cousin Mickey was my bookie. He operated out of a small room in the back of Mr. Stumpy's barbeque joint. For a while I felt like God had given me a gift as I could pick the big winners. The cash I was makin' went to pay for your Mama's medical bills."

Roger began laughing and said, "You mean to tell me that the man who gets bent out of shape if I leave the light on in our bathroom was a gambler?"

"I had it down to a science, son. Every day durin' my lunch break I would meet with Mickey and I would place my bets. Many nights after you and your Mama were asleep, I was checkin' the box scores and schedules in the *Oak Bay Gazette*."

"So how does this play into Mama findin' out about you and Dianna?"

"It's simple. Remember the Miracle Mets of 1969?"

"Sure I do."

"The Miracle Mets sent me to the poor house. It was the first time in my brief gamblin' career that I bet with my heart and not my sports mind. I absolutely loved the Baltimore Orioles. Pitcher Jim Palmer was my guy. I was convinced that they would sweep the Mets easily. The people in Vegas thought the same way before the World Series started. I was also at a point where I was gettin' antsy about winnin' only a few hundred dollars on a big bet. I met with Mickey for several days and finally arranged for him to help back me for a five thousand dollar bet on the World Series. In all reality, Mickey vouched for me that I would be able to cover the bet. When Baltimore smacked them good in the first game of the series I just knew that I had hit the big time. I even went down and looked at a new bass boat thinkin' it was a done deal. Of course, you know what happened. When the Mets scored two runs in the eighth inning of Game Five I threw up in the bathroom for over an hour. I had no earthly way to pay Mickey back that money. That game was on a Thursday. The next day I went to see Mickey about how I was goin' to get out of such a big hole. Evidently, Mickey was partly playin' with House money from an outfit out of Atlanta. Those guys in dark blue suits were not happy when they made a little visit all the way here to Oak Bay. I will never forget it. It was Saturday, October 18, 1969, when the blue suit dudes approached me in the parking lot of the hardware store. They said in so many words that unless they received the seven thousand, five hundred dollars in one week, some people would be dead. When I asked who was gonna be dead, they laughed and told me that it would be me and my entire family."

"I thought you said it was five thousand dollars?"

"I did, but the extra fifteen hundred was for interest and a collection fee."

"What did you do? I assume you got the money because we are still alive."

Mark James laughed and sat down on the top porch step with his son. He leaned over a little and said, "I had no other option except to go to the only people in town that I knew would lend me the money."

"Who was that?"

"Teddy Branham and his father at the One Spot."

"You have to be kidding me. You mean to tell me you borrowed that money from Jeannie's daddy?"

"I sure did. It took me only about five minutes to explain myself and he and his father had no problem giving me the money. They both knew the story about how my Grandfather and myself tried to save Dianna from Crazy Dave. Because of that, they were glad to help me out. To this day I am pretty sure Teddy never knew that me and Dianna were once in a relationship. If he knew, he never said a word about it. The only thing he said to me was that I would need to pay them back whatever I could each and every week until the debt was paid. His old man also told me that if he ever heard of me gamblin' again before the debt was paid, he would have me shot dead. However, in just a few months everything changed."

"What do you mean?"

"I received a phone call at the hardware store one day in January of the next year from Dianna. She was very upset and couldn't hardly talk to me. Finally she was able to tell me that your Mama barged into the One Spot and wanted to know who I was seein'."

"You lost me there, Dad. How did Mama find out?"

"She saw my checkbook behind my back. When she saw entries in my checkbook ledger for several checks made out to the One Spot, your Mama began diggin' for more information. Your Mama might be crazy at times, but she is not stupid. She knew what the One Spot was all about, and she thought I had to be seein' a lady of the night with all the money that I was shellin' out. She knew that I wasn't spendin' all that money on booze because I never came home drunk. The day she went down there, Dianna was the first person she approached at the One Spot. Your Mama just came out and asked her if she was havin' an affair with me. In Dianna's defense she had no idea what your Mama was talkin' bout. Not knowin' what to say she simply said that our relationship ended several years ago. That is when the crap hit the fan. By the time I got home that afternoon, your Mama's mind had already begun to spin out of control. I tried to explain, but she was uncontrollable. You may not remember this but she tore up just about everything we owned. I finally had to take her to a hospital in Charleston. Three weeks later, in what amounted to a four hour long therapy session, I had to explain the entire situation to your Mama. So, when you left on Sunday to go to church with the Branham's, your Mama went fool. I admit that I am the stupid one in all of this because I never should have let you go. At the time I didn't think much about it. It had been almost ten years since I had thought about all of that. Now I think you know why a relationship with Jeannie Branham can never happen."

Chapter Eighteen

The next morning every member of the O.T.C.C. was already assembled in the Main Street Amoco station lounge when Roger James arrived at 7:03 am. Stumpy looked at Coach Hutchinson and whispered loud enough for everyone to hear, "Don't mention the game last night, Coach."

Roger forced out a smile when he said, "I heard that, Mr. Stumpy. It is all right. I will be the first one to admit that I stunk it up at the end of the game."

Coach Hutchinson, while pouring himself his first cup of coffee said, "I don't know why Coach Fugate didn't take you out sooner. For God's sake, you were throwing a no hitter going into the seventh. There wasn't much more you could have done without any help from the offense. Whenever our boys did swing, it looked like our bats were full of holes except for yours, Roger."

Rainey, standing next to Roger, gave him a slight push and whispered, “Here it comes. I told you that you are the Golden Boy to these old men.”

Carl then spoke up and said, “He might be a helluva ball player, Coach Hutch, but he sure can’t tell time. Three minutes late ain’t gonna cut it round here.” The veteran of Vietnam then looked over his reading glasses and asked, “You hear me, boy?”

Roger shook his head and acknowledged his boss and then whispered to Rainey, “Golden Boy?”

Carl then made everyone get quiet before he began with an unusual morning pep talk of sorts. He said, “Some of y’all may remember the hell we went through in 73 the last time we had a gas shortage. Don’t be surprised if some old lady cusses you out or some teenager decides to shoot ya the bird. People are gonna be upset so just let them vent. Do not respond to any verbal attack, but the first SOB that lays even a pinky finger on ya, you have my blessin’ to whip some B-hind. Let me be more clear. Do not hit a woman. I don’t care how she attacks you.”

He then assembled the members of the O.T.C.C. and gave them their orders like he was a military General preparing for battle. The oldest member of the O.T.C.C. Gene Purdy turned up his hearing aid before he interrupted Carl by saying, “Carl, I don’t think it's right for you to tell these boys to hit a woman.”

Stumpy just shook his head and said, “Dang it, Gene, you really need to consider an ear transplant.”

Darryl looked at Rainey and said, 'When I arrived here this mornin’ I noticed that you left the keys in the fish car. Somebody could have stolen that car.”

Carl quickly replied before Rainey could respond when he said, “Ain’t nobody gonna get within 10 feet of that car. If Rainey does get the smell out, it will be a miracle. Rainey, you and Hot Rod take some time after the mornin' rush dies down and get to work on it."

Right before the Main Street Amoco officially opened for business, Hank Burrows turned the station's homemade TV antenna just enough to get a clear picture of the CBS Tuesday Morning Show. When he turned up the volume, they were shocked to learn that actor John Wayne, known as the Duke, had died of cancer the day before. Stumpy took off his hat, placed it over his heart and said,

"If that don't beat all. That Duke is one lucky guy. I can't believe that he will get the chance to meet our friend Kirby. I bet those two are already sittin' at a bar up in heaven havin' a helluva time."

Darryl shook his head and replied, "If the Duke is up in Gloryland having a drink with Kirby, I'm pretty sure it will be the Duke who picks up the tab."

Luther spoke up and said, "Y'all hush. There ain't no drinkin' up in heaven."

Stumpy laughed and said, "Luther, some in here would say that if there is no drinkin' in heaven they may not want to make the trip."

Luther growled, "Then they just need to pack their bags and head straight to hell."

Coach Hutchinson laughed with the others in the O.T.C.C. and then said, "Luther, Stumpy sure knows how to push your buttons."

Before he walked out of the station lounge, Luther looked at Coach Hutchinson and said, "You and the rest of this gang are the problem cause y'all listen to that fool all day long."

Stumpy took a ceremonious bow and then said, "I do live to get into Luther's head. God love him. I love Luther like a brother."

Customers were already lined up at both pump aisles when Carl told everyone to go ahead and open the station. Rainey and Roger worked together on Full Service aisle two while Carl and Luther worked Full Service aisle number one. Stumpy worked the cash register while Hank Burrows directed traffic. Coach Hutchinson, one of the most loved men in Oak Bay, was in charge of public relations. The rest of the gang manned the station lounge and helped with anything that Carl told them to do. It was organized chaos along with the sounds of horns honking, people yelling at each other as well as them yelling at the staff of the Main Street Amoco. Rainey's cardboard box sign on the main marquee which simply read, 8 Gallon Limit per Vehicle, had customers cursing up a storm while Coach Hutchinson tried to calm their nerves. One elderly lady looked at Carl and said, "I hope like hell you are happy now."

Some of the worst people in town were unbelievably polite. Some of the most Christian people in town were more than unchristian. Rainey and Darryl heard the 'N word' more than once while Roger was told by one customer that he sucked at baseball. Luther was told that he was going to hell while Stumpy was told that he ought to be ashamed of himself for working with a bunch of pirates and thieves. Hank Burrows was almost run over by an old friend while Gene threatened to hit an irate woman with his cane. It seemed that all hell had broke loose at the Main Street Amoco by 8:30 am.

Thirty minutes later, Carl went inside the station lounge and made a call to the Carolina Petroleum Company in Charleston. He asked how long it would be before they could drop off a load of gasoline. He shook his head several times and then said, "I understand, Partner." He slowly and gently placed the phone receiver back on top of the black rotary phone and then looked at Stumpy with a face full of worry saying, "We are up the creek. They won't be able to deliver any gas until Friday."

About an hour later, it appeared that the morning onslaught of people wanting their eight gallons of gasoline had begun to wane.

After taking six dollars from his last customer, Rainey yelled at Roger and said, “It’s Fish time.”

A few minutes later, Rainey began the process of administering Carl’s homemade remedy. With the seats of the Camaro already disassembled along with all of the mats placed outside of the car, Rainey told Roger, “Take that tube of toothpaste and dab a little on the floorboard and in the trunk about every two or three inches.”

Mixing a concoction which included mouthwash and Lysol, Rainey poured Carl’s secret into a ten gallon metal sprayer. He then sprayed down the entire car. Roger asked, “What is with the baking soda?”

“That will be the last step in this process. It is amazing.” Rainey then asked, “So how are things with you and Jeannie?”

Roger then explained to him his dilemma regarding his family history. Rainey interrupted him and said, “I saw what happened at the game last night. I thought your mother was going to try to kill Mrs. Dianna. No disrespect, but my money would have been on Mrs. Dianna.”

Roger laughed and then replied, “I really don’t know what to do. It just seems that there is too much baggage between our families for it to work out. Besides, she has a college boy from the Citadel who really wants to be with her. I don’t see this happening.”

Rainey smiled and then said, “Not to mention that many people in this town get all bent out of shape when they talk about the Branhams. If I were you, I would steer clear. She is one beautiful girl, but if I brought her home, I have no doubt that my mother would have a problem with it.” He began scrubbing down the backseat and continued by saying, “I don’t know, but like I told you yesterday, there is just something strange about them. I can tell you that there are not too many Brothers from the Bay going out of their way to make friends with the Branhams. The few Black girls who work at the One Spot are the only Black people I know that venture down to that place. In the Bay some people think those River Indians who hang out at the One Spot have the power to cast spells on people with voodoo or black magic. Many uneducated people have prejudged them for no reason at all. Others simply believe many of those Indians still live in teepees and thatched huts down on the river like a bunch of primitive aborigines. My own preacher makes no bones about his disfavor of them. I once heard him tell some of our church members that they needed to keep their distance from those River Indians because they weren't Christians. That on top of the fact that Teddy Branham is one mean dude, doesn't help your cause."

Roger asked Rainey, "Do you really think they are all bad people?"

"I am really not sure, but I say all this to you because in reality there are a lot of white people in this town who will not be comfortable with their "Golden Boy" dating a girl from a family that is questionable in their eyes. If you don't believe me just ask Carl, Stumpy or your boy, Coach Hutchinson. They might give you a pat on the back for messing around with the girl, but there isn't one of them that will tell you it is all right to get serious with her. If you want to disappoint Coach Hutch, tell him you are about to get engaged to Jeannie. He would be heartbroken. He and the rest of these old-timers are no different than most of the men in this community. A lot of men in this town have always thought that it is acceptable to go down to the One Spot and have their way with one of those girls. Some men equate having sex with those girls as nothing more than a sporting event. As far as they are concerned, it's one thing to tag one of those girls in the One Spot, but it's another thing to bring one of them home to meet their mother. Think about it. We have local politicians and deacons of churches, who frequent the One Spot while pretending that they are God fearing family men. I know it is all stupid, but you will have to decide if the ridicule you will face is worth the relationship."

"There is no relationship. She won't even give me the time of day."

Back in front of the Main Street Amoco, Stumpy walked out to Full Service aisle number one and brought Luther a cold six ounce Coca Cola and said, "Here, good buddy, looks like you need some refreshment."

Luther took the Coca Cola, but he did not respond. Stumpy then laughed and said, "You know I love ya, Luther."

Luther noticed a very well-dressed man climbing out of a new Impala parked on the Main Street curb across from the station. Sporting a three-piece suit and a fifteen dollar looking haircut he walked toward the station carrying his professional leather briefcase. Luther wiped his glasses to get a better view of the man. As he approached Luther the man said, "Hello, how are you doing today?"

Luther replied, "I'm sorry. Do I know you?"

The professional extended his hand and replied, "It's Shane Walker. Don't you remember that I met you the other day when I dropped off a U Haul truck with my wife."

"That's right. You are the new lawyer in town. You sure do clean up nice, young man."

"Thank you Luther. I took your advice and decided to get a good shave and a haircut."

"I have to say that I would have never recognized you. It is amazin' how a good barber and some fancy clothes can make a man's appearance change so dramatically. How in the world can we help ya today?"

"Well, I'm here on business."

"What kind of business?"

"I need to speak to Carl Norman. Do you know where I can find him?"

"What is all of this about?"

"I'd rather not say. I need to speak to Mr. Norman."

Stumpy, who was standing next to Luther looked at Oak Bay's newest lawyer and said, "Come on, Hot Shot and follow me. He's in here."

Standing behind the station lounge cash register, Carl was busy checking and signing the invoice for a High Alloy Crankshaft Sprocket that was delivered from the Oak Bay Ford Auto Parts Department. After handing the invoice back to the overweight, thirtyish looking courier he said, "Ok, Partner, that should do it. When you get back to the Dealership, tell Brooks that he needs to go ahead and send me last month's bill. I ain't seen one yet."

Stumpy standing with young attorney Shane Walker then spoke up and said, "Hey, Carl, this lawyer man needs to speak with you."

Shane Walker then introduced himself and asked, "Are you the sole owner of this station?"

"I sure am."

"Well, sir, I represent the law firm of McCloud and Turner. I sure would like to have a private word with you if that would be possible."

"We are pretty busy 'round here this mornin'. Maybe you can come back another time."

Shane Walker adjusted his neck tie and then replied, "No, sir. I was told by Mr. Turner that I had to speak to you now."

Carl looked at Hank Burrows who had just walked into the station lounge and said, "Gosh Almighty, what in the world could be so important that Mr. Turner needs this young buck to come talk to me?"

Hank threw up his hands in a gesture indicating that he had no idea. Carl then sat down on a stool behind the station counter and said, "Hell, boy, I really don't have the time, but if it's that important go ahead and spill your guts. I am all ears."

Shane Walker replied, "I really think we should go and talk in private."

"Oh, hell no… Whatever you have to say will be found out by all of these people because there is really no such thing as a secret in this town."

"All right then. Well, as I said earlier I am representing the McCloud and Turner law firm. We have a client who has decided to make a claim against your business."

Stumpy asked, "What kind of claim?"

"A wrongful death lawsuit."

Carl took off his service station cap, scratched the top of his balding head and replied, "What the hell are ya talkin' bout, boy?"

Shane Walker explained, "It seems that the estate of Mr. Kirby Davis, the deceased who passed away in your station lounge yesterday, has decided to bring a lawsuit against you and this station."

Hank Burrows shook his head and said, "So Kirby did have a last name."

"Yes, sir, I am afraid that Mr. Davis actually had two distant relatives who live right here in Oak Bay. It appears that the legal executor of the estate has decided to bring this lawsuit."

Stumpy asked, "What estate? Old Kirby didn't have a dime to his name."

Shane Walker nervously cleared his throat and replied, "It may have appeared that way, but I am here to tell you that Mr. Davis has real estate, bank accounts, stock, and gold worth more than four million dollars. His assets are quite impressive."

Coach Hutchinson laughed and said, "I don't want to tell you how to do your business, Mr. Walker, but you evidently have the wrong Mr. Davis. Old Kirby went around this town eating out of trash cans, drinking Vicks 44 cough syrup, sleeping under bridges and bathing in service station restrooms. Our Kirby didn't have more than a few dollars on him the day he died."

"No, sir, we have the right Mr. Davis. He may have been a crazy coot for the last part of his life, but when he was a young man, Mr. Kirby Davis became one of the most respected commercial real estate entrepreneurs in the city of Baltimore. From what I have read about him, after making a fortune in architecture and the building of factories, he was responsible for the building of the Glen Martin Aircraft Plant which produced many of our bombers in World War II. While in Baltimore he fell in love and was set to marry a young lady from Philadelphia who was much younger than him. One week before their wedding, the love of his life was evidently robbed and stabbed to death in broad daylight on High Street in downtown Philadelphia. Caught only a day after the crime, the man who committed the murder confessed that he only got away with about four dollars. From what we know, Mr. Davis never recovered from his loss. Grief stricken, he basically decided to disappear from society. At the time of his decision to exit life as he knew it, his parents had already passed away. As an only child who never had children, he really did not have many relatives. He ended up giving away most of his fortune to the Boys' Club of Baltimore, the Salvation Army, and an Animal Hospital in Minneapolis. He also kept a good portion of his sizable fortune in various trusts and interest bearing accounts that he designed for the sole purpose of distributing the proceeds to other charities. However, for some reason he made the decision to retain another portion of his fortune, specifically for one of his only surviving heirs who lives right here in Oak Bay."

Coach Hutchinson quickly asked, "And who may that be?"

"His first cousin. Y'all might know her. Her name is Mrs. Essie Hudson."

Luther almost dropped his Coca Cola when he asked, " Did you say Essie Hudson?"

"Yes, sir."

Carl laughed and then asked, "You mean to tell me that Mrs. Essie, who can't barely remember her last meal is the one who is bringin' this lawsuit?"

"Not exactly."

Carl shook his head before he asked, "What does that mean?"

Before Shane Walker could reply, Luther spoke up and said, "It is her crazy nephew, Bob Blankenship."

Shane Walker nodded in agreement and said, "Mr. Blankenship now has Power of Attorney over all of Mrs. Hudson's affairs because of her failing health. Although Mr. Kirby Davis's will names Mrs. Hudson as the executor of his estate and the only benefactor, legally it is now Mr. Blankenship who will be in charge."

Carl looked over the entire O.T.C.C. when he said, "Don't say that Crazy Bob didn't warn us. He said that we would be sorry for messin' with him, and I'm afraid he may be right."

Before he walked out the main entrance of the Main Street Amoco station lounge, Shane Walker said, "I know this is not good news, but I want y'all to know that it is not an open and shut case. We don't even have the results back from the autopsy. If I were you, I would hire a lawyer for your immediate protection."

Carl laughed and said, “Now this is gonna be interestin’ since Kirk McCloud is my attorney.”

Shane Walker smiled and said, “That is precisely why they sent me over here to give you the news. They wanted me to explain that there is a conflict of interest. Because Mrs. Hudson has been a client longer than yourself, they are going to be obliged to represent her interests in this matter.”

Stumpy growled, “Those SOB’s. That is just their fancy way of saying that they are goin’ to side with the client who has a clear path to a jackpot.”

Shane Walker in a most professional manner replied, “I can honestly say that Mr. McCloud sent me here as a professional courtesy. He truly wanted you to know that you have plenty of time to mount a good defense. All of this is preliminary. There hasn’t been one document prepared or filed concerning this case. Mr. McCloud is in no hurry. Mr. Blankenship on the other hand seems to be one determined soul.”

Chapter Nineteen

Once Shane Walker left the station lounge to make his way back to the McCloud-Turner law firm, Coach Hutchinson said, “Carl, I know a good hot shot lawyer over in Charleston, who I can call if you want me to. A lot of people down there say that he is a silver-tongued devil who gets results.”

Gene Purdy surprisingly heard Coach Hutchinson and responded by saying, “Carl doesn't need a lawyer. It’s the service station’s insurance company that will handle all of this. That is why you pay for the insurance.”

Carl laughed and then said, “That is exactly right, Mr. Gene. The insurance company would be responsible for most of it. The only problem is that I have the highest deductible you could ever imagine. Your son-in-law talked me into the cheaper premiums with the higher deductible.”

Stumpy cried out, “What the hell, Carl?”

Carl smiled and replied, "I just couldn't afford to pay those premiums. I have never needed to file a claim since I established this joint, so I just thought it was a waste of money. I have already read the policy and the fine print. If Crazy Bob is awarded a ton of money this place is done."

Darryl spoke up and asked, "Are you cryin' over there, Stumpy?"

Stumpy cleared his throat and said, "Hell yeah, I'm cryin'"

. Darryl asked, "Why are you cryin'?"

"Because if this place goes under, I will have to spend all my time at home with my old lady."

Hank Burrows screamed, "Shut the hell up, Stumpy. This place ain't goin' anywhere. No matter what happens with Crazy Bob's lawsuit we all know enough people who can make sure that this station stays afloat."

Stumpy continued to cry. Darryl asked, "Why are you still cryin', Stumpy?"

Stumpy wiped his nose with his handkerchief, smiled a big smile and then answered by saying, "Because my friend Old Kirby left a pile of his money to a dad blame animal hospital. All the times I took him down to the drug store and bought him a bottle of Vicks 44, and he didn't leave me a single dime."

Coach Hutchinson said, "I did catch that. Now that I think of it, I used to see a lot of dogs near Shiloh Creek following Kirby like he was the pied piper."

Gene Purdy woke up and said, "That is because when he was on a Scope Mouthwash binge for several days the dogs wanted to lick his beard. To those dogs he was a walkin' candy cane."

Taking a break from working on the fish car, a conflicted Roger walked over to the corner of Main Street next to the station and entered a Bell System phone booth. He pulled out a quarter, slid it into the large phone's coin slot, quickly dialing the phone number of Jeannie. As the phone began to ring, Roger began sweating because of the heat and humidity inside of the glass phone booth. It was as if he was in a sauna. His heart began pounding when Jeannie picked up on the third ring. He first apologized for his mother's behavior when Jeannie interrupted him by saying, "It is all right, Hot Rod. My mother explained to me why your mother acted the way she did. She is embarrassed for the way she lost her cool. Actually it was me who lost it because I couldn't understand why my mother was just sitting there letting your mother keep going on about the godless Mormons. Then once my mother got fired up, it was on."

"What exactly did she explain to you?"

"She told me the whole story. Although Dianna has always been upfront with me, it was a real shocker when she divulged this information. She and I stayed up almost all night as she explained her relationship with your father. I understand why she kept all of this from me, and I completely understand why your mother reacted the way she did. It was actually your old girlfriend, Patty who upset your mother. I completely understand why your mother became so upset."

"Jeannie, I'm sorry for all of this"

"Don't be sorry. How cool is this?"

"What do you mean?"

"You know. It's not every day you find out this kind of information."

"I don't know. I was pretty shook up when my Dad spilled his guts to me last night. Don't you think it is a little creepy?"

"Not at all. I think it is cute. Who knew?"

Roger smiled, paused for a few seconds of awkward silence and then asked Jeannie, “Does your father know about this?”

“Sure he does. Don't worry. He is cool with it. He and my idiot uncles idolize your father. Way before I knew anything about this, I can remember all of them talking about how your father was a legend at Oak Bay High.”

Roger laughed and then said, “Well, that’s good. I didn’t want my Daddy to be in any trouble with your father.” He then paused and asked, “Do you think we can get together after baseball practice tonight?”

“I guess so, but only as friends. You know that we can’t ever be anything more than friends. She then paused before asking, “What time and where?”

“Why don’t I meet you up at your house around seven-thirty?”

‘That might not be the best idea. Why don’t I meet you in the parking lot of the Old South Motor Court on the Pee Dee Highway?”

“That’s a date. I mean just a friendly visit with each other.”

“Sounds cool.”

Once Roger hung up the phone he could hear the station bell ringing like a fire alarm was going off. He turned around and could see that many vehicles had begun pulling into the station during a mad lunchtime rush. Rainey, Luther, and Carl were pumping gas and servicing vehicles at a record pace. Carl caught a glimpse of Roger in his peripheral vision when he cried out, “Help out Rainey with that Pinto, then hustle your rear end into the station and bring out another case of 40 weight motor oil.”

Luther yelled, “Bring out a couple of cans of power steerin’ fluid while you're at it.”

Although the cussing and the fussing continued from customers they knew and those they didn't, the staff at the Main Street Amoco began to take it all in stride. Rainey looked at Roger and said, "This has become funny. Some of these people are losing their religion over a couple gallons of gasoline."

Roger replied, "Speakin' of religion, look who has just pulled up."

Over on Full Service aisle number one, the pastor of the Oak Bay Baptist church, Vince Smith, jumped out of his Lincoln Continental and began shaking hands with Luther. Roger could tell that Carl was doing his best to avoid having a conversation with the man of the cloth, but eventually after a few minutes he was forced to acknowledge his presence. Fashionably dressed far above the standards which most people in town were used to, the energetic preacher approached Carl and said, "Brother Carl, I just heard about the tragic death that occurred here at your station. I want you to know that I have been prayin' for all of you boys since I heard the news. Tragic… It is simply tragic."

Carl, who continued to check the oil under another customer's Pontiac nodded his head and replied, "Thank ya, Preach'a."

Preacher Smith then said, "I sure would like to pray for you and all of the boys if you have a few minutes."

Carl smiled and replied, "That sure is nice of ya, but I think you can appreciate that we are slammed right now."

"You're right. Y'all are pretty busy. If you don't mind, I would like to put up an advertisement poster in the lounge before I leave."

"What kind of poster?"

"Our church is havin' an old fashioned tent revival camp meetin' this Saturday down at the Oak Bay Fairgrounds. I would love for you and the boys to come and fellowship with us."

Carl carefully sidestepped the invitation by saying, "Not a problem, take that poster inside and Mr. Stumpy will help you out."

Before he made his way to the station lounge, Preacher Smith stopped next to Luther and said, "I know y'all have limits on how much gas each customer is allowed, but Brother Luther this fine runnin' machine begins to knock if it runs on a tank that is half full. I sure would appreciate it if you and Carl could allow this humble servant of the Gospel to have just a few more gallons of gas."

Luther walked over to Carl and whispered to him the request by his own preacher. At first Carl shook his head, denying the request. Then Luther looked at him over his glasses in a most pathetic way. Without saying a word, Carl reluctantly gave in to avoid any further discussion with the man of the cloth.

Once the pastor of the First Baptist Church of Oak Bay drove away, Carl told Luther, "That preach'a is a piece of work. I have a feelin' that he is gonna be diggin' deep into the pockets of his members durin' his time in this town. I don't know, Luther, but I have always had a problem with those Bible thumpers who go around callin' everyone 'his Brother' or 'his Sister'. This cat here reminds me of a used car salesman. I know you like him, but he has that glazed look in his eyes. I have no doubt that he has a touch of mental illness just waitin' to reveal itself."

Before Luther could respond a loud booming clap of thunder exploded near the back of the station. They had been so busy servicing vehicles that none of the station crew noticed that a thunderstorm was trying to make its way through downtown Oak Bay. Darryl walked out of the station lounge and yelled to everyone, "The news on the TV just said a storm is a comin.'"

Only a few minutes later, Roger and Rainey took turns servicing the vehicles on Full Service aisle number two while Carl and Luther stayed dry under the station awning which only covered Full Service aisle number one. The lightning became so bad that Carl finally had to tell them all to get underneath the awning which basically shut down half of the station. Rainey looked at Roger and said, "Holy crap. I forgot about the fish car."

Before Roger could respond, Coach Hutchinson yelled out of the station lounge, "Hey everybody, take a look. It is snowing on the other side of the station."

The downpour associated with the thunderstorm along with Carl's secret concoction of various cleaners created a mountain of soap suds that flowed out of the car into the side parking lot of the Main Street Amoco. Stumpy yelled out, "It's Christmas in June right here in Oak Bay."

Chapter Twenty

A slow moving front continued to produce pop up thunderstorms all over Oak Bay County the rest of the afternoon. The steady summer afternoon rains drastically slowed down the flow of customers at the Main Street Amoco. After checking the gasoline reservoir levels in the afternoon, Carl was relieved that his business would be able to stay open at least one more day. Rainey, who gave up working on the fish car for the rest of the day, was told to leave early after he completed an afternoon oil and lube job. Right before he left that afternoon Roger was not disappointed when he received the news from Coach Hutchinson that American Legion baseball practice was canceled by Coach Fugate. The cancellation of practice gave Roger some free time before he was supposed to meet Jeannie.

His mother was startled when Roger barged into his mobile home. Halfway dozing through an afternoon episode of the television soap opera, *The Edge of Night,* Juanita James jumped to attention when Roger walked into the wood paneled den. 'You scared me," she cried out while he jumped on the couch next to his mother.

"I hear you, scaredy cat. I see what goes on around here when I'm not here."

"I'm not really into this if you want to change the channel to the *Match Game.* I can miss a week's worth of these *Edge of Night* episodes and pick right up where I Ieft off in about ten minutes."

"I'm good, Mama. I just want to rest a little here on the couch. How are you feelin' today?"

'You know, I get a little down in the dumps whenever it rains, but other than that it has been a pretty productive day. I finally got the oven cleaned, and I went and paid the electric bill. Those folks over at the Pee Dee Electric Company think very highly of their power. I still can't believe we got charged forty-one dolla's last month. I told them that I wanted them to come out here next week and check our meter. There is no way on earth we should be payin' so much for electricity."

Roger then tested the waters of his own home when he asked, "Did you have a good time at the game last night?"

"You know it's funny that you ask that. Did I miss something special last night because Sheila at the Electric Company told me that she was sorry she missed all of the fireworks last night. Did they shoot fireworks after the game?"

After telling his mother that there were fireworks at the game, Roger sat wondering if his mother was simply an abuser of drugs or if she had a mental disorder too severe for him and his father to handle. He had experienced years of her emotional meltdowns as well as her defiant denial of events only to be rebuked for suggesting that she was incorrect. At an early age he and his father made an agreement to limit other children from making overnight stays so as to avoid the possibility of the children experiencing one of her episodes. He loved his mother and wished he could wave a magic wand to help her mind heal from whatever hurt and pain she once experienced. Wrestling with his feelings toward Jeannie along with his father's new revelations about his secretive past, Roger made the selfish decision to go ahead and meet Jeannie one more time.

Using his good friend Stew as the veil of his secret encounter, Roger told his parents that he and Stew were going to hang out with some of the other local teens at the Oak Bay Pizza Hut. Roger was surprised that his father offered very little resistance to him going out. He waited for his father to ask him to have a talk on the front porch, but the invitation never materialized. Instead his father wrapped himself up in the pages of the *Oak Bay Gazette* and a liquor drink too strong for most. His mother cleaned the kitchen spotless from the evening meal while praising Jesus.

Pulling into the parking lot of his anticipated encounter, Roger James knew that the Old South Motor Court was once described as a hidden jewel of grace and hospitality by Northern tourists heading to Florida. Coach Hutchinson once told him that the place built in 1951 was nothing short of being a modern marvel of construction. Amenities including a multi-tiled swimming pool, a Southern style restaurant and grill, a fully operational truck stop along with a gift shop were advertised in national publications and billboards as far north as Boston. Two generations of tourists experienced the culinary excellence of their famous Carolina Pecan Waffles, Pee Dee Boiled Peanuts, Carolina Stone Milled Grits, Granny's Homemade Butter Biscuits, and thick slabs of Carolina Salt Cured Ham. When traffic began flowing freely down Interstate 95 in 1976, the Old South Motor Court began dying a painful death like other businesses along the Pee Dee Highway.

Waiting for Jeannie for only a few minutes, Roger took note of the deterioration of the once proud Southern destination for families and truckers in need of a good night's rest on their way to Florida. His own father talked to him about the place where local Oak Bay residents would pay fifty cents to swim in the pool for an entire afternoon. He thought of the honest hard working people who had vanished from this once vibrant place of business. It pained him to see the old place was now cluttered with the evidence of neglect disguised as empty beer cans, liquor bottles, and broken glass from the once numerous window panes. In only three short years, a new modern route of travel had reduced the thriving place of business to a bankrupt heap of disrepair. He remembered the times as a young child where he and his mother would browse through the Gift Shop with its assortment of tacky Rebel yell hats, Nothing Could Be Finer Than To Be in Carolina t-shirts, Palmetto tree ashtrays, Confederate Battle Flag license plates, and beach towels. In his mind, he could still picture one of Oak Bay's best entrepreneurs, Mr. David Carraway with his slicked back dark hair, sporting his tight white, button down shirt and black tie, handing him a bag of fireworks purchased for the fourth of July. The taste of his first ever Coca Cola flavored Icee still lingered in his mind. It pained him to know that Mr. Carraway, like many other businesses up and down the Pee Dee Highway really thought that their loyal tourist following would never abandon them for the convenience of a newly built Interstate speed track which only offered the view of pine forests and thick swamps. Mr. Carraway gambled that Southern hospitality along with the flavors of locally made fruit cakes and pies would be enough to keep the masses off the new, faster route which had no stop lights or small towns in the way to slow down traffic. Mr. Carraway held on as long as he could until the bills crashed on top of him like the weight of the world. They found him in the kitchen of the Old South Restaurant one clear morning before Christmas of 1977 swinging from a rope which offered him his only escape from creditors; some as far away as New York City.

Wiping a reminiscent tear away from his cheek, Roger noticed a large sign on the entrance of the Old South Motel which read: Help Wanted- Cooks, Waitresses and Diesel mechanics. He pondered curiously as to how long that sign had been in place. Moments later, he was suddenly startled when an older looking black man knocked on his driver's side window. The man motioned for him to roll down his window. Roger looked in his rear view mirror and side mirrors to see if anyone else was around. He then slowly began rolling down his window. Once the window was cracked, the elderly man said, "Son, I hate to tell you this, but you have a flat rear tire."

Roger, who was still startled by being parked in the abandoned Motor Court, didn't know what to do. He was scared. He didn't know if he should trust the man. He thought the worst right before the elderly man said, "Come out son, I will help you change this tire."

The man's calming tone of his voice, lured Roger out of the car. Once he shut his car door, he looked down at the rear tire and had a dual emotional reaction of both happiness and sadness. He was happy that the elderly man was actually trying to help him. He was sad because Jeannie was supposed to show up in a few minutes.

"Buzz Belton is my name. Sorry about your tire, but when you pulled in here, I knew you were in trouble."

"Thank you, Mr. Belton. My name is Rog.."

The man quickly interrupted him by saying, "Roger James. Yes, sir, I know your Daddy, Mark. Best linebacker that ever put on the Green and Gold. Excuse my language, but damn if you don't look just like old Mark. You can call me Buzz."

"Forgive me, Buzz, but how do you know my Daddy?"

"Hell, Roger, everybody in Oak Bay knows your Daddy. I even remember him bringing you and your mother here to the Motor Court when you were a small chap. You sure have grown up since the last time I remember seeing you."

Roger felt awkward as he began helping Buzz with the changing of the tire. He then said, "I'm sorry that I didn't remember you."

"No problem, Roger. It has been a long time since you stopped here. It's been a long time since there has been any business here."

"I hope you don't mind me asking, but why are you out here tonight?"

"Let's just say that an old man sometimes likes to visit the past. I live across the highway back behind that old shed. I worked here for almost thirty years. Everything was good and then the Interstate came. I watched Mr. Carraway do everything he could to save this place. It was sad. I come over here sometimes and pray for his soul. You know he wasn't in his right mind when he hung himself."

"I didn't know that."

"Mr. Carraway was a good man. He was the first White person in this town to really help Black folks. I mean to tell you he really helped people out in a lasting way. A lot of White folks in this town did not like him because of it, but he didn't care. Mr. Carraway loved every soul he met no matter where they were from or what color they were. He gave a lot of Black folks around here, jobs, store credit, and even helped some people go to college. The man was a saint, and nobody in this town even remembers him. When he hung himself it was like he never existed. The "good folks" of this town both Black and White turned their backs on him. They thought he had committed the unthinkable sin."

"That is a shame."

"What brings you out here in the middle of the night, Roger?"

"Well, I am supposed to be meeting a girl out here."

"I see… Be careful with sneakin' round with girls. That can be dangerous."

Roger smiled and replied, "She is already late. I really don't think she is going to make it."

A few minutes later after the spare tire was secured and put in place, a car drove up into the parking lot. It didn't take Roger long to realize that it was Bridget Lee's Volkswagen. She immediately jumped out of her car and said, "I have some bad news for you, Hot Rod. Jeannie sent me here to tell you that she can't come here tonight. Her mother is sick, and she has to work tonight at the One Spot. She tried to call you on your CB radio, but she did not get a response."

Roger shook his head and said, "That's just great. I'm not sure that she even likes me."

Bridget laughed and said, "Me either. That girl has all kinds of problems."

Buzz Belton then spoke up and said, "It sounds like the girl you need to be with is right here."

Roger shook his head no and Bridget yelled, "No way Mr…"

"Buzz Belton is the name and changin' tires is my game."

Roger then turned toward him and pulled out his wallet. He then said, "I'm sorry, Mr. Belton. Let me give you five dollars for your trouble."

Buzz smiled and then began walking away before he said, "No money needed, Roger James. You just tell your Daddy that old Buzz said hello and that he will always remember the best linebacker that ever played at Oak Bay High."

Once Buzz walked away, Bridget said, "That was weird."

"Yes, it was. So why did you say that Jeannie has all kinds of problems?"

Bridget replied, "I would love to talk to you about all of this, but can we go somewhere a little safer? People have been robbed at this old Motor Court. Hop in my car, and we can ride while we talk."

Jumping into her Volkswagen, Roger was dejected but he wanted to know more about Jeannie. Bridget whipped her car around in the parking lot and took off. She asked, "Where to?"

Roger asked her, "Do you know how to get to Rust Bottom Creek?"

"Sure, it's only about five miles from here."

While the rain intensified on their brief journey, Bridget unloaded what she knew about Jeannie. She said, "I don't know any of this for sure, but I have a pretty good suspicion that Teddy Branham beats Jeannie and her mother."

"What makes you say that?"

"At the beach, I saw some bruises around her ribs when she was undressing. Obviously I got nosey and kept asking her about it. That is why she was wearin' a one piece bathing suit. She told me that her Daddy had punched her a couple of times. I kept pryin', and she shut up about it. The only other thing she told me was that her mother got slapped all the time."

"Do you think that she and Dianna are prostitutes like some folks say?"

"I don't think so, but everyone in town does think that way."

"What other problems does she have?"

"Her Daddy, Teddy, seems to be her biggest problem. When Teddy gets on a big bender, she and her mother have to run the business without him. Everyone in town knows that is a fact."

Driving a few more miles, they came up to the small bridge that ran over Rust Bottom Creek. Roger yelled at Bridget, "Stop the car."

Doing as he said, she then looked at him and asked, "What now?"

"Back it up. I think that the dirt road before the bridge is where we need to go."

Backing down the small bridge without any traffic in sight they both could see the dirt road and the open pasture that was next to it. Bridget put her car into second gear, let off the clutch and drove slowly down the road. Roger then yelled, "Pull the car over here into this pasture. This is the place."

"What place?"

For the next twenty minutes, Roger explained to Bridget the story of his father and Jeannie's mother's teenage love affair. Once he was done talking, Bridget looked at Roger and asked, "Do you want to see if there is any magic here at Rust Bottom Creek tonight?"

Instantly, they both leaned over, and they began slowly kissing each other. Bridget thought about the many times she had dreamed about kissing the best looking guy at Oak Bay High. Roger thought about the many times he wondered how it would feel to be with Oak Bay's prettiest cheerleader. At the very same time, they both pushed away from each other. Bridget smiled and asked, "Any magic?"

Roger laughed and said, "It was good."

"But no magic?"

"I wouldn't describe it as magic, but it was good."

Bridget smiled and said, "You don't know how many times I wanted to do that. I don't want to be mean, but there was absolutely no magic for me."

"You really do know how to hurt a guy's pride." He then leaned back in the passenger's seat and continued by saying, "I hope you know that I care a lot about you. Ever since we were in Mrs. Simon's

English class together, you don't know how much I enjoyed it when she would make us read Shakespeare out loud together. I have also enjoyed our times together on the Prom Committee as well as serving together on the Student Council. I think maybe...

Bridget took her hand and placed it over his mouth before saying, "Look Roger, I love you like a brother. I wouldn't want to do anything to ruin our friendship."

Roger interrupted her and said, "I understand. I feel the same way. We gave it a shot, and now we know. What we don't know is if Jeannie is in trouble, if she likes me, or if she and I being together just isn't in the cards. Can we still be friends?"

"We will be friends forever, Roger James."

Chapter Twenty-One

The next morning, a low lying Carolina fog was already trying its best to roll out of Oak Bay when Luther arrived at the Main Street Amoco. Being the first person to arrive, he was somewhat startled when he walked by the Men's Restroom. Taped to the door of the Restroom was a poster board which had the words, MURDER TOOK PLACE HERE, professionally painted on it. His first inclination was to remove the poster, but after a second thought he decided that Carl needed to see it before it was removed. Rounding the corner of the station, he could hear the telephone ringing in the station lounge. Luther fumbled around for his station lounge key. The large Saunders and Haddon key dangled with about fifteen other keys which were all attached to his chrome plated, Rand manufactured retrievable key chain set. Hanging from his belt, he almost pulled loose a belt loop trying frantically to find the key. Once he unlocked the door and made his way inside the station, he answered the telephone. After saying hello he listened to a frantic lady pleading with him to send help to get her car started.

"Slow down, mam. I need an address… Thank you...We haven't opened up yet, but as soon as one of our automotive technicians arrives I will send him your way."

Once Luther hung up the phone, Roger James came through the station lounge with his service station shirt untucked and his hair still wet from his morning shower. Luther took one look at him and said, "If you want to soar with the eagles, you can't hang out all night with owls… You look like you had a late night on the town."

"No, sir.. I just couldn't sleep last night."

"Well, tuck in that shirt, then take the service truck and go see if you can get a car started at 115 Washington Street."

By the time Roger had cranked up the station's service truck, Carl, Rainey and a few more of the O.T.C.C. had arrived for their morning coffee to start the day off right. Stumpy growled at Coach Hutchison, "I thought you said you were gonna bring the donuts this mornin'?"

"I thought Gene said he would do it."

Over behind the station lounge counter, Carl began pulling cash out of a grease stained Bank of Oak Bay zipper bag to put the day's start up change in the cash register. Luther interrupted the donut debate when he asked, "Did anyone take down the sign on the Men's Restroom when y'all came in?"

Stumpy replied, "What sign?"

Luther cried out, "What sign? Are all of y'all really that blind?"

Like soldiers following their commanding officer, all of them walked behind Carl who led them outside to the Men's Room. Stumpy took one look at the sign and said, "That Crazy Bob ain't gonna let this thing alone."

Hank Burrows said, "Nobody touch it. We might be able to lift some prints off the Duct Tape."

Carl laughed and then swiped the sign off the Men's Restroom door before saying, "Crazy Bob is too smart for this. Whoever put up this sign is just piggy backin' off this accident. I'm not so sure somebody else don't want to see us fail."

Stumpy looked at Coach Hutchinson and said, "I wouldn't be surprised if the CIA and President Carter didn't have somethin' to do with this. They might have bugged us. Who knows? They may be mad about the way we talk about the President and his brother Billy around here."

Hank Burrows just shook his head and said, "I can't believe I spend my time up here with such ignorance."

Stumpy shot back, "Don't think that ain't a thing. Look at old Tricky Dick Nixon and Watergate. There ain't no tellin' how many folks Tricky Dick has killed to save his own hide."

Rainey laughed at all the foolishness he was hearing when he said, "Who knows, Mr. Stumpy, it might have been some aliens from Mars who landed here last night in Oak Bay."

Stumpy growled back at him, "Don't think that ain't a thing either. I for one have actually had the pleasure of witnessin' a flying saucer one night in Myrtle Beach."

Darryl quickly responded, "You mean a UFO."

"No, Darryl, it was a real flyin' saucer."

Hank cried out, "Good grief, I am surrounded by stupid."

Parking the service station truck in front of the car with a dead battery over on Washington Street, Roger immediately noticed something strange about the 1971 dark green Plymouth Barracuda parked in the driveway. It eerily reminded him of the car that his best friend, Stew Turbeville drove. When he jumped out of the service truck, he began walking toward the car. Before he was able to make his way to the car, he could see a woman standing in the doorway of the house. She yelled out, "Please, hurry."

He immediately recognized the lady and called out to her. He asked, "Is that you Mrs. Stanwick?"

Pausing for a moment she replied, "Is that you, Roger?"

"Yes, mam. Are the keys in the car?"

"I think so."

The middle aged woman then disappeared back into the house for a moment, giving Roger enough time to approach the front door steps of the house. When she reappeared dressed in a robe she opened the screen door, and tossed Roger a set of keys. He tried to say something to her, but she slammed the front door leaving him without saying a word.

Walking back to the car he thought it was strange that the woman who once served as his Sunday school teacher and who was also in a prayer group with his mother would not take the time to speak to him. It wasn't until he walked over to the back of the car that he understood why she didn't want to speak. The faded South Carolina Gamecock bumper sticker on the back of the car gave it away. Roger knew this car better than most. It was definitely Stew's car. He wasn't sure what to think while he opened the hood and began to look at the battery. While he cleaned the corroded battery posts, he wondered why his best friend's car was at this woman's house. A few minutes later his answer came when Stew Turbeville came flying out of the front door wearing a pair of gym shorts, a worn out Carolina Baseball t-shirt and a pair of sandals. He looked at Roger and said, "Don't look at me like that."

"Like what?"

"You know that look you always give me when you are mad with me."

"I'm not mad with..."

Stew yelled, "Hurry up, Damit, before somebody sees me here or before Mr. Stanwick gets home from workin' third shift at the poultry plant."

"What are you doin' here?"

"I know what you are thinkin', but it just happened a few months ago when she was pickin' up a pizza at the Pizza Hut. The next thing I know we are throwin' down in her car parked in the back parkin' lot."

"Isn't she your mother's best friend?"

"Not only that, she is my girlfriend's Godmother. Now get this thing cranked up before I get shot."

Roger laughed and said, "We will have to jump it off, but the salt and sand from the beach have done a job on your engine. You need to sell this car."

Once they were finally able to start Stew's car, he slapped a ten dollar bill into Roger's hand for the service call. Roger quickly put away the jumper cables while Stew drove away like a mad man. Roger then crawled into the service truck and was about to put it in reverse. He heard a banging on the window of the truck's cab. Looking up he saw Mrs. Stanwick standing there motioning for him to roll down his window. Before he could roll the window all the way down, she screamed at him, "Don't you say a word to your mother or anyone else about this, Roger James. You keep your mouth shut."

Back at the station, the morning rush was back on by the time Roger parked the station service truck. He hustled up to help out Luther who was having a hard time replacing the windshield wipers on a Datsun truck. Roger took over the task while Luther started talking to one of his church members over on Full Service aisle number two. Roger heard the elderly church member say, "Revival Service this weekend at the Fairgrounds is gonna be somethin' special. The Preach'a told Deacon Frank that what he was gonna preach about might turn this town upside down."

Luther asked, "And what would that be?"

"He didn't say. He just told me that the Preach'a told him that the Good Lord had actually paid him a visit a couple of times last week."

"Who? Frank or the Preach'a?

"The Preach'a."

"Now ain't that somethin'?"

"Yes, sir, Deacon Frank said the Preach'a told him that he picked up the Almighty, who just happened to be walkin' down the Pee Dee Highway dressed in one of those tie-dyed t-shirts and a pair of Levi jeans. He went on to say that he took the Almighty to the church parsonage and actually had a cup of coffee with him."

'You have to be pullin' my chain."

"No, I'm not, Luther, Deacon Frank said the Preach'a told him that a Revival was about to sweep over this town like we ain't never seen."

Luther later told Roger, "Either Deacon Frank has done fell off the wagon again or Preach'a Smith has some loose screws in his head. I don't care what anybody says. There ain't nobody been drinkin' coffee with the Good Lord who is in their right mind."

Inside the station lounge, Hank Burrows quietly asked Carl to take a break and go outside with him. Carl, who never questioned Hank, immediately put down a box of spark plugs which had just arrived from a NAPA auto parts delivery boy. He then obliged the most respected law man of Oak Bay without question. Walking around the corner of the building next to the U Haul trucks and trailers,

Hank looked at his friend and said, "Carl, I had an interesting conversation with Stan Hawkins yesterday. He told me about y'alls little chat the other day concernin' the Happy Mart that they are buildin' across the street."

"Is that right?"

"Carl, I am worried about this place. Stan is right. You may need to really think about sellin'."

"Not happenin."

"What are you goin' to do if you lose this possible lawsuit?"

"Honestly, Hank, I have no idea. I have put so much into this place I don't even know."

"I know you are not goin' to like what I am about to suggest, but I think it might be a good solution to your financial problems."

"What?"

"Let me call the man who sells the video poker machines."

"Oh, hell no... "

Hank, who never lost his cool, grabbed Carl by his arm and yelled, "Just listen and let me explain."

Some of the customers in the gas line couldn't help but notice Hank when he took hold of Carl. Some of the locals initially thought Hank was making an arrest, but were relieved once he let go of Carl. Hank continued by saying, "I have been thinkin' about this for a few days. The way I see it is that if you don't start video poker, the Happy Mart will. I say you get a head start on them and go ahead and get a loyal followin'. That way when they open up, our loyal video poker customers won't be tempted to go there and buy their gas. This will kill two birds with one stone."

"I don't even know if those machines are legal."

"From what I have found out, they are goin' to be legal statewide at the first of the year; however, all you have to do right now is to get a local judge to sign off, and you can start operations."

"Where would we put those machines?"

"We can take out one of the couches in the station lounge and put two or three machines there. Then if things go well, we could jam about four or five of them in the back storage rooms."

Carl scratched his head before saying, 'I'm not sure we could find a judge who would sign off because of the One Spot bein' the only place in the county where gamblin' is legally overlooked."

"In six months it ain't gonna matter. The General Assembly of the Great State of South Carolina has already spoken. Video poker is comin' to town, and we need to be the first ones with those new machines."

Carl shook his head and then said, "The only way I will do this is if you will agree to be in charge of the operations. You know I will pay you for your help."

"I really don't' want another job, but I promise to get you up and runnin'."

"I guess you need to set up an appointment with Mr. Peterhead."

"I'm way ahead of ya. Mr. Peters will be here bright and early this Friday mornin'."

Over in the station lounge, Stumpy and the rest of the O.T.C.C. peered out through the lounge window when a brand new 1979 Jaguar XJ6 pulled up to Full Service aisle number one. Rainey winked at Roger and then said, "We both need to help Mr. Luther with this one."

Gene Purdy stood up from his chair and almost pressed his face up against the station lounge window saying, "Good Lord, I bet that dang car costs more than my house."

Stumpy asked, "What kind of car is that?"

Coach Hutchinson replied, "It is British made. It is called a Jag as in Jaguar."

Gene began purring like wild cat. He cried out, "ROUW, ROUW."

Darryl said, "Gene, you need to shut the hell up before your dentures fall out."

Two hot shot looking men quickly stepped out of the fine looking car. They looked like twins as they both stood tall with dark hair, wearing a pair of Ray-Ban sunglasses, khaki pants, heavily starched white shirts, expensive looking Italian shoes, and enough gold around their necks to cause suspicion. The driver asked Luther to fill her up. Luther spoke up and said, "I'm sorry sir, but we have an eight gallon limit per vehicle. The driver turned toward Luther and pulled out his wallet, flashing him a one hundred dollar bill. Luther smiled and said, "That is nice. It's been a while since I've seen one of those around here. Obviously you misunderstood me. We have an eight gallon limit per vehicle."

The driver replied, "I heard what you said, but I am offering to pay you one hundred dollars for a fill up."

Luther shook his head before saying, "Alrighty then. Hold on. Let me go and ask my supervisor."

"Suit yourself, but as far as I am concerned you can keep the change as a tip."

Walking toward Carl, Luther took only about three steps before Rainey sprinted up to him and said, "I'll go ask Carl for you."

Once Rainey explained the situation to Carl, he sprinted back and yelled out to Luther, "He said a fill up today will be one hundred and fifty dollars. Not one cent less."

The driver of the Jag with New York plates didn't even bat an eye when he said, "That will be fine, but make sure not to allow water to spill on my hood when you wash my windshield."

Walking into the station lounge without saying a word, the two men headed straight for the station's soft drink vending machine. After retrieving their cold drinks, Stumpy asked, "Did you buy that car around here?"

The two men looked at each other momentarily, but did not reply to Stumpy. Coach Hutchinson stood up from his chair and said, "Mr. Stumpy didn't mean to offend you, two gentlemen; it's just not every day we see a fine car like yours at this station."

Finally after a long pause, the driver of the car smiled and asked, "Who is the owner of this establishment?"

Stumpy asked, "You mean this gas station?"

"Yes."

All of the members of the O.T.C.C. pointed at Carl, who was walking toward the station lounge. When Carl entered the station lounge he said, "I'd like to shake the hand of the man who just purchased twelve and a half gallons of the Amoco Oil Corporation's best gasoline for one hundred and fifty dollars."

The driver of the Jaguar smiled before he extended his hand for Carl to shake. Applying a tight grip to the hand of the stranger, Carl said, "I haven't seen a deal like this since a series of requisition snafus I witnessed over in Saigon in 1968."

All of the members of the O.T.C.C. laughed at Carl, but not one of them had the nerve to say anything, sensing that Carl was in a most serious mood because he mentioned Vietnam. Stumpy immediately whispered to Coach Hutchinson, "I don't know who these cats think they are, but when Carl starts talkin' about Nam they better watch their step or he may flashback on their fancy asses."

After shaking the hand of Carl, the driver of the Jaguar said, "My name is Wilson Martinelli. This is my brother and business associate, Francis".

Carl laughed and said, "My name is Carl, and these old fools in here are my business associates."

Wilson Martinelli smiled briefly then said, "I'll get straight to the point. Our company based out of New York City is in the business of buying and selling properties for clients who wish to remain anonymous until closing. It just so happens that I represent a client who is interested in buying your property."

Carl shook his head and replied, "Is that right? So you mean to tell me that somebody from this town wants to buy this station? Do they think they can run my station better than me?"

"Not at all. The anonymous investor is not even from this state and without saying, I do know they have no intention whatsoever in using this property in the same manner."

Coach Hutchinson asked, "What sort of business do they want to put here?"

"I'm not at liberty to say at this point of the negotiations, but rest assured it will be a business that makes everyone in this town proud."

Stumpy growled, "We already have a good barbeque joint in this town, and there is no need for another."

Gene woke up and cried out, "I can't even imagine another business on this property. I remember when they built the Blue Star Service Station way back before Carl took over this place. We have always had a gas station right here, and I don't think that will ever change."

Wilson Martinelli took one sip out of this cold drink and said, "Gentlemen, the winds of change are about to blow over this town, and this prime piece of real estate will become a part of this fantastic change."

Hank looked at him with a look of animosity and said, "You may be right about change sir, but this one sacred spot in Oak Bay has survived through three wars, two hurricanes, and seven Presidents. Carl will never sell this property."

Carl then smiled and asked, "Have you been in contact with Stan Hawkins, Oak Bay's largest real estate developer?"

"We are aware of Mr. Hawkins, but he has nothing to do with this business venture."

Carl raised his voice when he asked, "You mean to tell me that the biggest real estate developer in this town is not involved with this? What kind of monkey business is going on here?"

Wilson Martinelli laughed and then replied, "I can assure you that there is no monkey business going on here. As I stated earlier, my client is not from this state and they try their best to operate without local interference or entanglements. They always feel that local people get too emotional from a business standpoint. Our clients obviously work very closely with the local citizens whenever they finally secure their properties but in the initial stages they choose not to do so."

Stumpy then cried out, "How much money are you willin' to shell out for this joint?"

"That will be a discussion for another time, but I do know that my client is prepared to make a quite generous offer for this piece of property along with a consideration for the valuation of this business."

Chapter Twenty-Two

Officially declared a rainout at Legion Field that evening, there wasn't a cloud in the sky when Coach Fugate told his team that the playing surface was still too wet for them to play a game. Holding a bag of kitty litter in his arms, Roger looked at his best friend Stew and said, "I wish Coach would have made his decision an hour ago before we raked, shoveled, and broke our backs to get this field ready to play."

Stew wiped a clump of clay away from his forehead before replying, "I think Coach did everything he could to get this one in, but the outfield is still like a sponge full of water."

Teammate Jed Courson, holding a field rake near third base overheard them and said, "I think all of the rain in that storm decided to end up on this field."

Roger looked at him and asked, "So how are things with you and Patty?"

"We are done. It is over. She left for the beach today and won't be back for at least a week. You're not headed to the beach this weekend are ya?"

Roger laughed and replied, "No, but if I was going to the beach, she would be the last girl on earth I would try to be with."

Jed walked a little closer to Roger and said, "I think I owe you an apology."

"For what?"

"I didn't even think how you must have felt when I started seein' her. I know y'all were broke up, and you didn't mind but...

"I promise it didn't bother me at all."

"I was such a fool. I really had no idea that she was usin' me just to get back at you. Can you believe she actually had the nerve to tell me that? Who does that?"

"Count your blessin's, Jed. That girl has snakes in her head. Some good old boy here in Oak Bay will be saddled down with her in a few years, and he will hate the day he ever looked her way."

Roger then began walking toward the dugout to pick up his baseball glove and to catch up with Stew. Right outside the dugout, he put his arm around Stew's shoulder and whispered to him, "We need to talk, and you know exactly what we need to talk about."

A few minutes later both of them were in the parking lot of Legion Field leaning against the back of Roger's Mustang bogged down in a serious conversation about lust and love. Roger looked at Stew and asked, "Where do you think all of this mess with Mrs. Stanwick is goin' to get you?"

Stew took out a wad of chewed bubble gum from his mouth and stretched it out with his fingers, leaving it stretched out in his left hand. He then grabbed a small portion of Red Man chewing tobacco out of a pouch in his back pocket. Like a pro, he smoothly wrapped the bubble gum around a clump of the shredded dark leaves before sliding the wad of tantalizing exuberance into his mouth. He then replied to Roger, "Man, I don't even have a clue."

"Are you in love with Mrs. Stanwick?"

"Hell, no! I don't think so… She is just lonely and needs some lovin'."

"Love? That old lady is a married woman. You have to know that this is not goin' to turn out good for you or her."

"If you knew the things she does with me you might understand."

"I don't want to know, but you are my friend, and I hate this for you because a lot of people are goin' to get hurt once people find out."

"The only person who knows is you."

"Right now, Stupid, but this is Oak Bay, by God. You know that secrets never stay secrets in this town. One of you will make a mistake or Mr. Stanwick will pop up at the wrong time. When that day comes, I would hate to be you. God help ya if your Mama finds out. "

"Yeah, I think it would kill her to find out, but I worry more about Sarah Beth. We have been a couple for quite a long time."

"Do you love Sarah Beth?"

"Sure I do."

"Then end this craziness with the lady who is the same age as your Mama. The same crazy lady who used to teach us in Sunday School."

"Speakin' of crazy, how is your Mama handlin' the idea that you might go out with Jeannie Branham?"

Roger then went into great detail telling his best friend about his family's secret history concerning the Branhams. After hearing the tales associated with Mark James's teenage romance, Stew began laughing. He then gracefully leaned over the side of Roger's Mustang and spit out a mouth full of tobacco juice before saying, “You mean to tell me that your old man used to be with Dianna Branham? Damit boy, your Daddy really was the man back in the day. No wonder your poor Mama spends half of her day cleanin’ that trailer like the Devil and the other half of the day wrapped up in prayin’ to Jesus. It don’t take a high priced doctor to understand that you goin’ out with Jeannie would be the ultimate flashback for her.”

“I know it, but I can’t help the way I feel about Jeannie. It is more than her good looks. I really think she is special.”

“Where do ya think all this mess with Jeannie is gonna get ya?”

Roger smiled and then replied, “Touché.” He paused for a moment and then continued by saying, “I don’t have a clue how this will play out.”

While the two friends kept talking in the Legion Field parking lot, there was a prelude to the weekend Camp Meeting Tent Revival of the Oak Bay First Baptist Church during Wednesday night services several blocks away. An unusually large number of people were in attendance due to a week-long culmination of the summer’s Vacation Bible School where children from all over Oak Bay made crafts and learned about God. Inside of the large sanctuary, where literally one hundred years’ worth of church goers had been baptized and eulogized, Preacher Vince Smith was leaning against the pulpit podium while he leaned heavily on the hearts of his congregants. He shouted, “I know that some of y’all think I have lost my mind, but Jesus did come and visit with me this week. I don’t know why he chose me to reveal his plan for our world, but while we sat in the church parsonage he spoke to me just as clearly as I am speakin’ to y’all.”

With only a smattering of ‘Amens” shouted back at him, he quickly walked down the steps of the elevated pulpit. He then shouted, “Jesus told me that Revival was gonna turn this world upside down.”

Some of the reserved congregants who wondered where he was heading with his message then shouted several more ‘Amens’. By the time he was ending his message of Revival he had them all on their feet clapping when he said, “If you are puttin’ all of your trust in the President or all of the corrupt politicians then you will leave this world one disappointed soul. Y’all make sure to be at Camp Meetin’ this Saturday because that is where I will reveal what Jesus told me.”

Later that evening, Roger was shocked when he was finally able to hook up with Jeannie over the phone. She told him that she was sorry that they had not been able to meet. She also told him in so many words that she did not think that a relationship between them was in their future. However, she did want for him to be her friend. He did not like the way the conversation was heading, but he made the conscious decision to go along with her offer of “friendship”.

While they continued talking, Roger kept staring at the February cover of a Sports Illustrated magazine cover which featured swimsuit model Christie Brinkley. He had taped that cover along with two previous years’ swimsuit cover issues in a straight line across the top of his wood paneled bedroom. Those swimsuit models were surrounded by a Miami Dolphins felt pennant, one for the Atlanta Braves along with an Oak Bay High baseball hat which hung on a nail right above them all.

During their conversation, Jeannie enjoyed looking at her lava lamp which sat on a night stand next to her cozy waterbed frame. She had no modern day posters on her bare walls. She had a large picture of her and her mother taken on her fifth birthday hanging next to the door. Over her bed was a small gold plated cross tacked into the wall which had a small string of beads and ritualistic looking feathers hanging from it. Next to her doorway, sitting on her dresser drawer set was a picture of her grandmother posing in her early twenties. Anyone who saw this picture would swear it was a black and white picture of Jeannie. It was one of her most prized possessions.

Continuing their conversation, Jeannie told Roger that she felt comfortable talking to him. Laughter brought tears. Tears turned into sighs of joy. They talked and talked some more. Roger began to pry a little when he shared with her that he knew about her making out with the quarterback from the Citadel at Myrtle Beach. At first, she seemed surprised that he knew about her brief encounter with a student from the military institution; however, she did not try to hide it from him. He asked her, "Do you like him?"

"I could see us being together in another world. Right now, he is way too old for me. Besides, he will be in Charleston while I am stuck here down on this river. Long distance romances never work out."

"You have that right."

Prying a little more he asked her about her relationship with the Tucker boy. There was a long pause, then he heard her sniffling over the phone. He felt like she was crying. She played it off as her allergies flaring up."

She kept crying for a few more seconds before replying, "I'm fine, but I don't want to talk about it right now. There are too many bad memories."

Quickly changing the subject, Roger asked, "Are you coming to my game on Friday night?"

He could hear her blow her nose before she replied, "I think I will sit this one out. I think your mother needs a break from me right now. Too many bad memories for her."

"I understand, but you could sit out near the outfield away from them."

"No, thanks. This girl is not going to hide from anyone."

"When do you think we can get together?"

"I don't know. We do have all summer. Maybe we can meet at the McDonalds parking lot one night when you don't have a game."

"Sounds good to me."

After hanging up the phone, Roger decided to take a look at the Journal he had been missing out on over the past few days. Picking up where he last read, he quickly learned that in the fall of 1774 Matthew James finally completed the building of the log cabin. For Roger, this was the proof he had been looking for about the age of the building that was now sitting on the back portion of his family's property. At that precise moment he wanted to go wake up his father and tell him the news. He did not do it. He kept reading. The more he read, he thought to himself that he was so glad that he had not yet revealed the book to his father. Roger did not quite understand everything he was reading, but he deciphered enough to understand that war was coming to the colonies in 1775; the Revolutionary War. Matthew James, his great-great- grandfather was now in the middle of a conflict which he had no control. What he did have control over was his allegiance to the King of Great Britain. It appeared to Roger that Matthew James became a Loyalist. Not only was he loyal to Great Britain, it appeared that Matthew was an informant for the British regarding the people of the backwoods of South Carolina. In layman's terms he would have been considered a spy.

This information from the journal was an emotional blow to Roger. He cried a few tears before he quit reading. Once he put the book away, he wasn't sure he wanted to read any more of a journal which had revealed a family history which seemed more tainted than revered. He was emotionally drained. Briefly dozing off, Roger was suddenly awakened when he heard the sound of a car outside of his trailer window. He jumped up and could see the lights of a car that was slowly moving down the dirt road behind the trailer. Mark James was already standing in the living room with a loaded shotgun when Roger walked out of his bedroom holding his own pistol. Without saying a word they both rushed out of the trailer while Juanita James followed in her pajamas, bathrobe, and bedroom slippers. Passing by the old barn, the car could be seen heading toward the back of the property. Mark and Roger picked up their pace as Juanita kept yelling, "Who do y'all think it is?"

By the time the car came to a stop, Mark and Roger were about ten yards behind on the passenger side of the car. The engine stopped while the car lights stayed lit. A woman dressed in blue jeans and a turtle neck looking shirt opened the door of the car and was immediately startled when she saw a shotgun and pistol pointed in her direction.

"Don't shoot", she screamed.

Before Mark James could respond, a tall slender looking man jumped out of the driver side of the car and yelled, "We are sorry to disturb you."

Mark James screamed, "What in the hell are y'all doin' at 12:30 in the middle of the night?

The man responded by saying, "We wanted to take a look at the log cabin."

Mark screamed again, "At midnight? Are you people crazy?"

The woman ran her fingers through her hair before saying, "We had no idea that people actually lived all the way out here. We were told that the log cabin was near the edge of the swamp."

Juanita screamed, "I knew we should have torn down that old house. It has brought us nothin' but a lifetime of misery."

Roger asked, "All y'all from around here?"

The man replied, "No, we are not. I am sorry to disturb you and your family. My name is Don Ellis from the University of North Carolina-Wilmington. Chad Emory of the Oak Bay Historical Society gave me a call and asked me if I could come down here for a few days to take a look at the place. This is my wife Doreen."

Mark laughed and said, "You and your wife sure picked a fine time to come and visit."

Doreen spoke up and said, "Like I said earlier, we had no idea that anyone lived here until we drove up this road. Ever since Chad gave Don a call we have been so excited. Don is an expert on antiquities and ancient relics. He teaches anthropology at UNCW. He is the leading expert on the history and habits of Native Peoples in the Southeast."

Juanita cried out, "That is just great. Now go back where you came from. This site is closed."

Doreen began apologizing again when Don Ellis finally spoke up and said, "Let's go, Doreen. We have already created enough confusion for these fine folks."

Mark spoke up and said, "I think that would be a good idea. You are more than welcome to come by tomorrow during daylight hours."

Roger and his family walked back to their trailer while the Ellis couple departed. On the top step of the trailer porch, Juanita looked at Mark and said, "This is a mistake. I do not want strangers coming to look at our place anymore." Roger tried to calm her down until Mark stepped in and said, "Honey, we will work it out."

"No, Mark, God will work it out."

"That's right, Honey, the Good Lord will work it out."

Early the next morning, Roger knew that the Good Lord had not yet worked out the controversy concerning the log cabin when he heard his parents yelling at each other in their bedroom. Right before he left for work, Roger saw his father walking down the hallway from his bedroom. He smiled at this son and said, "She is still bent out of shape."

By the time Roger jumped into his car to head to work, the steamy Carolina humidity was already rearing its ugly head in Hogtail Swamp. When Carl arrived at the Main Street Amoco, Stumpy was already standing by the station lounge door carrying two large bags. Carl asked, "What's in the bags, Stumpy?"

"I bought the boys one of those new Steak Biscuits from Hardees. Everybody says they are out of this world."

"That's awfully nice of you, Stumpy. I can't remember the last time you brought any food up here except for a few bags of peanuts and some leftover birthday cake."

"I am always tryin' to make sure all these old geezers stay healthy. Feed 'em too much and they will be goners. No, sir, you never see any fat people in the nursin' homes. Fat folks don't make it that long. We need to start eatin' healthy around here."

Carl smiled and said, "Those steak biscuits ain't exactly like eatin' a salad. I'm pretty sure they would not fall into the category of health food."

"The hell you say. Steak is as healthy as it gets except for pork barbeque. I always say that people who eat salads or grass need to look at cows. Cows eat grass all day long, and they are all pretty fat."

Once the rest of the O.T.C.C. arrived at the station, Coach Hutchinson was the first one to ask the most pressing question on their minds when he asked, "Do you put ketchup or mustard on these biscuits?"

Darryl replied, "It depends on how you were raised. Some like ketchup while some like mustard."

Stumpy said, “It don’t matter. You can’t go wrong with this biscuit.”

Hank Burrows stood up from his chair and changed the subject when he asked, “Are you all goin’ to make it to Kirby’s funeral tomorrow afternoon at the Church of Christ?”

Stumpy asked, “Do they already have his body back from Charleston?”

Carl replied, “They say his body will be back by tomorrow afternoon.”

Darryl said, “I had no idea Kirby was a member of the Church of Christ. I guess you never know everything about the folks we see every day.”

Gene said, “I try not to judge religions, but I have to say that the Church of Christ crowd is a little different. No piano playin’ is allowed in the church, and they just seem a little too happy for me.”

Hank Burrows laughed and said, “I never knew Kirby to be a church goer so I’m guessing that is where Mrs. Essie attends church.”

Darryl said, “You know people are dyin’ today that have never died before. In all seriousness, it really doesn’t matter where your funeral takes place. Once you're gone, it doesn't matter.”

Stumpy stood up from his chair and said, “Now that ya mention it, y’all know what scares me about dyin’?”

Hank replied, “Boy howdy… I can’t wait to hear this.”

Stumpy took another bite of his Hardee’s steak biscuit before saying, “I’m scared as hell of Eugene Fillard and his weird actin’ brother at the funeral home proddin’ and probin’ around on my naked body. On top of that, I really don’t want Eugene pulling up my underwear and pants over my fat rear end. Do y’all know how embarrasin’ that is gonna be for me? I am gonna be one pissed off soul if I find out those brothers really are queer.”

Luther spoke up and said, "You can worry about somethin' else because even if they are a little light in the loafers, no man or woman in their right mind would ever look at you in a sexual way, you old Fool."

Hank held up his hand and said, "I vote with you, Luther. Sex and Stumpy are not anything somebody would ever consider."

Stumpy laughed and said, "Don't be jealous. I had one gal at the Big Pig Barbeque Hut tell me one time that instead of wantin' to go to Disneyland; she wanted to go to Stumpyland."

Rainey spoke up and said, "Paying customers always get told whatever they want to hear, Mr. Stumpy. I bet that lady cost you a fortune."

Carl laughed with all of the members of the O.T.C.C. before he spoke and said, "Don't let us forget that today is Flag Day. We need to take a moment to honor Old Glory before we start the day."

Every one of the old-timers shuffled over to the center of the station lounge and faced the American Flag which was hanging on the back wall behind the cash register. Carl brought it home with him from Vietnam, and it was the first thing he put up in the station lounge when he began business. On this most solemn of occasions, everyone began reciting the Pledge of Allegiance once Gene Purdy yelled out, "I Pledge Allegiance…"

Once the Pledge was recited, Stumpy put his arm around Carl and said, "She still looks good after all these years."

Carl wiped a few tears away from his eyes before saying, "I still wake up each mornin' and thank my lucky stars for allowin' me to get back home in one piece."

Darryl, who had earlier been reading the station's June issue of *Life* held it up and said, "It says here that Marlon Brando will be starring in Apocalypse Now which is a movie about Vietnam coming out later this summer. There is also a big article about the Scariest Roller Coaster Rides. I can't wait to read about that."

Stumpy cried out, "Y'all know I have a lot of folks who tell me that I look just like Marlon Brando."

Hank spoke up and said, "I'm out of here on that one. I have some business down at the Courthouse."

All of the chatter and laughter of the O.T.C.C. came to a screeching halt right before the station officially opened as the station bell began ringing loudly. Carl cried out jokingly, "Best go ahead and report to your battle stations. We might as well open up and get this crowd out of here."

People were already lined up for gas when the pumps were turned on. Tempers over the price of gas were still flaring as Carl and Coach Hutchinson did their best to calm the nerves of customers who felt betrayed by the high price of gasoline. Out on Full service aisle number two, Roger and Rainey were doing their best to convince one of their local patrons that Carl was not some oil baron controlled by sheiks from the Middle East. Local farmer Claude Witherspoon, who was purchasing five gallons of gasoline for his Jon Boat sitting on a trailer hooked up to his pickup truck, proclaimed loudly, "Old Carl has sold us out. He chose money over servin' the people."

Hearing this exchange, Luther walked over to Full Service aisle number two and smiled at his old friend before saying, "Claude, I have to give you credit. You have figured it out. Carl Norman went to the jungles of Vietnam, got shot, came back home to Oak Bay, opened a gas station, joined the Middle Eastern Oil Mafia, and is now going to move to Arabia to become a sheik with a harem full of women by his side. Yeah boy, you are the smartest SOB in all of Oak Bay."

Rainey couldn't help himself when he looked at the old farmer and said, "Don't tell anyone Mr. Witherspoon, but when Carl dresses up in his new thawb and head scarves; he looks like he belongs in the Middle East."

Carl, who missed the Middle Eastern allegations against him, was busy standing next to the 'Fish Camero' in the station's parking lot. Billy Bradford, who had come by with a nephew to pick up the aromatically challenged vehicle, looked at Carl and said, "I don't smell anything out here, but I am scared to open it up and get in."

Carl replied, "Rainey and Hot Rod Roger did a good job. I've tried all morning to find even the slightest whiff of fish, and so far it is good."

Stumpy added his two cents by saying, "Those boys had a helluva time gettin' all of the fish scales out of the carpet and upholstery."

Billy smiled at Stumpy and said, "Lord knows I tried, but every time I got in this car, I would almost puke." He then looked at his twenty-five year old nephew and motioned for him to jump in on the passenger side of the car. They both sat in the car for a few minutes before they began sniffing all around the seats like two trained hound dogs. With one last good sniff, Billy yelled out, "It is a miracle. I don't smell a thing. How much do I owe ya?"

Without pausing Carl quickly replied, "One hundred dollars."

Billy Bradford smiled, pulled out his wallet and handed the money to Carl. He then said, "I will be back for my money if the smell returns in the afternoon heat."

Carl smiled and said, "All work at the Main Street Amoco is always guaranteed."

By the time Carl and Stumpy walked back into the station lounge, Hank Burrows walked into the station, returning from the Oak Bay Courthouse with some news he wanted to share with the O.T.C.C. He was smiling like a chessy cat when he said, "I talked to several people at the Courthouse and found out some interestin' news."

Gene Purdy woke up and said, "Well, spit it out, Hank."

Hank said, "This station is not the only property the Martinelli Brothers would like to purchase. They have already bought the vacant lot a block away and have made offers to almost everyone in a two block radius. I have never seen Stan Hawkins so upset. He can't believe these New York city slickers have come down here and are beatin' him to the punch."

Coach Hutchinson asked, "What are they trying to do?"

"Stan said he found out what they were up to when they closed on the vacant lot owned by Old Man Tiller. The deed of record was written to a Company called New Image Partners, Ltd. out of Chicago."

Stumpy growled, "What do people in Chicago want with this station?"

Hank laughed and said, "Y'all ain't gonna believe it. They aim to put one of those new fully covered shopping malls right here in the middle of our town."

Gene cried out, "The world is comin' to an end. A mall here in Oak Bay? That is the dumbest thing I have ever heard."

Carl said, "There is no way they could handle all of the traffic that goes along with a shopping mall."

Hank Burrows looked out of the station lounge window and pointed to the side of the building. He then said, "They have thought of everything. They aim to put a three story parkin' garage right over there."

Stumpy screamed, "Carl, don't you sell this place. This town will never be the same once they bring in those fancy boutiques, food places, and electronic billboards. We will spend our last days sittin' on fancy store benches, havin' to make sure we dress proper, and havin' to watch what we say in public. Life in Oak Bay won't be worth livin'."

Carl laughed and said, "Worry about somethin' else, Stumpy. They will be pumpin' gas at this station long after we all kick the bucket."

Stumpy smiled and replied, "That is what I like to hear… A man with vision."

Chapter Twenty-Three

An hour later, the Oak Bay County Coroner made his way to the Main Street Amoco. Everyone in the O.T.C.C. knew exactly what he had in his hand when he made his way out of his car carrying a big brown envelope. Roger and Rainey who were busy servicing two cars and a truck on Full Service aisle number two made eye contact with Luther who then walked over to them and said, "I guess the results are in. I bet Carl is as nervous as a whore in church."

Carl, who was busy patching a tire in mechanic's bay number one, looked up and yelled at Stumpy, "Tell the Coroner to come on out here and give me the news."

Once Coroner Calvin McDavid was directed by Stumpy, Coach Hutchinson and the rest of the O.T.C.C. made their way closer to the mechanics bay entrance so they could hear the results. Coroner McDavid stepped into the bay and said, "I have some good news."

The Coroner, whose formal training was his experience as the Manager of the Meat Department at the Oak Bay Piggly Wiggly before being elected ten years prior, smiled and said, "Forgive me for being late, but the Sheriff had me in his office for a big meeting with SLED. It looks like they are about to make an arrest concerning the murder of Senator Broadway. They are pretty sure they have their man."

Carl smiled and replied, "That is good news. Who is it?"

"I can't say right now, but the news people are camped out at the courthouse. I'm pretty sure they will make the announcement today." He paused and then continued by saying, As far as your case goes, I don't think there will be a judge in these parts who will entertain any of this once they have a look at these results. Kirby Davis registered a BAC well over the state's legal limit for being considered intoxicated."

"Is that right?"

Coroner McDavid looked around into the station lounge understanding that he had the attention of the O.T.C.C. when he concluded by saying, "I have to admit that I was surprised. All I can say is that Mr. Davis had to be drinkin' a lot of Vicks 44 or Listerine to have such a high alcohol level if he wasn't slippin' into the beer or hard licka. I didn't ask the boys in Charleston, but I would think his liver had to be pickled."

Stumpy cried out, "Who cares what he drank. The most important thing is that our town drunk lived up to his obligation of bein' drunk when it counted the most.

Coach Hutchinson said, 'God bless, Old Kirby."

Gene Purdy laughed and said, "God bless whoever helped him get so drunk."

Darryl laughed and said, "I think we need to call this VB day."

Stumpy yelled, "Why VB Day?"

"Victory over Bob, of course."

A few minutes later Coach Hutchinson walked out to Full-service aisle two and yelled at Roger saying, "Roger, you have a phone call. It sounds like a sweet little girl. You better hurry."

Roger walked into the station and picked up the phone receiver. The entire O.T.C.C. including Carl watched him while he answered the phone. Roger said, "I see. Well, I guess I can. Calm down. I will be there in twenty minutes." He then hung the phone up and looked at Carl before he asked, "Carl, would it be all right if I leave a few minutes early today?"

Carl smiled and asked, "What's wrong. Are you havin' some lady problems, Hot Rod?"

"More than you could imagine."

A few minutes later, Hank Burrows yelled out to everyone at the station, "Y'all come in here and look at the television. They have made an arrest for the murd'a of Senator Broadway."

The entire O.T.C.C. and several customers crowded around the station lounge television set and listened as a young news reporter from Channel Five in Charleston made the announcement from the Oak Bay County Courthouse only a few blocks away. He said, "Two men have been arrested for the murder of State Senator Dennis Broadway. The senator was killed almost two weeks ago. Today the lead investigator from the South Carolina Law Enforcement Division, Cabe Ivey announced that 51 year-old Brian "Buzz" Belton and 50-year old Theodore "Teddy" Branham have been arrested. Authorities tell Channel Five News that Belton and Branham killed

Senator Broadway at the One Spot Bar and conspired to cover up the murder by staging a fake automobile accident on the Billy Richardson Bridge on the edge of the Oak Bay city limits. This is Frank Rivers reporting for Channel Five News in Oak Bay."

Luther looked at Roger and said, "You better go see that girl. I bet she is devastated."

Carl hopped right in by saying, "Go, Hot Rod. Go right now."

Roger sat in the Hardee's parking lot for about ten minutes before Jeannie arrived in her mother's Ford Torino. He could tell by the way that she looked that she was troubled. Before she made her way out of her car, he could see her putting out a cigarette. He could barely hear her due to the noise of the traffic going down Main Street when she said, "Thanks for coming here." She then began to cry like a little girl. Standing in between their cars, Roger put his arms around her and let her continue to cry. People inside of the restaurant peered out while he embraced her. She cried hard and long. He could not get her to calm down. He thought he might have to call somebody to help him. He was at a loss. She then suddenly held her head up and said, "They took my father away this morning. I think my mother is in shock."

"I heard. I am so sorry."

Roger then walked her over to a cement bench next to where they were parked. Once seated, Jeannie looked at him and asked, "Can I trust you?"

"Sure, Jeannie. You can tell me whatever is on your mind, and I will never tell a soul."

He knew that she needed to talk, but once she began talking he wished like hell that she had never confided in him. Fighting through a few coughs and many tears, Jeannie Branham unbottled some deep dark secrets that had been driving her crazy. Crazy Daisy began laying her troubles on Roger while looking at the ground most of the time. She said, "You may not know this, but my father has been making me work on my back since I was fourteen years old. I tried to resist for a long time, but Teddy was brutal. My mother gave in a long time ago. She said I would get used to it. They both made me feel like it was my responsibility to help out with the family business. I'm so ashamed of what I have been doing. Excuse my language, but I have serviced truckers, low-life suckers, and some pretty bad mother fu…" Roger interrupted her by placing his index finger over her lips. She quickly removed his finger and continued by saying, "My father has made me be with men old enough to be my grandfather." She then held her head up and looked Roger in the eyes before saying, "You need to know all this because I am rotten to the core. I have done things that are the absolute worst. I'm not like you and Bridget. You two are good people. Roger, you have a good heart and everyone in this town idolizes you. I say all this because as much as I care for you, I know that I could never let someone as good as you be involved with me. I hate my life! I even once planned to kill myself until I met Dale Tucker by accident a few years ago at the Peach Basket Ice Cream Shop. When Dale and I started going out with each other, I took a chance and told him what my Daddy was making me do. Dale was a really good guy. He was a lot like you." She stopped and then said, "I don't know why I am telling you all this."

Roger took hold of her arm and said, "Go ahead and tell me. I swear I will not tell anyone. You obviously need to get this off of your chest."

Fighting back tears, Jeannie then said, "Anyhow, Dale confronted my father one night at the One Spot and let him have it regarding me. They ended up fighting in the One Spot right in front of the main bar. Dale ended up getting the hell beat out of him, but not after hurting my father pretty bad. Before I was able to get Dale out of the One Spot, my father told him that he was a dead man. A few weeks later Dale ends up getting killed while I am sitting in his truck. Do you know who ran over him?"

"No, I do not, but I thought it was an accident."

"The other person they arrested today, Buzz Belton, was the same man who ran over Dale."

Roger asked, "Why do you think he ran over Dale on purpose?"

" Because I know he did."

"How do you know that?"

"Because a few weeks ago I saw him talking to my father in the One Spot. I immediately recognized him from the accident. I had never seen him there before. I thought it was odd that he would be talking to my father. They talked for a long time. When I finally asked my father about it later that night he told me to mind my own damn business. He seemed rather disturbed that I was asking about this man. I began thinking and wondered if Dale's accident was really an accident. I then remembered that Buzz Belton never tried to brake when Dale was killed. Of course, he said he never saw Dale at the scene of the accident, but I questioned that several days after Dale's funeral. Then I remembered that my father told me back then to get over it. He said I was being stupid moaning over a piece of crap like Dale. The night after I saw Buzz in the One Spot I asked my father again after he was good and drunk. My father can't keep his mouth shut when he drinks so he told me what I already suspected."

"What was that?"

"That he paid Buzz Belton to kill my boyfriend."

"Your Daddy had Dale Tucker killed?"

"Yes, he did. Once I found out, I went off the deep end. My father slapped me around a little and then told me to get back to work. My mother later told me that Buzz owed my father so much money from gambling at the One Spot years ago that my father had him over a barrel. Once the Old South Motor Court went out of business evidently Buzz couldn't pay my father back what he owed."

"This is so crazy. I just met that guy the other night. He seemed like a nice guy." Roger paused for a moment and continued by saying, "I know you are upset that your Daddy may go to prison or the electric chair, but you should be a little happy that you are now out of the situation."

Jeannie looked at him and said, "It's not that simple."

"What do you mean?"

"My father did not kill Senator Broadway."

"Who killed him?"

"I did."

With those words, Roger almost fell off the cement bench. He looked at Jeannie and asked, "You did what?"

With her eyes filled with some of the most tormented tears he had ever seen, Roger listened to her with alarming curiosity when she replied, "That night when my father slapped me around, my next customer was Senator Broadway." She then threw her hands up before she continued to say, "He just happened to be in the wrong place at the wrong time. On that night when he was done with, me, he threw his money at me and said, "I can't believe I drove all the way from Moncks Corner for that. My wife puts on a better show when she is drunk."

Jeannie continued, "I don't know what happened to me, but when he said those words something raged inside of me. I think that at that moment I lost my mind. I quickly went over to my purse that was next to the night stand and pulled out a knife. I always keep it in my purse." She then reached down and opened her purse where Roger could see the knife.

Roger cried out, "Hold on, don't pull that out right here." Closing her purse, Jeannie then continued by saying, "I stabbed him right in his back while he was putting on his shirt. I stabbed him many more times before we both fell to the floor. It all seems like a blur now, but the next thing I remember is my father and Buzz Belton standing over a dead man planning a way to get rid of his body. They both had been drinking and argued for several minutes about what would be the best way to dispose of the body. After cussing me out several times, they decided that they would push his car off the bridge to make it look like an accident. Of course, we know now that they should have just buried him. My idiot father had Buzz go up on the Richardson Bridge late that night and cut loose several steel beams directly over the rocky portion of the river. While Buzz was working on the bridge, my father made me help him load up the trunk with several jugs of gasoline from our shed. They thought that when the car hit the rocks, it would explode and the authorities would not be able to tell what happened to the Senator. It was a stupid idea, not very well thought out. After cutting the bridge, Buzz came back to the One Spot to help my father drag the Senator's body outside to his car. My father made me go with him and watch the whole thing. Buzz almost went over that bridge before he jumped out of the Senator's car. Some of the steel railing became tangled under the front axle not allowing the car to fall into the river. Buzz and my father then pushed the car over the bridge. We waited for a few minutes hoping for an explosion. There was no explosion. When we looked over the bridge, we all realized that the car bounced off the rocks and flipped into the water. We then drove Buzz to his house. By the time we returned to the One Spot, the police had been contacted about a wreck on the bridge."

Roger did not know what to say. He sat quiet for a few minutes before Jeannie said, "I'm sorry that I told you this, but I had to tell somebody."

Roger asked, "So you had just gone through all of this when I saw you at the beach?"

"Yes, that's right. That is why I went to the beach. My mother thought it would be a good idea if I left town for a few days."

"So how did the law figure all this out?"

"I'm not quite sure, but I think it had to do with one of his aides who told the authorities that he knew that the Senator was at the One Spot that night. SLED and the Sheriff's Department have been camped out there ever since. I am sure that somebody must have seen the Senator that night because he was a loud and obnoxious man who drank like a fish. Also that night when they were putting the Senator's body in his car, somebody was in the parking lot and saw them. Before my father and Buzz could catch up with whoever it was, they had vanished. I have to believe that the mystery person may have turned them in."

After a few minutes of not saying a word, Roger looked at Jeannie and said, "I would think that your Daddy would keep his mouth shut trying to protect you from going to prison."

"You don't know Teddy. He would sell his soul to the Devil if he thought he could get out of this. I have no doubt that it won't be long until I am arrested."

Later that evening after American Legion baseball practice ended, Roger wanted to tell somebody about Jeannie's insurmountable problem. He felt like she immediately needed a lawyer and possible psychiatric help down the road. He did not know which one she needed the most. It was killing him not knowing what to do. It was the one time in his life he wished he could talk to his Daddy. Deep down he knew that his Daddy would steer him in the right direction. He came within an eyelash that evening of spilling his guts to his Daddy when his mother began raising some hell at their trailer. Out of the blue, she verbally assaulted Mark James worse than usual. She insisted that he get rid of the old house. She was convinced that God did want it on their property. The taming of her distorted tongue could not be squelched no matter how many times Mark told her that he would take care of removing the log cabin. Roger thought to himself that his father had to be a saint for the way he calmly handled his mother. He wondered why his father stayed in a marriage that was so one-sided. It was the first time in his life where Roger would not have blamed him if he decided to pack his bags and leave.

Once his parents finally retired for the evening, Roger went to his bedroom in hopes of getting a good night of sleep. He tossed and turned as he kept thinking about Jeannie and thinking about all that he learned. He now began to question whether he wanted to be involved with a girl who had murdered a man. He thought- if she could murder once, she certainly could do it again. All kinds of thoughts rushed through his head. He was very tormented.

Not being able to sleep, he decided to look again at the journal under his bed. Knowing that his relative, Matthew James, was a Loyalist informant for the British, Roger was not too interested in what else the journal would reveal until he began reading further. To Roger's surprise he learned that Matthew was involved in helping a few Patriots hide in and around Hogtail Swamp to avoid being captured by a regiment of British troops who were desperately looking for them. Deciphering what was written, it then occurred to

Roger that Matthew was playing both sides of the fence early in the war, but had made the decision to help with the Revolution.

Matthew wrote about a fierce battle at a place called Mingo Creek in the Lowcountry where many American troops had to flee for their lives. Some of those soldiers fought with American Revolutionary War hero Francis Marion. The group of men were hidden and aided by Matthew and the local Indians known as the River People.

Once Francis Marion found out that his men were protected and survived during an usually cold November, he wanted to show his gratitude by protecting the people who had risked their own lives to help his troops. Matthew, who believed he owned the parcel of land he was living on was later told by Francis Marion that there was no record of title showing that Matthew was the proprietor of the land deep in the backwoods of South Carolina. When Matthew told Francis Marion that he had bought the land from a British land regulator named Simon, Francis Marion informed him that the land regulator had been hanged in Charleston for his misdeeds of fraud and corruption.

Francis Marion then took it upon himself to write a treaty to give the land in question to Matthew James. He also went a step further when he gave unsettled lands around the Pee Dee River to the scattered tribe he called the River People. As Roger kept reading he learned that the documentation regarding this so-called “treaty” was buried on a high piece of ground in Hogtail Swamp in a chest specifically made for the protection of the parchments. Roger could not believe that his ancestor specifically mapped out how to find this treasure chest at a place he was very familiar with. He was so excited he wanted badly to go in the swamp that very moment and see exactly what was in that chest.

He thought long and hard for about ten minutes before he realized that he was now in way over his head. Sanity prevailed when he decided the best thing to do was to reveal what he had learned from the journal to his father. Two hours later he tiptoed into his parent's room and gently shook Mark James. His daddy looked up at him and asked, "What time is it?"

"Four o'clock."

For the next two hours Mark James was given a rundown on a journal that he never knew existed. When Roger gave him the news about their Swedish heritage, Mark James looked at his son and said, "Oh, well, I guess we can call ourselves Vikings."

Once Roger showed his father the writings associated with the parchment chest, Mark said, "The best thing we can do now is to get Chad Emory and that archeologist from UNC-Wilmington involved. Even if we were to find it, they would know exactly what the parchments mean. I will get in touch with them this morning."

By the time a sleepy Roger walked into the station lounge the next morning everyone wanted to know how Jeannie was holding up. Roger did not have much to say so they left him alone. A few minutes later they all began congratulating Coach Hutchinson on being named to the Oak Bay High School Hall of Fame. Stumpy held up the front page of the *Oak Bay Gazette Sports* Section which prominently displayed a picture of the retired coach and administrator. He yelled, "Congrats, Coach Hutch. To the best coach this town has ever seen, we all salute you."

Coach Hutchinson, who did not like being recognized one bit, choked up when he replied, "Our success at Oak Bay High was because we had good players who were also fine young men of character."

Carl laughed before saying, "He sure ain't talkin' about me. He used to call me a dumb ass at least once a day."

Coach Hutchinson smiled and then said, "You all know that is not true."

A stunned Rainey spoke up and asked, "You played football for Coach Hutchinson?"

Carl smiled before replying, "I sure did, and I hated his Yankee ass for a long time. Then when I went through basic training at Fort Jackson, I quickly realized that there wasn't a thing my Drill sergeant could say or do to me that Coach Hutchinson hadn't already done. That's when I began to appreciate Coach. Now don't get me wrong, I was one of the worst football players who ever suited up for Oak Bay High, but Coach Hutch will tell y'all that I would fight better than most."

Coach Hutchinson laughed and said, "Carl would fight, but most importantly he would do whatever I asked him to do. I remember one game against Wallace High School where I told Carl he needed to kill their center. Carl literally tried to kill the poor boy. He karate chopped the Wallace starting center in his throat on the second play of the game. They had to cart the boy off the field while Carl got thrown out of the game. We ended up winning handily because they couldn't handle a snap from the new backup center. After the game, I looked for Carl in the locker room and in the visiting stands. I couldn't find him anywhere. I thought he may have hitched a ride home. Walking to the team bus, I noticed that it was cranked up and running. I thought that was strange since I had the bus keys in my pocket. As I got closer I saw Carl sitting in the driver's seat of the bus that he had hardwired to start the engine. That evening the most valuable player of the game ended up driving us home knowing that he had done what I asked him to do. I also knew then he was definitely mechanically inclined."

Roger whispered to Rainey, "My Daddy says that Coach Hutch was so mean in his younger days that he would paddle his players during practice when they missed a block or screwed up an assignment. He said that Coach Hutchinson would make them bend over right in the middle of a drill and take their licks from a big wooden paddle that everyone in Oak Bay called 'The Rainmaker'."

Rainey whispered back, "Why did they call it the Rainmaker?"

'Because there wasn't a boy at Oak Bay who had ever been hit by that paddle who didn't shed a few tears or cry like a little girl. Daddy says that a blow from the Rainmaker was like setting your ass on fire."

"That sounds pretty brutal. It kind of reminds me of slavery. I bet he couldn't get away with that these days."

"Why do you think he is retired? He used the Rainmaker one time too many on the wrong person when he became the Principal at Oak Bay High."

Raney then asked, "So how is Jeannie taking the news about her father?"

Roger cleared his throat before saying, "She is taking it pretty hard. It is a mess."

Right before the station bell began to ring with the day's first customers, Carl said, "I checked out the pump reservoirs this mornin', and we will be lucky to stay open till lunch time. Because of that, we will shut down early. This will also give everybody time to get to Kirby's funeral this afternoon."

Once outside of the station lounge Luther walked up to Roger and said, "Now don't feel like you have to go to Kirby's funeral today. I know you have a big game tonight."

Before Roger could reply, Rainey yelled from mechanics bay number one saying, “Carl wants me to service this Chrysler truck right now. I will be out there once I am done.”

Looking over at Rainey, Roger was almost run over by a white Corvette which came in for a landing on Full Service aisle number two. Roger was about to yell at the older gentleman driving the Corvette when Luther yelled, “What the hell? You almost ran over this young man.”

The elderly man wasted no time in opening his door and jumping out of his car. Roger thought for sure that the man was going to attack Luther so he quickly made his way toward them. The driver yelled out, “I apologize. I thought I was pressing the brake, and I guess you know I didn’t.”

Luther growled at him, “You need to be more careful. That is how people get killed.”

The driver smiled and replied, “You are absolutely right. Please accept my apology.”

Roger stepped in and asked, “What can we do for you, sir?”

“You wouldn't happen to be Hot Rod Roger James would you?”

“Yes, sir. That is me?”

“You move pretty fast on this concrete. I have heard you also move pretty fast on a baseball diamond along with some other qualities that are pretty impressive.”

Roger laughed and then said, “I guess that all depends on who you talk to.”

“My name is Dan Dudley. I am a scout for the Atlanta Braves baseball organization.”

Luther asked, “ Are you here to watch Roger play ball tonight?”

“Actually I just drove here to get some good gas. I’m just kidding. Yes, sir, I am here to watch Roger. I arrived here late last night after watching a game in Cheraw. I watched a kid named Ty Gainey who is an unbelievable player. I hope we have a shot with him in this year's draft because I know we would be lucky to get him. The folks over in Cheraw also had great things to say about Roger. They said he's not only a good pitcher, but he carries a mighty powerful stick when he goes to bat. "

Roger smiled but not nearly as much as Luther who said, "He's not only a great ball player; he is a great young man."

"That's what I've been told. I assure you that the Atlanta Braves would not be wasting my time if our organization didn't think Roger was a special young man. I didn't drive here last night just because some local yokel from Cheraw said I needed to come to Oak Bay. I've had Roger on my radar for quite some time." He then looked at Luther and asked, "Are you related to Roger?"

Without hesitation Luther replied, "We are not blood kin, but he is like a grandson to me."

While taking the handle and hose off of the gas pump, Roger couldn't help but notice a radar gun in the backseat of the Corvette sitting on top of two cases of Levi Garret chewing tobacco. He asked the scout from Atlanta, "Is that a hand held radar gun in your car?"

"Why, yes, it is. We are now using these new babies when we scout. Have you ever been clocked on one of these guns?"

"No, sir. I've never seen a real one except at the County Fair. I knew that gun at the County Fair was screwed up when it recorded me at 119 miles per hour last year. I won a big teddy bear that night and received a lot of pats on my back, but I knew that gun was a piece of junk." Grabbing a windshield squeegee Roger then continued by saying, "Coach Hutchinson tells everyone in town that I throw harder than anyone he has ever coached."

"Did you say Coach Hutchinson?"

"Yes, sir."

"Is that old son of a gun still coaching ball?"

"No, sir, he has retired, but he is sitting inside of the station lounge if you would like to speak to him."

"The keys are in it. Fill it up, then pull it around to the parking lot while I go in here to see an old friend. I haven't seen that son of a gun in years."

A reunion of old friends took place in the Main Street Amoco lounge when Dan Dudley surprised the legendary coach from Oak Bay who was still being talked about by Stumpy as being the greatest coach of all time. After Roger parked Dan Dudley's car, he walked into the lounge with Rainey. They both wanted to see the reunion of old friends. After the two friends from years past shook hands and hugged, Coach Hutchinson asked, "What brings you to Oak Bay?"

He pointed over at Roger and said, "That young man right there. We just met a few minutes ago."

Coach Hutchison smiled and said, "He's a good one. Are you still scouting for Cincinnati?"

"I haven't been with them for about two years now. They tried to put me out to pasture, but thank God the Braves still thought that I knew a little something about baseball."

Stumpy interrupted the conversation by saying, "You just missed it, Dan. Old Coach Hutchinson just learned that he was being inducted into the Oak Bay High School Hall of Fame."

"That is outstanding! Congratulations, Hutch… I sure would like to be at the Induction Ceremony. Lord knows I would love to tell some of the stories I have on this guy."

Stumpy laughed and then asked, "How do you know Coach Hutch?"

"Oh, we go way back. I've known this rascal since we were in high school together in Upstate New York. A little thing called World War II sent us on our separate ways." The professional baseball scout who had a lifetime of ballpark sun ground into his skin smiled and said, "A funny thing happened that I still can't believe. Two boys from a small town in New York end up fighting in Europe for three years without a scratch on us. I ended up with an Airborne Division of the Third Army. As fate would have it, I missed my landing mark and found myself in the woods right outside of a town called Dinant in Belgium. The next thing I know, I am being chased through a thicket near a farm by about ten or fifteen Nazi soldiers. I made it to a large barn where I jumped into a water trough and covered myself in hay. I guess they saw me go into the barn because a few minutes later, they were blasting the barn with every bullet they could fire. I laid in that trough and prayed like I have never prayed. I could feel the bullets popping over my face, underneath me, and all around the barn, but I stayed still and motionless. A few seconds turned into what seemed to be about two hours. Then in one more rapid succession of fire, the top of the water trough was shattered so badly the top railings were blown up into a pile of splintered wood chips. If it wasn't for the steel tips in the top of my boots I would have lost all of my toes. The tops of those boots were blown to shreds. Just as I thought the shooting had ended, one more shot rang out and it hit me in my right elbow." Laughing for a second or two, Dan continued by saying, "I haven't been able to straighten it out since that day. When I yelled due to the pain, I knew I was a dead man. I closed my eyes and boom; the biggest explosion I have ever heard sent a wave of heat over my body. A few seconds later the shooting stopped, and I began to hear the sound of a large truck. I crawled out of what was left of that water trough and looked outside through a crack in the boards of the barn.

I was so excited to see a tank from the US Second Armored Division. Once outside of the barn I heard a voice coming from the tank yelling, "Hey, Dudley, is that you?" I took a closer look, and there was my old high school buddy from Glen Park, New York waving at me from the top of an armored division M24 Chaffee Tank. Coach Hutch's dead-eyed shot from a tank in the woods of Belgium saved this old boy, and I will never forget it."

Coach Hutchinson coughed a few times and then said, "Now that's enough of that. Dudley has always been known to tell a good tale."

Gene Purdy cried out, "Damit, Hutch, this is the first time I have ever heard this story. I didn't even know you served in combat."

Coach Hutchinson said in a stern voice, "I drove a tank, Mr. Gene. I simply drove a tank. I wouldn't exactly call that combat. The real heroes are those boys like Luther, Carl, and Dudley who had their boots on the ground. They are the ones who had to actually fight. All I did was drive a tank."

A few minutes later standing next to Full Service aisle number one, Rainey asked Luther, "Did you know about Coach Hutchinson serving in World War II?"

"I did know because he is a member of the Oak Bay VFW post and the American Legion. Obviously I didn't know about him drivin' a tank. That is the first time I have ever heard anything about his service during the war."

Roger laughed and said, "That is what drives me crazy about you, old guys. All of you seem to keep all this stuff of great significance all bottled up. I have known Coach Hutchinson all of my life, and I didn't even know he served in the war. On top of that, I also learned today that Carl played football for Coach Hutchinson. My own father has never shared any of this with me."

Rainey shook his head and said, "Roger is right, Mr. Luther. How come, you old guys, never talk about the things like serving in the war or many other events which describe your personal achievements?"

"I don't know. I guess it's because nobody ever asks."

Roger said, "That's what is wrong with you, old guys. It really seems like it is hard for y'all to express yourselves."

Luther smiled and replied, "That's what is wrong with your generation. Y'all don't know when to keep your mouths shut. You two better learn that not everybody wants to hear about your emotions or your darn feelin's. The sooner you learn that, the better off y'all will be. My generation believed that we were just a part of the world. Your generation believes the world should revolve around each of you."

Roger asked jokingly, "What other treasures have you kept hidden from us?"

Luther laughed and replied, "Well, let's see... Did you boys know that the American Legion has fielded a baseball team right here in Oak Bay since 1931?" After pausing and receiving no reply he continued by saying, "And I guess that you did not know that American Legion Baseball was started so that young people could have the opportunity to develop their skills, personal fitness, leadership qualities, and to have fun."

Roger asked, "How do you know all this?"

Luther laughed and then said, "Because if you did not know it, I played on the team in 1937 that lost to Shelby, North Carolina in the Regionals. I played second base and the memories of those games are something I will never forget."

Roger turned and whispered to Rainey, "We don't know nothing about these old-timers. They just go about their business and keep their mouths shut about themselves."

Mr. Dan Dudley had walked out of the station lounge when Carl and Hank Burrows noticed Paul Peters of the American Amusement Corporation entering the parking lot of the Main Street Amoco. Carl looked up at the Pennzoil station clock hanging on the wall of the lounge and said, "I forgot all about this joker comin' here today."

Before Mr. Peters could enter the station lounge, Hank quickly met him on the station's entrance's curved concrete sidewalk. He shook his hand and then motioned for him to walk over near the U Haul trailers and trucks parked on the side of the station. Once Carl appeared, Mr. Peters said, "Good sir, let me just start by saying that I appreciate your military service to our great nation."

Carl interrupted him and said, "There is no need for all that. All I did was fly in a chopper. It's not like I did any real combat. He then paused before saying, "So Hank here tells me you think you can get us started with some Video Poker machines. Tell me all about it."

For the next fifteen minutes while they sweated through the thick mid-morning humidity of downtown Oak Bay, Paul Peters explained the ins and outs of a new business that was about to invade the great state of South Carolina. Sealing a deal he already knew was a reality, the fast talking entrepreneur from Virginia said, "You have two options. You can buy the machines yourself or you can rent them from me with no cash out of pocket. I highly recommend renting where you pocket sixty percent of all the profits. We are only a phone call away from servicing your machines if you have any problems. This way you will be able to get your business up and running smoothly without worrying about money. The machines sell themselves once you are able to lure the customers in the door. Later on, you certainly have the option to purchase the machines. He paused momentarily before continuing by saying, " So let me get this straight, on Monday you would like for us to deliver four of the Deluxe Full House machines and three of the King of Black Jack models. Is that right?"

"That's right, and I would like to rent."

"Have you been able to speak to a judge in town who is willing to sign off for you to legally give cash payouts?"

Hank smiled and said, "I have the paper right here."

By the time the gas pumps finally gave out around noon, Carl officially closed the station on a Friday for the first time anyone could ever remember. Rainey made a cardboard sign and replaced the eight gallon per vehicle sign with the new one which simply read: WE ARE OUT OF GAS. Several customers were still driving up to the station looking for a fill up when Carl and Luther locked all of the doors. Carl said, "I hope this Video Poker saves us from goin' under."

Luther smiled and said, "I think you know how I feel about it, but if you think it will save the station, you won't hear a word from me. Now my preach'a might be another story."

Luther then walked over to the station parking lot where he saw Roger and Rainey talking next to Roger's Mustang. He yelled over at them and said, "Hold up, you two. We have been so busy around here that I forgot to invite you both to our church's Camp Meetin' Revival on Saturday night."

Roger replied, "I'm…"

Luther interrupted him and said, "I know you both probably have better things to do on a Saturday night, but it sure would mean a lot to me if y'all came. I sure do think the world of both you and a little Jesus won't hurt y'all at all."

Luther did not get a response from either one of them but when he left the station to go home and dress for Kirby's funeral, Roger looked at Rainey and said, "You know I don't want to go to that Revival Meeting, but I think it would really make Mr. Luther happy if we went. He practically told that baseball scout from the Braves that I was his grandson."

Rainey laughed and said, "I don't know, Roger. Although Mr. Luther seems to have had a change of heart about me over the past few days, I know there are still a lot of people in that church that will not want the Colored Boy from the Main Street Amoco to attend their special church service."

Roger laughed and then replied, " Well, you will be my guest, and we can see for ourselves if the love they always like to preach about is for real. If they ask you to leave, I will blast them in the local newspaper or on the radio the next time I get an interview after a game."

Rainey smiled and said, "Ok, but remember all this big talk at your own funeral."

Roger laughed and said, "Speaking of funerals, we better hurry up."

CHAPTER TWENTY-FOUR

A makeshift choir of ten people were singing "Amazing Grace" when Roger and Rainey entered the entrance of the Hampton Street Church of Christ to pay respects to the best town drunk that the people of Oak Bay had ever known. Walking into the church it occurred to Roger that Carl may have exaggerated a little about the gas levels at the station as an excuse for shutting down the place so they all could attend this funeral.

Sitting next to Luther and Stumpy, Roger whispered to Rainey, "That is Crazy Bob Blankenship sitting next to his Aunt Essie on the front row."

Rainey whispered back, "I sure do hope a few more people show up for Mr. Kirby. It looks like we are the only non-family members here."

On the last stanza of the old Christian hymn, "Amazing Grace", written by an Englishman in 1772, people from all over Oak Bay began making their way into the church. Roger and Rainey recognized many of them. A lot of them were customers of the Main Street Amoco. As more people arrived, the members of the O.T.C.C. had no idea that so many people in Oak Bay had a connection to Mr. Kirby Davis. Stumpy turned around and looked over at all of the people coming into the church and then whispered to Luther, "Crazy Bob must have paid folks to show up here. I sure hope this makes my friend Kirby happy today."

Eugene Fillard of the Fillard Funeral Home stood up at the front of the church looking somewhat nervous. Speaking in an effeminate sounding voice which carried an undeniable Southern twang he said, "The family would like to thank y'all for takin' the time to honor Mr. Kirby Davis. The family has also requested that if anyone knew Mr. Davis, they are more than welcome to come up here and speak about him today. Once everyone has had time to express their thoughts, the service will be concluded with a prayer from Pastor Quinlan. Burial will take place in a private ceremony following this service. Once Pastor Quinlan prays, y'all may be dismissed."

One by one they stood up and testified about their relationships with a man who was never known to experience even the slightest of coughs. Some laughed at Kirby's love of cough syrup and mouthwash while others shed a few tears about a man who once took it up himself to ride a severely injured Boston terrier through an ice storm on his moped almost ten miles to the local veterinarian. It was said of him that he gave when nobody was looking, and he gave without wanting anything in return. His love for the local stray animals of Oak Bay was revealed by many who said that Kirby raided the local trash cans so he could provide enough food for his furry friends. On the human side of things, it was Kirby who collected soda bottles along the Pee Dee Highway so he could give the money to needy children for Christmas. Each week before Thanksgiving he would wander through the town and ask local residents for just two cans of canned food. He took those cans and gave them to the most underprivileged in the community. One lady testified that he had told her that if everyone gave two cans he could feed the whole town. Through his sorrow from a past life nobody knew anything about, he transformed himself into a man who survived on little while giving so much.

After the closing prayer, everyone in the church seemed to be happy. Stumpy pulled out a handkerchief and blew his nose before saying, "My friend was one helluva guy."

Coach Hutchinson said, "God rest his soul. What a great guy."

Once the Main Street Amoco crowd had made their way outside the church, a voice cried out from inside the church, "Hey, Carl and Luther, please wait up for a minute."

The members of the O.T.C.C. were shocked when they realized it was Bob Blankenship who was calling out to Carl and Luther. Almost running down the steps of the church, Bob immediately walked up to Carl and Luther before saying, "I need to have a word with y'all."

Carl looked at Luther before replying, "No problem, Partner. How can we help ya?"

Bob in a nervous sounding voice said, "I need to tell you and Luther that I am very sorry for the way I acted at your station the other day. I have been under a lot of pressure with my Aunt Essie's health getting worse. God knows what I will do …"

Luther interrupted him by saying, "It's all right Bob. Everybody has a bad day."

"No, Luther, I was having more than a bad day. I even went as far as trying to bring about a lawsuit against the station. I even paid someone to put up a nasty sign on your station. I can't begin to tell you how sorry I am. There is no excuse for my behavior."

Carl shook his head and asked, "So why the big change of heart, Bob?"

Bob Blankenship cleared his throat and replied, "When I went to clean out Kirby's small trailer the other day I found the most peculiar thing. Everyone in this town knows that Kirby led an eccentric life, but what most people will never know is that ever since he left Baltimore, he wrote."

Luther asked, "What did he write?"

"You name it, and he wrote about it. He had literally hundreds of notebooks filled up with every thought in his peculiar mind. What is amazing is that when I looked over the first few notebooks, they were the most recent collections of his writings. As I began to pour over those most recent notebooks, I was blown away at how well written he described his life in Oak Bay. He wrote in great detail about how all of you at the Main Street Amoco treated him. When I read the stories he wrote about each of you, it brought me to tears. He wrote about everyone at the station including their families. He described all of the kindness that was shown to him. He even described how he prayed for you all every day. After reading just a few of his notebooks, I feel like I know all of you. One of the most treasured lines he penned described how the men at the Main Street Amoco were his earthly family. My aunt and I can never thank all of you enough for the way you treated him. We tried for years to get him professional help, but he refused. I want all of you to know that the money he has left my aunt will be used to help the homeless and downtrodden in Charleston and right here in Oak Bay. I will be expanding my outreach efforts to help as many people as possible.

My mission outreach has struggled for years, but Cousin Kirby's money will be used to help it grow."

Luther said, "We had always heard that you were a fancy businessman in Charleston. I had no idea you were doing mission work."

Bob laughed and then said, "All that talk most likely came from my Aunt who seemed to be a little embarrassed by her nephew; the same nephew who only wanted to help people after serving a few years in the Peace Corp. I am sure that when people asked, she told them I was something other than a community organizer who spent all of his time helping the homeless and the mentally ill. I think she worried that I was becoming just like her favorite cousin, Kirby. My prayer is that we can all become a lot more like Cousin Kirby in our giving and kindness to others."

As they walked away from the church, Carl looked at Stumpy and Luther and said, "Now that is a big lesson learned. Never again will I judge a book by its cover."

Stumpy laughed and said, "Me, too. Man, did I have old Bob pegged wrong. I know old Kirby must be pretty proud of his cousin today."

Luther laughed and said, "I sure wish Kirby would have let us know who he really was. We might have been able to help him more."

Carl smiled before saying, "If we would have known I have to believe that his life would have been a lot different. Just think about all the fightin' and fussin' that may have taken place over his money. No, for whatever reason, Kirby kept his secret because through his deep despair he must have felt that he had not done enough for others."

Stumpy added, "That's right, my friend will be remembered as the Mystery Man of God's Plan who gave of himself."

By the time Roger made his way back home, he couldn't help but notice the construction crew workers who were busy building a foundation for the new brick home which would replace his grandmother's old house. Once parked, he walked over near the construction site and watched as a concrete truck backed up next to the east side of the freshly dugout foundation. When a few workers with shovels made their way toward the cement truck, Roger was able to clearly look at the log cabin which sat about fifty yards behind the new construction site. He immediately noticed the professor from UNC-Wilmington, his wife Doreen, Chad Emory, and his father all talking at the cabin. Roger then walked over to them. He was surprised to see that his father had already brought out the large journal which was sitting on the steps of the old home. After reintroducing himself, Roger asked Professor Don Ellis, "Is there anything in particular that interests you about this cabin before my Dad takes you into Hogtail Swamp?"

Don began smiling before replying, "The wooden pegs covered by a mixture of clay and horse hair is a strong indication to me that this structure was built around the time period of the 1770's up to the 1790's. The craftsmanship of this structure is outstanding. There was a lot of love and care put into the construction of this home."

Roger, already knowing the exact date of the structure's completion, laughed before asking, "That seems about right. How do you know all of this?"

"Believe me when I tell you that Doreen and I have been to many places over the years and she is better than me when it comes to archeology. I might hold the degree on paper, but she is the one who is pretty accurate when it comes to dating a site."

Roger smiled before asking, "So why are you so interested in this particular cabin?"

Doreen laughed before replying, “Are you kidding me? There are an incredible number of structures that are classified as Georgian and Greek Revival architecture in the Eastern Carolinas, however this structure is very significant because we have never seen anything quite like it.”

“What do you mean?”

Doreen laughed before saying, “This is not just a cabin. It was built as a combination house; meaning it was built part-cabin and what we refer to as Salt Box style.”

Mark James grinned before saying, “You lost me there.”

Don Ellis spoke up and said, “In layman’s terms - whoever built this house used two entirely different methods of construction in its design. In all my years of looking at old homes, this one is clearly unique. Although it was built with a simple design, the layers of construction were done in a manner in which future additions to the home could be done without ever any damage to the original structure. In my line of business we would consider this a work of excellence. It was well thought out by whoever built it. What I am trying to say is that this is not your typical backwoods log cabin. It is a treasure for archeologists like ourselves.”

Doreen then spoke up and said, “You both are so lucky to live next to a home that was built so long ago. Think about the events of history which could have destroyed it. Withstanding fire alone all these years is unbelievable. Think of all the storms, wars, and one of the South's worst enemies when you ponder over how incredible it is that this particular structure has survived for about two hundred years.”

Roger smiled and then asked, “What is one of the worst enemies of the South?”

“Termites, of course.”

After looking over the journal, Ron Ellis could not believe it. Chad Emory almost fainted when he read about Francis Marion. Doreen said, "I can't believe your ancestor went through these great lengths to hide those documents. I think it will be very interesting to see what those parchments produce."

Leaving his father and the professionals to venture out into Hogtail Swamp, Roger walked over to his trailer to get ready for his baseball game. Once inside he found his mother sitting on the couch. With no book in hand or television blaring he asked, "Are you okay? Before she answered him, he recognized that she had been crying. He spoke louder when he asked, "Mama, what's wrong?"

Not answering at first, she pointed toward the door. She then said, "I can't take it anymore."

"Take what?"

"Those people are here again today."

"Do you mean the people looking at the log cabin?"

Nodding her head up and down, she then replied, "This has to stop."

For the next ten minutes Roger tried to explain to her how wonderful the old house was to so many people. He did most of the talking. He soon realized that she was buying none of what he had to say. He tried to reason with her several more times when she finally said, "God is in control, and he is not happy about this at all."

Once the Almighty had been brought into the conversation, Roger knew it was of no use to speak any further on the subject. He did all he could do to cheer her up without any success. He then left her to dress for his game. Roger knew that his mother was not good. He prayed that his father would be able to calm her down once he and the historians made it back from the swamp.

That night at Legion Field, about thirty minutes before the scheduled start of the game, Atlanta Braves scout, Dan Dudley was being given the royal treatment by Coach Hutchinson and the Oak Bay American Legion Baseball Committee. They allowed Coach Hutchinson's old friend to sit directly behind home plate. Coach Hutchinson reminded him that he would be sitting within spitting distance of Oak Bay's mascot, Big Papa, but it did not dissuade him from moving to another seat. His main concern was to make sure he would be able to record an accurate reading on his new radar gun when Roger James began pitching.

Warming up with his friend and catcher, Stew Turbeville over on the left field side of the field, Roger stopped to pull up his stirrup styled socks. Pulling a shoe string through the top loop of his Pony cleats, Roger then looked at Stew who was staring over in the stands.

"Who are you looking for?"

Stew took the baseball and rubbed it across his shoulder before saying, "I ain't gonna lie to you. I heard my mother on the phone this afternoon. She invited Julie to go eat at McDonalds and then come to the game."

"Who is Julie?"

"Mrs. Stanwick."

"Oh, hell. That will be awkward."

'Tell me about it. On top of that, my crazy mother invited Sarah Beth and her mother to go eat with them."

Roger laughed and said, "That will be even more awkward. One day I would love to be at Thanksgiving Dinner when you all get together."

'You are such a smart ass... Just start gettin' warmed up before Coach Fugate comes down here."

The boys in blue from the Lake City American Legion team were a mouthy bunch when they began taking their infield warmup. Several of the Lake City players kept saying loudly,

"Oak Bay is goin' down… Oak Bay is goin' down."

Roger, who was walking toward the dugout, heard the third baseman and yelled over him saying, "Look out for the fast ball. I hear the pitcher is a little wild tonight."

The third baseman laughed and then yelled back at him, "Okay, Big Guy. You tell the pitcher that I will make sure to take his fastball and blast it back up his ass."

Coach Fugate heard the verbal exchange and came running over to Roger yelling, "Are you talkin' trash? We don't ever talk trash here in Oak Bay. You hear me James? Boy, ya better answer me."

"Yes, sir."

"We never run our mouths at Oak Bay."

Up in the press box the play-by-play announcer for WOKB started the coverage of the game by telling his loyal listeners, "It's hotter than a bright red bikini at Myrtle Beach here at Legion Field tonight as Oak Bay takes on Lake City. We are only five minutes away from the first pitch on the Oak Bay Radio Network."

After the playing of the National Anthem, Roger James spotted Dan Dudley sitting behind home plate with his Radar gun ready for action. Roger thought to himself, "I am going to throw nothing but off speed pitches during warm-ups so when I throw the first pitch he will be surprised."

Coach Hutchinson was sitting next to Dan Dudley when Dan squeezed the trigger of the radar gun on Roger's first warm up pitch. Dan just shook his head when he said, "76 miles per hour."

Coach Hutchinson smiled and said, "He is just warming up."

Dan with a smirk on his face turned to his old friend and said, "We will see, but most of the time you can only add about ten more miles per hour once they start the game. That one clocked in at 72."

Coach Hutchinson barely pushed his friend on his arm when he said, "Look over there. It looks like you have company tonight. That's old George McRoy from the Red Sox."

"I know, and that little guy right next to him is a new scout from the Cubs. They have been following me from Virginia Beach down to Savannah. This is such a slimy business."

A moment later when Big Papa made his famous entrance, Roger James prayed that his heat would be as accurate as it was fast. He did not disappoint himself or the crowd that had assembled on an Oak Bay Friday night. When the first pitch was recorded, Coach Hutchinson chuckled when Dan Dudley looked amazed at the numbers on the radar gun which recorded a 97 mile per hour fastball. On the second pitch, Dan Dudley stood up in his seat and looked baffled when the gun registered a 100 mile per hour strike right on the outside corner of the plate. He cried out to Coach Hutchinson, "This thing must be broken."

Big Papa looked at Dan Dudley and yelled, "Sit down, White Man. Big Papa needs his visual powers to rattle these boys from Lake City." He then yelled even louder, "Hey batter, batter - get ready for the Heat, you piece of meat."

On the next pitch, Roger James shook off his catcher's signal for a curve ball before delivering a pitch that had everyone in the stands buzzing. When the umpire declared it a strike, Dan Dudley stood back up and yelled at Coach Hutchinson, "This damn thing says he threw a pitch at 102 miles per hour."

People in the stands including Roger's father, Mark James started making their way toward the man who was holding a radar gun. Even

Big Papa was interested in seeing what many knew were the fastest recorded pitches ever thrown at Legion Field or maybe the entire state of South Carolina. Even the two scouts from the Red Sox and the Cubs made their way down in the stands to get actual proof that what they were seeing on the field was matching up with major league baseball's newest piece of technology. Roger James could tell that he had stirred up a hornets' nest before he unleashed the next three pitches which all were recorded at speeds that ranged from 98 to 102. Roger James gave the local people the actual proof that what they had been witnessing for years was indeed reality. He gave the scouts the evidence that they needed to call their bosses long distance to get permission to offer a whiz kid out of Oak Bay a professional contract. The excitement was so contagious that by the last batter of the inning, a note had been passed to the WOKB radio play- by- play announcer who shouted out to his listeners, "And it is now official... I have just been informed that Roger James's last series of pitches were accurately recorded to be over 100 miles per hour.. I repeat -100 miles per hour... Folks, we are witnessing history tonight at Legion Field as Roger James is throwing pure Carolina Heat."

Walking off the mound after pitching nine of the most perfect pitches God had ever allowed to be witnessed, Roger saw his mother standing next to his father. She yelled, "That's my boy. That is my baby boy."

Stew walked up to him and said, "Damit, boy, my hand ain't gonna last all game with the way you are hummin' that tater tonight. Are you on some kind of drug?"

While the scouts had scrambled outside of the stadium to fight over the only pay phone within a half of a mile, they heard a roar from the crowd and did not know that Roger James had just sent a Lake City fastball deep over the centerfield fence for a Grand Slam.

When he crossed home plate, he was greeted by every last one of his teammates. Taking the turn back toward the dugout, he could see the proud look on the face of his father. Stumpy who was sitting next to Carl and Luther yelled out, "Make us proud, Hot Rod. Keep makin' us proud."

Next to the dugout Roger caught sight of his new friend Rainey who simply gave him the thumbs up. Roger James felt like he was experiencing the closest thing to perfection a young man could ever imagine in his dreams.

Two innings later the professional scouts along with the rest of the crowd could not believe that Roger James had only pitched a total of 18 pitches. Not one of the Lake City batters even came close to fouling off a pitch while Roger James never threw anything but a fastball right over the corners of the plate. Dan Dudley, who had already been introduced to Mark James by Coach Hutchinson, looked at the father of pitching perfection and said, "I've traveled through Georgia, Virginia, and the Carolinas for many years, and I have never seen anything like this. It's not like he is pitching against the Sisters of the Poor. Those boys from Lake City can play some ball."

Although Big Papa was getting into the head of the Lake City pitcher with his wild dog barking impressions and duck calls, the boys from Oak Bay could not muster enough offense to add any more runs by the end of the third. In between the third inning as the crowd was quiet, all hell broke out in the stands. Roger and Stewart could see and hear the dog cussing that Stew's mother was putting on Mrs. Stanwick. They later found out that Julie Stanwick's lapse of judgment came when she decided that Jesus wanted her to repent of her sins by confessing to her best friend. She was mistaken. Mrs. Turbeville and Stew's girlfriend had to be restrained by several men who had never seen such a cat fight. Stew looked at Roger and said, "The gig is up. Mr. Stanwick is gonna kill me."

Roger held back a smile and whispered, "He's not going to kill you. He is gonna kill Mrs. Stanwick."

Stew's girlfriend, Sarah Beth, then ran up to the dugout and shouted to Stew a few choice words that would make any sailor cringe. She then yelled even louder, "You make me sick, Stew. I can't believe you laid up with that old woman! It's over, Stew Turbeville. Don't you ever call me again!" She then threw a perfect strike with his Oak Bay High School Class Ring which hit him squarely in between his eyes.

While Stewart bent over in pain to retrieve the ring of partial gold and a fake emerald, Roger said loudly, "I guess that pretty much ends that relationship."

Regrouping after the incident in the stands, Roger kept bringing the heat, but the boys from Lake City kept fighting. Finally the Lake City third baseman hit a solid ground ball right down the first base line. The crowd held their breath while Oak Bay's first baseman scooped it up and stepped on the bag to record the last out of the inning. The Oak Bay fans cheered loudly when they realized the perfect game being pitched by Roger James was still alive.

Still up only by four runs, Roger came to bat in the sixth inning with two outs already in the books. The WOKB play- by- play announcer held tightly to his microphone when he said, "Roger James is now up to bat. He is working on a perfect game and now after already plating a Grand Slam and a third inning double, Hot Rod hopes to add an insurance run. Another blast over the Vineyard would be outstanding."

No sooner had the announcer made his call, Roger James smacked a line shot to right center that would have gone out of any other ball park. The ball hit the very top of the old fencing and made solid contact with a vine that hadn't been disturbed in many years. It seemed like the old vine threw the ball back toward right field. As the ricocheted ball took an evil bounce off the glove of the right fielder, Roger James knew that ball was heading toward the right field goal post. As he rounded second base he could see that not one player from Lake City had caught up to the ball which had a wicked spin. At that moment, Roger James made a decision that he would regret for the rest of his life.

Coach Fugate was holding up both of his arms as he rounded third, but the Golden Boy from Oak Bay had other plans as he headed for home plate. Only a few yards away from an inside the park home run, Roger James could see the ball bouncing off the clay infield right in front of the plate. He had to make a split second decision to either slide or try to run over the catcher. He chose to run over the catcher.

Later that evening when Roger James came to his senses, he could barely see the emergency room doctor at the Oak Bay Hospital who told his father, "The X-rays tell me his shoulder socket is crushed. I've seen car wreck victims whose X-rays look better. He will need surgery. He will need to spend the night here in the hospital, and it will be a few days before we will be able to do the surgery."

An hour later after waking up with a little pain, Mark James and Coach Hutchinson gave him the news. Coach Hutchinson looked at Mark and said, "You go ahead and tell him."

Mark, with tears in his eyes said, "Son, you don't know how hard this is to say."

Roger took hold of his father's arm and interrupted him saying, "I can tell this is not good news."

Coach Hutchinson was the one who gave Roger the medical details because Mark James couldn't bring himself to tell his son that his baseball career was definitely over. There were tears followed by laughter when Mark told his son that the catcher had dropped the ball, and Roger had safely made an inside-the-park homerun.

He said, "Lake City came back and almost won the game, but your inside the park homerun was just enough for the win."

Coach Hutchinson said to him before he left the room, "They are going to let you go home later this afternoon. Get some rest. I want you to know that I have already told your father that all of us at the Main Street Amoco will do whatever we need to do to make sure that you can go to college."

CHAPTER TWENTY-FIVE

Later that morning when Roger was more coherent, Mark told Roger that they had found the chest lodged in between two roots of a four hundred year-old cypress sitting on a small, elevated portion of land in Hogtail Swamp. Roger asked, "Did you open it up?"

Mark smiled and said, "They wanted me to open it, but I couldn't do it without you. For Pete's sake, you are the one who did all the research. It would only be fitting if you are the first one to see it."

Carl, who had slept in a chair next to Mark in Roger's hospital room, woke up and told them he was going to work. The veteran of Vietnam made his way over to the Main Street Amoco two hours before the Saturday morning opening of the station. He had already talked to the Carolina Petroleum Company about making sure the gas shipment arrived at 6:30 am so that the morning customers wouldn't have to wait on their fill up. Turning down Main Street he was hurting for Roger, but he was relieved to know that gas prices had stabilized at 89 cents per gallon. He had never been more confident about his chances of making a good living from the gas station he had built with hard work and determination along with the help of his friends.

Unlocking the back door to the station like he had done so many mornings before, Carl felt the unusual feeling of having a pistol stuck in his back. He was told not to turn around and to go ahead and unlock the door. The next verbal instructions pissed him off when he was told to go to the cash register. He said calmly, “No problem, Partner, but I think you are gonna be disappointed when you see what little cash we keep in this joint.”

It wasn't until he entered the station lounge and turned on the lights that he could see his assailants in a clear reflection from the station’s large glass window. Dressed in all black with thick wool stockings over their faces, they remained silent. While he wondered who they were, they pushed him closer to the cash register and ordered him to open it. Carl’s mind told him to comply with them and hand over the small amount of cash in the register. His inner soul nudged him enough to make him believe that he would rather die than to give over his cash without at least a fight. Banging the old cash register with his left hand, he slipped his right hand down on a spring-loaded board concealed under the edge of the station lounge counter he installed during the first gas crisis in 1973. In one quick swoop Carl Norman went Vietnam on his assailants. He pulled out his double barreled sawed off shotgun and pulled the first trigger. Hitting one of the men right above his thigh with a blast of buck shot the other assailant fired his pistol, hitting Carl near his collar bone. Several shots later while dragging his bleeding buddy out through the station lounge, the masked robber had every intention to go back into the station lounge for the money. He decided differently when Carl hunkered down behind the station lounge counter and fired his second load of buckshot through the station lounge's large window

Spooked and on the run, the shooting from the unharmed robber quickly ended. For a few seconds Carl Norman, a Veteran who had survived the jungles of Vietnam thought he might actually die on the floor of the Main Street Amoco lounge.

If it wasn't for the arrival of the early shipment of gasoline from the Carolina Petroleum Company and the quick thinking of the truck's driver named Moses McKnight, Carl may have bled to death.

Mark James, who was buying a cup of coffee from a downstairs vending machine at the Oak Bay Hospital saw the ambulance which brought in Carl. Rainey and Luther came running into the Emergency Room entrance only a few minutes later .

Mark saw them, walked over to them and asked, "What happened to Carl?"

An out of breath Luther replied, "It looks like he was being robbed, and they had a shootout."

Rainey spoke loudly when he said, "From the looks of things in the station lounge, Mr. Carl was able to shoot them with his shotgun."

Mark replied, "I hope they catch 'em soon. The good thing is that I think Carl is going to be fine. Bill Howard with the Fire Department said he would make it. He is one lucky man."

Rainey asked, "How is Roger doing?"

Mark replied, "Thanks for asking. He had a rough night, but the doctor says he can go home this afternoon. He will have to have surgery to repair all the damage."

Luther asked, "How bad is his injury?"

"Pretty bad. The doctor says his pitchin' days are over."

Upstairs at the Oak Bay Hospital, Roger heard someone knocking on his door. Before he could respond the door flew open. Standing with a big smile on his face was his childhood friend, Stew Turbeville. Stew ran over to his bed and said, "I saw that nurse outside when I came in. You definitely need to get her number."

Roger said, "If you are talking about that sixty-year old nurse, I think she is more your speed since you are into older women."

"Touché."

Roger then asked, "How did you make out when you got home last night?"

"Oh, you know the deal. Mama went crazy on me for about an hour before my Old Man came in and told her to shut up. Before it was over, most of the blame had been thrown on Mrs. Stanwick. Mama wanted to call the Police and press charges until she realized there would be a court case, and I would have to testify. My father convinced her that it would be better to leave it alone. I have also been grounded until I die. That about sums it all up."

'What about Sarah Beth?"

"Obviously she was hurt, but when she realized that an older woman took advantage of me, she forgave me."

"She forgave you after that scene she created at the game?"

"Nobody in this town will ever remember that after the way you played last night. I hope you have seen the mornin' paper. The headlines of the Sports Section read: James Steamrolls Oak Bay to Victory "

Roger laughed and said, "I wish like hell that I would have slid into home plate. I guess you heard about my prognosis."

"Your old man told me. Man, I am so sorry. I'm just sorry that my children will never get to see the best pitcher in the nation play in the big leagues."

"Did you say the best pitcher in the nation?"

Stew stepped a little closer to Roger's bed and then said, "By God, as long as I live, I will never forget that streak of fast balls you sent my way last night. I will go to my grave tellin' everyone that I caught the best pitcher in the United States of America."

"You are so full of it. Nobody will ever believe the guy who still believes that wrasslin' is not fake."

While the hospital staff was busy taking care of two of Oak Bay's local heroes. Hank Burrows and every other member of the O.T.C.C. made a decision to open the Main Street Amoco once they found out that Carl was going to make it. They took it upon themselves to make sure that Saturday's customers would be able to have their fill of Amoco gas without any gallon restrictions. Stumpy and Darryl worked their tails off cleaning up the glass and blood in the station lounge while Gene Purdy set up a makeshift register with ten Coca Cola wooden bottle crates stacked on top of each other. By the time Rainey and Luther arrived, they couldn't believe how the old guys were running the place. Luther looked at Rainey and said, "Carl needs to go on vacation more often."

"You are right, Mr. Luther, the O.T.C.C. is killing it."

Pretty soon as the news of Carl's heroic standoff made its way around town, people came to the station to offer support. Some came to buy gas while others brought food for all of the members of the O.T.C.C. Coach Hutchinson even had some of the ball players from the Oak Bay American Legion baseball team come by to lend out a helping hand with pumping gas so that Rainey could concentrate on oil changes and lube jobs. With a broom in his hand, Stumpy walked over to Luther on Full Service aisle number one and said, "I hope Carl is happy with what we are doin'."

Luther smiled and replied, “You done good, Stumpy. You done good.”

Over near the U haul trailers and trucks parked on the side of the Main Street Amoco, Hank Burrows was busy talking to the current Oak Bay Chief of Police concerning the early morning robbery. Chief Lollis said, “Hank, it looks like those jokers parked a block away near the Pecan Orchard. We found blood, and we found tracks, but with only Carl as a witness we don’t have much to go on right now.”

“Have you checked the hospitals around the state?”

‘We have checked everywhere. From all the blood in the station lounge and from what Carl told us, one of those jokers may be dead by now.”

Later that afternoon the Main Street Amoco looked like a big party. Gene Purdy sat down in his chair inside of the station lounge and cried out, “I ain't never seen so many people up at this station in all my years.”

Stumpy laughed and replied, ‘That's because your old ass is always asleep.”

Luther, who had walked into the station lounge said, “It is almost three o’clock, and I think we are gonna shatter the record for the most gas sold in one day.”

Rainey, who had worked up a good sweat, yelled through the mechanics bay saying, “Ten oil changes isn’t no joke either, Mr. Luther.”

Darryl laughed and then added, “And we have sold more sodas and Lance crackers than the law allows.”

Coach Hutchinson yelled out, “Well, look who has arrived this afternoon.”

Walking into the station lounge, Carl and Roger approached the old- timers as they wore matching slings on opposite shoulders.

Stumpy cried out, "Now someone take a picture of these two one armed bandits."

Hank Burrows said, "Hold on, Stumpy, don't start up with your craziness."

Luther said, "You two need to be at home restin'. We have this place covered."

Carl shook his head and said, "I wanted to take a look at the place before I went home. Hot Rod wanted to do the same."

After hearing about Carl's early morning ordeal, Stumpy said, "Well, we are just glad you are alive. We will let Hank find out who those fools were and once he does, you let Old Stumpy handle them."

Gene Purdy laughed and said, "What in hell do you think you can do?"

'Stumpy Justice is what I will do."

Darryl said, "I can't wait to hear this."

Stumpy laughed and said, "It's the kind of justice where you take those fools down to the swamp, strip them naked, tie them to a cypress stump and pour honey all over 'em. Oh, the hell they will pay when those fire ants and other swamp critters get hold of 'em. That, my friends, is what we call Stumpy Justice."

Coach Hutchinson immediately changed the subject when he said, "Now let's not forget about that incredible performance Roger put on last night."

Gene Purdy said, "That's right. Roger, I can't begin to tell you how excited I was listenin' to the radio last night. Best game I've listened to in twenty years."

Luther said, "I wouldn't have believed it if I didn't see it with my own eyes. When I saw that radar gun record a readin' of 102 miles per hour in the second inning, I almost fell down the bleacher aisle."

Roger smiled and thanked them all and then said, “Well, that is the end of baseball for me. The doctor says I will never be able to throw a baseball again once I recover.”

Stumpy yelled out, “That don’t matter, Roger. What you did last night will never be forgotten in this town as long as you live. One day about forty years from now somebody will come up to you out of the blue and remind you of the night he saw Hot Rod Roger James throw a baseball over 100 miles per hour, hit a Grand Slam, and an inside the park home run to win the game. It may not seem important now, but from a bunch of old men who could never even dream of such a thing, we all can tell you that it will be important once you are our age.”

Rainey, who was standing next to Roger whispered to him, “He’s right, Golden Boy, but now the Good Lord has other things in store for your life.”

CHAPTER TWENTY -SIX

Later that afternoon, people from all over Oak Bay County were parking their vehicles and making their way up to a big Carnival sized tent at the Oak Bay Fairgrounds. Bibles were being carried along with platters of dinners prepared for the masses who were coming to feed themselves both physically and spiritually. Rainey couldn't believe that Roger had agreed to participate after his baseball injury. Rainey, who agreed to drive Roger's Mustang, looked over at him and said, "You are one crazy white dude. You should have stayed home. Mr. Luther would have understood."

"I'm fine. I promise that I am not in any pain. Besides, I might need a little religion after the news I got today."

Rainey laughed and said, "We are thinking alike. I decided to come with you just so I could pray for my sick mother. I sure hate to watch her slip away and suffer like she is doing now."

After parking the car, the two young men from the Main Street Amoco were greeted outside of the Revival Tent by Luther who was excited to see them. Walking with Luther all the way down to the front of the large assembly, they all heard a man in the crowd say, "Look there, Luther has brought in a Colored Boy to the Revival.

Roger and Rainey took one more step before Luther stopped, turned around and walked over the old White man. Luther said, "This is my Grandson, you old fool. Don't you know that it's not polite to call anyone a Colored Boy? I suggest you show my grandson some respect and apologize to him right now before I begin to act unchristian."

The old man quickly apologized to Rainey who then looked at Roger and whispered, "God sure has done his work on Mr. Luther."

While the choir sang several songs, Roger James looked back at the largest crowd of people he had ever seen in his hometown. He took a quick peek at Mr. Luther and Rainey. He thought back to the beginning of the week where he could have never imagined that those two would be sitting next to each other in a church service. He then prayed a simple prayer regarding Jeannie. He knew she was devastated, but he wondered why she had not called or reached out to him after his injury like Bridget had done.

Roger had never been to a Baptist Revival meeting and some of it seemed very strange to him. Rainey, on the other hand, seemed to be really moved by the singing and the people who stood up and gave their testimonies. Luther looked like a proud grandfather sitting with his grandsons. Then when they had heard the last long prayer of the night, Preacher Vince Smith took center stage when he rolled up his long sleeves and began hammering out a story about how Jesus had come to visit him in Oak Bay, South Carolina.

There was no doubt to anyone listening that Preacher Vince Smith believed that Jesus spoke to him. Roger James was not yet convinced. Throwing in a few New Testament scriptures during his message the Baptist preacher had the crowd all riled up when he said, "God is comin' back quicker than y'all think."

Shouts of Hallelujah and Amen were heard all over the large assembly under the tent. Continuing with a story which described a plain looking man walking down the Pee Dee Highway, visiting with Preacher Smith, only to reveal himself as the Almighty, the fiery man of the cloth leaned into the microphone and cried out, "Y'all are the lucky ones; Jesus told me to tell y'all the truth."

Ten minutes later the preacher who had been in Oak Bay for less than two months revealed the most controversial revelation ever when he yelled, "Jesus told me he is comin' back for us this Friday at 12:00 pm Eastern Standard Time."

There has never been any place more quiet than when Preacher Smith gave the date and time of the return of Jesus Christ. The eerie and awkward silence ended a few seconds later when an old farmer from the back of the assembly yelled, "What does that mean, Preach'a?"

"I'm glad that you asked Brother Ross. It means that you can get your family prepared for the ride to Glory when Jesus returns next Friday."

The farmer yelled out again, "Where did he tell you that we needed to meet him?"

"Brother Ross, he told me that we all needed to be out in front of the Oak Bay Baptist Church ready to go on Friday with nothin' but the clothes on our backs."

'Another lady in the church stood up and asked in a pitiful voice, "Preach'a Smith, Lord knows I am ready to go to Heaven, but what are we supposed to do between now and Friday? My property taxes are due on Wednesday. Do I need to pay my taxes?"

Preacher Smith didn't miss a beat when he replied, "Go tell everyone you know that the time is near." He then paused before saying, "There will be no need to pay for anything if you know that Jesus is about to take you away. No more credit cards and no more bills. Jesus said you can leave your checkbook here because there will be no need for it in Gloryland...Hallelujah"

That evening the Oak Bay Baptist Church was split right down the middle. Half of the members thought their preacher had revealed the truth while the other half thought he needed to be committed to a mental institution. Before Roger and Rainey could make it back to Roger's Mustang, they witnessed two major fights in and around the big Revival Tent. Luther wasn't buying one word of it, but he was so busy trying to calm down people in his own church, he totally ignored his 'grandsons' from the Main Street Amoco.

Once Rainey started up the car, Roger asked him, "Don't tell me you bought into any of that bull from that preacher?"

Rainey replied, "No, but what if…"

Roger interrupted him and said, "You are the smartest person I know in this town. Don't even go there with me."

Rainey laughed and said, Sike… I had you for a moment. There is no doubt that Mr. Luther's pastor has lost his mind."

Ten minutes later, Roger and Rainey leaned up against the hood of his Mustang in the McDonalds parking lot. They laughed at the old Oak Bay ritual of teens riding down that section of Main Street in what everyone called 'Cuttin' Town'. Roger said, "It's funny, but my Daddy talks about Cuttin' Town when he was my age."

Rainey said, "You know Cuttin' town for my people has always been different. The young Black teens have always Cut Town in the

Bay near the Tobacco Warehouses. It has only been a few years that any of us would ever dare come to this section of Main Street to Cut Town."

Roger said, "That is so stupid to me."

Rainey laughed and said, "You do know that some of the worst fights between Blacks and Whites in this town had to do with black teenagers riding up to this section of Main Street during the 1960's. Blacks were not allowed to cross those railroad tracks after dark."

"That is hard to believe."

At that moment a group of White teenagers from Oak Bay High rode past them on Main Street with a large Confederate flag attached to a pole on the back of a pickup truck. Roger looked at Rainey and said, "They do love that flag."

Rainey laughed and then said, "Yes, they love that flag, but I want you to look around and see how many Black teenagers you will find driving around here tonight with a flag of Malcom X or Martin Luther King. You won't, and if you did see it, there would be trouble in this town."

Roger replied to him, "I get your point. I wish I could change the past, but hopefully the hearts of people in this town will continue to change. Like I told you before, I know that this world would be a much better place if people like you and me would just sit down and talk. I want you to know that I am so glad that you are my friend, no matter what the rest of the world thinks."

Rainey smiled and said, "I was only being your friend when I thought you were going to the Major Leagues. I was trying to become your agent… Sike." Rainey then changed the subject when he asked, "So how is Jeannie doing now that her father is in jail?"

"I'm not really sure. It is a complicated mess."

Once they had eaten a couple of burgers and headed for Roger's trailer, Rainey slowed down as they crossed the Billy "Cotton" Richardson Bridge. He looked over at Roger and said, "It is hard to believe they decided to throw the Senator in the river."

Passing over the bridge they were both shocked when the disc jockey for local radio station WOKB made an announcement. He said, "We have learned that local authorities have arrested another person in connection with the Senator Dennis Broadway murder. A seventeen-year-old female has been taken into custody."

For Roger there was no guessing as to who it was by the time he and Rainey made it to Roger's trailer. Mark James was sitting on the front steps of the trailer porch when they arrived. Mark looked at Roger and said, "They have arrested Jeannie. Hank Burrows just called me and gave me the news. He wanted you to know."

Without betraying Jeannie's trust in him, Roger shook his head before saying, "I need to go and see her."

Mark and Rainey both talked him out of it. They convinced Roger that he could see her the next day. Mark then said, "I have already planned for Chad Emory and Don Ellis to come over here tomorrow afternoon to open the chest. Rainey, you are more than welcome to come as well."

Rainey looked at Mark and asked, "What chest?"

For the next thirty minutes Roger explained to him what he had found. After hearing Roger's explanation, Rainey laughed and said, "Golden Boy, it appears to me that you have found a treasure. I wouldn't miss seeing what is inside that chest if my life depended on it."

Chapter Twenty-Seven

Early the next morning, Roger and Mark made their way to the Oak County Detention Center where Jeannie Branham was being held under tight security. Roger knew that Jeannie most likely wouldn't say much to him with his father by his side. He was hoping that his father may offer her some advice like which attorney she needed for her defense.

Dressed in a grey colored jumpsuit accessorized with shackles on her wrists and ankles, the most beautiful girl in Oak Bay did not look so beautiful that morning when she walked into a small conference room for a brief visit. Keeping her head down most of the time, she said very little. She looked physically exhausted. It was apparent to Roger and Mark that she did not want to talk. Roger said, "Keep your spirits up. You need to talk to a lawyer and tell your side of the story."

She mumbled, "I told you this would happen."

Roger replied, "It will be fine."

She only nodded in affirmation before she was taken back to her cell. Jeannie Branham's spirit had been crushed.

Walking out of the Detention Center, Mark stopped Roger in the parking lot and said, "I know you want to protect her, but you need to let me know what is going on. I can't help if you keep me in the dark."

Roger with a serious look on his face said, "She made me swear that I wouldn't tell anybody."

Mark smiled and said, "Well, thank God, I'm not just anybody. I know I have raised you to be a man of your word, but this is serious business. We are talking about this girl fryin' in the electric chair. Whatever she has told you - you need to tell me right now. If there is any way she can be helped, now is the time to figure it out. Keepin' secrets like you are in elementary school will not save this girl from Old Sparky."

Roger reluctantly gave in to his father's request. The dark secrets of the One Spot were now revealed to Mark James. Driving slowly down the dirt road which led to their trailer, Mark looked at his son and said, "I'm not sure there is much we can do. There will be many people who want her to receive the ultimate punishment. Killing a bum at the One Spot is one thing. Killing a state senator is not something people turn a blind eye to."

Two hours later Roger found himself sitting on the second to the last pew of the First Presbyterian Church of Oak Bay with his family. He was feeling a little pain in his shoulder when his mother leaned over to him and whispered, "Do you need to take another pain pill?"

Roger politely told his mother he was fine while his pastor was concluding his sermon. Before he ended his message of love and hope, the pastor calmly brought up what had occurred the night before at the Baptist Tent Revival. Rebuking his fellow clergyman for preaching blasphemy to his Baptist followers, he then said, "The Scripture from the Gospel of Matthew found in the 24th Chapter is very clear on this subject. The Scripture reads: 'But concerning that day and hour no one knows, not even the Angels of heaven, not the Son, but the Father only'. He then looked up and said, "Please don't get caught up in the foolish talk this man has stirred up in our town."

It wasn't until an hour later, near the end of the James family's Sunday lunch in their trailer that Roger and Mark James knew that Juanita James was buying what the Preacher from the Oak Bay First Baptist Church was selling. Standing in front of the sink while she filled up an ice tray with tap water, she said, "I want you both to know that the Lord has spoken to me just like he did the pastor from the First Baptist Church."

Mark James's eyebrows shot up as he looked over at his son. He then asked, "What did he say to you?"

"The Lord spoke to me while I was at the hospital's Emergency Room waiting for Roger."

Roger held back his laughter before asking, "What did he tell you, Mama?"

"He told me that he was coming back next week."

Mark James licked the fried chicken grease off of his fingers before he replied, "Well, if that is the case, then I might as well take the week off from work, and we can all go down to Myrtle Beach."

She cried out, "What we need to do is to spend our time readin' the Bible and prayin'."

Roger stood up from the table and walked over to his mother and patted her on her back before asking, "Why would we do that when we have the rest of eternity for all that?"

His mother turned around and took her hand, placed it on top of his head, and looked in his eyes before replying, "So we will have time to watch television in heaven."

Leaving Juanita James in the kitchen to wash the dishes, Mark James took his son outside on the front porch. He looked at Roger and said, "She is gettin' worse every day. I don't know how much longer I can leave her here by herself."

Roger shook his head and replied, "You better not leave your checkbook or credit cards with her any time soon. She may decide to spend all of our money since we won't be needing it in heaven next week."

"You know she went through somethin' similar to this several years ago when she was convinced we needed to take a trip to the Holy Land. Don't you remember her goin' to the Dream Maker Travel Agency and scheduling a two week stay in Jerusalem?"

"I do remember that. I forgot. What happened?"

"There was no trip to the Holy Land. I ended up takin' her' to a hospital in Charleston for three days and two nights. It then took me two weeks to get all of that cleared up with the travel agency. Those folks over at Dream Maker wanted me to pay them a thousand dollars."

"You paid them a thousand dollars without making the trip?"

"You must have been too young to remember. I had to round up several of our friends and family members to take a trip down to Myrtle Beach. We had to agree to sit through a two hour sales pitch about buyin' a beach condo. It was a fiasco at the Condo real estate office where this fast talkin' salesman had your Mama convinced that we needed to go ahead and buy a condo right on the waterfront. She kept sayin' yes and I kept sayin' no. The salesman kept sayin', 'That I didn't love my family if I wouldn't agree to buy. I finally had to threaten to bloody his nose up against this silly looking bell that they would ring in their office every time they made a sale. Finally that fool gave up the ghost. It was quite a scene where I had to calm down your Mama who couldn't understand why I didn't love my family."

Roger laughed at his father and then asked him, "What do you think we need to do now, Dad?"

"I guess we are goin' to have to keep a better eye on her. Since you will be sidelined here for a few days after your surgery, you can be with her most of the time. If she gets any worse, we will have no other choice except to have her committed."

A few hours later, Roger and Mark James led a group of historians and Rainey over to the old tractor shed to open the chest which had been retrieved from Hogtail Swamp.

Mark James picked up a hammer and chisel from his work bench and walked over to the chest which was sitting on a thick metal table. Don Ellis yelled out, "Oh no...Please stop. Please let me do it."

Pulling out a pair of clamps along with some other assorted small chisels out of a carpenter's sack, the professor of anthropology began a meticulous, yet cautious handling of the chest along with his wife Doreen. Brushing away rust with a small paint brush after using a clear liquid in a spray bottle, it appeared that they would take all night to open the chest. Mark laughed after a few minutes and said, "I can go find a blow torch if you need it."

Professor Ron Ellis was not amused. He did not reply as he stayed focused on the task at hand. Fifteen minutes later he and his wife had the lock completely disassembled. Before he opened the chest he said, "Don't be surprised if all we find is one big pile of rust. I have been down this road before."

He and his wife then slowly lifted the lid of the chest where a large completely yellow looking piece of parchment sat rolled up; bound by two pieces of thin ribbon sized cloth. Gently removing the historical relic out of the chest with surgical-like precision, Ron Ellis said in a low voice, "The contents of this chest have been protected by an ancient method of waterproofing. Using a concoction of tree saps and thin pieces of wood, old Native peoples have been known to use this method of preservation which was quite effective. This is quite a remarkable find."

He and Doreen then began removing the rolled up parchment. A few inches from the top of the chest Chad Emory of the Oak Bay Historical Society noticed two other relics. Although excited, Ron and Doreen masterfully went ahead and carefully extracted the parchment. Once the parchment was placed on the metal table, Ron leaned back over the chest and took out what appeared to be a metal button with a pair of surgical tongs. Lifting the button into the air near a large lamp that Mark had placed in the shed, Ron Ellis cried out, "This gives us pretty clear evidence about the time period as this is a Revolutionary War era button from the Continental Army." After inspecting the button for a few minutes, he then reached back down into the chest and retrieved what appeared to be a large dagger in a silver-plated sheath. Turning over the sheath under the light of the lamp he noticed an inscription which read: A TOKUN of Friendship THRU Blood- The 3rd day of the first month of our Lord, 1781.

He then yelled out, " This is unbelievable."

Roger asked, "What does it mean?"

Ron Ellis replied, "I'm not exactly sure, but I would bet that if we can read this parchment we will find the answer."

After slowly cutting away the ribbon sized cloth that secured the parchment roll, the esteemed professor of anthropology began unrolling in a painfully slow manner. Once completely rolled out, they all were astonished to find a total of seven large sheets filled with incredibly small handwritten words which filled the entirety of each page. Looking at the very last page Doreen said, "We do know that the document was signed by Revolutionary War hero Francis Marion and Matthew James. It was also signed by a Native man who appears to have been named Three Bryson Osinkowatta. It says he was the representative of The Peoples of The River. Matthew James is listed as a witness. Francis Marion is listed as the Representative for the Continental Army of the United States of America/ Second Continental Congress via the Articles of Confederation."

For the next thirty minutes, Ron Ellis and Doreen quickly read over the document. The legal looking document revealed an agreement pertaining to an encounter occurring in November of 1780. He then said very loudly, "We need a lawyer to look this over. If this is what I think it is, the Native descendants of this area own not only a section of land near the river; they own a good portion of the city of Oak Bay, South Carolina"

Chad Emory almost fell over before asking, "What makes you think this?"

"Look at this rudimentary drawing of this survey plat. Do you see this boundary line?"

"Yes."

"This boundary line well exceeds the official city limits of Oak Bay as it goes to the most northern portion of the county which is bounded by Shiloh Creek. You have to understand that Oak Bay had not been established when this was written."

Roger asked, "How did Francis Marion agree to give up all of this land? Was it even his land to give away?"

"Evidently he thought at the time that he had the authority to do this. What you have to understand is that he was counting on the

British being overthrown. This is why a lawyer who specializes in land titles needs to look at this. Although this looks like a legal document, only a lawyer will be able to determine if this is valid."

Chad Emory spoke up and said, "Professor Ellis is exactly right. There are many legal factors involved. First and foremost would be to establish the legitimacy of the descendants of these people. Although you and I know that this document is describing the people we know who live near the river, the state of South Carolina or the United States has never legally recognized them as a tribe or as a legitimate group. This would be a major hurdle for anyone making a claim. Secondly, there may be a restriction based on a statute of limitations. Basically, time may have run out for the descendants to make a claim in court. Lastly, it would have to be determined who would be responsible for paying restitution or settling the case. Would it be the State of South Carolina or would it be the Federal government of the United States? What concerns me is that this agreement was made with the first government of the United States which was governed by the Articles of Confederation."

Mark asked, "Why is that important?"

Rainey quickly spoke up and said, "Because in all reality the outcome of the Revolutionary War had not been decided. This means that when Francis Marion ceded this land to the River People and Matthew James, the United States did not technically exist as an independent government. His agreement was a promise that if they won the Revolutionary War this document would be valid. Although they did win the war, it could be argued in court that Francis Marion gave away land that he had no authority to give away."

Ron Ellis laughed and said, "Rainey, you are correct. It looks to me that you need to think about going to law school. Your explanation was very good."

Roger then spoke up and said to his father, “Dad, we may need a lawyer to determine if you really have a claim to this property. I sure would hate to find out that the State of South Carolina actually owns this farm.”

Chad Emory said, “I don’t think this will be a problem, but it wouldn’t hurt if somebody took a look at this.”

Juanita James, who had walked into the shed a few minutes earlier, spoke up and asked, “Do you mean to tell me that we may not own this land?”

Mark quickly responded by saying, “We own this land, Juanita, You don’t have to worry about this.”

“That is not what I just heard. I distinctly heard Mr. Emory tell you that you needed a lawyer to look at this document.”

Roger spoke up and said, “It will be fine, Mama.”

Juanita James looked at Mark before she began walking back to the trailer and said, “Everything associated with this house is evil. I knew the day you decided to keep it, we would have problems.”

CHAPTER TWENTY-EIGHT

On Monday morning Coach Hutchinson was busy putting on another pot of coffee in the Main Street Amoco station lounge when Stumpy arrived with Luther. The legendary coach turned around and said, "When the Cat's away, the mice will play."

Stumpy growled, "What is that supposed to mean?"

Luther laughed and replied, "He is tryin' to tell us that we are late to work."

Hank Burrows laughed and said, "Old Carl decides to sleep in today, and everyone comes in when they want to."

Stumpy shot back, "I ain't on the payroll at this joint. Luther ought to be ashamed of himself."

Gene Purdy woke up and yelled back, "That's the problem, Stumpy. You eat up all the profits. Carl can't keep enough food up here for you. You might need to think about payin' Carl for allowin' you to spend your time here."

"Your insults today will not deter me in the least, you old fool. But keep it up and I will be puttin' a Stump Grinding' on your old deaf head before the day is over. Did ya hear me or do I need to use sign language?"

None of them paid any attention to Gene's reply as they became distracted by a huge eighteen wheeler that pulled into the station's parking lot. Jammed tight almost against the side of the station, the large truck's engine made the whole building shake.

Stumpy yelled, "What the hell?"

Hank Burrows yelled back, "I almost forgot. The new Video Poker machines have arrived."

For the next thirty minutes before the station officially opened for business, Hank took charge in leading the men of the O.T.C.C. in rearranging the station lounge which hadn't been renovated since Carl took over the place. The big sofa was moved to the other side of the lounge next to the large glass window while Darryl and Stumpy did their best to collect the loose change and Lance Cracker wrappings that fell out of it onto the station lounge floor. Out back, Rainey and Coach Hutchinson moved boxes of transmission oil and power steering fluid in the storage room which needed more than a broom and dustpan to make it clean. By the time the very first customers of the day began to sound off the station's air bell, the newest poker games in Oak Bay were plugged in with lights flashing.

Ten minutes later, the men of the O.T.C.C. found themselves arguing over which one of them would be the very first Video Poker customer of the great city of Oak Bay. Coach Hutchinson said, "It only makes sense that Hank should be the first since he will be in charge of the operations."

Stumpy growled, "Hank don't even like to gamble. I think it should be me because I will definitely put in more than one quarter like the rest of you, tightwads."

Gene cried out, "Age trumps everything. I should be the one."

While the argument over who should have the credit for such a momentous historical occasion became even more heated, nobody in the station lounge noticed that a gas customer named Shaq McCray had popped in a handful of quarters into the machine next to the station lounge's main entrance. As the cards were shuffled and the deck cleared for action, the lights on the Deluxe Full House model began flashing when Shaq pushed the Deal Button. All of the men of the O.T.C.C. began laughing when they noticed the very first customer of Video Poker. Shaq McCray, a thirty-one year old African American electrician and faithful customer of the Main Street Amoco took it upon himself to invest one dollar in quarters in hopes of hitting a jackpot.

Darryl cried out, "You did good, Shaq."

Shaq turned to Darryl oblivious to the great historical debate and replied, "No, sir. I need another Queen or a Jack of hearts."

Before Hank could put out the new advertisement poster which came with the machines, all of the machines were being played. Stumpy, who was perched on a stool in front of the last machine in the station lounge, cried out, "Somebody needs to go to the bank or the Piggly Wiggly to get more quarters. This is great."

Exactly twenty-two minutes after the first quarter was played, the Deluxe Full House model machine that was being played by Shaq McCray hit the Jackpot. Whistles and sirens went off like firecrackers on the fourth of July. Shaq jumped up and down like a young school kid as the machine gave notice on its shining screen that a winner had won one hundred dollars. Stumpy jumped off his stool and was the first one in the station to pat Shaq on the back. He cried out, "Dammit boy...You done hit the jackpot."

Shaq with a pure look of joy on his face looked at Stumpy and asked, "Who pays me my money?"

Gene pointed at Hank. Beginning to feel slightly sick, Hank began to calculate the input versus the output. He then sheepishly opened the station's cash register and slid Shaq McCray one hundred dollars in cash. Stumpy quickly picked up the station's Polaroid camera asking Shaq to pose for a picture. He yelled in excitement, "We need to put up the picture of all the winners right under the O.T.C.C sign over the door. That way people will see that the machines do have real winners."

Hank, who had a more than uneasy look on his face, walked up to Stumpy and whispered, "We are already in the hole. At this rate Carl will go broke before he ever gets started."

Stumpy, a successful entrepreneur of a Pork Barbecue empire laughed at his friend and replied, "Calm down, Hank. Don't get your taters tangled. I have actually been to the big casinos in Las Vegas. I learned out there that a few jackpots are just like throwing blood into the water. Once people find out these machines pay out cash jackpots, the sharks won't be able to stand it."

By that afternoon the members of the O.T.C.C. were more concerned about who was hitting 21 or a Full House more than who was buying good quality Amoco gasoline. As Stumpy predicted, when word got out that Video Poker at the Main Street Amoco was paying out cash jackpots, people started coming to visit. Rainey had already gone to the bank once for quarters when Stumpy ran out of the station lounge and yelled, "We need more Quarters!"

Rainey yelled back at him, “You will have to send somebody else. I have two oil changes waiting on me.”

Carl, who had just walked into the station with his shoulder still sporting a sling, could not believe his station lounge looked more like a casino than it did a gas station. He whispered to Coach Hutchinson, “Where did all these people come from?”

Coach Hutchinson replied, “A young man hit the jackpot earlier this morning, and the news about his fortune has spread all over town like wildfire.”

Carl asked, “Where is Hank?”

“He is in the back room with a gang of customers.”

Carl began laughing when he noticed Gene Purdy playing one of the machines with two rolls of quarters propped up on top of it. He yelled, “Hey, Mr. Gene, what the hell are ya doin’?”

Gene smiled and then yelled back, “I haven't had so much fun since the honeymoon with my third wife.”

Walking into the back room of the station, Carl was shocked to see the people waiting in line to have their shot at winning a big jackpot. He looked at Hank, who was taking another ten dollar bill from a customer in exchange for a roll of quarters. A few seconds later the bells and whistles of the King of Black Jack machine in the far corner began going off as another patron hit a big Jackpot of one hundred and thirty five dollars. Carl could not believe that Hank was counting out the cash payout like he was giving away Monopoly money. He walked over to Hank and grabbed him by his shirt collar before saying, “What the hell, Hank? We’re about to lose our ass in this business.”

Hank smiled and said, “Now calm down. I thought the same thing earlier, but Stumpy said that a few jackpots would bring in the masses. Guess what? He is right. We are takin' in a lot more than we are shellin' out."

"You took the advice of Stumpy?"

"I sure did. Carl, Stumpy was right. These people can't get enough of these machines."

Out on Full Service Aisle number one Roger James came by to visit Luther on his way to see his doctor. He found Luther somewhat aggravated about what was happening inside of the station lounge. Luther said, "I hope Carl knows what he is doin' with this Video Poker mess. I've already seen folks in here that have never set foot in the place before."

"Isn't that the point, Mr. Luther? Aren't we trying to bring in more customers?"

"You listen to me, Roger James. Not all business is good business. I've seen those shops that sell those nudey magazines, and I have seen the fancy beer joints in the big cities. You remember that when you sell yourself to the Devil, you will eventually have hell to pay. I'm afraid that is what Carl has done."

"Speaking of hell, what is going on with your church and Preacher Smith?"

Luther took out his red grease rag from his service station uniform pants pocket and wiped his glasses before saying, "We have a Deacon Board meetin' tonight to discuss what we are goin' to do with him. In all my years, I have never had so many people call me about what was goin' on at the church. The bad thing is that some of them really believe the end of time will be this Friday."

Later that afternoon Mark James and Chad Emory had arranged for Oak Bay's most esteemed attorney, Kirk McCloud to meet with them at his law office to discuss the historical documents that had been retrieved from Hogtail Swamp. Newly hired attorney Shane

Walker greeted them when they arrived. Looking at Mark James, who was carrying a large black bag which held the parchments, Shane Walker said, "Y'all come into this conference room. Mr. McCloud will be with you in a few minutes. He tells me that you have found a very important historical document. I can't wait to see it myself."

Kirk McCloud, who was Oak Bay born and bred smiled big when Chad Emory began to roll out the parchment pages. He said, "I can't believe you found this in Hogtail Swamp. It is in excellent condition for its age." Peering through his thick reading glasses, the long-time attorney's facial expression turned serious when he read the details surrounding a treaty signed by Francis Marion.

Shane Walker, who was specializing in real estate law, looked at his boss and asked, "What do you think?"

Looking specifically at the rudimentary land plat that detailed the property lines of the treaty, Kirk McCloud looked at Shane Walker and replied, "There is no doubt about it. A good portion of the town of Oak Bay is in question."

Reading further, the esteemed man of the legal community again spoke up when he said, " I think the direct ancestors of this group of people may have a legitimate claim to all of this property. However, I would estimate that it would take years of court proceedings before this could be settled. The main problem I see is that those people would have to make an individual claim against every single landowner in this county unless the Courts decide that the State of South Carolina or the United States government was responsible. There is also the question of tribal acknowledgment since these people are not really recognized by the United States government as a tribe. This could end up going all the way to the Supreme Court before it is settled."

Mark asked him, "Do you think I need to worry about my property?

Kirk McCloud laughed and said, "Not one bit. You and your family have been there too long for anyone to care. Even if they cared, there would be nobody alive to lay claim to the property."

Chad Emory asked, "What about the River People who live near the river? Do we need to contact some of them to see if they would like to make a claim?"

Kirk McCloud replied, "I am a greedy man, Chad, but I wouldn't stir up a beehive just to get a few cups of honey. In my opinion, Mark needs to keep this as a family treasure or sell it to someone who buys antiques. Other than that, I really don't see it going anywhere in the legal system."

Mark said, "Well, that is a big relief. I guess this wraps it all up. I thank you for your time."

After shaking hands and making their exit, Shane Walker quickly followed Mark and Chad Emory out of the building . Once out the front door, he yelled, "Mr. James, do you mind if I have a word with you?"

Mark looked at Chad Emory and said, "I bet this youngster wants to buy this."

Chad smiled and said, "If you ever do decide to sell it, you make sure to give me a shot at it. I would love to have it."

The young looking Shane Walker then approached Mark and said, "I don't know if you know this, but our firm is representing Jeannie Branham who has been arrested for the murder of state senator Dennis Broadway."

"I wasn't aware of that."

"I also bet you weren't aware of the fact that Jeannie decided to tell me all of the details surrounding the murder."

"No, I did not."

"She told me that the only other person she spoke to about this was your son, Roger."

Mark became visibly nervous and said, "Now look here- don't bring my son into this mess."

Shane Walker took his hand and said, "I have no intention of bringing Roger into this, but I do need your help."

Mark pulled away from him and asked, "How can I help?"

Shane Walker stepped a little closer and said, "Teddy Branham and Buzz Belton are going to fry for this murder. After talking with Jeannie, I don't want the same for her. I believe what she told me is true. I think she is a victim of her circumstances."

"I would agree with that."

"Then help me, help her."

Chapter Twenty-Nine

The next day, Roger James went under the knife to have a crushed shoulder socket repaired from a historical slide into home plate. Mark James had to bring his wife to the hospital so he could keep watch over her as she was continually telling him that they were all about to make a grand trip to heaven on Friday. Unfortunately she and Preacher Vince Smith were not the only people in Oak Bay who were planning for an eternal journey. Over at the Main Street Amoco Luther began to notice a few of his church members who were hunkered down in the station lounge shelling out ten dollar bills to play a game which had them hooked. He was disappointed to find out that they had decided to live up their last few days on the planet by spending their hard earned money on Video Poker.

He also confided to Rainey that he couldn't believe that his Deacon Board had decided to hold off on firing Preacher Smith. In one of the longest debates in the history of the Oak Bay Baptist Church, the majority of the deacons thought it would be a good idea to wait and see what Friday would bring. They decided that it would be easy to fire him on Friday afternoon if Jesus did not return. They also thought it would be much harder to explain to Jesus why they fired the preacher if he did return in all of his Glory.

Carl was still not himself when Oak Bay Chief of Police Lollis stopped by to give him some good news. In front of most of the O.T.C.C., he explained that the two young men who had attempted to rob Carl had been apprehended. The two were caught when they showed up at a veterinarian's office in Charleston demanding medical attention. The vet notified the police after he was able to see their license tags along with giving an accurate description of their vehicle. After their arrest, they admitted to a week's worth of stealing and writing bad checks. Chief Lollis said, "They told the Sheriff in Charleston that they wanted to steal some new tires from the station when Carl startled them."

Gene yelled out, "All that fuss for some tires? I hope they fry."

Chief Lollis smiled before saying, "They won't fry, but they sure will hate the day they ran into Carl Norman."

Hank Burrows, who had been working in the station's Back Door Video Poker Lounge, walked into the main station lounge right after Chief Lollis made his way back to his police cruiser. Hank quickly asked Carl to walk outside with him. Once outside he said, "Carl, we have a problem."

"What now?"

"It's your neighbor, Jack Cauthen."

"What about him?"

"His old lady Anita will not leave?

"What do you mean?"

"Carl, she is poppin' quarters into those machines like she has an unlimited checking account. I don't know where she is gettin' all that money. I have begged her to leave. I bet you she has dropped over five hundred dollars in these machines since yesterday."

"Has she won yet?"

"Only about fifty or sixty dolla's."

Carl shook his head and said, "It's really none of our business how people decide to spend their money, Hank."

"Come on, Carl, he is your neighbor, and he is a really good guy. Do you mind if I give him a call over at his dry cleaner business or do you want to talk to her?"

"Give him a call."

Once Carl left Hank to deal with the gambling addiction of his neighbor's wife he was surprised to see Wilson Martinelli standing next to the entrance to the station's Men Room. The slick looking young entrepreneur had a friend with him who Carl had known all of his life. Oak Bay's most successful Real Estate developer, Stan Hawkins stepped closer in front of Wilson Martinelli. Carl's old friend spoke up before Wilson Martinelli could speak. He said, "Thanks to you my friend, Mr. Martinelli has agreed to get me involved in his very lucrative project that is goin' to make this town turn upside down."

Carl laughed and then said, "You have that right. Putin' a shoppin' mall on Main Street will turn this place upside down."

Stan Hawkins smiled before saying, "Carl, I know how ya feel, but it really is time for you to go ahead and sell."

"Sell? Look at this place, we are doin' better right now than we have ever done."

Wilson Martinelli laughed and stepped up a little closer before saying, "No disrespect, sir, but once that Happy Mart across the street is built your sales are going to decline quickly."

Stan Hawkins lit up a cigarette before saying, "Carl, I told ya that you needed to sell. Trust me when I tell you that this is your Golden Ticket. This outfit out of Chicago is goin' to build a mall in this town, and it might as well be right here. What they are willin' to offer you and the rest of the people around you is incredible. You need to do this for your family. Look here, man, I watched your poor old Mama and Daddy work themselves to an early grave. God Bless 'em. This deal could change your life."

Carl looked at his childhood friend and asked, "How much money are we talkin' bout?"

Wilson Martinelli pulled out a paper from the inside of his blue blazer and handed it to him.

Carl read it for only a few seconds when he smiled and said, "Only a damn fool wouldn't jump all over this."

Later that afternoon, Rainey drove over to the Oak Bay Hospital to check on his new friend. The receptionist at the front desk told him, "Please remember to bring back your visitors' pass when you leave."

Walking into Roger's room he immediately recognized Stew Turbeville who was saying his goodbyes. Roger, who was feeling much better, sat up in his bed asking, "Do you two know each other?"

Stew stepped closer to Rainey and gave him a high five before saying, "Are you kiddin' me? I met Rainey at Skateland last summer. This dude could play ice hockey the way he skates. All the brothers in the Bay say he could be a professional roller derby skater."

Roger said, "Who knew?"

Rainey smiled and replied, "Skating is something nobody should ever brag about."

Stew said, "I don't know my man; you are a legend at Skateland." Before leaving the room, Stew continued by saying, "Tell your Dad I said hello. I'm glad you are all right."

"Thanks for coming by to see about me."

When the door shut to Roger's hospital room, Rainey walked a little closer to Roger's bed and then said, "Your boy Stew has been spending a lot of time in the Bay."

"In the Bay? I don't understand."

"I have a cousin who is a big pot dealer. Stew has been a good customer the past few weeks."

"Not Stew. I have known him to drink a few beers but.."

Rainey interrupted him and said, "I didn't want to tell you, but your friend needs some help. If he keeps hanging down in the Bay, he will end up in jail or shot. My cousin says he is buying enough to be a dealer himself. You know they don't play in the Bay."

After bursting Roger's bubble, Rainey then asked, "Have you spoken to Jeannie?"

"Not really. I can't even begin to imagine what she is going through."

Rainey replied, "I know what you mean. One thing is for sure, Friday is going to be an interesting day in this town. Mr. Luther's preacher has the whole town in an uproar. I even know a few old ladies in the Bay who have decided that Friday is the last day."

Roger smiled and said, "Let's hope not."

The rest of the week Stumpy and Gene Purdy played Video Poker so much, Carl became worried about them. He finally told Hank Burrows to put a cap on their spending. Stumpy went to Carl and protested by saying, "Don't screw with my lucky streak."

Gene went to him and said, “Let an old man have a good time.”

Luther went to Carl and said, “I've got church members who are hooked on this worse than people who get hooked on dope.”

Once Friday finally came, Roger and Mark James sat in the Oak Bay County Solicitor’s Office with Shane Walker and Kirk McCloud. Mark brought with him a historical document which had been placed under a cypress tree in Hogtail Swamp by his great grandfather many years ago. The large black canvas bag carrying the old parchments was a very noticeable item as it sat on the table in front of him. Once Solicitor Marvin McDowell walked into the small conference room he looked at Kirk McCloud and asked, “What’s in the bag, Kirk?”

Ten minutes later Solicitor McDowell looked up after intently studying the parchments. He said, “This may be one of the most incredible documents I have ever read in my life, but what does all of this have to do with Jeannie Branham?”

Once Shane Walker explained that Jeannie was a direct descendant of the River People, Solicitor McDowell became very interested. He asked, “So you want me to give this girl a plea bargain in exchange for this claim to land going uncontested. Is that what I am hearing from y’all?”

Kirk McCloud spoke up and said, “This girl may or may not have been the one who stabbed the Senator, but she does not deserve to spend the rest of her life in prison. She is willing to testify against her own father about the murder of Dale Tucker as well as testify about the illegal prostitution that has been taking place at the One Spot. I would suggest you cut her a good deal before we all have to go to court to protect our own property.”

Solicitor McDowell laughed and said, “I never would have thought that my office could be blackmailed in a case involving the murder of a State Senator. I understand where y'all are coming from. How does ten years with the possibility of parole in seven sound to y'all?

Shane Walker spoke up and said, "Six years with the possibility of parole after three sounds much better."

Solicitor McDowell laughed and said, "Sounds good to me. It's a deal, but only if these parchments stay with me and my office."

Mark James spoke up and said, "Now hold on here. Those parchments have real sentimental value for me and my family. I can promise you that I will never sell them or allow anyone to use them."

Solicitor McDowell replied, "You used them today, sir. It's plain and simple- no parchments -no deal for Jeannie Branham. The county of Oak Bay cannot afford to allow these documents to be used in future land claims. The ball is in your court, Mark."

Mark James did not hesitate when he looked at his son and said, " A few weeks ago we never knew these parchments existed. If it can help a young girl to avoid spendin' the rest of her life in prison, then to me it served its purpose." He then handed the Solicitor a treasure written by his great grandfather.

Over at the Oak Bay First Baptist Church a much smaller crowd than what was expected sat in lawn chairs outside near the front steps of the church while deacons of disbelief sat in their cars across the street keeping a watchful eye on their prophetic pastor. With only a few minutes left before their trip to Gloryland, the faithful followers began singing "Jesus Loves Me" as loud as possible. Then like an Apollo mission to the moon, they began counting down. With each second that passed, the group of about one hundred people became louder. They cried out, "22, 21, 20."

When they reached the twenty second mark, a woman parked in a car right next to the church ran out from her car totally naked and shouting, “It’s time- It’s time.” She ran right up into the arms of Preacher Vince Smith, who was as shocked as everyone else.

The crowd shouted, “Three, Two, One”.

Nothing happened. One old lady yelled at Preacher Smith, who was trying to cover the naked lady with his sports coat. She cried out, “Do you think the Lord might be on Central Time?”

After a few more minutes the disappointed crowd began to disperse while Preacher Smith, a man of the cloth for over twenty years, begged them to stay a few more minutes. A few minutes later, a few of the deacons, church members, the pastor’s immediate family, along with the Oak Bay Chief of Police watched Preacher Vince Smith pull out a silver plated .33 caliber revolver and fire the gun into his mouth. It was a tragic scene as the blood from his face stayed embedded into the mortar of the front step bricks of the Oak Bay Baptist Church many months after the incident. Fortunately for him, the gun slipped when he pulled the trigger, and he was able to survive with only half of his face blown off along with all of his ministerial integrity being shot to hell. Several good people in the community ended up losing their religion while others became more inclined to follow what they read in their Bible instead of what they heard during a sermon.

Mark and Roger were called by Chief of Police Lollis to come and pick Juanita James up from the Oak Bay Detention Center on Roger’s CB radio. Once they arrived at the Detention Center the Chief hated to inform them that Juanita was the lady who ran up the steps of the First Baptist Church in her naked glory. Chief Lollis also informed them that the Hogtail Swamp Volunteer Fire Station was at their farm where they were finishing putting out a fire which destroyed the two hundred year old log cabin. Juanita had set the fire before she drove into town.

Roger ended up riding with his father to take his mother to a mental hospital in Charleston. Stopping to fill up at the Main Street Amoco for the long ride, Carl, Luther, Rainey and the entire O.T.C.C. wished the two James men good luck on a most difficult journey while Juanita James slept like a baby in the backseat.

Chapter Thirty

Almost forty-one years to the day he worked his last day at the Main Street Amoco, Roger James found himself on the front steps of his parent's home near Hogtail Swamp having a serious chat with his father and best friend. It was a talk that he had been dreading for several days. His father who was talking through a mask said, "She passed away peacefully in her sleep. You know your Mama loved you and those grandchildren. She lived a good life. I am really gonna miss her."

Sitting a few feet away and also wearing a mask, Roger James became choked up before he said, "It's all right, Dad. I know you are going to miss her."

Mark James looked at his son with only his eyes showing when he said, "Once we were able to get her medication straight all those years ago, you know she never had another major episode. I just wish we could have figured all that out earlier. Those doctors in Charleston did a great job of helping your Mama."

"You did good, Dad. No other man would have gone through the hell you went through. I don't know how you did it."

"I don't know about all that. I loved your Mama. Now, I am glad that I'm in the fourth quarter of this life with all this Covid and wearin' masks. I don't know how much longer I can take this. I hate that the children and Bridget could not make it because of Covid. How are they doin'?"

"They are all doing good. You know Mark Roger just graduated from the University of Central Florida. Dean is about to finish at the University of Georgia, and Marie is in her third year of Medical School. Of course, my sweetheart Bridget is still driving me crazy. Then again, she does work at the Tampa Mental Health Center. Covid has me really worried for her."

"I know what you mean. When your Mama came down with it, I knew for sure that I would be the one who would go first. It just blows my mind how I haven't shown any symptoms, and she went into a tailspin in just a few days. The hardest part out of all it was that they would not let me into the hospital to see her. That will be on my mind for the rest of my days."

Roger smiled and then said, "I'm sorry, Dad. I know that had to be tough on you."

The two James men talked for a few more minutes about the weather and other newsworthy events of the day when Roger looked at this father and asked, "I hope you don't mind me asking you this, but I have been curious about something we have never talked about."

"What would that be?"

Roger laughed before he said, "Dad, I knew growing up that you were a big time athlete in this town. Everywhere I went somebody would tell me how great you were. You were a legitimate hometown hero. How come you never once bragged about your accomplishments to me? I really can't remember you ever talking about it. Why?"

"That's simple, son. I lived in the shadow of many great men. We just didn't brag about things like that. I never told you this, but my old man used to drive me like a mule when I played ball. No matter what I did, it was never good enough for him. I guess he had been saddled with the Dairy when he was young and never had the chance to play ball. Deep down I knew that my success in football was somehow his success. Our relationship suffered because of his unrealistic expectations. I swore that if I was ever able to have a son, I would not push him like that."

"Thanks, Dad. You have always been a great example to me over the years."

Mark James then stood up on the top step and asked, "Have you called Rainey today?"

"No, I have not. He told me that he would make time to take me to lunch."

"He sure has been a good mayor here in town. He has this place lookin' good."

"You have that right. When I drove past the old Main Street Amoco yesterday I couldn't believe they had built a new Starbucks at that location."

Mark James laughed then said, "Yes, it's hard for a lot of us old-timers to believe that the old station turned into a fancy coffee shop. I can testify that their coffee at Starbucks is nowhere near as good as the coffee that Carl used to have in that old service station."

Roger laughed and said, “Now I know you are senile. Carl’s coffee was so strong it may have killed some small children. Speaking of the station, what ever happened to all the old guys from the O.T.C.C.? I kept up with them over the years, but it's been so long ago I have forgotten some of those people. Remind me about those people.”

“Well, I’m sure that you remember that old man Gene Purdy and Stumpy got put out with Carl one day and decided to run off to Las Vegas for a few weeks of fun. Don’t you remember that those two gambled and hit the nightlife? They stayed out there in Vegas for three weeks until Gene died of a massive heart attack after he won a big card game. He died right on the table with a smile on his face, while holding a royal flush. You were in college when that happened. Old Stumpy ended up coming back home and helped Carl for a few years until Carl got rid of the Video Poker business at the station.

“Once the Happy Mart finally was built, Carl hung on as long as he could. He never sold out to the Mall people which is the reason why the Mall is on the property next to the Walmart on the outskirts of the town. When Carl finally realized that the Happy Mart was goin’ to suck him dry, he renovated the old station and bought a Blockbuster Video Franchise. That’s where Coach Hutchinson and Luther worked until they passed away. Carl took good care of those two old guys. A lot of people in town say that when Coach Hutch passed away, Carl never got over it. It hurt me too, when Coach suddenly died, but evidently he and Carl had a love hate relationship which was very deep. Of course, you were there at Luther’s funeral. I’m not sure who had the biggest funeral between him and Coach Hutch. People in this town loved both of them. Darryl was the very last member to work at Blockbuster. He later opened up a UPS store which he sold before his death a few years ago. People around here say that Darryl ended up being one of the richest men in this town. He also gave a lot of his money to his church."

"Didn't Mr. Stumpy die just a few years ago?"

Mark laughed and replied, "With a smile on his face."

"What happened again?"

"He was at the Bottoms Up Gentlemen's Lounge in Myrtle Beach gettin' a lap dance when his second wife Laura Ann came in there and found him in the act. She walked over to him, pushed the girl off his lap, and fired a pistol right between his eyes. They had a big trial after they arrested her. Every television station in this area covered it. Laura Ann got off pleadin' self-defense. She said Stumpy had been abusin' her which everybody in town knew was a lie. The jury didn't see it that way, and now she is runnin' the Big Pig Barbeque Hut. She even had the nerve to take down that big paintin' of Stumpy that used to be in the main dinin' room. None of us old-timers ever go there anymore, but on Saturdays that place is still packed. I sometimes wonder how Stumpy fared when the Fillard brothers got hold of him at the funeral home."

Roger laughed and then asked, "How is Carl doing these days?"

"Hell, Carl is still going strong as he spends most of his time riding his Harley. Can you believe that he and his old lady got matchin' tattoos and matchin' Harleys? That nut has told everyone that they are plannin' to go to that Sturgis Motorcycle Festival in one of the Dakotas in a few months."

"Even with Covid getting so bad?"

"Carl don't believe Covid is real. He told me back in April that people had lost their minds over this thing."

Roger shook his head and said, "I guess we could testify that it is real. I sure would like to see him while I am here."

"You can catch him on your way back home. He is in Daytona this week. I can't believe they rode all the way down there."

"Thanks, Dad, for taking me down memory lane. I wish you would move with us to Tampa now that Mama is gone."

"I'm too old to move. You know a James has lived on this property for a long time. Besides, I would just be a burden to you and your family. "

"You mean that an Erickson not a James has lived on this property for a long time. They both laughed before Roger continued by saying, "Dad, you would never be a burden to us."

Mark James smiled before saying, "Those grandkids would end up hatin' this old Dinosaur. Besides, I'm just gettin' the hang of those Zoom Meetin's I have been on with your family. Those Zoom meetin's have changed my life."

Roger laughed at his father before saying, "I think I will go and try to find Rainey if it's all right with you. I will be back later."

"Take your time, but do me a favor and stop by a store and get me some coffee and shuga."

Driving down by the Oak Bay Courthouse, Roger James couldn't help but notice that the old statue of Confederate General Micha Jenkins had been removed. Making his way up to the office of the Mayor, he couldn't believe the new modern City of Oak Bay Municipal Center. After having his temperature taken at the main entrance, the security guard said, "Please keep your mask on while doing business inside. You know we have a mandatory mask policy in all city buildings."

After climbing a set of winding stairs, he found himself standing in front of a receptionist who was completely boxed off from him behind a plexiglass barrier. He asked, "Is Mayor Thomas available?

"No, sir. The mayor had to leave town this morning. His daughter became sick at Clemson University, and he went to bring her home. Don't tell anyone, but they think she may be positive. Chances are that he will have to quarantine once he comes back."

"No problem, I will call him later on his cell."

Walking outside into the courtyard adjacent from the Old County of Oak Bay Courthouse, he dialed his old friend on his cell phone.

Rainey answered on the first ring and said "What's up, my main man. I guess you know I am on my way to Clemson."

"I heard, Mr. Moving on Up. How is Shante?"

"You know, she told her mother that she had lost her sense of smell. She can't taste anything. I'm pretty sure she has it. I am going to take her for a test, and then we are coming home. She was taking a summer class, but they have now gone all virtual so it won't be a big deal if she leaves her apartment for a few weeks."

"You better mask up around her. You know you're not as young as you used to be."

Rainey laughed and then said, "Hey man, I am so sorry about your mother. She was a good lady."

"Thanks, I appreciate that. I'm standing out here next to the Old Courthouse, and I have to say that you have this place looking good."

"Obviously for political purposes I will take that, but to be honest with you the secret to our success is something that you and I talked about many years ago."

"What's that?"

"We used to talk about how if people could just take the time to sit down and talk, things would get better in this town. Don't get me wrong. We still have a long way to go, but unlike a lot of other places our people do talk to each other. You would have been proud of the way our Cultural Heritage Committee came to a consensus to remove the statue of the old General and build the new Veterans of Wars Museum near the Interstate. That is where the old General and his horse reside today."

"Since you are the politician, who is going to be the President next year? Biden or Trump?"

"It's hard to say. I think it is going to be down to the wire."

After catching up a few more minutes with his old friend, Roger found himself several blocks away from the Courthouse. He stopped in the old Piggly Wiggly which had been converted to a very upscale Fresh Market. Stopping at the coffee aisle, he pondered for a few minutes as to which of the various brands his father would like. The decision over which coffee brand to purchase would have been complex if it weren't for him noticing a sale on Maxwell House. He looked up and a very familiar face partially hidden behind a mask stood right in front of him. It was somewhat awkward, but he had no choice but to acknowledge Jeannie Branham.

"Well, hello, Hot Rod Roger James. It has been a long time."

"It's great to see you, Jeannie. How are things at the Native American Cultural Center? Rainey told me that you were the new director."

"Things are going fantastic. You know that I stay busy."

"I never thought that you would end up back here. I just pictured you being anywhere but here in Oak Bay."

"You know when I graduated from Berkeley, I spent about fifteen years in Los Angeles where I met my husband Tom."

"I heard. Isn't he into agriculture or something along those lines?"

"Sort of. Tom is a horticulturalist who helps me with our gardens at the Cultural Center and our own tree farm."

"How about the kids and your mother?"

"The kids are a handful. You know better than me that after you have two it gets hard. Dianna lives in Myrtle Beach. She is still working, but in a much different role. She works on the gambling boat at Little River. Covid has them shut down right now. How are your kids?" Before he could respond she interrupted him and said, "Oh, I am so sorry about your mother. She was such a sweet soul. I tried to come to the funeral, but with Covid they said there would be no service."

"Thank you. I appreciate that."

"So catch me up on your exciting career and family."

"You know most of it. Let's see- you know I graduated from the University of South Carolina with a degree in Business. Coach Hutchinson and his friend Dan Dudley helped me to become involved in baseball where I did an internship with the Houston Astros. I never dreamed that I would be working on the business side of baseball when I was growing up here. The next thing you know, I am working with the Cincinnati Reds in their front office. Now I am an assistant GM with the Devil Rays in Tampa. The children are all about to finish college, and my oldest is in medical school."

"How is Bridget?"

"She stays busy like you. Of course, you remember that she became a therapist."

"Is it true that you two didn't start dating until you went to college?"

"That's right. We did not keep in touch after our high school graduation, but as fate would have it, we ran into each other at a tailgate party before a Carolina football game. She and some of her College of Charleston's sorority sisters were visiting some friends. People laugh at me when I say this, but when I saw her that day, I knew she was the one. I fell hard for the girl I knew all my life. The rest is history."

They talked for only a few more minutes before they parted ways with an awkward, Covid fist bump. As he turned back to pick up the Maxwell House Coffee, he noticed that his hands were sweating. He smiled and thanked God that he had been taken away from her when forty years prior he thought he was going to die when she headed to prison. He thought about the same experience his father once had a generation before in the exact same location with Dianna Branham. He pondered over the probabilities of the odds that he and his father would experience the same exact type of emotional reunion a generation apart.

A few minutes later, while he was standing in the checkout line his old friend Stew Turbeville walked up behind him and cried out, "Hey big guy. The prayer your Dad prayed for your mother was beautiful at her funeral service. I'm glad I was able to visit with y'all yesterday."

"I don't think I will ever get over you becoming the minister of the First Presbyterian Church of Oak Bay. God does work in mysterious ways."

"That is exactly what Sarah Beth says. I thank God every day for allowing me to get my life straight. Playing baseball at the Citadel was the best thing that ever happened to me. You do remember that during my freshman year me and JFK got into it, and I told him that I was the one that threw his car keys and wallet into the ocean."

Roger laughed and said, "I forgot all about that. Didn't you become good friends?"

Stew laughed and said, "He and General Eisenhower loved giving me hell my knob year, but we have remained friends all these years. You know, we Citadel boys are thicker than thieves. By the way, Sarah Beth hopes that you and your Dad will be able to come and eat with us before you go back to Tampa. We can grill up some burgers and hotdogs. We can eat outdoors unless you are too used to that big city food and fancy restaurants. Bring the journal with you. I would love to look at that thing again. You know my favorite part of that journal was when Matthew James describes why he decided to write the journal. You remember he wrote, "I write so that I will always remember how God saved me from the rope of treason. Hopefully the adventure of my life will be indoctrinated many years after I have been with my Lord." Stew paused and said, " What a legacy. Your ancestor was quite a dude."

Roger nodded in agreement and said, "We will definitely come over and take you up on that offer. Dad needs to get out of the house. If the weather is good, we will do it."

They spoke for about fifteen more minutes outside of the Fresh Market before Stew was called away on his cell phone to visit with a parishioner. Walking to his rental car, Roger James, once the Golden Boy of Oak Bay, heard a voice in the parking lot calling his name.

"Hey, buddy, aren't you Hot Rod Roger James?"

Roger looked at the homeless looking man who reminded him of someone he once knew by the name of Kirby. He said, "Do I know you, sir?"

"Not sure, but I know who you are. My name is Frankie Wardlaw. I'm pretty sure you don't remember me, but you were my hero when I was a kid. I was about ten years old playin' in the Pit at Legion Field the night you threw the ball over one hundred miles per hour. To this day, your performance that night was one of the greatest things I have ever witnessed. When you hit that Grand Slam, I thought I had gone to heaven. But when you hit that catcher and scored the winnin' run, I knew I was in heaven. That experience has always been a treasure for me. I still tell people about it, and they think I am crazy. God Bless you"

"No, sir, thank you for making my day."

They talked for a few more minutes as Roger listened to a man who had once been a successful carpenter. Many years ago he fell from a roof and injured his back. Several surgeries later he fought to stay afloat financially, but could not fight off the constant pain of his injury. During his recovery he was hooked on a pain killer called Oxycodone. Then to make matters worse he became hooked on a Video Poker machine in the back of the Happy Mart convenience store that he thought was going to turn his luck around. He lost a job, a wife, and a place to live twenty years ago; the same year the state of South Carolina outlawed Video Poker.

Roger was touched by his appreciative attitude where he took the blame for his misgivings and thanked the Lord for one more day. Roger was saddened by his story of financial ruin.

Roger then took the time to listen to a few of his jokes before saying to him, "You may not believe this, but a few days after I played in that game, a wise man here in town predicted that I would run into somebody forty years later who would remember that special night. Today is that day. God Bless you, sir. I didn't think there was anyone in this town who remembered that night." Roger James then reached into his pocket and gave the man a twenty dollar bill.

The man thanked him, laughed and then said, "God bless you, Mr. James. It has been my pleasure talkin' to you after all these years. You takin' the time to speak to me is a treasure I will never forget. I promise this twenty doll'as will go to good use. I'm goin' into this Fresh Market and buy me some Vicks Formula 44 Cough Syrup and a large bottle of Scope. Then I will ride my moped over to the Kirby

Davis Animal Shelter where I feed the dogs and cats every afternoon."

The End

About the Author

W. Scott Jones is a high school Social Studies teacher and football coach. He has served in various public and private schools in South Carolina during his thirty plus years in education. A former Social Studies Teacher of the Year, Coach Jones has also been blessed to serve as a Head Football Coach and Athletic Director. Selected to coach in the Shrine Bowl of the Carolinas in 2010, Coach Jones has been fortunate to be a part of many championship teams along with many great players and wonderful coaches.

Born in Alapaha, Georgia, Coach Jones grew up in a rural area near Sumter, South Carolina. He attended North Greenville College and is a graduate of the University of South Carolina. He loves to write, motivate young people, tell a good story, and have fun. He has been married for thirty plus years to his wife Bridget, who is a successful Licensed Professional Counselor. They have three incredible grown children.

The Treasures of a Carolina Summer is his second novel. The first novel, **A Storm in the Carolinas** has received excellent reviews and continues to be a growing success. To find out more about the author follow W. Scott Jones at www.wscottjonesauthor.com or follow him on Facebook at W. Scott Jones Author.

Made in United States
Orlando, FL
10 September 2022

22262006R00183